WHERE THE LEAVES Fall

AIESSA HOLLAND

This is a work of fiction. Names, characters, places, and incidents either are the product of the author's imagination or are used fictitiously. Any resemblance to actual persons, living or dead, events, or locales is entirely coincidental.

Copyright © 2025 by Aiessa Holland

All rights reserved. No part of this book may be reproduced or transmitted in any form or by any means, electronic or mechanical, including photocopying, recording or any information storage and retrieval system now known or to be invented, without permission in writing from the author, except by a reviewer who wishes to use brief passages in connection with a review or an article.

This book represents the personal views and opinions of the author and does not reflect the positions or opinions of past, present, or future employers with which the author is affiliated.

Scripture taken from the New King James Version®. Copyright © 1982 by Thomas Nelson. Used by permission. All rights reserved.

First paperback edition October 2025

Book design by Jackie Dras

ISBN: 979-8-9929045-0-5 (Paperback)

ISBN: 979-8-9929045-1-2 (E-book)

Contents

Sensitive Themes	1
Dedication	2
Part One: Freeport	3
1	4
2	10
3	20
4	31
5	35
6	42
7	50
8	63
9	78
10	86
11	94
12	101
13	105
14	111
15	117
16	122
17	129

18	137
19	146
20	154
21	158
22	165
23	169
Part Two: New Hope Bible Camp	173
24	174
25	184
26	193
27	210
28	216
29	222
30	228
31	240
32	246
33	255
34	264
35	279
36	286
37	292
38	297
39	304
40	316
41	329
42	334

43	338
44	343
45	347
Acknowledgements	353
Hymns/Songs	357
Scripture References	358
Discussion Questions	361
About the Author	363
Also by Aiessa	364

SENSITIVE THEMES

This story is ultimately one of hope, faith, and finding peace in Jesus, but it also explores real themes that might be sensitive for some readers. Please see the list of sensitive themes below.

- Bullying and emotional manipulation
- Struggles with identity, self-worth, and anxiety
- Troubled family relationships
- Addiction
- Memories of grief and loss
- Spiritual doubt
- Mental and emotional healing

Dedication

For the sweet souls in foster care who inspired me to write Lena's story. You've all faced more challenges in your young lives than many of us face in one lifetime. Your resilience and ability to find joy in the ordinary in spite of the hurt you've had to endure has been so encouraging to me. This book is my hug to you and a reminder to set your sights on Jesus because He loves you and will never let you walk alone.
Keep your eyes on Him and you will be unshakable in every season of life.

PART ONE: FREEPORT

1

The sound of lockers slamming down the hallway made me jump as students hurried from one class to the next. My nerves were shot after a full day back at Freeport High, the last place I wanted to be. Grabbing my Spanish and Geometry books from my bag, I swapped them for the American history textbook tucked inside my locker.

Just one more class left, I thought to myself. If I could have morphed to the size of an ant, I could have wandered the halls without being seen. Yet, no matter how small I tried to make myself, the whispers and sidelong glances I received since first period were a dead giveaway that being invisible wasn't going to be an option for me this year.

Today was only the first day of senior year, and already my worst fears were coming true. Three tragically slow periods had already crawled by, each one spent dodging stares I couldn't ignore but when the lunch bell finally rang, I fled to the quiet sanctuary underneath an old oak tree in the quad. Now, as I packed my bag to leave after the final period, I just wanted to escape.

I turned to do a quick scan of the hall and noticed the cheerleaders just feet away. The second I stared back at them, every head turned in the opposite direction as the group began whispering behind their hands. With a quick zip of my bag, I lowered my head and mentally recited the verse I memorized yesterday from Isaiah 41:10 for these exact moments.

Fear not for I am with you, be not dismayed for I am your God. I will strengthen you. Yes, I will help you, I will uphold you with my righteous hand.

No one knew how I had spent my summer. They still saw me as Lena Harris, Ronni Dice's best friend and Lacey Lockhart's mortal enemy. The three of us spent all of junior year at each other's throat's leaving chaos in our wake. As much as I hated their whispering and taunting stares, I could see where my peers were coming from now. After my summer at camp deep down, I knew I'd react the same way if anyone lashed out at Carter, Jojo, Denny or Theo. I would want the person trying to hurt my friends to know there's power and numbers. The biggest difference between me and the rest of Freeport High was that I could try to move on and quit stirring up the past. I had to keep reminding myself, though, that *they didn't know what I knew.*

As I slid past the group of girls, it took all my effort to hold my head high as their whispers swirled. But now that I knew the gospel, I understood how they still felt about me, knowing all that I had done to Lacey last year. I kept this in mind even when the giggling from the group caused my gaze to shift.

To my surprise, Worthy Clarke stood among them, staring back at me though the look in her eyes told me she didn't share the same sense of humor as the others. Without a second glance, I spun away and hurried to my next class, wondering where Worthy and I had gone wrong.

She was both naturally and effortlessly beautiful, but her kindness truly set her apart. Worthy had kind eyes, a kind voice, and a kind spirit, but when I considered all of those attributes I could never understand how she and I had become strangers. When Worthy started making other friends freshman year, I boiled it down to the fact that she was someone who had always made friends easily, and by the end of the year she seemed to know someone in every circle. Even though we stopped hanging out, the two of us still saw each other when Mom and I were at church. Worthy and her grandmother, Miss Pearl, had been our closest friends in the congregation ever since we moved to Freeport.

I only noticed a change in her when Mom got sick. Once the rumors started to swirl, Worthy started acting differently around me. She was still kind and polite, but instead of hanging out the way we used to, we hardly talked. Over time, I realized that Worthy likely shared the same opinion as everyone else. My mom was an addict, and no one wanted to be around an addict.

Camille and Lacey drifted away not long after Worthy. My texts went unanswered, and their invitations to hang out stopped coming. I felt like my family's shame had seeped into me, marking me as someone to avoid. While everyone else steered clear of me, Ronni showed up. Once the war with Lacey began, Ronni was the only one who defended me after Lacey turned on me for exposing her boyfriend for who he really is. Despite Ronni's reputation, I clung to our so-called friendship like a lifeline.

On the surface we seemed like your average teenage girls—shopping, hanging out, going to the movies, but with Ronni nothing was ever that simple. Shopping meant *shoplifting*. Hanging out involved *drinking* or *experimenting* with things I couldn't even name. Going to the movies wasn't about catching the next blockbuster but about letting Ronni use me for my employee discount.

Our friendship had always been one-sided where Ronni took what she wanted and I let her, grateful just not to be on my own. She lived like rules didn't apply to her, hiding behind her family's money and the steep disbelief that she could get away with anything. That recklessness was magnetic, and with Mom unraveling at home, Ronni's friendship was my only escape.

Until it became a trap.

Last year, Ronni's spiral dragged me down with her. In her obsession with getting back at Lacey, she crossed the line by hooking up with Lacey's boyfriend, Javier. When the truth exploded in the most humiliatingly public way, Lacey set her sights on both of us. Even when I cut ties with Ronni, that still didn't stop Lacey. She egged our cars and decorated our windshields with cruel slurs. Lacey's final act of revenge sparked one last act of payback when Ronni and I rolled her house. The plan was supposed to end the war, but when everything went sideways, Ronni bailed, leaving me to take the fall alone. Caught red-handed by the Lockharts. I found myself in the front seat of my Dad's truck on the way to his last attempt to set me straight, *New Hope Bible Camp.*

The most amazing part was that my dad's plan worked. Camp changed everything for me. This summer had been the best of my life, but now being back in Freeport, I was facing the consequences of the girl I used to be. Everyone still saw me as the girl caught up with the wrong crowd, not the girl who had been transformed.

After giving my life to Jesus, I knew I was different now but no one else had caught on yet. As I sauntered into history class early, I found an empty seat in the back of the first row by the door. The good thing about avoiding my peers was getting the pick of the seats. Within minutes, others filed in as I kept my head down, staring aimlessly as I flipped through my history book.

Once class began, Mr. Francis closed the door and started to call roll. When he called my name, I felt a blush creep up my neck and face, attracting even more attention from those around me. To my left, I recognized two guys from the varsity football team, both friends of Javier and Lacey. I watched as they exchanged a glance and chuckled before turning back to Mr. Francis.

Just when I started to feel relieved to not have any more of Lacey's close friends in my classes this semester, the door opened and my stomach plummeted. Ronni entered the classroom and looked almost unrecognizable. I hadn't seen or talked to her since we rolled Lacey's front yard. She sported ripped jeans, a baggy black tee; her face was almost bare of makeup, and her usual multi-colored hair had been bleached to a single shade of blonde.

"Name?" Mr. Francis asked her. This took me off guard because everyone knew who Ronni was. The girl basically came from Freeport royalty.

"Veronica Dice," she answered. "But you can call me Ronni."

The guy who snickered at me let out a whoop as the others clapped him on the back. I had always known her to be the queen of comebacks, but Ronni said nothing and quietly made her way to the front seat by the far window. As Mr. Francis reviewed the syllabus, I kept stealing glances in her direction. Seeing Ronni again felt surreal. The carefree, reckless girl I once knew seemed to be replaced by someone completely different.

Throughout class, her behavior was even more bizarre. Instead of doodling or cracking jokes, she was actually taking notes like she planned to study them instead of copying someone else's answers. I had no idea how her summer had gone. All I knew was that Ronni had changed... *dramatically*.

I was jolted back to reality once the bell rang, and as I scrambled to collect my things and dash out the hall, Ronni was just as quick. Our eyes met once we reached the door at the same time, but she quickly cast her eyes to the floor and moved over to make room for me.

Without replying, I darted forward and felt my shoulder roughly brush hers as I burst through the door. I had taken only a few steps when the roar of the crowd faded behind me. Spinning on my heel, I turned to see Ronni headed in the complete opposite direction, seeming as eager to escape the day as I was.

2

After surviving the first day of school, spending the rest of the day at work felt like a cakewalk. After camp, I had promised Dad I would find a job when I got home. I knew he saw it as a way to keep me on the straight and narrow, but I honestly saw it as an escape. I had dreaded coming home to Freeport this summer, not because I didn't miss my dad, but because of all the reminders of my past. Camp offered me a fresh start and a chance to become the person I wanted to be, but returning to Freeport felt like resuming a life I was trying desperately to leave behind.

The day I came home, my past hit me like a stinging slap in the face. As Dad and I drove home from Meadowbrook, we entered Freeport and passed the Stop-N-Shop, but all I could think about was the last time I had set foot inside that store. At the time I didn't know what was happening, but suddenly Ronni grabbed me by the arm and pulled me behind her as we fled the store after she shoplifted a pack of cigarettes. The next day, Dad had stopped in to get gas only to have the manager warn him to keep his thieving daughter away from his store.

Next up, I saw the MoviePlex still standing in all its glory with a packed parking lot. The owners had fired me last year after a co-worker reported me after I had lied about being sick and skipped my shift just to spend the day with Ronni. Now, driving home felt like a movie montage of all the poor decisions I had made chasing Ronni's friendship. As we drove out toward the city limits, I saw a large sign that read:

SALTY PATH AQUARIUM: SEASONAL HELP WANTED

I didn't know the owners, and it had been years since I had gone inside since the place was always crawling with tourists, but that sign felt like a shining ray of hope welcoming me to start over. The next day I went in as soon as they opened and filled out an application. Anthony, the manager, offered me a job on the spot. The following day, I picked up my work polo and began cashier training at the gift shop, where I've spent every afternoon since.

One of the best parts of my job was that I didn't have to work with other kids from school. The rest of my co-workers were local college students who worked outside the gift shop in different departments and didn't know me. Work was the one place in Freeport where I felt like I could actually be myself without being haunted by my mistakes.

As much as I hated to admit it, being home wasn't any easier. Me and Dad had developed a polite night routine in the evenings. When I got home, the two of us would make small talk about our day, have dinner together, but then I would always retreat to my room. The house felt even bigger than I remembered before I left camp with just the two of us, and I hated how empty the ghost of my mother made everything feel.

Within the first week home, I had taken down all my music posters and photos of Ronni to stare at a blank canvas of white walls. As if removing the past could somehow make the present easier to face. My room became my bubble from the rest of the house, where photos and traces of my mother were still everywhere.

On my first night back, Dad updated me on my mom's treatment. Instead of coming home after finishing her five-week program, she opted to continue her treatment through exposure therapy offered for recovering addicts. Dad said she had had a rough first week trying to transition to the new facility, which struck me as odd considering the way she'd spent most of my childhood as a coast guard wife often relocating. Even though Dad tried not to show it, I knew he was devastated by the news. I knew I should also be concerned for her, but as I thought about how much she had hurt us, I was partly relieved to hear that she was the one struggling for a change.

My mom had battled her alcohol addiction in silence for years before it finally became public. I think my dad felt guilty after learning that she had struggled far longer than anyone realized. I tried to get over it but what stung the most was the way she lied and then left us without saying a word.

In this new phase of treatment, Dad said Mom was allowed one point of contact in the early stages, and I fully supported him being that person. I knew Dad was ready to forgive and forget, but I wasn't even close. Sometimes I wondered if my mom thought about how her choices had truly affected us because everyday I felt like I was living with both the consequences of her mistakes and mine. I couldn't pretend anymore that what she did to us was okay.

When I pulled into the driveway after work, I glanced out at our quaint white house where my dad's old pickup sat in all its rusted glory. I turned off the engine and climbed out of the car as the sound of water blasting in the backyard caught my attention. As I made my way over, I found Dad standing at the helm of an old boat he had been working to restore over the summer.

"Hey kiddo!" Dad greeted me, wiping his sweaty brow on his sleeve. His tattered, Salty Path Sea Tours hat was just as soaked with sweat as his gray t-shirt. "Did you have a good first day back at school?"

He tried to sound cherry but underneath I could still hear the concern in his voice. I wondered if he'd been expecting a call from school just like last year when the principal probably had him on speed dial with all the drama Lacey and Ronni caused. In that moment, I knew I wasn't the only one still struggling to adjust to the new me.

"Just a little chaotic," I replied, hoping to give him an honest yet positive answer. "First days are always busy. How was your day?"

I watched as his shoulders sagged in relief. "Good, I've just been working on this old girl," he said, turning off the hose. "I think I finally came up with a name for her."

"Really?" I asked, trying not to laugh at the excitement in his voice. I had only ever seen my father look at one other person the way he admired his boat.

My mother.

"Don't keep me in suspense; what did you come up with?" I asked.

With a big grin, Dad answered, "Gone With the Wind."

I fought to keep a smile on my face as soon as Dad spoke the words, but I knew exactly why he had chosen the name. *Gone With the Wind* was my mom's favorite movie. Growing up Mom and Dad had watched the movie together so many times they could randomly quote it to each other. When I got older, I could finally watch it, but I could never sit through the entire film. The movie was way too long, and Scarlett O'Hara, who my mom always fawned over, got on my nerves.

"I think your mom's going to love it," Dad beamed, tapping the side of the boat affectionately.

Just seeing how excited Dad was at the prospect of my mother coming home, knowing that she had chosen yet again not to, was enough small talk for me for one night.

"Well, I've got a ton of homework to do, so I think I'm just going to turn in now. Dad.*

"Sounds good, hun. There's some sandwich stuff in the fridge if you're hungry," he said before turning the sprayer back on.

After spending the summer at camp, I understood wanting a fresh start. Yet, seeing how my dad hoped the boat might be a fresh start for him and my mom, was too much for me. Dad still thought she would come back home, but the longer time passed without her, the more I lost faith in her.

Once I was back inside the house, I followed Dad's suggestion and gathered sandwich supplies from the fridge. As I layered meat on top of two slices of bread, I tried to shake off the bitterness I felt about my mom and focus on the good in my life right now. I had come home from camp a different person; my faith was no longer shattered, and I owed that to Aunt Lou and Carter. This summer they refused to let me stay stuck in my past and gently guided me back to the truth that I had turned my back on.

The friendships I had made at camp rooted us in sharing something real, which was a foundation I didn't think my parents had ever established. Even though Mom had grown up a Christian, somewhere along the way, she'd lost herself. My whole life I never really heard my dad talk about his belief in God, and the more I knew about their relationship, the more I wondered how two people with such different values could have ever truly made a marriage work. The more I thought about the faith they didn't share, the more I missed my friends and the summer we spent together that completely changed my life.

I closed my sandwich and reached to return the deli meat to the fridge when the local pizza menu magnetized to the door caught my eye. I froze and felt a familiar ache blooming in my chest as the menu pulled me right back to the first night I spent in Meadowbrook after camp.

✳✳✳

The morning everyone left camp, I had braced myself to say goodbye. After I hugged my friends and loaded up my belongings, Dad and Aunt Lou pulled me aside and told me that they had talked it over, and if I wanted I could spend one extra week in Meadowbrook staying with Aunt Lou.

I didn't even hesitate to accept their offer.

After four unforgettable weeks together, the thought of more time with my friends felt like winning the lottery. As much as I missed Dad already, he reassured me it was okay because he'd have me for the entire school year. Deep down, I think he could see just how much it hurt to let go of this place and the people so soon, but I knew my dad just wanted to see me happy.

That August afternoon as we all went our separate ways, agreeing to meet up the next day, I started to settle in at Lou's house when my phone rang.

It was Carter.

"I'm picking you up and we're all going to go for pizza," Carter insisted, not leaving any room for debate. *Not that I would have said no, of course.*

For the first time since we met, I finally had the chance to see him without being a sweaty camp mess. After a quick shower, I swapped out my usual t-shirt and shorts combo for a cute top and jeans from Lou. That night, I wore my hair down and even added a little makeup. When Carter pulled up and laid eyes on me, his smile said everything.

Aunt Lou waved us off from the porch as we headed out. Carter and I held hands the entire drive to the restaurant, where Jojo, Denny and Theo were already waiting.

"Well, well, well, look who finally showed up!" Denny announced our arrival. I saw how he draped his arm over the back of Jojo's chair. The two of them looked as though this was the most normal thing in the world, as though they had been a couple for years. Saying the two of them together was as satisfying as finishing a five-thousand-piece puzzle.

Grabbing a seat to Theo's right, Carter pulled out my chair and sat down next to me, close enough that our shoulders touched.

"You made it seem like we were late, Dennis." Carter accused Denny, sitting across from us. Denny tapped an invisible watch on his wrist, which only made Carter narrow his eyes at him.

"Don't you dare accuse me, dude. You know I would never be late for pizza." Carted defended us.

Jojo and I laughed while Theo shook his head and asked, "So are we going to decide what to order together like normal or am I the fifth-wheel doing my own thing tonight?"

There was a slight edge to his voice, but when I glanced over at him, Theo waggled his eyebrows and shot me a daring glance. With one look, I knew he was just being his typical sarcastic self.

"We can totally split a pizza," Jojo offered as our server came to take our drink orders. All of us ordered water except for Denny, who asked for sweet tea.

"You always have to be different, don't you?" Theo teased him.

With expert precision, Denny ripped off a piece of paper from the edge of his straw, inserted the end into his mouth and fired it, striking Theo directly between the eyes.

"Bullseye!" Denny cheered as he tucked the straw into his drink.

"Always the picture of maturity, aren't we? Dennis?" Theo groaned, swatting the paper from his face to the floor. "Just for that, I'm going to pick out the pizza."

Denny and Carter instantly argued, while Jojo leaned over the table as if ready to lecture a small child. "No fair, Theo. You picked last time!"

"I am not eating cauliflower crust again," Denny said, shooting an accusatory look at Theo. "I just spent this summer at camp. I *need* real food."

Theo rolled his eyes as if he had heard this thousands of times before. "You were the one who said you needed to weigh in for football and wanted to shed a few pounds. You act like I poisoned you."

"Um...you did," Denny muttered, gazing over Jojo's shoulder at the menu in her hands.

"Keep talking, and I will," Theo muttered under his breath.

Carter leaned over the table, calling for a time-out. "All right, kids. How about we let Lena choose this time? It's her first time here with us, and that seems fair."

"Sounds good to me," Jojo beamed across the table at me.

"Way to pick favorites," Theo verbally jabbed, keeping his eyes locked on the menu in front of him.

"So, what'll it be, Lena bug?" Denny's face brightened once the server arrived with our drinks. "Do you like cheese, pepperoni, buffalo chicken, or supreme?"

"Do we need a few more minutes to look over the menu?" Our server asked expectantly while I was still surveying all the options before me.

Denny eyed her before motioning over to me. "She's the one who's deciding what pizza we'll split, but can I put in an order of mozzarella sticks?"

"Sure," the lady jotted down as my eyes landed on my favorite combination.

Glancing back at my friends, I asked, "Are you guys okay if I order ham and pineapple?"

As I gazed around the group, they were pin-drop silent, and suddenly all eyes started to Denny who suddenly tensed in his seat.

"Shots fired." Theo grimaced, holding up his menu to hide behind.

Carter shifted in his seat beside me, but before he could speak, Denny shot daggers my way. "You are a monster."

I stared at him in disbelief. "What? No, I'm not. Do you not like ham and pineapple?"

Running a hand down his face, Denny glared at our stricken waitress and waved for her to lean down. He lowered his voice before threatening, "If you bring any fruit on any pizza to this table, I will write a Google review about you attempting to poison me."

"Oh, don't be dramatic. Denny," Theo argued, lowering the menu as Jojo just put her head in her hands, overcome with embarrassment.

"I'm not being dramatic," Denny snapped. "I don't know what you all eat down there at the beach, Lena, but you just came from Bible Camp, girl. Fruit on pizza is blasphemy!"

Carter waved his hand, motioning for the server to come his way as he tried talking over the bantering boys. "Can you just bring us pepperoni and cheese, please?"

I caught her jotting down his order before Carter added, "And can you hurry with his mozzarella sticks? Denny's not himself when he's hungry."

Our server chuckled as she made her way back to the kitchen while Denny and Theo continued to argue about what toppings truly belonged on pizza. I peered over to see Jojo shrinking in her seat, sipping her water as though trying to hide.

Carter put his arm around me then, and I could feel his laughter vibrating through me as I burrowed into his side as I couldn't hold back from laughing any longer.

"Aren't you so glad you decided to stay here with us this week?" Carter asked, his whisper tickled my ear as I felt his lips brush my skin.

I glanced up at him, and our faces were so close, I could see tiny flecks of amber in his chocolate eyes. "I'm exactly where I want to be."

Under the table, Carter's fingers brushed mine as he reached for my hand. I held on, interlacing my fingers with his as he prayed once our food arrived. When Carter released me so we could eat, I hurried through dinner, eager to hold his hand again because letting go of him was the last thing that I wanted to do.

3

The warmth of that night in Meadowbrook vanished as my reflection did in the fogged up mirror while I got ready for bed. I slipped into my pajamas and towel dried my hair but as I stepped into my room after my shower I froze.

Dad stood near my bed setting down a package I hadn't been expecting.

"Hey hun, I forgot to tell you that this came for you today."

Crossing the room, I peeked down at the box as a huge smile spread over my face. In the top left corner, the return address held the name *Lou Rivers*. Immediately I tore open the box to discover a variety of goodies packed inside. First, I pulled out a cozy knit short and shirt set followed by a pair of lavender earbuds and a small plant whose pot read: *Oh the places you will grow!* Underneath I grabbed a devotional book for high school seniors, then a notebook, gift cards for fuel and coffee, and an umbrella.

Dad pointed out the umbrella adding, "Make sure you put that in your bag and take it with you to school tomorrow. A tropical storm is heading our way."

Living on the coast meant we were no strangers to hurricane season. Obediently, I put the umbrella away as Dad leaned in and kissed the top of my head.

"You should call your aunt and thank her. Oh, and don't stay on the phone with Carter too long tonight."

I glanced up in time to see Dad tilting his head as if daring me to argue with him. Carter and I spoke nearly every night unless his soccer schedule interfered. His soccer season just started a week before the school year leaving him with little free time.

"He's at an athletic banquet tonight thank you very much," I explained smartly, "I think he said it was some celebration for seniors, but don't worry, I'll give Lou a call, and I promise I won't keep *her* too long."

Dad stuck his tongue out at my response. Even though he rooted for us, I knew Dad wished I'd spend less time on the phone with Carter, but we were determined to make our relationship work. Without constant communication, I had no idea how else we could possibly maintain long distance. At the end of the summer, we had made a promise to each other that as long as we tried, we could make things work, and so far we had both kept our word.

"Sweet dreams, kiddo," Dad said before moving to the door and closing it behind him.

I sank onto my bed and pulled the package onto my lap before reaching for my phone. When I swiped the screen, I found one unread text message from Carter.

> Rosie: I miss you, Dutch! <3 <3

I bit my lower lip trying my best to contain my excitement, knowing I was on his mind despite the busy night he had ahead. I instantly replied.

> Me: I miss you more! <3 <3<3

Then, I scrolled to find Lou's name listed in my Favorites. I pressed the call button beneath her name and listened as the line rang twice before she answered.

"Hey sweetie," she greeted me with the usual cheer in her voice.

"Hey Lou!"

"How's my favorite niece?" She asked. The question always made me smile because I was her only niece, which automatically made me her favorite.

"If I'm being honest, I'm feeling just a little spoiled tonight." I confessed, feeling the soft material of the knit shorts between my fingers. "Thank you so much for the gift box you sent. You didn't have to."

"Nonsense," Lou disagreed. "You're only a senior once, and this is a huge milestone in your life. You deserve to be celebrated."

I wished I felt the same way Lou did, but I knew I could match her enthusiasm when I graduated in the spring.

"I love the gifts," I said, sorting through the box again. "Everything is perfect, and I'm excited to read the devotional book you sent."

I picked up the pocket-sized hardcover and flipped it over. On the back cover in big block quotes was the Bible verse Philippians 4:13, which said *I can do all things through Christ who strengthens me.*

"When I was at the bookstore, I had to get it for you," Lou said. "I know you haven't been able to go to church since you got back with your busy work schedule and all, but it's important to stay in the Word."

Even though I knew she didn't say it to hurt me, Lou's words hit deeper than she knew. When I got back to Freeport, Dad's first order of business was for me to find a job, no exceptions. At first, I wondered if we were still struggling given Mom's extended time in treatment, but as I settled in, I could tell he was worried I'd fall back into old patterns. Dad had only had a few days to see that I was doing better, but even then he had every right to be concerned.

Last year had been tough for both of us, but at the end of the summer, I finally realized Dad hadn't sent me to camp to punish me. He sent me away hoping I could get back on track. Dad was a firm believer in both responsibility and integrity, and getting a job was his way of keeping me in line. Mom used to joke that his time in the Coast Guard made him obsessed with structure, but I also knew that work was Dad's form of discipline. Me finding a job wasn't just about responsibility; working was also about keeping me busy and out of trouble.

Dad hadn't been at camp to witness my transformation over the summer, and even though I didn't have anything to prove, I knew that he was still adjusting to the new me. I couldn't blame him, especially not after everything I had put him through last year. His form of discipline worked out for me though, especially since work had become my escape.

When I was at the aquarium, I didn't have to think about my mom. I didn't have to see her in family photos hanging in our living room, or in the way I instinctively separated my colors from my whites while doing my laundry, just like she had taught me. I didn't have to drive past the beach and remember how she used to build sandcastles with me or, worse, at the church off Sandy Shores Drive where we used to sit side-by-side every Sunday before she left.

I couldn't tell Lou that, though. She and I had been through so much over the summer together, and I didn't want her to worry about me. I knew Lou would listen if I needed her to, but coming home had been much harder than I expected. She was all the way in Meadowbrook, and I couldn't burden her with my problems, especially with everything she had going on with work. I tried to tackle things as they came, but church was the one thing I still kept putting off by working during service times.

"The book is great, Lou," I finally said. "I can read a passage in the morning as a good way to start out my day."

"That sounds like the perfect plan," Lou encouraged. "While we're on the topic, how was your first day?"

I wanted to be grateful for the subject change, but school wasn't exactly my favorite topic either. If there was one thing I appreciated about my aunt, it was that she never pushed, especially when she understood how hard it was for me to come back to Freeport. Since I had come home, she tried to encourage me in all the ways she knew how, through a morning Bible verse, pictures of Cobalt Bluff to remind me of Meadowbrook. Lou probably didn't know, but her small acts of service always came at just the right time.

"School was fine," I said. "Nothing out of the ordinary." Though technically my first day was normal, I had hoped for a better outcome than being the target of all of Freeport High's gossip.

"Do you like your classes?" She asked.

"So far," I mentioned vaguely. I wasn't about to tell her about Ronni being in my history class, so I opted for a new subject. "How's everything going in Meadowbrook?"

"Busy, but good!" Lou said, keeping her tone bright. "Hannah's first day was today, so I'm excited to have some part-time help around River Ridge."

Lou never complained about her job, but I knew the family real estate business kept her constantly moving. When I was younger, I remember hearing her and Mom talk about running the family business together once my Dad got out of the Coast Guard but those dreams never came true. Even though my Dad did leave the service for Mom, it wasn't exactly for the reasons either of them had hoped. Helping Mom get over her addiction had taken everything he had, and still it hadn't been enough.

All things considered, I was glad Lou finally had someone to help now, even if Hannah wasn't exactly family.

"I'm glad you finally have help." I told her. "How was Hannah's first day?"

"She's doing really great," Lou replied. "Hannah is such a fast learner and has always been a tremendous help at camp. I think she's going to thrive at River Ridge."

"I bet she will, too. Tell her I said hey." I told my aunt, remembering just how much I had always admired Hannah.

"I sure will." Lou said. "Is there anyone else you would like for me to pass a message to?"

I chuckled, already knowing where she was going with this. "Sure. If you see Jojo, give her a big hug for me."

On the other line, I heard Lou giggle. "Consider it done. Anyone else?"

This time I laughed out loud. "Okay, okay, you can give Carter a hug too.

Lou snorted. "Finally, there it is. You know, every time I see him, he fills me in on how you're doing. Any chance we can change that so I'm not learning about my favorite niece through someone else?"

"I'm sorry," I said, although I couldn't help smiling at the thought of Carter bringing me up in conversation. "I think it's just because we talk every day and I know you're busy, so I don't want to bother you."

"Honey, you could never bother me." Lou said, letting out a soft sigh. "I got so used to having you here this summer, but now that you're back home, I just miss you. Know that I am never too busy for you though, kiddo."

At that moment, I wished I could reach through the phone and hug her tight because I missed her too. "I know that, and I promise I'll do better about calling Lou."

"I'm holding you to that," she said with a smile in her voice. "All I want is for you to keep putting God first and remember that I'm always here for you. No matter what you need, whether it's school, work, boy stuff, or anything else. I mean it, Lena, okay? You can always talk to me."

Her words meant more than I could describe, because Lou knew just how much I'd been struggling, and I knew I wasn't alone. Me and Dad hadn't been the only ones my mom had left behind when she walked out. Before the summer, Lou and I hadn't really talked in years, not after the argument she had with my mom at my Gramp's funeral.

My mom and Lou didn't speak for a long time, but this summer had changed everything for us. Reconnecting with Lou showed me just how much my mother's decisions had impacted more than just me and my dad. Now that my aunt was back in my life, I wasn't about to let any amount of distance come between us again. Lou wasn't the kind of person who broke promises, and I knew when she said she would be there, she would show up for me every time.

"Thanks, Lou," I told her. "And I do mean it, I promise I'll do better."

"We both will," Lou replied lovingly. "Now go get some sleep, sweetie, tomorrow will be here before we know it. I love you, Lena."

"I love you too," I replied, wishing I could hug her close.

When our call ended I glanced back at the package sitting on my bed and heard Lou's voice once I stared back at the devotional book on top of the box.

Stay in God's Word.

With that reminder, I picked up the book and began flipping through the pages as the soft flutter of the paper took me straight back to the first quiet morning Lou and I spent together in Meadowbrook this summer.

***

The couch let out a soft creak as I plopped down next to Lou, who was busy flipping through an old photo album. She paused occasionally, peering down at a faded image as the smell of dusty paper inside a time-worn leather cover filled the air.

"These pictures are from most of my summers at New Hope." Lou said, and I caught the way her voice filled with nostalgia.

I watched while she ran a finger along a photo of a rustic wooden cabin surrounded by teenagers laughing and tossing a frisbee. Camp was much less developed in the picture, and the cabins appeared smaller and more weathered. To my surprise, the lake was freestanding without a dock in sight, and I couldn't help but smile at how much the place had grown since her time as a camper there.

"Did you guys even have electricity back then?" I teased. "What did you guys do all day?"

Lou laughed but narrowed her eyes at me. "We spent time together without technology and made up our own games using this amazing gift that God gave us called an *imagination*."

I playfully stuck out my tongue at her while she turned the page and froze. Staring back at us was a photo of her with my mom; both of them were around my age and sitting on a bench. Mom's hair was lighter in the summer sun, but her smile was wide and carefree, just like I remembered her. It broke my heart all over again to see her so full of life in the picture, because I didn't remember the last time I saw her like that.

"Your mom used to love going to camp," Lou said softly as if she was reading my mind. "Natalie was the loudest singer during song services and she always made friends with almost everyone by the end of the summer."

I gulped as I forced back the tears and worked to keep my voice steady. "She looks so happy there."

"She was." Lou said matter-of-factly.

Lou held the page open for a moment longer before flipping to the next photo. This time, Lou was in the photo standing with the group of campers singing. I had to look closer and squint to try to make out the familiar tall, scrawny guy in the back who had shaggy hair and an awkward grin.

"Wait, who is that?" I asked, pointing to the photo.

Lou stifled a laugh before answering. "If you can believe it, that's Max Adler."

"You mean Max as in Max's diner *Max*?" I asked, staring back at her wide-eyed.

"The one and only." Lou beamed at me, still trying not to laugh. "He was so awkward and lanky back then, but he's always had a magnificent singing voice. Me and Max were always a team, especially for the camp talent shows."

That grabbed my attention. "There used to be a camp talent show?"

Lou gave me a half-smile, still eyeing the photo. "We used to have a talent show during the summer, but when the end of summer banquet came about, the show was kind of ruled out except during other camp events and retreats. The talent show was always a great way to lighten the mood."

Having spent the summer at camp, I knew just how heavy the mood could get.

"Max and I did some of the craziest things when we were campers," Lou shared as she reminisced. "We started off singing duets, but eventually Max got tired of singing and dared me to branch out. There was this one year where we tried a synchronous juggling routine, but it went so horribly because I couldn't hold on to the tennis balls. The two of us laughed so hard we couldn't even finish the act."

I noticed just how much Lou's eyes lit up while she talked about Max and their friendship. "So you two have always been close, huh?"

Lou gave me a small smile but didn't elaborate as she reached for another photo album on the couch beside her. "Here," she said, setting the book in my lap. "I found some pictures of you and this one from vacation Bible school when you were little."

Before I turned my attention to the book in my lap, I caught sight of another photo in the album we were just looking at with her, mom, Max and someone who looked instantly recognizable.

My brow furrowed as I asked, "Wait, that can't be Theo Lockwood, right?"

Lou gazed back down at the book but shook her head, chuckling. "No, that's Grant Lockwood."

My mouth fell open at the sight of him, and I couldn't believe the spitting image Theo was of his father. "So does this mean you and Mom were friends with Grant?"

Lou's mouth twitched before she replied. "Your mom and I grew up with Grant. All of us went to the same school, church, and camp too."

I stared back down at the picture, now piecing things together. "That makes sense. My dad and Grant seem to know each other too, or at least that's how it seemed when they saw each other at camp." When I suddenly remembered the tension between the two of them, I added, "Though they didn't exactly seem happy to see each other."

Lou fell quiet and rested her fingers on the edge of the page, but I didn't miss the flicker of hesitation that crossed her face before she simply said, "We all used to be good friends."

I suddenly thought about just how different things were now and how complicated they seemed to be. None of the kids in the photos had stayed close, but I knew life had a way of happening to everyone. When I glanced back down at the picture again, I felt my heart warm at the idea that maybe things could come full circle.

"It's kind of cool though," I told her thoughtfully. "When I think about Theo, we could be like the second generation of friendship."

Lou's smile was soft but encouraging. "Maybe so."

Turning to pick up the VBS album in my lap. I grinned as soon as I saw the first photo. There I was, no older than seven, wearing a glitter-covered paper crown with Jojo, Denny and Theo beside me, all of us covered in face paint.

"Wow! I can't believe how tiny we were!" I laughed, taking in the sight of us as kids.

Lou snickered and leaned in to peer over my shoulder. "Not that long ago those boys were fighting over you like they do everything else now."

I grimaced, throwing Lou a look of disbelief. "What? No, they didn't!"

"Did too," Lou insisted with a mischievous smile. "Denny and Theo used to argue about who was your boyfriend, and Jojo would get so jealous."

I stared at her for a moment before I couldn't stop myself then burst out laughing. "That's so ridiculous! I can't believe how long Jojo and Denny took to finally figure things out.

"Love isn't always something we realize at first," Lou said, her smile soft but knowing as she stared back down at the photo of us. "Sometimes, it feels like it could take forever, but other times love hits us head-on when we're least expecting it."

As she turned the page, I let her words settle over me but kept silent while I wondered if she was only talking about Denny and Jojo or someone else.

4

With each day that passed, my summer memories began to blur beneath gray skies and the school bell. Dad had been right about the tropical storm because the rest of the week was a wet, dreary mess. Friday after school, I slowed my roll toward my car when I saw a group of boys playing soccer on the rain-soaked field. As they played, the boys slid through the mud, laughing and shouting completely unphased by the nasty weather. I stood there for a moment, mesmerized as something about the scene pulled at me, instantly reminding me of Carter.

Before I met him, soccer meant nothing to me, but at camp I noticed the way his face lit up every time he talked about the sport. Carter said the game taught him discipline and teamwork, but it also felt steady after all he had been through before the Roses adopted him. The game wasn't just a game he played; soccer helped shape who he was.

Over the summer in Meadowbrook, I didn't hesitate when Carter invited me to his and Theo's scrimmage against Valley View's biggest rival. Denny and Jojo came along, and the three of us huddled together on the bleachers ready to cheer the guys on.

"I have to confess I know nothing about soccer," I admitted while I watched the guys race down the field.

Denny scoffed, wiping sweat from his brow as we sat unshaded beneath the scorching sun. "Me neither, but that's mainly because soccer isn't as awesome as football."

Jojo elbowed his ribs and glared at her boyfriend. "Those are our best friends out there. You can't just trash talk them."

Denny barked out a laugh. "Since when have you known me to not trash talk, Jojo Bean?"

I put a hand over my mouth to stifle my laughter but noticed the way his nickname for her sent a blush creeping up her neck.

"Besides, I trash talk them so that when the other team does their comments don't knock the boys off their game. As long as we're the ones trash talking, people assume we know what we're talking about, just watch this."

Me and Jojo sat on the edge of our seats as Carter sprinted down the field, weaving between defenders with quick precision. His red number eleven jersey billowed as he sped across the turf, but just as he swung his leg back for a pass, suddenly a player from the other team cut in and stole the ball out from under him. The momentum shifted as both teams charged in the opposite direction.

Denny groaned and cupped his hands around his mouth, shouting, "Hey eleven! Was that a pass or a donation to the other team?"

As the whistle blew, Carter slowed to a stop with his hands on his hips and turned to shake his head at Denny's not-so-subtle commentary.

I pursed my lips trying to hide my smile, but I couldn't stop staring at my boyfriend in astonishment. Carter's presence on the field was unforgettable as his red jersey and black shorts highlighted his build, and his tanned skin held the proof of a summer spent outside. As I admired him, I knew there was so much more to Carter than just his looks that held my attention. I loved the way he played the game. Every movement was intentional, and every pass stayed measured and precise. He poured his heart into soccer just as he did with everything else.

During the next play, he and Theo were charging down the field while the other team had possession. The ball traveled so quickly that it was hard to keep up, and when the other team missed the goal, Danny's trash talking only got worse.

"Hey blue shirt! Were you aiming for the fans or the goal?" He shouted, still cupping his hands around his mouth. "Because if that's your best pass, I'm going to need a map to find it!"

Jojo and I doubled over on the bench, clutching our sides as Denny ranted while a few people nearby stared back at him. One woman even clapped along with his heckling.

This behavior was so typical of him because Denny was always the first to crack a joke, or just dive into something headfirst even though his only intention was to make someone else smile. Beneath all of his goofiness, there was so much more to him. I'd seen it over the summer in the way Denny would carry the heaviest sports gear without being asked, or how he would listen to others without interrupting. He always showed up for his friends without question, and although Denny could have intimidated just about anyone with his size alone, not once had I ever felt that way around him. He was a giant teddy bear with a heart that melted for the sweet girl beside me.

As I turned to gaze back at the field, the ref finally blew the whistle for a time-out. I watched Carter stand near the sidelines, tipping his head back as he drained his water bottle, then wiping his face with the back of his arm. The moment he glanced up and caught me watching him, he froze, but just for a second. Carter held my gaze, and I saw the small smile I recognized so well spread across his handsome face. My stomach flipped just like it always did when Carter looked at me like that, like somehow even in a crowd of fans I was the only person he could see.

As I watched him jog back onto the field, a quiet certainty struck me. After our time together over the summer, here we were, just like we promised on the last night of camp, making our relationship work. When his eyes found mine again from across the field, I watched as he wiped at his brow, then caught that same knowing smile spread across his face that always filled my stomach with butterflies. Carter and I were really real, and I was in Meadowbrook supporting him just as he had done for me since the day we met.

When the whistle blew, the game resumed as Denny, and Jojo stood.

"Hey, we're going to go get some snacks. Do you want to come?" Jojo asked.

I shook my head because the truth was I didn't want to go anywhere. As the two of them took off down the bleachers, I watched Carter sprint ahead of his teammates as a dull pain filled my heart. I wanted to stay in Meadowbrook, in this exact moment forever. But in an instant, the memory faded. Meadowbrook dissolved around me and I realized I was still stuck in Freeport, standing alone in the school parking lot as the torrential rain poured down on me.

5

That night, the moonlight filtering through my curtains cast soft shadows as I sat curled up on my bed with the devotional book Aunt Lou gave me. The rain had finally settled into a soft, steady drizzle outside as I sat freshly showered and wrapped in a warm blanket, trying to focus on the words in front of me.

How do you think your relationship with the Lord needs to grow or change this year?

A few weeks ago the answer would have been obvious, but now everything felt more complicated. I tapped my finger on the page as I thought about all the things I had been avoiding that made me uncomfortable. If I was honest with myself though, I knew I needed to stop letting my circumstances stand between me and God. I felt the sting of guilt gnawing at me until a soft knock pulled me from my spiral.

"It's open!" I announced, knowing it was Dad.

As expected, Dad poked his head in before fully entering. "Hey honey, I was just finishing up on the boat and found another package for you on the porch." He crossed the room and held out a small box.

I sat up in an instant and set my book aside as Dad handed the box to me. My heart flipped when I saw Carter's name scrawled across the return address.

"I'm starting to think that filling up your gas tank wasn't nearly sentimental enough for a back-to-school gift," Dad joked with a grin.

I chuckled as I glanced up at him. "No, Dad it was perfect. You didn't have to, though."

Dad sighed, offering me a shrug. "I figured it was the least I could do for someone who thinks that the *E* on the gas gauge means there's enough in the tank."

Rolling my eyes, I replied, "That's not true! I don't like running on empty; I just hate stopping to pump gas."

Dad chuckled as he reached out to ruffle my hair. "Your mom is the exact same way."

I knew he didn't mean for the comment to sting, but his words landed like a slap across the face. Without saying anything in response, I peered back down and started to open the package. "I guess we should see what it is."

Before I could even dig into the box, Dad added, "Let's be clear, just in case that's some kind of promise or engagement ring situation, the answer is no.

My jaw hit the floor. "What? Dad, no!"

"Oh, and you have to finish college first," he added, already moving toward the doorway. "Better yet, you have to *start* college first."

I felt the red hot heat of embarrassment flush over my cheeks as I gaped at my father.

"Dad, we haven't even been dating that long." I protested, rushing to defend both Carter and myself.

Dad only shrugged once more. "I knew your mother was the one the moment I met her, but that doesn't change the rules, so pass that along to Mr Carter. Good night, honey."

Before I could respond, Dad shut the door, leaving me both speechless, and a little mortified. After a moment it dawned on me that Carter and I had been together for over a month and even though it had only been a short amount of time, I felt like I'd somehow known him forever. Carter had become my favorite person. He was the first one I wanted to talk to in the morning, and the last I wanted to hear from at night. Suddenly, the urge to hear his voice took over, and I grabbed my phone to check the time. *10:28 p.m.*

Carter had an away game tonight, and I wasn't sure if he was home yet, so rather than calling I just snapped a photo of the package and texted it to him with a heart emoji.

The box was small, and I tried not to let my mind wander after the ridiculous ideas my dad had just planted in my head. As crazy as I was about Carter, we were far from discussing the rest of our lives together.

Before I could finish opening up the box, my phone lit up with an incoming FaceTime call, and I saw Carter's name pop up.

"Hey!" I answered, squinting at the but all I could see was a dark silhouette. "Um... I can't really see you."

"Yeah, I'm sorry about that," Carter replied. "We're still on the bus heading home, but it's pitch black in here. Give me a second."

There was a pause on his side as he adjusted the lighting, and then a second later I could see his face, dimly lit but smiling.

"There you are," I smiled back once he came into focus.

His grin appeared even brighter than usual on the dark bus. "Now, tell me about this mystery box you got."

I smiled and held up the box to shake near my ear but heard nothing rattle. "I don't know; some guy sent it to me."

Carter's grin spread even wider. "Is this guy cute?"

"The cutest," I replied coyly.

I watched as turned his head from side-to-side as if looking around before focusing back on me. His voice came out in a whisper. "I heard this guy also has a really great taste, so you should open the box."

I felt my stomach somersault and my neck grow hot while he watched me struggle to open the box, before I gave up and put down my phone. "I'm going to need both hands for this task," I explained as I tore into the package and pulled out a small white box.

For a moment, the sight of the small container made my heart race, but I shook away the thought and tried to play it cool. I shimmied the lid off and stared at a necklace sitting in a cotton-like mesh. The pendant held a mountain range, and in the center was a small orb that caught the light in my dimly lit bedroom.

"Carter, this is beautiful," I gushed, holding the necklace to the light. "I can't believe you got this for me"

His face softened, eyes lingering on me with his usual quiet warmth. "Correction there, Dutch. I had it made for you."

His confession took me by surprise, but slowly my heart melted in my chest.

"You should look at the small circle in the middle and tell me what you see," he instructed.

Doing as I was told, I lifted the pendant and turned it gently between my fingers. As the light caught the orb; I leaned in and gasped. The orb in the center held a photo I had only seen one time before, but had never forgotten. Inside was a picture of Carter and me sitting on the dock at camp with his arm wrapped protectively around my shoulder.

This was the photo that got us into trouble at camp over the summer.

Carter and I had broken the rules by spending time alone without an adult nearby, but we had done nothing inappropriate. The dock had simply become our spot. It was the place where we could talk, laugh and just spend hours together with our toes in the water and our hearts wide open. That dock wasn't just where I got to know Carter, but it's where I began to truly understand him. There on the dock, I saw his quiet strength and his deep love for God.

With wide-eyes I stared back at him in disbelief. "Where on earth did you get this picture?"

I caught the mischievous smile playing over his face despite the dark. "I just thought...since we're not at camp anymore that I could ask Lou for it, so I did."

My jaw dropped as I pressed a hand over my mouth, barely able to contain my shock. "After all the trouble we got into over this photo, Lou just handed it over to you?"

Carter glanced around before lowering his voice, trying not to disturb any sleeping teammates.

"You and I have pictures together, sure, but I wanted this one." He explained. "It's just the two of us in our spot, and even though your Aunt Lou was a little reluctant at first, I eventually wore her down."

"How?" I pressed.

Carter dipped his head closer to the phone and kept his voice low. "Lou is someone I can be completely honest with, and I told her even though we broke some rules, I wasn't sorry."

"You really said that to Lou?" I asked, feeling stunned.

"I wouldn't lie to you, Dutch. Carter replied as the dim light from his phone cast a soft glow, lighting up his sincere, midnight eyes. "When I look at that picture, I don't think about us getting into trouble. I just remember all the time that we spent getting to know each other this summer. Sitting with you on that dock is my favorite memory from camp. I want to carry that moment with me wherever I go."

I almost melted into a puddle watching as Carter sat taller, fiddling with something beside him before aiming the camera back so we were face to face. Carter pulled out a small silver chain and held up a similar small pendant like mine, but this time there was an ocean wave with the same small orb at the center.

"This is mine with the same photo of us inside." Carter explained, draping the chain around his neck. "I only take it off when I'm playing so it doesn't get broken."

"I honestly don't know what to say, Carter." I told him as he adjusted the chain around his neck. "This is the sweetest gift ever, I love it."

"You just said all I needed to hear, Dutch." Carter replied with his grin returning. "I just want you to remember that no matter how far apart we are, I'm right there with you. Maybe the necklace will help."

Meeting his gaze, my heart fluttered again and all I could do was say," thank you."

Carter's eyes locked onto mine and for a moment I thought he was about to say something else until his lips twisted into a playful smirk. Then in the worst pirate accent, I'd ever heard he growled, "Me sea lass."

I almost doubled over clutching my stomach while I watched him dramatically rub the pendant hanging from his neck like some kind of pirate treasure. Carted chuckled, though he tried to stay quiet so that he wouldn't disturb any sleeping teammates. "I knew that would make you smile," He said warmly.

When I recovered I cleared my throat and gave my best attempt at a growl replying, "Me mountain lad."

Carter winced and I watched his entire face crunch up while he bit back a laugh. "That was even worse than mine."

I cackled even harder but as my laughter faded, I noticed the serious shift in his expression. "I miss you, Dutch."

I stared back into the screen watching Carter's onyx eyes and I wished more than anything that I could hold him so he knew just how much I missed him back. But with the distance between us, I knew I had to settle for words that didn't quite feel like enough.

"I miss you too, Rosie." I replied softly.

The charge between us evaporated once his teammates behind him started to ooh and ahh. Some threw in kissing noises before a hand flew past Carter's head to wave in front of his camera.

I watched as his phone shook before Carter regained his composure. "Sorry about the guys, they're just jealous."

I chuckled and shrugged as his teammates ruined our moment. "Don't worry, I'll let you go now and hopefully they don't give you any more trouble."

Carter beamed. "I scored the winning goal tonight. They won't be giving me a hard time anytime soon."

"Congratulations! I cheered quietly. "Enjoy your win with the boys but we're still on for tomorrow night, right?"

Carter smiled brightly. "It's a date, Dutch."

6

Long distance dating was beginning to teach me to appreciate the small things I had taken for granted, like choosing an outfit for someone who couldn't actually see. After spending half an hour fixing my hair, I was still standing in front of the mirror twisting an unruly curl around my finger in an attempt to tame the wild strand. For the past five minutes I had debated whether to leave my hair down or go ahead and toss it into a ponytail. Even though I felt a little ridiculous getting ready just to FaceTime Carter somehow the ritual of getting ready for a virtual day made me feel... normal.

When the microwave beeped I dashed the kitchen to save the popcorn before it burned. The buttery scent hit me the second I opened the door and I gave the bag a quick shake and tore it open to pour the snack into a bowl. I hurried back to my room where Carter was waiting patiently from his perched spot on my phone

"I can't believe you forgot the good snacks," Carter shook his head while taking a bite of a piece of chocolate.

As with all of our virtual dates, I took a seat at my desk to face my phone while streaming a movie from my laptop. Carter had a similar setup but was lying on his bed watching the TV in his room.

"I know, but I was in a hurry after work and I didn't have time to just stop by the store," I explained. "But isn't popcorn the perfect snack for any movie?"

Finishing his chocolate Carter shook his head disagreeing with me. He liked to plan themed snacks based on whatever movie we ended up watching. The night we watched *The Princess Bride* together we ate Twizzlers as a reference to the vines in the fire swamp. The week after, Carter chose movie gummy sushi which was much more fitting that my choice of pretzel sticks while we watched *The Karate Kid*.

For tonight's feature, we watched as Forrest Gump sat on a bench with a box of chocolates in his lap. As he offered the candy to the nurse next to him, Carter, in time with the movie, mimicked Forrest Gump, saying "life is like a box of chocolates, you never know what you're going to get."

I couldn't help but giggle as I watched him smile before popping another candy into his mouth. "How many times have you seen this movie?"

"Just enough to quote it," Carter chuckled

"So, you're going to pull a Denny tonight?" I teased laughing as I popped a handful of popcorn into my mouth. Over the summer I discovered Denny had an affinity for memorizing movie lines which drove Theo crazy.

Carter waved a hand dismissively. " Forrest Gump is iconic, Dutch. There's so many brilliant lines from this movie. I mean, the guy tells his whole life story to anyone who sits next to him. Forrest Gump is basically *Evangelism 101*."

I'd heard the term before mostly from church and camp, but I always thought of those guys that went door-to-door selling stuff. "Are you talking about telling people about Jesus?"

Carter popped another piece of chocolate into his mouth and nodded. "Evangelism just means telling people about what Jesus did. He died for us so we could be forgiven and his sacrifice was the ultimate victory. Dutch, think about this summer when you started reading the Bible for yourself and decided to follow him. Through baptism you symbolically put the old you to death and rose up as a new creation."

I still remembered the passage I had read at camp over the summer. In Romans chapter six, Paul talked about a new life in Christ. Reading those verses pricked my heart and I immediately knew what I had to do.

As Carter spoke, I remembered the moment vividly as he asked the pointed question while I stood in the pool beside him. *"Lena, do you believe Jesus is the son of God?"* A chill ran through me as I said yes before Carter immediately submerged me in the water. I remembered being given a clean slate as soon as I rose up from the pool at camp.

Remembering my choice made me reflect on what took place when Jesus died. Despite being buried in a tomb Jesus rose again in a miraculous display that simply defied death. Being submerged in water that day was a symbolic washing away of my own sins, a reminder that Jesus' sacrifice covered me and made me new. I still got chills thinking about all the Lord had done for me.

"We all have a story to tell," Carter said. "That's one of the main reasons I love this movie. Even though it's far-fetched, we get to watch this amazing life Forrest led. The guy was an underdog, but his journey impacted so many people, and that's the thing I think we all need to remember. Even when we can't see the impact we have on others, all it takes is telling one person who can do the same thing and change the lives of dozens more."

As young as Carter was, I couldn't help but feel awestruck whenever he talked about his faith. I smiled and said, "I don't think I would have picked up on all that just by watching this movie myself. I've always just remembered Lieutenant Dan and thought Forrest was nuts for running across the whole country."

"Or maybe he was just a good example of never giving up and facing his problems head on," Carter smirked.

"See, now you're just showing off," I teased him. "Really though, how do you just do that so easily? No matter what, you can just see the meaning in everything."

"I've probably watched this movie a hundred times, Dutch. I notice something new every time," Carter said, popping another piece of candy into his mouth. "That's kind of how reading our Bibles works too."

"True," I murmured, letting my gaze drift back to the screen.

A comfortable silence fell between us, broken only a moment later by Carter. "Speaking of revisiting things... when do you think you'll be able to go back to church?"

The question caught me off guard and when I glanced over, his steady gaze suddenly made me feel like I was under a microscope.

I gave him a small shrug and replied. "Work's just been so busy since I started. I'm still the new girl so I don't want to be the one who's already asking for time off."

There was a crinkling noise on the other end of the video call as Carter said his box of chocolates aside. "Well maybe if you asked to work around church times your manager can help you."

"I just don't think it's that simple," I mentioned a little sharper than I should have. My shoulders tense as I turned back to face the screen even though I could still feel Carter's eyes on me.

Only a beat passed before he spoke again, gently but hesitantly. "Did something change Dutch? You loved being at church while you were here in Meadowbrook."

Keeping my eyes glued to the screen. I didn't answer him but the weight of his words settled in my stomach like a stone.

Now Carter pressed. "Does it feel harder to be there now that you're home."

Still, I said nothing, and just kept my eyes on the computer screen. I had enough guilt over missing services that I didn't want anyone else making me feel bad about it.

A moment later, Carter's voice dropped lower. "Is it because of your mom?"

The question landed as smoothly as a plane crash, hitting me harder than I expected. Carter was done guessing now, he could probably see it from a mile away. I had told him bits and pieces over the summer about my past and he'd seen glimpses of my hurt but not like this. There was nothing that could have prepared me for the way people whispered behind my back at school or how walking into church again would open up far too many questions that I wasn't ready to answer.

I turned and opened up my mouth to speak but I couldn't form the words.

Seeing my hesitation, Carter leaned back and fixed his eyes on the ceiling. "Before the Roses adopted me, I messed up all the time. I was so angry at the world, and I didn't care what anyone thought of me." Just then he glanced over at me, keeping his voice soft. "When I got to Meadowbrook, I finally felt like I had a clean slate because no one here knew the old me, and I got to be someone totally new."

His honesty hung in the air between us, and somehow his words comforted me more than I expected them to.

When I met Carter at camp, he never judged me for my past. Instead, he had shared his own struggles and helped me feel safe opening up to him. Carter had told me about the choices he'd made before Amy and Jack Rose had adopted him, but he also freely spoke about the love they had poured into him by showing him God's love.

Not once had his opinion of me been shaken even when I shared some of my past. *So why was it so hard for me to talk to him now?*

"Setting foot in church... it was weird for me at first," Carter continued. "I did so many dumb things before I was adopted that I didn't feel like I could fit the mold of a Christian."

I glanced over to face and finally met his gaze as he said, "I honestly thought I'd burst into flame stepping one foot in church with all the sin I had in my life."

I couldn't help but laugh at his confession.

"I thought people were going to be able to see right through me and know how much of a mess I was, but instead they welcomed me. Everyone treated me like I belonged and that hit differently because I was so used to feeling like I was a constant disappointment." He exhaled as he turned away from me.

Carter had never been afraid to be open with me and his vulnerability always had a way of connecting us on a deeper level. I was starting to believe that when he saw me struggle he knew if he shared, he could pull out my truth, too.

"Things have been different for me," I finally said. "Coming home was harder than I thought because I think people still see the old me and not the girl I am now."

Carter stared back at me with a thoughtful gaze. "When you say you don't want people to see you at church because they might judge you, I get it, Dutch. I was afraid of the same thing. But what if church is the one place where people won't see you for who you were, but for who you are?"

"No one has seen me differently since I got home." I replied, staring off as I remembered the whispers in the halls at school that still followed me. *Nothing had changed there so why would church be any different?*

I thought about the last time I'd been to church here in Freeport. I felt acknowledged by others but it all hit on a surface level. Church members asked me how I was but the conversation always seemed to turn back to my mother. When I thought about it, I realized it wasn't their judgment I noticed but something else entirely.

Everyone pitied me.

Our family situation wasn't a secret here in Freeport, everyone knew what was going on. My mom had spiraled when her addiction pulled her under and when I showed it for services alone, I could see the sorrow in their eyes. Even though they didn't mean to, their pity made me feel more alone than showing up by myself ever could. I knew I wasn't ready to face that kind of pressure again or to even talk about my mom.

Carter bit his lip and offered a one shoulder shrug. "Look, I know my story is different because I got a fresh start in Meadowbrook and no one saw me differently."

My mouth tilted in a mischievous grin. "So, what you're actually saying is I should move away and start over?"

Carter chuckled but slowly shook his head. "Think about Forrest Gump, Dutch. After everything he had been through, he went home but he was a changed man. What if it's the same for you? You're different now and you owe it to yourself to live the way you promised, even if people still see you how they want to see you."

I sighed as his words hit deeper than I expected. "What if the people at church still only see me as an alcoholic's daughter?" I whispered. "Or as the girl who still just shows up all by herself?"

The questions didn't even seem to bother Carter and I watched as a slow smile spread across his face. "But, what if they see you for you?"

"They won't," I insisted, shaking my head. What he was saying sounded too good to be true and I didn't have the energy anymore to play the *what-if* game.

"You'll never know if you don't find out for yourself, Dutch," Carter replied, his soft eyes searching my face again.

As silence filled the room, the only audible sound was the movie playing on this screen, even though neither of us was really watching anymore. Then, just as I turned back to face him, I saw Carter watching me. When he spoke again, I noticed his voice was quieter this time.

"I see you, Lena."

He glanced back at the movie, and picked up his chocolates again while his words planted themselves in my heart.

I really wanted to believe him but as we sat in silence for the rest of the movie I couldn't focus. All I could imagine was the scene Carter described, where I returned to church and was welcomed with open arms. Laughing with all the other church members like no time had ever passed.

His earlier question soon felt unshakable just like at camp when he first challenged me to read the Bible.

You'll never know if you don't find out for yourself.

What if he was right? Maybe I did owe it to myself to find out.

7

The next morning just after 8:00 a.m. I was rushing through my morning routine thanks to my snooze button. I was moving faster than I had ever moved before brushing my teeth with one hand and putting on mascara with the other to avoid being late. With only one eye complete, I stopped mid-swipe when I saw my manager's name flash across my phone screen. Quickly I spit out my toothpaste and dropped my toothbrush on the counter to take the call.

"Hello?" I answered on high alert.

"Hey Lena, it's Anthony."

"Hey Anthony!" I said, slipping into my best professional voice. "How are you?"

I braced myself already dreading what was coming next. Even though I enjoyed working at the aquarium, I had quickly learned that a high turnover was why they had hired me on the spot.

Anthony cut right to the chase. "Good listen! We've hit a minor snag this morning with an electrical issue so I've called someone in to take a look. Assuming it's nothing major we'll still plan on opening, just later. Can you plan on coming in at noon?"

"Uh, yeah. Are the animals okay?" I asked, feeling completely taken by surprise.

"They're fine," he said, brisk as ever. "I'll shoot you a text once we're good to go. For now, just plan on being here by noon. If you're up for it we could use you until close. Does that work?"

Not really, I wanted to say. The idea of another long shift on my feet made them ache already, but what choice did I have? Anthony's favors weren't usually optional.

"Sure," I said, trying to hide my reluctance.

"Outstanding! I appreciate the flexibility Lena. You're a rockstar." Then before I could even respond he hung up.

I stared at my phone for a beat then glanced at the time: *8:13 a.m.*

That's when it dawned on me, today was Sunday. Worship at Sandy Shores Drive would start soon and for once work wasn't the thing stopping me from going. I stood there holding my phone, feeling conflicted. *Had Carter and I somehow spoken this moment into existence with our conversation last night?* That thought made my chest tighten with guilt.

Weeks ago I would have jumped at the chance to go to church in Meadowbrook, but here in Freeport the desire wasn't the same.

The small white church had been where my mom used to sit beside me in the back pew helping me read hymns we'd sung for years with my grandparents. I used to watch her flip straight to the right scripture and follow along in her Bible reading the notes she'd written in the margins as we listened to the sermon. When there were potlucks Sundays, we would bake casseroles and desserts together to share after worship. Those memories were eventually eclipsed by all the following Sundays that I sat alone while she was too hungover to leave her bed. Singing the same familiar hymns without her warm and steady harmony beside me. When people would hug me or shake my hand they would always say, *"Tell your mother we missed her."*

The more services she missed, the heavier those words felt. Though I knew the church members meant well, they had no idea how isolating their comments could be. I had gone from being part of me and my mom's dynamic duo, to just being the poor girl with an alcoholic mother.

At one point, I'd considered visiting a different church, but Freeport was small and no matter where I went, others would know who I was. I would just be in a new pew with the same odd glances, with members casting the same judgment.

Still, after my conversation with Carter, last night I couldn't shake his words from my thoughts.

What if they see you for you?

I stared at myself in the mirror, noticing the aquarium polo tucked into my khaki shorts, hair done, makeup fixed. My uniform had become a shield for me to hide behind but I didn't have to go to work yet, and without that excuse I couldn't ignore the nagging feeling inside me anymore. I tapped my phone and saw that I had almost an hour before services started. Just enough time to change, grab something to eat and actually go to worship this morning. My stomach twisted as Carter's voice came back to me once more.

How will you know if you never see for yourself?

Leaning over-the-counter, I studied my reflection one more time. All summer I had struggled with the thought that I wasn't enough for God and not for the people at camp who welcomed me so easily but I had been wrong. Running had only distanced me from the very thing my heart needed most, and I wasn't going to make the same mistake again.

The question from Lou's devotional book suddenly popped in my head next.

How do you think your relationship with the Lord needs to change your growth this year?

The answer was simple, I had to move forward. At camp this summer, I had learned how God had given His only Son for me so that I could have the hope of heaven with him someday.

Didn't he deserve one hour of worship from me?

Without bothering to let the fears of judgment creep back in and make me reconsider, I pushed all thoughts from my mind, crossed the hall to my bedroom, and began looking at my dress options. As I sifted through my closet, a Bible verse I had read this week popped into my head.

I will never leave you nor forsake you.

The thought filled me with a similar sense of peace I had experienced over the summer. I couldn't help but ask myself, *how had I been so quick to forget God's promises?* I knew as long as I walked with him I would never be alone again, not in a pew or anywhere else.

***

When I pulled into the church parking lot, the last ounce of bravery I'd left my house with had faded. Now I sat frozen in the driver seat of my car white-knuckling the steering wheel as the early September sun poured through the windshield, too bright for how uneasy I felt. Showing up seemed easier when it was just a thought, but as I was driving over, the closer I got, the smaller I began to feel.

I let go of the wheel and lowered my visor to check my reflection, only to see my scrunched waves had lost their shape in the humidity, though my makeup held. I normally didn't wear much but given the extra time this morning, I wanted to make an effort.

I snapped the visor back into place and scanned the parking lot where more cars were already pulling in as everyone headed toward the entrance. I exhaled slowly trying to breathe out the growing tightness in my chest.

Glancing down at the clock, I saw that it read: 9:52 a.m. I had eight minutes until service started. My fingers hovered over the key but before I turned the engine off I lowered my head and quietly whispered a prayer: *God please be with me and help me to be brave.*

As I raised my head, I decided to just rip off the band-aid so I opened my door and climbed it out. I clicked the lock on my key fob and slowly marched across the crowded parking lot, taking each step one-by-one. My sandals clicked against my heels as I climbed the concrete stairs to the front door. As I reached for the handle, the solid front door flew open forcing me to dart backwards to avoid being hit.

Once I found my footing, I glanced up and felt a jolt ricochet through me as I spotted a girl I knew well standing before me. Her sundress made her rich caramel skin seem even more perfect as her tight coiled curls framed her beautiful face. Worthy Clarke looked just as stunned to see me as I felt seeing her.

"Oh, I-I'm so sorry." She stammered, but her words were rushed like she was in a hurry.

I started to reply, but the door opened again, and the jingling of keys caught both our attention. Miss Pearl, Worthy's grandmother swung up in the door and held out her keys to her granddaughter. "Here, baby, don't forget these. The bag is in the trunk."

Worthy's eyes flashed back to me, as she pointed and said, "Hey Nan, look who I just ran into."

Miss Pearl turned toward me and froze, and I watched as her eyes widened in surprise, locking on mine. For a moment she seemed shocked to see me and neither of us moved, but then something shifted in her expression and a slow, sweet smile spread across her face.

"Oh my, Worthy girl," Miss Pearl said, stepping closer. "Are my eyes playing tricks on me or do you see sweet Lena, too?"

Before I knew how to react, Miss Pearl wrapped me in a hug as if no time had passed. Her embrace was as comforting as I remembered as the soft scent of honeysuckle surrounding me. When Miss Pearl pulled back her hands slid down my arms to grip my hands gently. Her beautiful cocoa eyes met mine and I was struck by her timeless beauty. The only signs of age on her were the silver strands threaded through Miss Pearl's long braids and the wrinkles on her hands now holding mine.

"Welcome back baby," she said sweetly, giving my hands a gentle squeeze.

I smiled politely at her but cut my eyes to Worthy as she shook the keys over her head. "Um, I'm just going to run to the car now. I'll be right back," she said, darting down the stairs to the parking lot.

Miss Pearl seized my attention again and motioned for me to come with her. "We've only got a few minutes before service starts. Let me help you get settled in with us."

I had forgotten just how forward Miss Pearl had always been. When my family first moved to Freeport, Mom and I found the little white church and quickly became members. Like mine, Worthy's dad had been in the Coast Guard, but when her mom was sick, her family was often hit or miss at church services. Worthy was just a little girl when her mom passed away from cancer. Miss Pearl moved in with them soon after to help raise Worthy, especially since her father was frequently away.

The day I met Miss Pearl, I was captivated by her. There was a warmth about her that reminded me of my Grams, but she also had a way of making you feel known and loved with just one look. Miss Pearl greeted people in the church as though she'd been a member here her whole life and when she met my mom she pulled her into a tight hug and introduced herself as Miss Pearl Clarke. Not Pearl but Miss Pearl, a name that immediately commanded respect, though respect was never hard to give to her.

The one constant that had never changed earlier in my mom's addiction was Miss Pearl. No matter what, she always seemed to be there, checking on me when I showed up for services alone and offering to bring a hot meal if we needed one. I hadn't appreciated her before, and looking back now, I wish I would have told her just how much her efforts had meant to me.

Now I let Miss Pearl lead me through the front door and into the foyer. The same dingy blue carpet lay beneath my feet showing less life than the last time I stepped foot on it. The mail slots were still located to the left for all of the members' families. I used to visit often to see what kind of mail my mom and I would get. Before I stopped attending services, I began emptying our slot to throw away the cards without looking at them. I didn't want to read notes or have people keep telling me just how much they miss seeing us or that they hoped my mom would return soon. No one knew just how much it hurt to be reminded of everything going wrong with my family.

A few older men stood by the double doors leading into the auditorium handing up bulletins. Each of them smiled kindly as we passed before entering the auditorium.

Miss Pearl took my hand and gave me a reassuring smile. "We've always got room on our pew for one more."

"That's okay, Miss Pearl," I tried to dismiss her. "I can just sit right here—"

My words trailed off as my eyes landed on the back pew I used to share with my mom. Sitting there now, I spotted a young mother with her two children quietly trying to wrangle them into putting their toys away before service started.

The sight took me by surprise but stung even more, launching me back to when I was just a little girl at church. Most of my childhood worship memories were made in Meadowbrook where my Gramps always had a stash of butterscotch or peppermint candies and Grams brought coloring books to keep me busy. Sometimes Jojo would come sit with us, and we would color side by side until we could run off to the playground after the final amen was said. I would give anything to be back there right now.

The little girl in the pew peered up at me, suddenly catching me staring. I felt my chest tighten as I tore my gaze away and found Miss Pearl now watching me expectantly.

"Honey?" She asked. "We should go find our seats, service is starting."

Reluctantly, I obeyed as she led the way up the aisle while a man stepped up to the podium to begin reading out the morning announcements. My heart was pumping louder and louder with each step we took. She slid into a pew five rows from the front, and I followed, only to pause again when I saw who sat on the other side of her. Cruz Clarke, Worthy's dad looked exactly the same as he did when I last saw him. He sported dark buzzed hair, and a neatly trimmed beard now brushed with gray. As soon as he spotted me, he leaned over Miss Pearl and reached out to shake my hand. His smile said everything his words didn't have to.

"It's so good to see you, Miss Lena," Cruz whispered.

I smiled politely in return, "It's good to see you too."

Once he let go, I noticed Worthy slip into the other side of the pew beside her dad. She appeared surprised again to see me as if she didn't expect me to be sitting with her family. A part of me wanted to shrug as if to say *your grandmother made me* or *Miss Pearl didn't really give me a choice* but before I could, she passed Miss Pearl's keys to her and focused her eyes on the front.

I tried to pay attention during the service as we sang songs, prayed and took the Lord's Supper, but during the sermon I found myself staring at the same page in my Bible mindlessly rereading the same verse over and over. Though I caught parts of the sermon, I was too distracted by Worthy's discomfort in seeing me. I wanted to hop up and find a seat in the back, but I knew that would only draw more attention to me, and I couldn't help but wonder if others were surprised to see me here, too. The town drunk's daughter returns to church after being sent away for the summer.

Did anyone even know?

Freeport was a small town, of course everyone knew. Over the summer my dad got a promotion at his city job, so he didn't have to work boat tours anymore just to make ends meet. If anyone had seen him over the summer and passing, I'm sure they noticed I wasn't with him. Our family had been at the center of Freeport's gossip ring for years, and I felt sure my absence only gave the town sending you to talk about.

As a short to gray-haired man stepped up behind the pulpit, I felt my stomach clench as he began singing a few closing acapella songs, but it was the last one that nearly broke my heart in two. The congregation filled the room singing the hymn, *God Will Take Care of You.*

The lyrics spun around me as if propelling me through a door I always tried to keep shut. Suddenly, I was back in that dark hospital room sitting beside the bed, holding my mother's limp hand begging God not to take her. Mom's skin had been so cold and pale, not warm and vibrant like I remembered. She used to sing the same hymn to me when I had bad dreams or cried while Dad was away at sea. This time as I sat with her I was the one singing willing her to come back to me.

The memory of singing those lyrics in that sterile room made my throat feel tight. I remembered just how the tears fell when I saw my mom's fingers finally move. She squeezed my hand and I knew she heard me singing.

Now, sitting here in a pew with the same words wrapping around me, I felt as uncomfortable as someone would wearing wet jeans. My hands twisted in my lap as I fought to stay present but the past only grew louder as flashes of memories pulled me through the months that followed. Just when Mom seemed to recover, I felt the pain all over again when she left.

The preacher's voice finally broke through my unwanted trip down memory lane as he offered the invitation to come forward, but when no one moved, the church sang one last song, said a closing prayer and then we were dismissed.

Immediately, I reached for my keys and climbed to my feet just when Miss Pearl and Cruz turned to me.

"How have you been, Miss Lena?" Cruz asked, a bright smile lighting up his face. "We sure have missed seeing you around here."

Cruz had always been a jolly soul, and I politely smiled back at him, unable to help glancing at Worthy who seemed as ready to go as I was.

"I've been good." I answered, hating the agonizing idea of small talk.

"Oh, don't give me that." Miss Pearl nudged me. "Tell us about your summer and where you've been hiding."

Just like that, I knew those around town had some idea that I hadn't been in Freeport this summer. I smiled as I tried to remain calm, though I felt anything but.

"I went to Meadowbrook for most of the summer break. My Aunt Lou grew up going to New Hope Bible Camp." I said carefully avoiding the mention of my mom. "This summer was my first time there."

Miss Pearl beamed affectionately, but I saw Worthy's demeanor as her face fell. "You went to New Hope?"

With a small grin, I tried my best to remain polite even though there was obvious tension between us. "Yeah, do you know it?"

I watched her give me a look like that was a ridiculous question. "Everyone here knows about New Hope Bible Camp."

Cruz chuckled and motioned to his daughter. "Worthy's been wanting to go for years."

"Oh that's great!" I continued trying to be polite. "You should go next summer."

"She should," Miss Pearl said, but her sidelong glance at her granddaughter alluded that there was more to that suggestion. "But sometimes we allow other things to get in the way."

When I glanced back at Worthy, I didn't miss the way she cut her eyes at her grandmother before murmuring, "Bible Camp cuts into cheer."

Before an argument could break out, Cruz asked. "Did you enjoy your time there this summer?

"I did." I answered almost dreamily as I talked about my favorite place. "I was baptized this summer and actually reconnected with some old friends there."

Out of nowhere Miss Pearl pulled me into a big hug and cheered in my ear, "Congratulations, baby girl!"

Cruz reached out next and gave my hand another quick squeeze as I noticed Worthy's interest in my camp experience began to shift. She no longer seemed wary of me but like she wanted to know more.

"That's so exciting!" Cruz cried. "How are your folks doing? I see your Dad around town from time-to-time but I haven't seen your mama lately."

The mention of my mom suddenly killed the mini-celebration we were having. I anticipated people asking about my mom, but hoped I could avoid those conversations entirely. Now, being asked point blank, I knew they were just making small talk, but I wasn't ready to open up about her.

"They're good." I answered flatly. Feeling the key fob in my hand, I clung to it, and decided that now was a good time to head out before they pressed me for more information. "I'm sorry to be short but I better run. Thank you for letting me sit with you."

Miss Pearl's brows furrowed as she caught me before I could turn. "Are you sure? We have a fish fry luncheon today and we would love to have you stay and eat with us."

"Thank you, but I'd better get going. I have to get to work this afternoon." I answered, instantly seeing Miss Pearl deflate. When I caught Worthy's gaze, I could see the familiar distance return.

"It's so good to see you, Lena!" Cruz reached out to me once more. "Remember, we have services at six tonight and at seven on Wednesdays. We hope to see you next time!"

I smiled and thanked them politely again before I turned to blend in with the crowd, filing out of the church. As I did, I waved politely and exchanged a few quick hellos with others who recognized me before finally escaping outside.

Once I made it to my car, I shut the door and released a heavy sigh. I had done it, I survived my first church service back in Freeport. My plan had been executed almost flawlessly, I faced my fears, avoided questions about my mom, and made it through services without crumbling into pieces.

Eager to focus on something else, I grabbed my phone and began checking my missed messages. I had a new text from Anthony that confirmed the aquarium was good to open and I was still needed at noon, but what caught my eye next was a Snapchat from Carter.

I opened a new SnapChat message and took in the sight of Carter, Jojo, Denny, and Carter's little sister Sadie crowded into the frame pulling goofy faces. Behind them, I saw the familiar sight of their lunch spot, Max's Diner. I felt my heart squeeze in my chest as I quickly typed out: *I miss you guys!* And then closed the app before I started to spiral.

Max's Diner wasn't just a photo; it was the place where Carter first prayed for dinner on our first date. The diner was where we shared our family history and enjoyed quality time together; finally, just the two of us. The memory made my heart race as it pulled me back to my favorite night in Meadowbrook.

8

The image of Max's Diner lingered on my mind, pulling me straight back to Meadowbrook and to my first real date with Carter. After weeks of living in jean cutoffs and sweaty camp t-shirts, dressing up felt foreign. No one ever cared about what you looked like at Camp, but on our first date I wanted to look nice for Carter.

The only decent outfit I had brought with me over the summer was my black skater dress that I had already worn days earlier to the End-of-Summer Banquet. Feeling panicked, I reached out to Jojo for help.

Trust me I'll be over soon. She had texted back.

By the time Carter arrived, Jojo had worked her magic. Loaning me a ribbed white tee, we paired it with a high-waisted skirt and an olive headband. Then, I touched up my makeup and helped tame my hair into loose curls. Finally, I borrowed a green jacket from Lou to pull my look together.

When Carter arrived, he saw me and smiled in a way that made my breath catch. Then, as we climbed into his car, he reached for my hand.

"You look amazing." He said, fingers sliding through mine.

I felt a blush creep up from my neck to my cheeks. "Thanks, you look great too."

He laughed lightly, and my stomach flipped. Carter wore a cream, short sleeve button down and dark jeans. He always appeared put together, but tonight there was something intentional about how he had dressed. His honey-brown hair had grown out, falling into soft waves, and his face was clean-shaven with no trace of stubble.

He really was beautiful.

Carter pulled into a spot downtown and parked, then stepped out and marched around to open my door with effortless charm. As I climbed out, I watched him drop a few coins into the parking meter and tap in four hours of time.

A flicker of panic rose inside my chest. "Um, Lou asked me to be back before eleven tonight." I said, nodding toward the meter.

Carter gave a small smirk and replied, "I know, but meters aren't exactly precise. I'd rather give us extra time than have to race the clock to make it back to the car."

I relaxed a little, returning his smile as he reached for my hand again. Fingers laced, we strolled past the shops downtown, places I'd seen nearly every summer or holiday I'd spent in Meadowbrook growing up. Not much had changed aside from the freshly painted storefronts and their displays, both keeping the small-town charm alive. As we strolled, I felt a memory trickle in of me holding Gramp's hand when I was a kid along these same streets that yanked on my heartstrings.

When we reached Max's Diner, Carter stepped ahead and grabbed the door for me. The familiar hum of chatter and clinking dishes spilled out, and I couldn't help but smile.

"After you, Dutch," he said with a playful tilt of his head.

The aroma of freshly brewed coffee and sizzling bacon hit me like a wave of nostalgia. Booths lined the walls, with tables nestled between them and the counter. The place looked the same as always. The counter was as crowded as usual, and since the restaurant was busy, the sign by the door urged us to seat ourselves. I followed Carter's lead as he chose a corner booth near the front, motioned for me to sit and slid in across from me.

"I hope you don't mind the diner," Carter said. "But it's the best place in town."

I grinned at him as I took in our surroundings. The diner blended modern simplicity with retro charm. I glanced up to see the high, white-paneled ceilings, which made the space feel open while large windows framed the golden hues of the setting sun, now casting shadows on the black and white geometric tile flooring.

"The Diner is perfect." I affirmed. "I used to come here all the time with my family."

"Just when I thought I was introducing you to something special," Carter joked.

"This place is special," I replied as a small blonde woman with a pixie cut and glasses approached. She greeted us with a sweet smile and handed over two menus.

"What can I get you two to drink?"

Carter motioned for me to go first, and I asked for water while he asked for sweet tea. As she spun on her heel, Carter turned his attention back to me, his eyes warm. "So what makes this place so special?"

I grinned again as I opened the plastic-coated menu. Max had expanded it from the two-sided handout he used to offer to a full breakfast, lunch and dinner spread. My gaze drifted back to the counter where I pointed at the small ice cream machine that still rested on top.

"My grandparents used to bring me in here for lunch all the time." I explained. "We came here so often, Max used to let me behind the counter when I begged to get ice cream all by myself."

Carter chuckled and threw me a teasing grin. "Are you admitting that you've always been stubborn?"

I stuck out my tongue at him and pointed to the large round booth across the restaurant behind him, currently filled with a family of six. "We used to visit often, and our family would sit in that exact booth after church on Sundays. Because our group was so large, that was the only table that could fit all of us. Oh, that and, um...Lou's ex-husband Ryan always preferred that booth."

Carter's eyes flashed with temporary shock. "Sometimes I forget that she was married. I think I heard her mention him to my mom once. Wasn't the guy a lawyer or something?"

I nodded. "Yeah, none of us have seen him in years. I just remember him being so busy, it drove my Gramps crazy. My Gramps was big on family time, and Ryan always seemed swamped with work."

"So, why did they get divorced?" Carter asked.

I leaned in and lowered my voice, as Carter mirrored my actions. "He had an affair."

As soon as the words were out of my mouth, Carter's eyes widened in shock. "On Lou? *No way!*"

I threw my hands up, feeling just as appalled as he was. "Right?! What made it worse was that the affair was with her best friend, *Max's ex-wife.* "

"You're kidding." He whispered, as his eyes narrowed in disbelief.

As if on cue, a man approached our booth with two drinks in hand. His short haircut was now flecked with gray, but his unmistakable grin was warm and aimed at me.

"Well, if it isn't little Lenny Lee back in Meadowbrook." He said, setting the drinks down with a thud.

I laughed and stood to greet him. "Hey Max, it's been forever."

Max spread his arms wide to take me in. "Get over here, kiddo."

I stepped into his hug, and just like that the years melted away. For a moment I was ten again, wild and carefree, darting around his diner begging to help behind the counter. His arms were strong and familiar, and I immediately realized how much I missed this place.

When he pulled back, Max's hands landed on my shoulders as he studied me like he was checking to see that I was real. "You're a Rivers girl through and through. I can't believe how much time has passed since I last saw you."

The name landed a little harder than I expected for it to. *Rivers was* my mom's maiden name and the one everyone in town knew my family by. Lou's business sign bore the family name in bold: *River Ridge Realty*, but I was just grateful that Max hadn't mentioned how much I looked like her, like everyone else normally did.

I smiled as he released me. "Yeah, I know it's been a while. How have you been?"

Max hadn't changed a bit. He was just as tall and broad shoulders as I remembered, though there were more lines around his eyes now.

"Living the dream." Max said with a grin. "Lou told me you were in town, but for some reason, I still pictured a little girl with messy braids and grass stains on her knees."

"Seventeen now." I corrected with a small laugh as I slid back into the booth.

His eyes widened as if really seeing me for the first time, then they shifted to Carter. "Well, look who you brought in with you."

"Hey Max," Carter said with a small wave.

Max narrowed his eyes as he lowered his voice. "I've got my eye on you."

I glanced back at Carter, whose tight-lipped smile showed he knew better than to talk back.

"So what'll it be tonight? Your usual chicken tenders and fries?" Max teased, looking down at me.

I cackled and held my hands to my face to hide my reddening cheeks in front of Carter. "I can't believe you remember."

"I never forget family orders." Max responded, and then it hit me just how close Max had always been to our family.

He always used to fish with Gramps and I remembered him sitting in the pews at church, always quick with a joke or a handshake. He treated my mom like she was his kid sister ruffling her hair whenever they crossed paths, and Max always greeted my dad with a clap on the back, and a hug whenever he could make it up for a visit.

With Lou, he was different, though, lighter somehow. The two of them shared old jokes and half-finished sentences, slipping into an easy banter that only years of friendship could build. Until this summer, I never truly understood just how precious that type of bond could be.

Now Max turned to Carter, but the warmth in his eyes quickly faded as he sized my date up. Carter shifted uncomfortably, then slid the menu across the table. "I usually order the bacon cheeseburger with fries." He answered, his voice steady but cautious.

Without another word, Max swiped the menus from the table and turned in one fluid motion. Carter's tense shoulders relaxed as he sank back into the booth. "I take it Max doesn't know my usual."

"Do you come here often?" I asked.

Carter smirked. "You don't have to try to pick me up, Dutch. We're already on a date."

I rolled my eyes and snorted. "You know what I mean."

Carter grinned as he shrugged. "I think I've been here enough with my parents and Denny to qualify as a regular. I always order the burger, it really is the best in town."

"I think so too," I said, tucking a loose piece of hair behind my ear. "Gramps used to say Max put a little taste of magic in everything he made."

Carter leaned in again, resting his forearms on the table, seeming curious. "Let's go back to the part where you were telling me about Max's ex-wife." He said, circling back to our earlier conversation.

"Everything makes so much more sense now. I never connected the dots before tonight but there has always seemed to be something going on between Max and Lou. "

I was mid-sip of water before I almost spit it out. "No way! They've always been best friends. Lou showed me old camp photo albums with tons of pictures of her and Max. Nothing romantic ever happened between them."

Carter raised his eyebrows and sipped his tea while I watched his eyes dance with amusement. "Are you sure about that?"

I narrowed my eyes playfully, "I'm sure."

He swirled the ice in his cup, tapping the straw against the rim. "I've seen Max sitting with Lou at church a lot recently. My mom teases her about eating at home less because she's always here at the diner."

I took another sip, letting the cold slowly slide down my throat. "Max grew up with Mom and Lou, and my Gramps even helped him open this place. I guess I just feel like he's always just been a part of my family."

Carter didn't press, but the knowing look in his eyes didn't fade either. Just then, the blonde waitress set our food down, and Max waved from behind the counter.

With another dimpled smile, Carter started assembling his burger, sliding the lettuce and tomato into place on top of the meat patty. "All I'm saying is Denny and Jojo were just friends, too... until they weren't."

When he finished and extended his hand across the table, I hesitated for half a second before reaching out to let my palm rest on top of his. His fingers curled gently around mine as he bowed his head.

"God," Carter began, dipping his head and lowering his voice to a gentle whisper. "Thank you for this food and the time that we get to spend together. Amen."

His words made my heart do a flip-flop in my chest, and I peeked over at him before he lifted his head. Just for a second, I saw myself outside this moment, like a younger version of me was looking in on a dream she'd only dared to hope for. Twenty minutes later, when Max slid the check onto the edge of the table with a wink, I finally felt like my feet were back on the ground.

"Lenny, don't be a stranger while you're in town, all right? I'll even reserve your booth in the corner if I know you're popping in."

"Thanks, Max," I grinned. Hearing him say *your booth* warmed my heart.

Max then turned his attention to Carter as he slid the ticket to him and glared. "Make sure you drive safely and remember I have eyes everywhere."

My gaze flicked back to my date as I watched Carter nod obediently before taking the check from Max. Then, with a final wink in my direction, Max slipped away behind the counter again.

"Wow!" Carter quietly exclaimed, staring down at the ticket.

"What?" I asked, wondering what was wrong.

Carter slid the check to me and my eyes darted straight to Max's chicken scratch right below the free charge of our entire meal. At the bottom, Max had scrawled: *Get her back to Lou's on time and keep your hands to yourself.*

I felt a slow smile spread over my face as Carter quickly slid from the booth. "Let's get out of here before he puts a hit out on me."

A laugh escaped me as Carter started for the door. As I climbed to my feet, I peered back over at Max, who caught my gaze. I mouthed a final quick *thank you* and watched Max dip his head slightly in acknowledgement. With a final small wave, I followed after Carter as he stood holding the door for me.

***

After dinner, Carter and I strolled hand in hand down the quiet streets of downtown Meadowbrook.

"So, how long has it been since you've been back here?" He asked, glancing at me as I pointed out a few of the newer shops tucked between familiar storefronts.

I paused, watching a flickering neon sign buzz to life at the corner ATM. "Two years at least."

For Gramps's funeral, I thought without saying out loud. Something in my expression must have changed though because Carter gave my hand a gentle squeeze and rubbed his thumb gently over mine. I glanced up and gave him a small, grateful smile as we continued down the street.

We passed the Meadowbrook Mercantile, the store's wide front windows glowing beneath string lights overhead. I stopped in my tracks, drawn to the familiar sight, and saw the same candy barrels that were still sitting near the entrance. As I scanned the shelves inside, they were still lined with an assortment of home goods, canned jams, outdoor supplies, and the toys I used to beg for. The store seemed exactly the same, like it had been frozen in time.

"This place always seemed so magical to me when I was younger." I said. "If Lou or my grandparents needed anything, somehow we could always find it here."

Carter leaned a little closer, looking through the window with me. "You should have seen Denny trying to find butter for his mom in here one time. It took him almost thirty minutes because he was looking in the non-perishable foods instead of the refrigerated section."

I flicked my gaze back at him. "You let the poor guy struggle?"

With a coy glint in his eye, Carter shrugged. "It was pure entertainment for me."

I laughed, then glanced a few doors down and spotted Peaks and Paperbacks. The store was more elegant than I remembered, with cheerful black awnings framed by lush flower boxes.

"My mom and Grams loved this store." I said and nodded toward the display. "They used to talk about their book characters like they were real people. "I would just sit and listen to them even though I had no idea what they were talking about."

Carter didn't say anything, he just peered down at me as if trying to read my mind. Seconds later, though, he asked. "Do you want to go inside?"

I shook my head and gave his hand a gentle squeeze this time and pulled him forward.

This one's probably my favorite store downtown," Carter said as we passed the pawn shop ahead. "Which probably makes me sound so lame."

I followed his gaze to the faded storefront where a buzzing neon sign in the window that read *COLLECTOR'S ITEMS* above a spread of vintage vinyls and antique instruments. On the shelf below, old devices and knick-knacks sat like forgotten memories.

"Only your use of the word *lame* is lame," I said, bumping his shoulder playfully. "Are you into antiques?"

Carter released my hand and motioned to an old army uniform in the window. "Kind of.... I'm really just into history. Sometimes this shop feels like stepping into a portal to the past."

I watched as Carter moved from the uniform to a shelf of old artifacts, spellbound by the collection. "I came in with my mom for the first time when she was searching for a globe for her classroom, but I ended up digging through stuff for hours. I found a pocket watch and this super old compass."

"That sounds.... interesting." I said, throwing him a teasing grin.

"Trust me it was," Carter said. "The watch was from World War One and the compass had coordinates etched on the back, like its original owner had gone on some wild adventure."

He glanced at me like he wasn't sure if he was geeking out too much, but I smiled.

"One man's trash..." I teased.

"Is another man's time travel device," he added, intentionally not finishing the line correctly. "I mean, isn't it cool to know that we can revisit the past by holding these things in our hands?"

Just as we were about to move on, something in the display made me stop short. "Wait, look at that."

Carter stepped closer as I leaned in toward a small music box nestled by a row of silver rings. The floral design on its lid was so familiar, It made my heart skip a beat.

"This looks like the one my Grams used to keep on her vanity." I said softly, eyes locked on the box. "She always used to let me listen to the music while getting ready because I love to wind up the centerpiece."

"What song would it play?" Carter asked gently.

"*Somewhere Over the Rainbow*." I said, feeling a small lump in my throat thinking about my Grams. "My Grandpa made the music box for her and then she passed it down to my mom to give to me someday, but Mom said it got lost during one of our moves."

Carter's gaze flicked from the box, then back to me. "Do you think this could be her box?"

I bit my lip. "I don't know, anything's possible, right?"

The store lights were off and a closed sign hung in the window, so I had no way of truly knowing.

"Do you want to come back and check later this week?" Carter offered as if he knew exactly what I was thinking.

"Yeah," I said quietly. "I'd like that."

He reached down and gave my fingers a light squeeze then grinned. "How about we go get dessert. I'm suddenly in a major cupcake mood."

I laughed, "You're always in a cupcake mood."

"Not true." He said, dragging me playfully down the next block. "Sometimes it's ice cream."

His quip made me blush as I remembered the ice cream fight he and I had on the dock before leaving camp. Catching the look in my eye, Carter threw me a flirty grin as he laced his fingers with mine then pulled me toward the Cupcake Cottage. The store's pink sign glowed under the streetlight and the striped awnings made it feel like something out of his storybook. He held the door open, and a bell jingled above us as we stepped inside where the warm scent of sugar and vanilla instantly hit me.

"Okay, this is dangerous." I whispered as my eye scanned the row of bistro tables and the glass case packed with cupcakes, cookies, and little cakes too pretty to even eat.

"The good kind of dangerous," Carter grinned, following me in.

A tall blonde girl came out from the back and I felt a tiny twinge of disappointment for a second. I'd hoped Jojo might be working tonight, but she was probably with Denny. I wandered toward the display while Carter headed straight for the counter like he owned the place.

"Hey Dutch," he called over his shoulder. "Do you see anything you want?"

I leaned over the glass and my eyes landed on a yellow cupcake topped with swirls of white frosting and rainbow sprinkles. "Birthday cake." I answered him, pointing to the dessert.

The girl behind the counter smiled and reached inside the display. "Is it someone's birthday?"

Before I could say a word, Carter tilted his head at me with that thoughtful look of his. "Not exactly," he said, "but we're definitely celebrating. My girlfriend here just became a Christian, so I guess you could say we're celebrating her *re-birthday*."

The girl beamed. "Then this one's on the house," she said as she rang us up.

Carter handed over a few bucks and waved off the change.

Outside, we tossed our boxes in the trash and leaned against the wall just outside the shop.

"Thanks, Rosie." I said, peeling back the wrapper of my cupcake. "For this summer and for the perfect night. I hope I've told you enough, but if not....I'm telling you now."

Carter's eyes softened as he gazed back at me. "I'd do it all again, Dutch. A hundred times."

He scooped frosting off his cupcake with his fingertip and popped it into his mouth. "Still unbeatable," he said around the bite. "Do you want to taste mine?"

I ran a finger across the top of my own and licked the frosting clean. "I think I'm good, I doubt I can even finish this one."

Before I knew it was happening, Carter reached over and smeared frosting across my cheek.

"Carter!" I gasped, stepping back. He was already laughing as he handed me a napkin like he was some kind of gentleman.

"Oh, come on!" He said, cackling. "We're celebrating!

I narrowed my eyes and backed up another step while he narrowed his playful eyes at me in return. "We clearly have different ideas of how to celebrate."

Carter took another dramatic bite of cupcake while still watching me. "Okay, then tell me how would you celebrate our first date?"

I raised an eyebrow and crooked my finger at him. "Come closer and I'll show you."

He blinked in surprise at my retort but took the bait and moved forward one slow step and then another. The next thing I knew, our faces were so close, our noses nearly brushed.

Then I struck, smashing my cupcake straight into his face.

Carter reeled back stunned as frosting clung to his cheek and nose. For one breathless second, we both froze before I doubled over laughing.

"You just wasted a perfectly good cupcake!" He accused, wiping his face. "That's a crime, Dutch!"

"I regret nothing." I laughed, already backing up, preparing to run from him, but I didn't make it far. Carter lunged and caught me around the waist spinning me to face him. He nuzzled his frosting covered face against mine as I squealed at trying to wriggle free.

"Truce, Rosie! I call truce!" I squealed, laughing breathlessly.

He stopped, but the happiness still danced in his eyes. "How can I even trust you now?" He teased me.

I slipped one arm free and held my pinky finger out to him. "I never break a pinky promise."

Carter quickly released me and linked his pinky with mine and brought our joined hands to his lips. The sight of his kiss sent a flutter straight through me before I kissed my own fist in return, just like we always did. He kept our hands clasped and pulled me toward him until our foreheads touched. Then his lips found mine soft and warm. I felt the world fade away as Carter kissed me gently, as if this moment meant as much to him as it did to me. With icing still on our faces and his lips still on mine I realized this wasn't just a first date.

It was a night I would never forget.

9

I clung to the memory of Carter while the weekend slipped by. Returning to church had been just as hard as I'd feared stirring up memories I didn't want to face. At home, Dad spent all his time sanding down his boat like if he just scrubbed hard enough, Mom would instantly reappear. No matter how sorry I felt for him, I was also a little envious because I wished I had something to distract me too.

When Monday arrived, I kept my head down as I moved through the school hallways doing everything I could to stay invisible. If I could just make it through the day without any drama, maybe I could hang on to the fragile peace I had worked so hard to rebuild over the summer.

By third period, I had things down to a science. Like someone in witness protection, I slipped between groups and avoided eye contact by making myself small. On the way to lunch, I took a wrong turn though and wandered too close to Miss Jones's office and Lacey's old locker.

I held my breath and glanced down the hallway, my pulse pounding in my veins. When I didn't see any sign of Lacey, relief swept through me as I picked up my pace and weaved through a knot of underclassmen.

Out of the blue I heard someone whisper, "That's her, that's the girl."

I didn't stop to see who they meant. I just kept moving as another voice carried asking, "You mean *Pickle?*"

Laughter broke out behind me like an unholy chorus. When I turned slightly just enough to see them, I realized the ones talking were on the varsity cheer squad.

Of course.

To my surprise, the squad didn't bother me, but the sight of Worthy did. She stood among them wide-eyed and guilty, as if caught in the act. Our eyes met across the hall, but I didn't wait to see what she'd say or if she'd say anything at all. I simply pushed forward past the administrative offices, through the main corridor, and into the cafeteria wing.

The lunchroom was already a zoo with two lines stretched beyond the doors. Walking in felt like stepping into a trap and my pulse quickened, at the thought that I could, at any moment, run into Lacey or Ronni. So I didn't risk it. I turned on my heel and slipped through the double doors that led to the student quad. With the sun blazing, I made a beeline for the shade of the live oak near the gym and sank to the ground. I tilted my chin up and inhaled deeply as sunlight dabbled through the tree above me as I tried to steady my racing heart, but I just couldn't forget what I'd heard in the hall.

Pickle.

The name still carried the brutal reminders of last year and the mistakes I wished I could erase. Senior year was supposed to be the best year, yet, here I was hiding from my classmates beneath an old oak. Desperate to quiet the noise in my head, I pulled out my phone and scrolled through Carter's texts from this morning. His messages were the perfect reminder that I wasn't who everyone still thought I was.

Right then, a new Snapchat lit up my screen. *Jojo.*

I opened it fast, eager for the distraction. She had sent a video of Danny and Theo at the lunch table dumping mashed potatoes, corn, and what looked like shredded chicken into one big pile smothered in hot sauce.

The caption read: *Boys will be boys...*

For the first time all day, a laugh slipped out, and I was busy typing a reply when footsteps slapped across the quad. When I glanced up, my breath hitched because Worthy was heading straight for me, crossbody bag bouncing against her hip. She wore a floral bodysuit, rolled-up jean shorts, and a navy cardigan. Worthy was always so put-together, unlike me, who was sitting in flannel and my faded Meadowbrook Mercantile tee.

"Is this seat taken?" She asked when she approached, pointing to the spot of grass next to me.

I blinked before I found the words to answer her. "Um...no. You can sit."

Worthy hesitated initially, then shrugged off her bag and lowered herself beside me, slowly and carefully, like she was as unsure of this decision as I was. Her eyes flicked to mine briefly, then away as silence stretched awkwardly between us.

I watched as she ripped up a blade of grass and started twisting it between her fingers. "I'm sorry about that back there, and about the girls...that was messed up."

I blinked at her, caught off guard. "You don't have to apologize."

Yet, even as the words left my mouth, they weren't true. I had hoped the drama from last year would have stayed buried, but clearly, that had been wishful thinking. If I was honest with myself, I understood where those girls were coming from. Before camp, I probably would have been right there with them, wanting the last word and needing someone to blame. Camp had been transformative for me though, offering me a new perspective.

"I've made a lot of bad choices," I admitted, eyes on the grass between us. "If I still feel the weight of them, I doubt anyone else has forgotten the things I've done."

With a focused gaze, Worthy tilted her head like she was trying to figure something out. "Did you really become a Christian this summer?"

The surprise in her voice as she asked the question only answered what I thought everyone believed about me. After last year it truly did seem unbelievable that I had decided to change. As I answered her, a sardonic laugh slipped out before I could stop it. "Yeah, I did."

Though the second I replied, I could see something shift as Worthy relaxed and finally gave me a genuine smile. "I thought so," she said, nodding like I'd confirmed a theory she'd been sitting on since yesterday. "Why?"

I glanced at her, taken aback, before Carter's words drifted through my thoughts from the night we watched Forrest Gump.

We all have a story to tell.

So that's what I did, I told Worthy everything, about the night Ronni and I rolled Lacey's house, and how my dad had sent me to New Hope as our last-ditch effort to set me straight. With just one question, Worthy cracked open the dam, and the events of my summer broke free, reuniting with family and friends, making new friendships, finding a place I belonged, and ultimately obeying the Gospel.

Worthy didn't interrupt, though, she just listened, her bright brown eyes softening the more I shared with her. While I explained everything about my summer at camp, I told her about letting go of the anger I'd been carrying toward God over what happened with my mom. How I'd opened my Bible for the first time in forever and felt something shift. How the people at camp welcomed me and prayed for me, and how, for the first time and what felt like years, I didn't feel like I had to carry everything alone.

"I spent so much of last year chasing all the wrong things," I said, my voice quieter now. "But this summer... I started chasing after Jesus instead."

As I shared my story, I glanced over at her, unsure how she'd respond, but behind her hazel eyes, I could see her really thinking about what I said.

"I don't think you should keep beating yourself up over last year, Lena." Worthy said finally.

I frowned a little. "What do you mean?"

She twisted another strand of grass between her fingers and then flicked it away. "I mean, if you've given your life to Jesus, then you've already turned a corner. You're not who you were, and that's what matters."

I gave her a sheepish smile. " I'm really trying."

"That's all any of us can do," Worthy said, a quiet smile playing on her lips. "Just keep showing up as the new you."

Her words settled over me gently, like something I didn't know I needed to hear. I studied her for a second, the girl I used to count as one of my best friends, wondering if maybe this was her way of making peace.

"Okay, but be honest," I said, nudging her gently with my shoulder. "You didn't come over here just to see if my story was legit, did you?"

Worthy laughed, brushing a piece of coiled hair behind her ear as the breeze lifted around us. "Partly yes, but mostly, I just wanted to see if you were okay."

"Why?" The question flew out of my mouth too fast, but Worthy's expression softened and I saw something vulnerable flickering in her eyes. I added, quieter this time, "I mean...why now?"

She sat up a little straighter, resting her elbows on her knees. "I guess I always felt like you didn't need me. You and Lacey were always this unstoppable duo, and I was just... there."

"That's not true," I said immediately.

She shrugged. "Maybe not, but that's how it felt to me. When things started falling apart between you two, I didn't know I fit. Things just got pretty messy for a while, so I thought it would be better if I stayed away."

I sat in silence as her words landed. I'd carried so much guilt for so long that I hadn't even stopped to see things from her side.

"You never said anything," I replied, my voice cracking a little.

Worthy winced as she offered me a helpless shrug. "I just figured... this school's full of people and we would all make other friends."

Slowly, I processed her words, but the truth hit me harder than I ever expected because I had never really made any other friends, at least not like Worthy had.

She hesitated again before adding. "When things got tense between the two of you, and you started hanging out with Ronni... I assumed you were the one that was causing all the drama."

I snorted, and even though I felt appalled, I could understand where she was coming from. "I guess you're not wrong."

She grimaced as she stared back at me. "I was, though. Lacey changed after dating Javier, but she's never been able to open her eyes and see the truth about him. I should have reached out and checked in on you instead of believing all the rumors."

I swallowed as her honesty started cutting through the walls I'd built around myself. Last year, I had wondered what I had done to deserve being abandoned by my best friends, but now, hearing Worthy's side of the story softened the blow. She had carried her own guilt, just like I had.

"I heard what happened with your mom," Worthy said softly. "But, I was so wrapped up in this version of you that I had in my head... I didn't think I could do anything to help."

"I'm not sure there was anything anyone could have done." I admitted.

"Maybe not." She said, shame filling her eyes. "But you were my friend, and I should have been there for you, because you deserved better than me not doing anything."

Her words struck me. Sitting here with her now felt a little like talking to a younger version of Miss Pearl. Like her grandmother, Worthy was direct but full of grace. The only other person I'd met like that was Carter Rose, and thinking of him suddenly made my chest ache.

"I'm sorry too," I said quietly, "for everything. I know I let a lot of people down, but the one person I disappointed most was myself."

"But, you're not that girl anymore," Worthy said gently, as if reassuring me.

I smiled as I agreed. "I still feel like a bit of a mess, but now that I'm home, I'm just... working on being a *redeemed* mess."

That made her laugh, and I watched as Worthy stretched out like she was finally letting the tension go. The air between us suddenly felt lighter too, like we'd finally made it through the storm of the past.

"So," Worthy said, grinning, "tell me more about the new Lena Harris. Oh, and don't hold out on me, were there any cute boys at camp?"

I snorted and felt my cheeks turn hot. "There was one."

Her eyes lit up. "Oh girl, you've got to spill that tea."

We laughed together the rest of lunch as Worthy caught me up on her life. I leaned against the rough bark of the live oak, letting the warmth of the moment wrap around me. A second, I felt a small weight lift off my shoulders before a familiar ache settled in my chest. Because the last time I felt this carefree, it was summer, and I was hiking Cobalt Bluff with my friends in Meadowbrook.

10

The early morning hike had been one of Theo's spontaneous plans. On our way to meet the group, Carter drove while I sat in the passenger seat adjusting the laces of the new hiking shoes I just bought from the Meadowbrook Mercantile.

Carter leaned slightly over the center console and asked, "How are they feeling?"

I had gone on nature walks with my grandparents before, but never a full-blown hike.

"Good, just different," I answered, finishing tying the laces. "They're stiffer than any other shoes I've worn."

Carter smirked, keeping his eyes on the road. "That's because they give you stability so you can reach great heights."

I leaned back and eyed him. The sun made his brown hair seem bronze underneath his backwards baseball hat, and as usual, Carter's easy-going smile pulled at the corner of his lips. When he had picked me up from Lou's in a dri-fit shirt and shorts, he looked like perfection. His scuffed hiking boots seemed like they had seen plenty of adventure, and I worried I might embarrass myself.

"Do you hike a lot?" I asked.

Carter shrugged, keeping his eyes on the road. "What's a lot?"

Chuckling, I added. "I don't know, frequently? Regularly? Enough to not get lost?"

The corners of his mouth rose as he reached for my hand. "Then, yes. I hike a lot."

I smiled when he reached over, intertwining my fingers with his. "Don't be disappointed if I can't keep up. We don't have all of this elevation where I'm from."

Carter ran his thumb over mine and added, "I've seen you climb bigger obstacles. Trust me, you'll have a good time."

I loved watching the sunlight and shadows dance on the road as we climbed higher and higher. My earlier worry morphed into a lighter feeling, like excited jitters. When we reached a clearing, Carter pulled into a gravel lot where Denny's Jeep was already parked. Denny, Jojo and Theo were already hopping out, stretching and grabbing their gear.

As soon as our car stopped, I opened the door just in time to hear Theo call out, "took you two long enough!"

He wore a faded t-shirt and gym shorts that matched his hat like they came as a set. Theo's boots appeared broken-in as he swung a backpack confidently over one shoulder like he hiked everyday.

Jojo lit up when she saw me. She was a walking color swatch with cut-off short-alls over a tee, bright mismatched sneakers, and a floppy sun hat that looked more like it belonged in a garden, than on a trail.

"Did you take the scenic route, or is that little beater too slow for mountain roads?" Denny chimed in, tossing a smirk in Carter's direction. He looked like Indiana Jones as he sported a boonie hat, crossbody water bottle, and way too much khaki.

Carter shook his head as he grabbed his gear. "You're just mad I drove instead of riding with you, Denbo."

"Lies!" Denny shouted. "You just wanted alone time with your girlfriend."

Without missing a beat, Carter snapped his backpack strap into place and grinned beneath his sunglasses. "That's exactly what I wanted."

I blushed as he lowered his shades and winked at me as we made our way over to join the others. Jojo pulled me into a quick hug instantly before pulling me away from the guys and leaning in. "So... how was the date?"

I tried to hide my smile as I thought about dinner at Max's and our cupcake fight afterwards. "We had so much fun, it was the perfect night."

"Good!" She gushed. "Did Grace give you a cupcake discount?"

I eyed her. "Do you mean the blonde from the bakery?"

Jojo nodded, and I tilted my head, wondering if there was more to the question. "Did you tell Carter to take me there?"

She shook her head, looping her arm through mine. "No, but I told Grace my friends might pop in. We can't keep day-old cupcakes, so a discount wouldn't have been a big deal anyway."

"Oh." I realized as she set me straight. "Thanks for that, although... mine didn't exactly make it."

Jojo's eyes widened and she smiled wide, spotting the mischief in my eyes. Leaning in, Jojo kept her voice low since we were nearing the boys again. "I'm going to need those details later."

We were giggling when we rejoined the boys who were now crowded around Theo's phone, arguing over trail maps. Carter leaned in close, still wearing that satisfied smirk, while Denny pointed at something like he knew a secret route to buried treasure.

"There's the Riverbend loop," Theo said. "It's flatter, but has the best water views. Or, there's Ridgeview, it's steeper but has a gnarly lookout of Cobalt Bluff."

Carter eyed Denny. "Ridgeview sounds fun, the view will be worth it."

Denny scoffed. "Are you trying to kill me? I vote for water."

"But we didn't bring a change of clothes," Jojo protested.

"And?" Denny asked, peering up at her. "What's your point, Jojo Bean?"

Theo gagged and cut his eyes at Denny. "Jojo Bean? Really dude?"

"Mind your business, Theodore," Denny snapped, "or you'll get your own nickname."

"What do you guys want to do?" Carter asked, looking at Jojo first, then me. "Water or the lookout?"

Jojo's face lit up with a slow smile as she glanced at me and suddenly, I felt like I could read her mind. Beads of sweat had already formed beneath her sun hat, and with one look, I knew what her choice was.

"You thinking what I'm thinking?" Jojo wondered.

I grinned, and together we replied, "Water."

***

An hour had almost passed while the five of us hiked along the trail. Sunlight filtered through the canopy of trees above, the heat, a gentle touch on my head and shoulders, as I took in my surroundings. Ahead of our group, Theo moved confidently, leading us along the hike. He pointed out roots for us to avoid and all the jagged rocks like he was a forestry expert.

Behind Theo, Jojo giggled as she clung to Denny's back, her arms wrapped highly around him as he carried her on a piggyback ride. When Denny stumbled off balance, Jojo squealed, and their laughter filled our hike with joyful noise.

Carter and I roamed slower than the others, my hand resting in his, as we trailed behind. The silence between us was easy, only occasionally interrupted by one of us pointing out animal tracks, birds, or stacked rock formations on the trail.

A squirrel darted across the path in front of us at one point, a flash of fur and motion that made me laugh. The creature vanished into the underbrush, and when I turned, I found Carter watching me instead of the trail. He glanced ahead, then back at me, and leaned in to steal a quick peck on my cheek.

I smiled, surprised. "What was that for?"

He shrugged slightly, eyes warm. "You look happy."

I was.

We kept going, but my focus shifted from the trees around us to the boy beside me. Carter kept his hand in mine, his thumb brushing gently against my skin now and then. He was quiet, but not distant, as he took in the views around us. That was something I loved about being with Carter, silence between us felt comfortable.

Since the moment we met, there had been this invisible pull between us, something I couldn't quite explain. Being near him was both effortless and easy, there was a steadiness in the way he walked beside me that made everything else feel less complicated. I wondered if Carter felt it too, the invisible thread between us, and the way moments like these made everything else around us fade away. Maybe he did and maybe that's why he held on to my hand and never let me go when we were together.

The sound of water rushing grabbed my attention as we approached a clearing in the path and a waterfall came into view. As always, the sight and sound of the water eased something inside of me as we stood taking in the view. Silently, Carter stood right beside me, his fingers laced with mine before gently lifting my hand to press a sweet kiss to the back of it.

"Do you remember at camp?" He started to ask, eyes still on the waterfall ahead. "When we talked about noticing what God created at the lake?"

My heart fluttered at the memory. "I remember."

We'd been sitting on the Med Cart, staring out at the lake when Carter asked what I saw. I told him, water, trees, and the sky, but I'd answered like I was just checking boxes. Carter pointed out all the things I had missed, reminding me that everything I had named was part of God's masterpiece to give us exactly what we needed; all because of His love for us.

Now, with the sound of water rushing, and the beauty unfolding before us at every angle, I knew what he was feeling because I felt the same way.

"In moments like this," Carter said, meeting my gaze, "how can we not see Him?"

Carter's smile was soft and certain like he was seeing more than just the waterfall. He gave my hand another quick squeeze before stepping closer to the water's edge. I paused to take in the sounds of the falls and the flicker of sunlight dancing on the water's surface like an open invitation to dive in. Everything seemed so alive and created for the perfect purpose.

The serene quiet was short-lived as Denny let out a rebel yell and charged toward the waters edge, leaping in with a splash. He surfaced moments later, grinning like a maniac. Then, before anyone could react, he lunged toward Jojo, grabbed her wrist, and yanked her in after him.

She squealed mid-air before going under. When Jojo came up, she wiped water from her eyes, already laughing as she lunged at Denny in retaliation. Neither of them seemed to care that their clothes were now drenched.

Carter laughed beside me, then turned with that mischievous glint in his eye that I knew too well.

"Oh no," I protested, backing away from him. "Don't even think about it."

He held up his hands innocently then casually peeled off his hat and slipped off his hiking boots.

"Carter!" I gasped as he jogged toward the water's edge and leapt in next, his splash was just as dramatic as Denny's. I stood there, hands on my hips, watching as the three of them treaded water and splashed each other, having the time of their lives.

Jojo pointed toward the waterfall ahead. "Let's go to the falls!"

Without hesitation, all three of them started swimming. I chuckled and stepped away from the riverbank, saddling up beside Theo who hadn't moved. His attention was glued to his phone, scanning a map with furrowed brows.

"Not tempted to join the chaos?" I asked.

He shook his head without glancing up at me. "Someone's got to make sure we actually know where we're going."

I nudged him gently with my elbow. "You know, you can have fun today too. You don't have to be so serious."

I grinned when I saw the crease between his brows smooth slightly as he relaxed and flicked his gaze to mine. "I find it ironic how we've already traded places. I thought I was the one always trying to cheer you up."

When I'd found Theo at camp, I remembered him as the boy I met on the church playground in Meadowbrook. He had been the little terror who teased me and threw sand in my face. At first, Theo had seemed like an older version of that boy, but as we got reacquainted, I realized that was just his way of lightening the mood and making me feel included.

"Looks like it's my turn to do the same," I replied.

Theo sighed, rolling his eyes before staring back down at his phone. "Leading the hike just helps me feel less like a fifth wheel." His voice was low. "Katie's all the way back home, and seeing you and Carter together, knowing you'll have to do long distance too, I just wish... I wish she and I could have had the same extra time you guys are getting."

My chest tightened hearing the pain in his voice. Theo had pined for Katie for years before this summer. He'd finally been brave enough to act on his chance at camp and luckily, she felt the same. They had been so happy in the short time they had together at camp, but Theo was right. Carter and I had been lucky enough to have an extra week together, but time was slipping away. While Theo busied himself with the map, my eyes drifted back to Carter who held up his hand waving me in.

I couldn't fight the smile spreading across my face. With what little time we had left, I wanted to spend every moment with Carter, even if that meant jumping into the water fully clothed and dealing with the consequences later.

Without overthinking it, I kicked off my shoes, took a running start and launched into the water. The cool rush hit me like a wave, washing away every lingering worry under the weight of the summer sun. I swam toward Carter, my toes brushing the rocks beneath the surface where he was waiting with his hand outstretched. When I reached him, he pulled me so close our noses touched. His soaked hair clung to his forehead, and that bright, familiar smile lit up his face.

Safe in his arms, we drifted with the river current toward the base of the bluff, where the waterfall roared, muffling the world around us. As the water poured over our heads, it felt like we were suddenly the only ones on the planet. Carter reached out and gently touched my cheek with cold, wet fingertips. When our eyes locked, I watched his gaze slowly drop to my lips before he leaned in. At first, our kiss was soft, but then it grew deeper, steadier as the waterfall rushed around us. Time could have stopped for all I knew as I sank deeper into Carter's arms, before getting completely lost in his kiss.

11

Daydreams of Meadowbrook were the only thing getting me through the following week. No matter how many times I tried to refocus during class, my thoughts kept drifting to Carter's laugh, the rush of the waterfall, and the lookout view once we reached the top of Cobalt Bluff. Compared to that day in Meadowbrook with my friends, everything here in Freeport just felt lonely and dull.

During history, my gaze drifted from the whiteboard to the view outside. The weather was so sunny and beautiful that being stuck in class felt like a waste. I fidgeted in my seat and sighed, attempting to focus, though my eyes wandered again, this time landing on Ronni. She sat perfectly upright, scribbling notes like her life depended on capturing them, but her sudden overachiever act still didn't make any sense to me. Since the first day of school, we'd successfully avoided each other, and I hadn't made any attempt to change that. Not after the way she bolted when our paths crossed that day.

I could take a hint.

Suddenly, my phone buzzed in my hoodie pocket, providing me with yet another great distraction. The classrooms were always cold, even when it was hot outside, so I pulled my sleeves down over my hands while I fished my phone out and hid it beside my textbook.

Theo Lockwood: SOS! The plan backfired.

I instantly felt my heart sink. The conversation I had had with Theo that day on our hike before I left still lingered on my mind. He had opened up about Katie, and I couldn't forget how the weight in his voice made me realize how easily a relationship could slip through your fingers. The thought only made me want to hold tighter to what I had with Carter.

Since then, Theo had reached out to me more than I expected him to. There were texts, updates, and plenty of questions about long-distance dating. He said he wanted advice on the way Carter and I were making it work, though I wasn't sure I really had any advice to offer him. I wasn't just some girl with an extensive dating history. I had one slimy ex-boyfriend, Chase Conway, who wasn't even in the same league as Carter Rose. Deep down, I knew where Theo was coming from, I was lonely without my friends, and I didn't want him to be lonely too.

> Me: What happened?

His reply came instantly.

> Theo Lockwood: I sent the flowers to her class, but she got in trouble.

I sucked in a deep breath and instinctively shook my head, too visibly because the guy next to me glanced over, brows furrowed as I sank back into my seat, flicking my gaze back to my phone screen discreetly.

> Me: Lockwood. that's not what I said to do!

> Me: Why didn't you send them to her dorm room like we talked about?

> Theo Lockwood: I needed a grand gesture. Go big or go home, right?

I thought about sending back a funny GIF to cheer him up when I felt a familiar ache settle in my chest just thinking about how Theo must be feeling. I first heard about their breakup from Carter after the first soccer game of the season. Katie had shown up late but stayed on the sidelines the whole game, then slipped out before the final whistle blew. Carter said little about the situation out of respect for Theo, but I could hear the frustration in his voice, he blamed Katie for how off Theo had played that night. The Vikings still won, but Theo had played so poorly, he ended up being benched. Later that night in the locker room, Katie called him. Theo thought she was calling to explain, but all she said was that they were better off as friends and ended things.

At first he was crushed, but Theo didn't stay down for long. With quiet determination. he was already working on a plan to win her back.

Before I could respond to his text, I heard my name and felt a jolt in my chest.

"Miss Harris," Mr Francis called out. "Would you prefer to keep texting or focus on how the events of the American Revolution influenced the writing of our Constitution?"

My neck burned as he glared at me, and I slowly slid my phone back into the pocket of my hoodie.

"Sorry," I said, redirecting my attention to the front.

"Do answer the question, Miss Harris." Mr. Francis instructed, crossing his arms, clearly trying to embarrass me.

"I, um…" I stammered, trying to recall the topic at hand. I knew we were talking about the constitution, but the details were a little fuzzy. Then, from the left side of the room, a familiar voice piped up.

"The writers of the Constitution wanted a strong central government, so the Constitution was written to protect the freedom of the people and balance the government's power," Ronni answered for me.

Mr. Francis seemed pleased until he turned back at me. "You'll do well to focus on the lesson instead of your phone, Miss Harris. Miss Dice won't be able to help you on next week's test."

The two guys near the front of class, chuckled under their breath, but I ignored them and went back to jotting notes. Out of the corner of my eye, I glanced at Ronni, she hadn't even looked at me once, her eyes stayed locked on the board, pen flying across her notebook like she couldn't afford to miss a word. It surprised me that the girl, who always rolled her eyes at homework, now seemed determined to become valedictorian of our class. The change in Ronni was so drastic I just couldn't believe it.

But then again... hadn't I changed too?

My thoughts drifted back to camp and to the quiet promise I had made to live more like Christ. That meant seeing people through a different lens, even the ones who had hurt me.

Ronni had been the only one to stand up for me against Lacey last year, and that kind of loyalty didn't fade easily. I could still picture us side-by-side, quietly plotting our rebellion, but that memory blurred quickly into the sting of watching her drive away, leaving me alone when everything fell apart that night.

I sighed as my thoughts shifted into a messy battle between who I used to be and the girl I wanted to become. Jesus said to love my enemies, and stand apart, and I knew if I was serious about following Him, that had to include how I treated Ronni too. Even if our friendship never returned to what it was.

When the bell rang, I resolved myself to take the first step and hurried after Ronni, who, as usual, made a mad-dash for the door. I reached her in the hallway and barely grazed her elbow before she pulled away, whipping her narrowed gaze back at me.

"Hey, sorry, I... just wanted to say..." My voice trailed off once she faced me.

The once vibrant, unstoppable Ronni Dice I knew seemed to have vanished as she watched me with an expression I had never seen her wear. The girls staring back held an unnerving glint in her eyes, that, to my surprise, was one I recognized.

Shame.

"Say what?" Ronni asked, narrowing her dark eyes at me. The sight of dark circles beneath her eyes softened the blow of her tone.

I adjusted my bag on my shoulder as I searched for the right words.. "I, um.... wanted to say thanks for the save back there."

Ronni's nostrils flared as she ran an anxious hand through her long blonde locks. "You don't have to thank me," She retorted. "Some of us just want to pass and not hold up everyone else's progress."

My jaw clenched as I felt my stomach clench. *She clearly wasn't ready for the olive branch I offered, so why was I even trying?*

The memory of her driving away from Lacey's house that fateful night flashed through my mind again, followed by her sprinting down the hall last week. Ronni had made it clear she wasn't in a rush to fix things. *So why did I feel this strange pull to be kind to her? Was this what it meant to follow Christ? Should I extend grace even when she didn't want it?*

Then, with one swift glance, the answer came to me. The pain in her eyes was unmistakable, it was the same haunted look of loneliness I had worn, and still did. Even if Ronni couldn't admit it, I recognized the truth she wasn't ready to face.

Ronni needed a friend.

Just like I had when she stood by me last year, when Lacey and her squad of torture first made school unbearable. I knew something was up with Ronni, though, and I couldn't ignore it.

Even if I was the last person she wanted to see, I wanted to make sure she was okay, or try to be there for her like she'd been for me.

Maybe this was what it meant to have my faith tested. Regardless of how she was treating me, I knew there was only one way to respond. I glanced down at my feet before summoning all the courage I had to keep going and offer the kindness I knew she needed. Taking a deep breath, still unable to meet her eyes, I focused on the ground and forced the words out.

"I didn't mean to interrupt the class," I said, then peered back up, meeting her stony gaze again. "I'm sorry I did though, and I just wanted to say thanks... for helping me out."

My words came out all fumbled, but apologizing made me feel better until she scoffed and rolled her eyes.

"I wasn't trying to help you," Ronni snapped back at me. She shifted her weight to the other foot and stared me down with hollow eyes. "Look, Lena, you don't have to pretend to care about me. I think we both know we're better off just going our own separate ways, like we did all summer."

For a moment I really thought I caught a small trace of the girl who used to stick her neck out of me, but I was wrong. Watching her stare back at me now was the equivalent of seeing someone stare straight through glass. She had made it too obvious; she wanted nothing to do with me.

"Trust me, Ronni, I get it. I just thought maybe we could be civil with each other this year." I offered, tucking my hair nervously behind my ear.

Ronni readjusted her bag then as she took a step closer to me. Out of the blue, I noticed a shift in her fiery gaze as she flashed me a snarling grin. "Oh, we can be civil," she agreed as her eyes flickered. "We can coexist within these walls until we're done with this stupid school, but I have a better idea."

She stepped closer, and I felt myself shrink beneath her gaze.

"Okay?" I asked, trying not to waver where I stood.

Then Ronni leaned in so close that I felt her quiet, icy words on my skin. "You should just forget about me just like you wanted to weeks ago, because trust me, I've already forgotten all about you."

My skin bristled as her harsh words washed over me. When she stepped back, Ronni took one last look at me before spinning on her heel and leaving me behind, just like she always did.

12

Some days, trying to do the right thing felt like walking into the eye of a hurricane. By the time I stepped into the parking lot after school, the weight of the day clung to me like a storm cloud. I told myself to shake off the conversation with Ronni, but her words still rang in my ears, sharp and uninvited. Turns out, loving my enemies had only earned me a verbal slap in the face.

I kept going, lifting my heart to God with questions I didn't bother sugarcoating. *Was that tiny flicker of compassion in my heart from You, God, or just leftover guilt? Am I really supposed to keep showing grace to people who clearly don't want it?*

Ronni's verbal attack paled in comparison to the silent response to my prayer. Sighing, I pressed my fingers to my temples, trying to massage away the pulsating throb, then reached into my bag for my keys. I glanced toward the far end of the lot to unlock my car and froze. A group of laughing students surrounded my car, sending a chill down my spine despite the afternoon heat. I slowed my steps as the air shifted, causing a tight churning low in my stomach. *Something was wrong.*

The closer I got, the louder my pulse drummed in my ears. As I held my key fob up and pushed the unlock button, the familiar beep sounded causing the group to scatter. There was a collective gasp as I pushed through the crowd, witnessing the scene before me. Sour liquid from pickles ran down the windows as they coated my car's hood and windshield.

All at once, there was a sharp ringing piercing my ears, and I stood there, my pulse pounding relentlessly in my chest. The laughter and commentary faded into a blur as I stared at my car, unable to move.

This year, I thought if I only maintained a low profile and kept to myself, I could fly under the radar, but I was so wrong. Standing here now under the leering gaze of culprits, I just wanted high school to end. Motion next to me made me flinch as Javier Diaz stepped forward, holding out his phone to capture the moment.

"You're going to go viral, Harris," he bragged, flashing a cruel smile. Instantly, I felt all my blood rush to my face as my hands trembled at my sides. Then, behind him, Lacey's cheerleader friends started snickering, and I noticed they were the same girls who had laughed at me behind their hands on the first day of school. Now they stood roaring with laughter without even trying to hide their handiwork.

My chest was tight with nerves, like my body was yelling at me to run or fight. On instinct, I took off my hoodie, wadded it up, and stormed over to my car, using it to clean up the mess. Behind me, a familiar voice asked what was going on, but I didn't glance back. The sour stench of pickle juice hit me full force, making me feel nauseous as I scrubbed.

"Oh gosh," the voice said, and it took me a moment to realize Worthy was standing beside me.

"Lena, are you okay?" she whispered.

I moved like I was underwater, feeling weightless in my own skin while scrubbing uselessly at the vinegar-slicked glass with my soaked hoodie. Tears stung my eyes as a warm hand landed gently on my arm.

"Here, Lena, let me help you," Worthy said, her voice soft but firm.

I didn't budge because not even her kindness could have broken through the storm raging inside me. To my surprise, Worthy didn't budge, and I wasn't sure where she had found it, but suddenly she appeared beside me with a towel in her hands to sweep the remaining pickles off the windshield.

Then she turned to face the gawking crowd with fire in her voice. "Unless you're helping, get out of here!" she yelled. "You heard me, leave her alone!"

Only when the crowd dispersed did I dare to glance up, but the moment I faced Worthy, I felt my stomach drop. The look in her eyes was one I had seen many times as she stared back at me like I was some fragile, broken thing. *Had I really convinced myself Worthy, and I were over our past just because of one lunch conversation?* The pity in her eyes was the icing on the cake of this miserable day.

A lump formed in my throat, but I swallowed it down, refusing to cry. Without a word, I ripped the towel from her hands, forcing myself to keep moving. I couldn't stop because I was afraid that if I did, I'd fall apart.

I felt Worthy's reach out one more time, but I shrugged her off.

"Just leave me alone, Worthy." I cried with quivering lips.

"Lena, come on, just let me help," she begged, resting her hand on my shoulder. "I promise I just want to help. I'm so sorry—"

I tore myself from her grasp again and whirled around, trying to hold back my tears. "I don't want you to feel sorry for me, Worthy," I told her, summoning my last ounce of courage. "If all you're going to do is pity me, then just go join your friends."

With shaky hands, I threw my hoodie and towel at her feet and reached for my keys.

"Lena, I can't believe they did this..." Worthy trailed off, staring at the sopping mess on my car. "But I—"

My chin quivered as I simply shrugged helplessly, feeling numb. "You can't?" I interjected. "Because the last year of my life has been like this, all because of *your* friends. They just can't let things go."

I remembered seeing the group that day in the hall when Worthy didn't say a word. Sure, she had sat with me at lunch after, but I knew the truth. She was one of them, and those girls were like wolves who didn't stray from their pack unless they were ready to pay for it.

Desperate to escape, I reached for my car door, but Worthy stepped in front of me. "Tell me what I can do to help," she pleaded.

I could only shake my head and tell her the truth. "Nothing," I whispered. "I don't want to cause problems for you, with the squad, your friends or any of them... Just forget this happened and don't worry about me."

Before she could say another word, I jumped into my and shut the door. Without a single glance back, I threw the gearshift into reverse and peeled out of the parking lot, eager to leave Freeport High behind.

13

Tears blurred my vision and my heart pounded in my chest the entire drive home. As soon as I pulled into my driveway, I rushed around back and hosed down my car, scrubbing so hard at the mess that the paint was bound to come off. The sour stench of vinegar still clung to my shirt, making me want to gag as humiliation soaked into every thread.

Once I finished scrubbing my car clean, I pulled my car back into its usual spot and sent a quick text to Anthony, letting him know I wouldn't be in for my shift at the aquarium this afternoon. His reply came back instantly in the form of a simple thumbs-up. Tucking away my phone, I headed straight for my bedroom, relieved that my Dad wasn't home. He'd take one look at me and demand answers that I didn't want to talk about or explain. I just wanted to get as far away from Freeport as I could.

As soon as I shut my bedroom door, the afternoon just crashed down on me. My legs felt like lead as I crossed the room and sank onto my bed. Curling up in the fetal position, I buried my face in my pillow, as the parking lot incident continued to play on an endless loop in my head. No matter how much I wanted to forget, the leering smiles of my bullies clung to me like a second skin.

My chest tightened as I sobbed into my pillow, remembering the way everyone just stood around taking pictures of me. The last time I had found myself in this position was right after my mom left. I had curled up into a tight ball for hours, trying to make sense of why she would just leave without saying goodbye. The only thing that soothed me was the song that once played from my grandmother's antique music box as I sat with her, knowing Grams' would have never chosen to leave my side.

I used to sing *Somewhere Over the Rainbow* anytime I needed to feel steady. I'd imagine how I could wish upon a star that everything bad in my life would simply vanish away just like the clouds in the song. But the day my mom left, I vowed to never let my comfort song, or any music, be tied to a person who could taint those memories. So, I stopped singing and put as much distance between that and anything else we used to do together.

Now, remembering how my mother walked out mixed with the events of today and caused a deep nausea to rise in my stomach. I sat up, clutching my knees to my chest to fight back the sickness, and squeezed my eyes shut as I pressed my forehead against my arms while the tears continued, willing myself to calm down and just breathe.

Gradually, the panic subsided, each exhale coming out a little steadier than the last. I scooted against the headboard, resting my head against the cool wall when I caught sight of something across the room. Just as I had left it, Carter's hoodie was still hanging over my desk chair like a lifeline in the perfect storm of my day.

I slid off the bed and took the sweatshirt into my hands. Lifting it to my face, I inhaled deeply, still able to catch Carter's clinging citrus and spice scent still clinging to the fabric.

The ache in my chest deepened as I stared down at the Viking mascot glaring at me from the front of the sweatshirt. I traced the letters of his school's name, Valley View High, with my thumb and for a moment, I wasn't in Freeport anymore. I was reliving the night Carter gave me his hoodie for safekeeping.

***

My final week in Meadowbrook was flying by, each passing day bringing me closer to the moment I would have to leave. At the end of the week, Lou let me invite the gang over for a movie night, and we got to work transforming her cozy living room into the perfect theater set up. Carter jumped in to help Lou with the popcorn, while Jojo followed close behind, navigating the space with ease, like she had grown up in Lou's house. Meanwhile, Denny and Theo stood by the couch, locked in an unending round of rock-paper-scissors, arguing over which movie to watch.

Denny, having won the most two-out-of-three matches, chose *The Sandlot*. When we were ready, the four of us settled together in front of the screen. Lou popped in every so often to check on us, but then headed back to her office. Business had picked up at River Ridge, and she was trying to get caught up with every spare moment she had.

In an oversized chair, Theo sat, absorbed in his phone. Denny was on the far right of the couch with a bucket of popcorn on his lap, with Jojo nestled against his side. Beside her, Carter reclined, resting his feet in the large ottoman while I sat directly to his left, with a bowl of popcorn between us.

The moment felt surreal, like I was living a life that wasn't quite mine. I knew I didn't live in Meadowbrook and couldn't stay, but I pictured myself always being with my friends and never having to say goodbye.

Denny's uncanny ability to quote almost every line from the movie impressed everyone except Theo, who finally cracked near the end.

"Dude, we all know you know every line, but can you stop quoting the entire movie?"

Denny gave him a wry smile in the dim light. "Heroes get remembered, but legends never die."

Beside me, Carter stifled a laugh while Theo rolled his eyes. "Denny, quoting The Sandlot doesn't make you a legend," Theo said. "It just means you need a life."

"Dude, how many times have you seen this?" Carter asked.

Denny shrugged, talking over a mouth full of popcorn. "Maybe like ten or twelve times."

Jojo elbowed him, subtly calling him out. We all silently stared at him until he groaned and confessed. "Okay fine, I lost count after thirty-two."

The rest of us chuckled as Theo propositioned him. "I'll give you a dollar if we can just finish the movie without you quoting another line. Deal?"

Denny only scoffed. "You're killin' me, Smalls!"

Laughter filled the living room until Carter climbed to his. "Sorry to ruin all the fun, but I've got to head home. Curfew and all."

My stomach plummeted at the thought of him, leaving.

"Still on a tight leash, huh, bro?" Denny asked, tossing more popcorn into his mouth.

Carter shrugged, then glanced back at me. "Care to walk me out?"

"Sure," I said, even though saying goodnight was the last thing I wanted to do. When Carter reached out, I took the hand he offered.

Carter and Denny exchanged their customary brisk handshake, then, on the way out, he messed up Theo's hair, which earned him a grunt. Carter opened the door, and the chilly mountain air rushed in, despite it being a summer night. I hugged my arms across my chest feeling goosebumps on my skin as I followed Carter down the steps toward his car.

He peered down at my hand, his eyes wide. "Wow, Dutch! You're freezing."

"I know; it's cold out tonight," I replied with a shiver.

Automatically going into problem-solving mode, Carter shrugged off his hoodie. "Here, take it."

I shook my head. "No, you keep it. I can just go back inside."

My protest only made him insist more. "Dutch, please take it."

Giving in, I slipped his hoodie over my head and breathed in his spicy citrus scent. Warmth radiated from the thick sweatshirt and I noticed a slow smile spread across his face while he admired my change of outfit. Carter took my hand again, pulling me close as he rested his back against his car door. I snuggled in close, feeling the softness of his hoodie and his added body heat warm me up.

"I could stay like this forever," he whispered, resting his chin on top of my head.

I pulled back slightly and stared up into his eyes. "Me too."

Our noses nearly touched but then Carter leaned down, closing the distance between us and pressing the sweetest kiss to my lips. It was a feather-light touch that sent shivers down my spine and when he pulled back, I saw the moonlight twinkling in his brown eyes.

"I think I'll keep you forever, too." He whispered, lightly kissing the top of my head, pulling me back into a hug.

"I'd like that," I whispered, snuggling back into his arms. We held each other just like that until he reluctantly whispered in my ear, "I don't want to, but I definitely have to go now."

We released each other, and I watched as Carter settled into the driver's seat, then immediately rolled his window down.

"Are you sure you don't want your hoodie back?" I asked.

He chuckled and rolled his eyes as a slight smile played on his lips. "I'm sure, Dutch. Besides, it looks better on you."

A small smile bloomed across my face as Carter's hand found mine for a quick graze.

"See you tomorrow?" I asked.

Carter winked. "Tomorrow."

The word hung in the air like a promise I wished we could always keep. He started his car and offered a small wave before pulling out of Lou's driveway. I pulled the sleeves of his soft hoodie over my hands, standing there until I could no longer see his taillights. When the car disappeared, I glanced down at the sweatshirt to see a menacing Viking staring back at me.

The soft sweatshirt felt wonderful against my skin as I pulled it over my face, inhaling his comforting scent again. Under the bright full moon, I braced myself, knowing I would inevitably have to say goodbye to Carter for real and leave Meadowbrook behind.

14

The memory of Meadowbrook faded, as I tried to scrub the events of my day but some things refused to wash down the drain. Afterwards, I pulled on a pair of shorts and Carter's hoodie, getting lost in its softness. I buried my face in the collar, hoping it would somehow take me back to that week spent in Meadowbrook which felt more like home than Freeport ever did.

Carter had soccer practice after school so we hadn't spoken since texting each other good morning. Not that I wanted to talk about how my school day had completely unraveled. There were no words to explain how it felt to stand in that parking lot soaked in shame.

I spent the afternoon in my room doing homework, desperate to forget the day's events. The house was still, quiet enough that the creak of my bedroom door later in the evening made me flinch.

My dad stepped inside with a cautious, worried smile. "Hey hun," he greeted me. "This is a pleasant surprise, I didn't expect to see you home so soon. Did you get the afternoon off?"

I shook my head, trying my best to be nonchalant. "I'm not feeling well, so I called out and came home after school."

Dad frowned, and I immediately felt the need to defend myself. Last year, I was fired for skipping work, but that wasn't the case today. *Didn't needing some mental health time count?* I felt a knot grow in my chest as I studied his face, searching for signs of disappointment.

"I told them I hoped to be in tomorrow, as long as I felt better," I offered, because honestly, the idea of going to work seemed one thousand times better than going back to school. I'd even spent the entire afternoon devising plans to avoid school indefinitely.

Hey Dad, how about I get my GED and just work until college in the spring?

Or, Hey Dad, you were in the Coast Guard, so you know about U.S. law. How hard would it be for someone to fake their own death and get a new identity, hypothetically, of course?

The last one would catch too much attention, and he would know something was wrong.

My favorite scenario was the last, but I wasn't brave enough to bring it up.

Hey Dad, if Aunt Lou agreed, could I move to Meadowbrook and finish high school there?

All I could do was picture Dad's face if I asked to leave, knowing Mom had done the same. The thought made me feel sicker than getting pickle juice thrown all over my car. He was fine with me visiting Meadowbrook, but moving away was a different story.

Suddenly, Dad crossed the room and rested the back of his hand on my forehead. Once he felt my temperature I watched him shrug dismissively. "If you don't feel well, kiddo, you don't feel well. You did the right thing by calling work. Can I get you anything?"

I shook my head, though inwardly I heaved a sigh of relief, and motioned back to my textbook. "I'm just going to get some homework done and get some rest."

I noticed the concern etched on his face, even though I forced a small smile.

"You're sure you're okay?" he asked as his eyes softened.

I nodded again, hoping to convince him. "I'll be fine."

Reluctantly, I watched as Dad crossed the room back to the door and paused. "I'll just be outside working on the boat if you need anything."

I offered him a small smile as Dad closed the door. Once I heard him slip out the back door, the house was quiet again, and I sank into my chair. I was glad for the space Dad gave me sometimes, but mostly I missed the way things used to be. Dad used to take me out on the tour boat after his shift was over, for daddy-daughter dates to have time for just the two of us. He taught me so much about how the moon controls the ocean waves and how the salt marshes capture carbon dioxide. All the time we had spent together only made the silences between us feel heavier.

Even though he was only in the backyard, I missed him. He was consumed with restoring the boat to have it ready when mom came home, *if she ever came home.* As hopeless as I thought his goal was, days like today helped me understand him better.

All afternoon, I wished Carter was here so I could fall into his arms and tell him everything about what happened at school. Carter always knew what to say, but when I picked up my phone again, there were still no new messages from him. Just as I was about to lock the screen again, I noticed a message I had missed from Jojo.

> Jojo: Hey friend! Is this you?

Beneath her text, I stared at the attached picture in horror of me and Worthy wiping pickles off the hood of my car. My eyes went blurry when I opened Instagram and saw multiple tags of the same picture under the hashtag: *#pickledprincess*

I felt queasy again, hearing Javier's ominous words back to me: *You're going to go viral, Harris.* I couldn't risk anyone else finding out, so thinking on my feet, I typed a lighthearted reply.

> Me: Nothing to see there, just a dumb senior prank.

With trembling hands, I cradled my head as fresh tears wet the words on the page of my textbook underneath. The thought of the picture going viral made my pulse pound. If Dad or Carter saw it, my life would be over. Dad would assume the worst, and Carter would never look at me the same. This day had only proved all my worst fears about returning to Freeport were coming true.

I climbed to my feet as my thoughts raced, trying my best to figure out how to make this day disappear. As I paced my room, I stared at the pictures I hung up from camp. There was a photo of me, Jojo, Denny, Theo, and Carter standing in front of the Dining Hall, but the one next to it made me pause. Lou and I were standing by her car in the parking lot on the last day of camp, and as soon as I saw her face, it hit me.

Call Aunt Lou.

I swiped at my screen and scrolled to Lou's name. Lou would know what to say, and she would know how to make it all disappear. I pressed her name and listened as the phone rang twice before Lou's chipper voice answered.

"Hey Lena. How's my favorite niece?"

Her voice alone was enough to make my emotional defenses crumble. "Lou, I need to talk to you."

Her tone shifted instantly once she heard the tears in my voice. "Honey, what's going on?"

***

An hour later, I felt like I could finally breathe after ending my call with Lou. She helped me report the images on social media to get them removed, but also talked me off a ledge. The pictures were gone before we hung up, and I felt the weight of the world lift off my shoulders. Her words lingered, reminding me that there was only one true opinion I needed to care about—*God's*.

"You are so much stronger than you feel right now," Lou reassured me. "You are *not* alone, okay?"

We were hours a part but Lou's words wrapped around me like a warm embrace. She listened as I cried, filling her in on what had happened, and confessed I didn't want to go to school tomorrow.

"Don't let those kids get to you," Lou had said. "People hated Jesus too, but that didn't stop Him from being about God's business. Remember *whose* you are, Lena."

Sobbing, I knew she was right, but I just kept wishing last year had never happened. There was so much I wish I could go back and change, and I couldn't shake all of the questions running through my thoughts. *What if I had just followed God instead of turning my back on Him? How much heartache could I have avoided if only I had relied on God instead?*

"Last year is in the past, honey." Lou had told me. "Stop looking back there, you're not going that way."

She was right, and as much I wanted the hurt to go away, I knew I had to focus on the present, and stay true to the promise I made to give God my full heart. No matter what happened, I wouldn't turn my back on Him again. As impossible as life felt, I was more determined than ever to cling to God and let Him direct my next steps.

Lou had prayed with me before ending the call, asking the Lord to heal my heart and give me strength to face those who hurt me. To remember to show them the love of Jesus because they didn't know the truth I knew. Before hanging up, Lou reminded me that high school didn't last forever, but my actions toward others would, whether I saw the results or not.

I really didn't want to love my enemies, and I had no clue how, but Lou reminded me that Jesus asked God to forgive those crucifying Him, and those words pricked my heart.

Forgive them, for they know not what they do.

Jesus' prayer for His enemies gave me the guidance I needed to walk into school and see the ones hurting me through His eyes and to remember He loved them, too. With Lou's advice, I was determined to cling to my faith now more than ever. After I finished my homework, I spent the evening reading my Bible.

Peter's words in First Peter chapter one reminded me to cast all my anxiety on the Lord. Chapter one of James showed me that being joyful during tough times would help me persevere through life's challenges as long as I held onto my faith. Then, after reading Isaiah, I felt braver knowing God's help and strength were with me.

As I studied, I felt like I could breathe easier. When I crawled beneath my covers that night, I prayed for peace and strength, knowing I wasn't walking alone, even if no one else knew who walked beside me.

15

The next week unfolded agonizingly slowly, like being caught in traffic when I was in a hurry to get off the highway. I could still hear the whispers swirling around me at school, but all I could do was keep my head down and remember Lou's advice that felt like a detour from my current reality. I clung to that hope, even when the school hallways felt like they were closing in.

Each night after work, I slipped through the front door like a ghost, retreating to the quiet of my room. Dad didn't normally ask questions, but one night, he paused at my doorway, eyes searching mine in that careful way of his when he seemed afraid of the answer.

"Everything okay, Lenny?" Dad asked, leaning against the doorframe.

I forced a tired smile, trying to act casual. "Yeah, I'm just exhausted."

He didn't push, but I didn't miss the crease in his brow lingering long after he'd shut the door. Dad wore the same expression I had seen on Carter's face nearly every night on FaceTime. Similar to my dad, Carter asked about my day, but I sidestepped his questions using vague replies and always changed the subject. He knew me too well not to notice what I was doing, but unlike at camp, Carter never called me out.

Just as Lou reminded me, I kept praying. I pleaded with God in each class to help me make it through and each time I bowed my head, I prayed for the strength to take the high road and follow Lou's advice. She told me to see those at school, the ones who gossiped and laughed at me, through the eyes of Jesus, and the more I tried, the more her plan worked.

As I snuck through the halls at school, I'd find myself singing a song my grandparents taught me when I was younger, *They Will Know We Are Christians By Our Love*. Every time I heard others giggling or whispering about me behind cupped hands, the song carried me down the halls, reminding me of the promise I made at camp: *to shine bright and remember whose I was*. But even though I was doing my best to push through, I still needed time to myself.

During lunch, I went outside and sat in my usual place under the old oak tree in the quad as a cool, salty breeze filled the air as autumn approached. Leaning against the oak, I peered up and saw the leaves beginning to turn yellow; then I closed my eyes, whispering a prayer I'd already said countless times.

Please, God, be with me and help me get through this.

Releasing a breath, I opened my eyes and sat up straight once I found Worthy standing above me, wringing her hands around her bag strap. My first instinct was to glance away, but her solemn expression grabbed my attention.

"Hi," Worthy said, breaking the silence.

My voice trembled slightly as I stared up at her. "Hey," I said then, avoiding her gaze, I reached into my bag to retrieve the sandwich I had carefully packed that morning.

Worthy let her cardigan fall onto the grass across from me, then eased herself down into the shade and adjusted her skirt.

"Lena, I—" Worthy began, staring down as she fiddled with her shoe lace. "I wanted to apologize again for everything that happened last week. I've been thinking a lot about what you said..."

I blinked, feeling caught off-guard by her apology. After what I'd said to her about her friends not letting go of the past, my heart sank as those words haunted me. She had tried her best to help me with my car, and I had punished her for it.

Worthy quietly sighed and kept going. "I've been thinking a lot about what it actually means to follow Jesus, and I've realized that I've been so focused on everything else that I've pushed God aside... and I'm just over it."

Her words reached deep inside me, and I knew exactly what she meant because I'd had the same revelation this summer. As I watched her fidget nervously, I could see how nervous she was as she bared her soul to me. I remember feeling the exact same way she did, because I still felt that way now.

"I know how you feel," I replied. "But why the sudden change of heart?"

Worthy played with her bag strap some more as she gazed out to the courtyard before us. "Because I messed up," she said, lowering her voice. "I thought if I stayed out of the drama with Lacey and the rest of the squad, then that meant I wasn't a part of it, but when I heard what you said... about me being one of them... I couldn't stand the thought of you, or anyone else, thinking of me that way."

"I wasn't trying to make you feel bad," I offered, wishing I could take back what I said.

Worthy turned and eyed me determinedly. "Lena, I needed to hear what you said, and truth be told, it felt like a wake-up call. Nan has been trying to tell me the same thing for a while now, but it didn't click until I heard *you* say it," she said, holding my gaze. "I haven't been the Christian I want to be; and I'm so sorry for not doing more to be a better friend to you. Can we move past the drama and just go back to the way things used to be?"

I paused, considering her words, because for a moment, my reflex was to say no. The hurt and bitterness I felt overwhelmed me, but I couldn't just not forgive her. I had been in the same place Worthy was in now weeks ago at camp. When I needed someone, I truly felt like God had placed Carter in my path. Remembering the fact brought on an idea that struck me. *Could I be someone who helped Worthy start over?*

Suddenly, her apology didn't just feel like she was waving her white flag, it seemed like a glimmer of hope. A small smile played over my lips as I thought maybe this was an answer to my recent prayers.

"Lena?" Worthy asked, eyeing me with visible concern. "You okay?"

When I stared back at her, I nodded quickly. "Sorry, it's just... the fact that we're having this conversation feels... I don't know, like providence or something."

Worthy tilted her head, trying to understand. "Like divine intervention?"

I smiled but shrugged away the thought. "Something like that, but, you know... I'm a fan of starting over, and would love nothing more than for there to be a clean slate between us."

Worthy smiled, eyes brightening. "Good, because my Nan and I are starting a weekly Bible study, and we want you to come."

I cleared my throat, surprised. "You want me to come to your house?"

She chuckled, as though my question seemed ridiculous. "We both do, and I think it's time I surround myself with people who share my faith instead of those who don't." Worthy said as she reached into her lunch bag, opened a snack-size chip bag, and casually popped one into her mouth. "Plus, Nan's been asking about you."

A lump formed in my throat, and I swallowed hard to fight back the tears at the thought of us picking up where we left off and becoming friends again.

"Okay, yeah." I smiled. "That sounds nice."

Worthy's face lit up, her eyes showing relief. "Good, I'll get more details from Nan, but you just let me know what night works next week though, okay?"

I beamed, trying to contain my excitement. "Sure, I'll text you once I know my work schedule. Is your number still the same?"

Years had passed since I had even bothered to text Worthy, but I had never deleted her number from my phone. She nodded slowly, and I watched the same realization hit her as regret flickered in her eyes. Worthy wasn't the only one with regrets, though, and I knew that together, we could help each other move past them.

"Thanks for inviting me," I said. "It's been a while since I've had a piece of Miss Pearl's wisdom, and I'm long overdue."

"It'll be like old times." Worthy smiled.

Once the bell rang, Worthy and I gathered our things, but I suddenly couldn't shake the sense that maybe God was behind Worthy's plan, and maybe things were finally beginning to look up for me.

16

Everyday for the past week, Worthy and I spent lunch together, but what surprised me most was how we picked back up where we left off, as if no time had passed at all. Hanging out with Worthy was like seeing a break in a cloudy sky. She had a way of keeping our conversations light and upbeat by sharing stories of show choir routines gone wrong or keeping me entertained by telling me about all the news she heard while working at the local coffee shop in town. The best part though was that Worthy never brought up my mom, so instead she would ask questions about summer camp and how me and Carter met. The more we talked, the more it felt like we were picking back up right where we left off.

Now, as the sun dipped behind the trees in the Clarkes' front yard, I sat on their creaky porch swing, letting the crickets serenade me. The scent of Miss Pearl's cooking still hung in the air after a dinner of roasted chicken and collard greens. Worthy had kept her promise and invited me for Bible study, but I should have known dinner would come first. No one left Miss Pearl's house without a full stomach.

Dinner went better than I thought considering our last awkward encounter at church. We talked about school mostly, but Worthy kept the conversation moving when I ran out of small talk. She caught them up on cheerleading and show choir, but no one mentioned the pickling incident at school, which I was grateful for. When Cruz asked if I'd be coming back to Sunday services, Miss Pearl jumped in before I had to say anything. She explained that tonight was the start of our weekly Bible studies to help me and Worthy deepen our faith together.

So here I sat, listening to the dishes clinking from the kitchen window, waiting for the others to join me. I hugged my knees to my chest and stared out at the still street, feeling lighter from the warmth of the Clarke house. When Miss Pearl finally stepped onto the porch, I instantly spotted the Bible tucked in her hands as she ambled over and took the wicker chair beside me with a satisfied sigh.

"Beautiful night, isn't it?" she asked, her voice soft as her gaze drifted to the last inch of sunlight beyond the horizon. As fall neared, the days grew shorter and shorter.

I nodded, offering a small smile. "It is, I love this time of year, especially when it's not so hot."

Miss Pearl grinned back wistfully as my gaze drifted to the worn cover of the Bible in her lap. The edges were dry and cracked from years of use that was such a stark contrast to mine. The leather version I carried was still new and stiff, a reflection of where I was in my journey with Christ. We enjoyed a nice quiet moment, broken only by the sounds of passing cars every now and then. The quiet was comfortable, not empty like home could be. Tonight, the Clarke's reminded me how warm and relaxed a family could be.

Finally, Miss Pearl broke the silence. "I've been meaning to ask, Lena. Tell me about New Hope Bible Camp. I know you spent most of your summer there, what was that like?"

I smiled brightly, feeling a flutter in my chest at the thought of camp. "It was amazing. I didn't expect it to be, but camp turned out to be one of the best things that's happened to me in a long time."

Miss Pearl raised her brows, encouraging me to explain. "And, what made it so special?"

I thought for a second, but the answer was simple. "The people, for one. I made some amazing friends and reconnected with some old ones. People there just felt real, you know? I was surrounded by others with their own struggles who talked about things so openly, without any judgment."

She smiled. "Sounds like you were surrounded by wonderful people."

"I was," I said. "My Aunt Lou was there too. We hadn't seen each other in forever, so getting to spend the summer with her..." I thought about how rocky things were at first, but once Lou and I cleared the air, she was really there for me. I glanced up at Miss Pearl, adding. "I think time was what we both needed."

"That's great, baby. Family is important." Miss Pearl mused.

I nodded thoughtfully as my mind drifted back to summer. "The lake there is beautiful, too. Me and my friends would just sit out on the sand and just talk or watch the sunrise. Everyone talks about how beautiful the beach is, but the ocean stretches on for miles. The mountains are amazing too in their own way."

"Aren't they?" Miss Pearl asked as I caught a twinkle in her eye. "When I was your age, I loved driving to see the fall colors in the mountains. Being up there was like seeing God's artwork on full display. There was something special to see anywhere you turned your head."

"I think so too." Hearing her talk about God's artwork immediately made me think about Carter.

Miss Pearl's smile was soft and knowing, like she could read my mind. "And I hear there's a boy in this story, too. Don't leave that part out."

I felt my cheeks redden as I realized Worthy must have filled her grandmother in. "His name is Carter."

"Ah," Miss Pearl's tone was light but curious. "Tell me about him. Is he the type of boy who can help you grow spiritually?"

My heart fluttered at the thought, and when I met her gaze, the conviction in my voice surprised even me. "If it weren't for Carter, I don't know if I would've found my way back to God this summer."

I could easily tell her about Carter, especially since he'd become such a big part of my life so quickly. As we talked, I thought about the evening devotional at camp after my baptism. That night, I had struggled to talk about how he had kissed me in the pool, but Carter didn't. He was so open in how he explained himself, and confessed his feelings for me, but what struck me more was what he said after.

You're going to Heaven with me.

As I remembered Carter's words, I knew at that moment he meant more to me than I could say.

Miss Pearl's eyes shone with approval. "Sounds like God placed him in your life at just the right time."

I grinned from ear-to-ear, feeling a familiar flutter in my chest. "I believe He did."

We sat together as the night stretched ahead of us, still and quiet. Finally, Miss Pearl reached over and rested her hand lightly on mine. "Lena, I don't want you to talk about it if you don't want to, but I'm aware of what you've been going through at school."

Her soft voice still made my heart ache. Miss Pearl was right, I didn't want to talk about it but what she said next surprised me.

"I want you to know," she said, leaning closer, bright eyes shining beneath the porch light. "I've noticed a change in Worthy, and I think a part of that is because of how you've handled yourself with everything going on at school."

I blinked, feeling stunned, unsure what to say. Part of me wanted to disagree because, if anything, my avoidance tactics had only improved since the incident in the parking lot.

With wise eyes, Miss Pearl continued. "No one deserves what you're going through, and I've got half a mind to go down to that school and give the administration a piece of what I think of them."

That made me smile.

"But I've been praying for you, and I need you to remember this," she said, gripping my hand. "Jesus didn't promise us that life would be easy. In fact, He promised the opposite, but He did promise to walk through this life with us."

She reached over with her other hand, gripping mine tightly.

I fought back the growing lump in my throat. "I learned that at camp this summer, and that's the truth I've been clinging to."

"You cling to God's truth, baby, and don't let go, no matter what happens. You hear me?" she asked, fiery strength igniting her eyes. "Don't let the opinions of those goons at school define you. Remember, you're a child of God. He sees you as a precious jewel, and that's who you are, Lena Harris, not any of those names they may call you or whisper behind your back."

Tears welled up in my eyes, but her words brought a smile as she continued gripping my hand.

"Thank you for saying that."

Miss Pearl stretched out a hand to stroke my cheek. "You keep shining bright for Jesus, baby," she said. "We may never know what others go through, but just remember, you may be the only Bible they ever see. Trust me, you're already shining as an example for all the Lord is doing in your life. If you don't believe me, just look at that girl inside."

Her gesture toward Worthy and Cruz, laughing together in the kitchen window, surprised me. I had no idea how much sharing my camp experience had affected Worthy, but I trusted Miss

Pearl to tell the truth. My faith gave me assurance that God was always beside me, guiding and shaping me, and placing others in my path to encourage me, like the Clarke family.

The porch light overhead suddenly flashed, and I blinked while my eyes adjusted.

"Y'all mind if I join you?" Worthy appeared, closing the screen door behind her. Miss Pearl turned, and we both spotted Worthy stepping out with two glasses of sweet tea, with her Bible tucked beneath one arm. She handed me a glass, then passed the other to her Nan, and took the empty seat beside Miss Pearl.

"It's so nice out tonight," Worthy said, just like her grandmother had as her eyes scanned the sky. "Brings back memories, doesn't it?"

The question brought back memories as I remembered us practicing cartwheels in the yard when we used to cheerlead together, while we waited for whatever Miss Pearl made for dinner. Outside of cheerleading, our friendship revolved around church. If we weren't enjoying a potluck, we enjoyed events the church hosted for the youth. Now, it dawned on me just how much time I had wasted being hurt and angry, turning my back on God and those who loved Him. Now I had a second chance, and I wouldn't waste it.

"Well, let's get started, girls," Miss Pearl said, pulling me from my thoughts as she turned her attention to her Bible.

I reached down and picked up the Bible resting beside me on the porch swing. As I did, the light shining from above the door caught the beaded bracelets circling my wrist—BESTIES, SISTERS IN CHRIST, PSALM 46:5, SHINE! The sight of them made me smile as I brushed a thumb over each one, pausing just above the band Carter had given me. I flipped through the pages absentmindedly until a highlight caught my eye.

You are the light of the world. A city set on a hill cannot be hidden.

Jojo's favorite verse.

I felt a slow smile creep up as I remembered real friendship spilling across the floor of Jojo's bedroom as we made beaded bracelets, our laughter stretching late into the evening. I remembered the way she gently placed the finished pile in my hand like they were something sacred. That night, I learned what it really meant to shine for Jesus.

17

One moment I was on Miss Pearl's porch; the next I was lost in the memory of a girls' day with Jojo and Aunt Lou this summer. We cruised down familiar streets with the windows down and the music cranked up. The day unfolded into one of those picture-perfect memories I would carry forever.

Our first stop was Max's Diner for lunch where clinking plates and the sizzle of grilled burgers greeted us when we stepped inside. Jojo and I slid into a booth across from Lou, all of us famished from an already full day.

"I've missed this place," Jojo said, scanning the menu like she didn't already have it memorized. "Camp food just doesn't stand a chance against Max's."

"You can't beat Max's burgers," Lou said with a wink, though her eyes flicked briefly toward Max behind the counter. It was quick, almost nothing, but I didn't miss the way Lou glowed when Max grinned back at her. If I hadn't been watching Lou, I might've missed their exchange. But then I remembered what Carter had said on our date, something about Max and Lou being more than friends. Now I couldn't help but wonder if Carter might've been right.

After we finished eating, Lou waved off Jojo's idea to order milkshakes. "Who needs a shake when the Cupcake Cottage is calling?"

Jojo's boss greeted us the second we sauntered in and insisted the treats were "on the house."

"I could get used to free cupcakes," Lou said, taking a dramatic bite of her red velvet.

"You and me both," I laughed, licking a smear of frosting off my finger. "Jojo, I seriously don't understand how you stay so skinny working here."

Jojo scrunched her nose. "Can you believe I'm actually tired of cupcakes?"

Lou and I shot each other a look before answering in unison, "No."

Our laughter carried down the sidewalk as we strolled through downtown, arms linked, discussing Jojo's so-called *secret recipe hacks,* and that's when I saw it.

The Meadowbrook Pawn Shop.

I slowed my steps without even thinking. "Can we stop in here for a second?"

Lou raised an eyebrow but offered me a one-shoulder shrug. "Sure, I haven't been there in years."

We stepped inside, and the scent of old wood and rusting metal danced around us like dust in sunlight. I focused on the glass case where the music box sat, the one Carter and I had spotted on our first date. As I made my way toward the case slowly, my heart picked up speed with each step hoping to still find the box on the shelf. After moving a couple of old trinkets around, I realized the music box wasn't there anymore. Disappointment settled in the pit of my stomach, though I tried to hide it as Jojo wandered toward a rack of vintage clothing.

"This place is like a cave of lost treasure," Jojo said, holding up a seventies-inspired blouse. "I might have to get this."

I managed a smile, trying to shake off the lingering sadness. "It suits you."

We left the pawnshop with Jojo's purchase in hand and headed into the heart of downtown, where the rest of the afternoon passed in a blur of laughter and shopping.

As the sun set that evening, Jojo stared back at me with a sly grin. "You're not going back to Lou's. You're staying at my house tonight. We're not done yet."

I grinned, and my heart felt like it had finally found some sunshine. "Deal."

***

That evening when Jojo and I pulled up to her house, I gazed out at the cute one-story with weathered wood paneling and a wide front porch. Hanging plants framed the deck, and stone lanterns lined the path to the door. Inside, the space was modest but inviting, a perfect blend of her mother's Korean background and her father's love for vintage decor. Suddenly, Jojo's unique style made more sense.

Jojo's mom was at the stove, swaying to music playing softly in the background. She wore a floral apron tied neatly around her waist, and her glossy black hair was in a loose bun. As she cooked, the house was filled with a welcoming scent of sautéed herbs and garlic. Jojo's dad sat at the table nearby with a cutting board and a bowl of onions and peppers in front of him. I noticed a towel on his lap and his walker resting at his side. Jojo had told me over the summer about his multiple sclerosis diagnosis. Even with the strain I didn't have to look hard to see, there was a lightness to him, especially when Jojo's mom leaned over to steal a kiss and a pepper slice.

"You beautiful little thief," her dad said before her mom swiped the bowl from him.

"I'll take that," she teased. As she returned to the sizzling skillet, they both noticed us in the entryway. Her mom immediately pulled us both into a hug like it was something she did every day.

"Lena! It's so nice to see you finally!" she said in a lilting voice that reminded me of Jojo's. Her eyes sparkled as she leaned back to take me in. "Jojo's been talking about you non-stop and I was so happy to hear about your baptism this summer. Congratulations!"

"Thank you," I said, surprised but touched by how genuine she was.

She pecked Jojo on the cheek and returned to the skillet.

Jojo motioned from her mom to her dad. "Lena, I'm not sure if you remember my parents, but this is my mom, Yeri, and my dad, Phillip."

"Phil," her dad corrected. He was now carefully peeling carrots and placing them in the bowl. His movements were slow, but when he glanced up, he was wearing a wide, serene smile.

"You've grown, Lena," Phil said simply, his voice gentle. "You used to run around the church like a wild thing with Jo."

Jojo laughed as she crossed the room, hugging him from behind. He chuckled and kissed her temple. Music still played softly, and her dad tapped his foot to the beat. Yeri wandered over and playfully bumped his shoulder, surveying his chopping skills.

"You missed one, chef," she teased, placing the bowl back in front of him.

He grinned, feigning offense. "I'm doing all the hard work over here."

"Sure, sure," Yeri said, then turned to us. "You girls hungry? I made oatmeal raisin cookies."

She held out the plate with a wink, and Jojo snatched two without hesitation. "You're the best, Mom."

"That will spoil their dinner," Phil joked.

Yeri brushed him off and lowered her voice. "Who says dessert can't come first?"

With a laugh, Jojo grabbed my hand and dragged me down the hall as her parents' warm laughter followed us, the sound filling their home full of love.

Jojo's room was just as unique and vivacious as she was. Fairy lights twinkled around walls covered in Polaroids, and behind her bed was a bold blue wall accented with wildflowers. The opposite wall held her vanity and an overflowing bookshelf cluttered with books, journals, and trinkets. Her closet door was open, the light on, and a pile of clothes sat in a heap on the floor.

Jojo spotted me eyeing the pile and began picking it up while I had a seat on the edge of her bed.

"Okay, so what's the deal?" She asked, returning a shirt to its hanger.

"The deal with what?" I asked.

Jojo popped her head out of the closet. "You and Carter, obviously. You two seem so dreamy and *in-love*."

I giggled at the way she said the last part but could feel my heart gushing. "It's just been the best week with him getting to be a real couple. I'm glad I got to spend extra time here with all of you, though. How's it going with Denny?"

Jojo smiled reflexively at the mention of her boyfriend. "That boy is something else! All day he's just been sending me silly SnapChat selfies instead of having a real conversation."

I smiled for a moment before the sound of shuffled beads filled the silence. Jojo exited the closet with a toolbox of beads and plopped down in front of me.

"Want to join me?" she asked, pulling out bracelet supplies from the box.

I slid off her bed and sat cross-legged beside her while she worked.

"I started working on some more for you to take home," Jojo explained.

"You didn't have to do that, Jo."

She glanced up at me with a sly grin. "Friendship bracelets are non-negotiable."

While she was working, I started helping her, cutting string and arranging beads so I could also make her a bracelet. Sitting there, I could feel the quiet strength of Jojo's family. Her mom was happily buzzing around the kitchen preparing dinner with Jojo's dad, who worked alongside her, trying to keep his hands steady despite the obvious tremor. They moved in sync, laughing softly, all while exchanging glances that showed just how in love they were. The warmth between them was palpable.

Seeing the way they lit up around each other, made me wish for the kind of love they had, the kind of love that was enough to hold a family together. It felt ironic to see how some families remained strong through tough times, while others fell apart.

"Hey Jo," I broke the silence. "How do you do it? How does your family keep it all together knowing your dad is sick?"

Jojo finished the bracelet, tying it in a tight knot before offering it to me. I smiled as I stared at the word spelled out in beads.

SHINE!

"It's not always easy, especially when Dad has bad days. Seeing him struggle is tough, but Mom and Dad always remind me of the light we have inside. They say our light needs to be reflected in all we do," Jojo answered.

I continued beading while I listened to her.

"One of my favorite Bible verses is Matthew five, fourteen through sixteen. It says *You are the light of the world. A city set on a hill cannot be hidden.*"

I glanced up at her. "So, you just choose not to hide behind your dad's health situation?"

Jojo was thoughtful before she said, "Sometimes we have to remember the blessings our trials bring and how God can use our lives to bring hope to others."

Her words left me in awe as she tied off another bracelet so quickly.

"My dad has gone through so much and still does, but he keeps pressing forward," Jojo explained. "It's hard to watch, and I struggle sometimes, but I try to remember God's promises. Even when it's hard, I know God will use these circumstances for good. He gives me strength, and I hope I can use my story to help someone else someday."

She handed me another bracelet that read BESTIES, and it made me smile. Thinking of our friendship, I hoped to have half the faith and strength Jojo had.

"I'm not sure I'll ever be that strong," I confessed, keeping my eyes downcast.

Jojo leaned over and nudged me, a teasing smile spreading across her face. "You're stronger than you realize. You just can't see it yet. But remember, you have everyone here to remind you."

I smiled and gave her a knowing look. "Thanks for reminding me. I needed that."

Jojo squeezed my hand. "Keep that in mind when you go home, too," she said. "Don't be afraid to let people see the light in you, Lena. Don't let the hard stuff dim it. When everything feels like it's falling apart, that's when your true strength shows the most. That's when you really shine."

Jojo's words hit me. Wise as she seemed, she was speaking from experience. Her cheery positivity had once annoyed me, but now it was what I loved most about her. Jojo's bright spirit wasn't a disguise for pain; it was a refusal to let her troubles weigh her down.

"I wish I could take you home with me," I told her, squeezing her hand in return. "You're a walking inspirational billboard. I could create an entire Pinterest board out of your advice."

She giggled, and I ducked as she picked up a handful of beads and tossed them at me. "Someone has to keep you from falling into a gigantic pit of despair!"

I picked up some beads and shot them back at her one by one. The two of us laughed as a bead fight broke out. All week in Meadowbrook, I had felt lighter and more like myself than ever before. Spending time with Jojo made me forget all about returning to Freeport as the night wore on. The two of us laughed until our stomachs hurt as we joked about everything from boys to embarrassing stories we shared.

Later, while Jojo cleaned up the scattered beads in her room, I joined in to help. The new stack of bracelets Jojo had gifted to me glinted on my wrist beneath the warm light of her bedroom. The bracelet that read *SHINE!* caught my attention again, but this time felt different. The word now held the weight of a promise and a challenge.

18

When October finally arrived, the leaves were undergoing a complete transformation, just like things were at school. A few weeks had passed since the car-pickling fiasco, which Worthy and I had officially dubbed as a *stupid senior prank*. She made it her mission to poke fun at the situation every chance she got, and, surprisingly, being able to view the situation that way helped me move past it. Over the past few weeks, Worthy and I had grown closer, and it made all the difference having someone in my corner.

Miss Pearl wasn't short on wisdom these days either. At Bible study, she shared a verse that stayed with me like a steady light guiding me through the halls of Freeport High. *Do not repay anyone evil for evil. Be careful to do what is right in everyone's eyes.* I clung to that scripture with each mocking glare or taunting whisper that came my way. Bible study at the Clarke house had become a weekly tradition I looked forward to, even though I knew it couldn't replace worship. I still hadn't worked up the nerve to ask for Sundays off yet, but deep down, I finally felt brave enough to, like I could face being at church again without being triggered.

The more I studied my Bible, the more I realized just how truly life-giving scripture was. Carter had always preached, *"Read it for yourself,"* and I loved that because no one else was responsible for my soul but me. Miss Pearl was the same way. When I asked a question, she would point me back to scripture for the answer every time. Her motto was, *don't take anyone else's word for it but God's.* She was right, and with every verse I read, my faith grew, leaving me feeling lighter and lighter with each study.

As I fell into my new rhythm, fall crept in. The days grew shorter and cooler, then one afternoon, Worthy suggested we find a place indoors to eat lunch. I hesitated at first, feeling sick to my stomach at the idea of subjecting myself to the cafeteria where the vultures awaited me, but she had a better idea. Worthy asked me to join her in the music room where the show choir usually hung out, and without hesitation I gave in. Something told me this could only be another step forward if I let myself trust it.

I already knew our show choir was talented, but lunchtime with them turned out to be total chaos in the best way. The music room was pure entertainment, and on most days, someone was rehearsing choreography or running through harmonies. Lunch was like a free concert, and before long, the choir pulled me into their orbit. I wasn't a part of the choir, but they viewed me as a constant source of feedback, and before long, they were asking me for performance critiques like I was an experienced judge on *The Voice.*

Even considering all the chaos, the music room became my refuge. Tucked between white brick walls and spontaneous solos, I found something I hadn't felt at school in years... *a sense of belonging.* Despite school still being low on my list of favorite places, I always looked forward to lunch. Whether I was listening to warm-ups or to the basses arguing over who could hit the lowest note, the show choir felt like my people.

One week, after hearing *"Defying Gravity"* on an endless loop, I caught myself humming the song as Worthy and I made our way to lunch. With each step we took, I worried about running into one of Lacey's friends, but the song lyrics calmed me.

"You know..." Worthy said, giving me a sly glance. "You used to sing all the time, and since you already hang out with us every day, why not join the show choir?"

I gave her a skeptical look. "Um...because one does not simply join a show choir. Besides, between school and work, I barely have time to study and talk to Carter, let alone add an extracurricular."

Worthy scoffed. "Show choir is always open to newcomers. We perform at school events but also compete at regionals and states. The more people that join, the better we are. You already spend every day with us, so why not join us?"

"Just because I hum doesn't mean I can sing." I replied.

With a narrowed gaze, Worthy gave me a look like I was ridiculous. "Do you not remember me just saying I know you can? I've heard you plenty of times, Lena. Remember the beach singing nights we used to have at church? I always loved sitting beside you and your mom while we all harmonized."

Worthy meant well, but she didn't know I had buried those memories in the sand. Music was once a huge part of my life, but along the way I let my love for it walk out the door with my mother.

I was quiet for a moment before I gave an awkward shrug. "Sorry but show choir isn't for me."

"Just think about it." Worthy nudged me with an encouraging grin.

I managed a small smile, grateful that she decided to back down, but the moment we stepped into the cafeteria, the roar of the room locked me in a chokehold. Whatever calm I'd felt dissolved as my defenses slid back into place.

The lunchroom aroma filled my nostrils as I trailed behind Worthy toward the dwindling line. Laughter burst from a nearby table, sharp and sudden, and when I glanced over, my breath hitched. Lacey was already glaring at me, whispering something to her friends. As the group suddenly burst into laughter, I felt my stomach sink and my neck grow hot.

"Are you okay?" Worthy asked, laying a hand on my arm.

"Yeah, I'm fine," I replied, though my voice cracked.

"Just ignore them," she said, grabbing my wrist and pulling me forward.

"It's okay," I said out loud, trying to calm myself. "Really, we go to the same school, and I just need to deal with seeing her and ignore all of them."

Worthy gave my arm a quick, reassuring squeeze before she grabbed a tray and made a beeline for the dessert station. "Good," she said over her shoulder. "Don't feed into Lacey's power trip and you'll fall off her radar. Kill her with kindness."

Agreeing with her, I stepped up and took the next tray from the lunch lady filled with chicken nuggets, fruit, and a slop of mashed potatoes. I appreciated Worthy's advice, but the words that stuck with me were the ones Lou, Jojo, and Miss Pearl had instilled.

Shine your light so others can see Jesus through you.

The reminder helped loosen the knot in my stomach after locking eyes with Lacey. I didn't know exactly what it would mean to shine my light, but I knew I wasn't alone. Taking a steadying breath, I stood behind Worthy while she paid. My plan was simple: keep my head down and get back to the music room as fast as humanly possible.

While I balanced my tray in one hand, I reached into my pocket to fish out a five-dollar bill, but when I handed it over, the cafeteria fell into a strange stillness that settled over the room. As the lunch lady handed me back my change, I turned just as a wave of ice-cold liquid splashed across my chest. I yelped, jumping as my tray slipped from my hands and clattered to the floor. The cold tea seeped into my shirt, its chill spreading quickly as the uncomfortable wet fabric clung to my skin. All of a sudden, the still cafeteria erupted in a sea of whispers as everyone stared at me.

"Oh, no!" a voice rang out, mock surprise threaded through every word. "My hand slipped."

I didn't need to look to see who ran into me; I would recognize that voice anywhere. Still rooted to the spot, I stared down at the puddle forming around my shoes as tea dripped from the hem of my shirt. The room quickly erupted in a wave of whispers and laughter, but all I could hear was fresh pounding in my ears as I slowly lifted my gaze to hers.

Lacey stood smiling, her hand covering her mouth like this was all just one big accident. Behind her the two girls standing there were the same ones I'd seen when Javier pickled my car. The sight of them only confirmed what I'd suspected all along. *Lacey had been behind everything.* To my surprise, instead of anger, something else rose up inside me, because when I saw beyond her flawless makeup and carefully curled hair, I could see all the insecurity Lacey was trying to hide.

The fun-loving girl I once knew back in middle school was gone. I barely recognized the person standing in front of me now. While I was trying to move forward, Lacey was still stuck in the same cycle of revenge we'd been caught in last year. This summer, I made a choice to lay my past down and let it go. Now, when I looked at Lacey through the lens of forgiveness, I didn't see an enemy. I saw a reflection of who I used to be. She had no idea about the kind of freedom I'd found in Jesus.

As I stared back at her, I wondered if this was how Carter had seen me at camp when we first met. A lost girl who just needed to be shown grace and to know that change was possible. Suddenly, I knew exactly what it meant for me to shine my light.

Worthy appeared at my side, shooting daggers with her eyes. "Really, Lacey?" she snapped. "This is funny to you?"

Feigning innocence, Lacey shrugged. "Like I said, my hand slipped."

Worthy took a step forward, but I placed my hand on her shoulder to pull her away. She glanced back at me as I shook my head.

"It's fine," I told her, hoping she could understand. *Lacey doesn't know what we know*, I tried to tell Worthy telepathically, *so this is how we show her.*

I watched as Worthy's brows furrowed, but before she could respond, I stepped over my spilled tray and handed my leftover change to the lunch lady. "Can this cover another cup of tea for her?" I asked, motioning to Lacey.

The woman stared back at me with wide eyes as she took the bills. "Are you sure?"

Smiling sheepishly, I nodded, knowing how strange I probably seemed to her. "Can I also get some paper towels to clean this up?"

She stared at me as if I were an extraterrestrial before shaking her head. "No, honey, you go get *yourself* cleaned up. We'll take care of this."

Worthy's mouth hung open, and Lacey seemed equally astonished when I turned to look at them. Lacey crossed her arms and stood like a pouting child, which made it even easier to summon the strength to face her.

"I forgive you," I said, staring into her dark eyes. "I'm sorry for what I did to get us here last year, but maybe someday you can forgive me, too."

Before she could have the last word, I stepped over the mess and scampered out of the cafeteria.

***

I headed for the bathroom at the end of the hall, only to be met by the unmistakable sound of someone retching in the first stall. I paused, almost gagging on the spot, until the person flushed the toilet, signaling they were done.

At the sink, I grabbed a wad of paper towels and dabbed at the tea soaking my shirt before catching my reflection. My shirt was soaked through, and my cheeks were red. Today felt so surreal, like I was watching someone else go through it instead of me.

Suddenly, the loud creak of a stall door pulled my attention from my reflection, and I froze, watching Ronni step out. *You've got to be kidding me*, I thought as our eyes met in the mirror, startling both of us. We stood there, gawking at each other in silence. Her face was pale and her forehead seemed to glisten with sweat, but I couldn't tell if the frown on her face was from being sick or seeing me.

Tearing her gaze from mine, Ronni made her way to the sink on the far side. I kept blotting at the stain, though it was useless. Ronni finally shut off the faucet and crossed the room toward me. When I glanced up, I caught her gaze on my shirt, but she didn't ask what happened, and my guess was she didn't have to. When Ronni began shaking her wet hands, I realized I was blocking the paper towels. I stepped aside, my pulse thudding as I braced myself for whatever might come next.

"So, did you fight back?" Ronni finally spoke, her question sharp. "Or did you just let Lacey walk all over you, like usual?"

Her words struck me and I watched as she balled up the paper towels and tossed them into the trash with more force than necessary.

"I walked away," I said, my voice steadier than I felt. "I didn't need to fight back. Walking away is about being the bigger person, not trying to even the score."

Ronni's expression tightened, like she was about to argue, but before she could, the bathroom door swung open. Worthy stepped inside, eyes moving quickly between us and the tea-stained mess on my shirt.

"Hey," she said cautiously. "I figured I'd find you in here."

Silence settled between the three of us for a moment before Ronni stalked past Worthy. She reached for the door but paused, before turning to face me.

"Here's to me being the bigger person, too," she said. We watched as Ronni stalked out, letting the door swing shut behind her with a dull thud.

Worthy frowned as she turned back to me. "Don't tell me Ronni Dice started something, too."

I slowly shook my head as Ronni's words came back to me, like she expected me to continue fighting Lacey. I couldn't pinpoint what had changed in her over the summer, but one thing was clear, the Ronni I'd once called a friend was gone. She wasn't the strong, unstoppable force I'd looked up to last year; she was a girl weighed down by life and shielding herself. Ronni's fight wasn't with me and I could see that now. Whatever she was facing was bigger than anything I could fix. If Ronni was pushing me away, there was a reason, but it wasn't up to me to solve her problems; she needed to find her own way, just as I had to find mine.

"No," I finally answered Worthy. "I'd say that door has closed, *pun intended.*"

Worthy scoffed before stepping forward to hand me a clean shirt. "I brought you this. I keep a spare in my locker because one time I forgot to bring a shirt for cheer practice and had to wear my dress shirt instead."

The thought made me smile as I took the shirt from her. "You're way too kind to me, Clarke."

I slipped into the large accessible stall at the end of the row to change.

"Someone has to be," Worthy called through the door. "You're not exactly kind to yourself... but maybe now's a good time to start."

I quickly swapped shirts, folding the tea-soaked one into a neat square before stepping back out. "I'm a work in progress," I said with a shrug.

Worthy rolled her eyes and nudged me toward the door. "Then let's start making some actual progress. How about trying to be a little more positive?"

I pulled open the bathroom door, only to freeze, causing Worthy to collide with me from behind and send me stumbling forward.

"Lena, what are you—" she began, but the words died on her lips as her eyes landed on the two adults standing across the hall.

Beside the principal, Mr. Hall, stood Mrs. Jones, the guidance counselor. "Girls, would you come with us, please?" Mrs. Jones asked calmly. Without waiting for a response, they turned and began walking down the hall.

My stomach dropped as I followed their lead, without needing to ask where we were going. Worthy moved quickly, falling into step beside me as we trailed behind them toward the main office.

"So...what were you saying about being positive again?" I whispered to her.

Worthy cut her eyes at me but remained quiet as we reached the end of the hall. Turning the corner, we followed the adults into the principal's office, where Lacey was already waiting.

19

I sat across from Mrs. Jones as the faint scent of lavender and chamomile drifted from the diffuser beside her, "*It's Talk Time*" sign perched on the edge of her desk. I shifted in my chair, but no position could make this feel anymore comfortable. The last time I sat in this room, it felt less like a safe space and more like a petri dish I was trapped in while my school counselor dissected me.

Mrs. Jones folded her hands and kept her steady blue eyes on me while I immediately gazed down at the floor. I recognized that look in her eyes. Every other time I had been in this office, Mrs. Jones had stared at me like that when she would mention my mom.

"Lena, how are you doing?" she asked, her tone calm but probing.

I shrugged, as I kept my gaze on the freshly opened box of tissues between us. "I've had better days, but as you can see, I'm fine."

"Hmm," Mrs. Jones murmured. "I'm not sure anyone in your shoes would be fine."

Chuckling, I shrugged off the thought, trying my best to seem unaffected. "It was just a dumb senior prank."

Mrs. Jones tilted her head curiously. "A dumb prank? Is that how you see it?"

"Yes, because that's what it was," I insisted, keeping my tone neutral. I refused to let anyone, including her or Mr. Hall, think Lacey's behavior had fazed me.

"Do you want to talk about what happened in the cafeteria?" Mrs. Jones pressed. "This is a safe space, Lena."

I almost rolled my eyes but remembered Ronni's advice from last year: *just play along.* If I let her think I had everything under control, she wouldn't drag me into her office for more "Talk Times." My goal this year was to move on and put this drama behind me, no matter how many times my past kept coming for me.

"Actually, I've been working through things outside of school with friends from church."

Mrs. Jones' eyebrows shot up. "That's wonderful, how's that been going for you?"

"Really well. I became a Christian this summer, and it's changed a lot for me," I said confidently. Her expression softened into something resembling genuine approval, though her demeanor never cracked.

"That's a meaningful decision," Mrs. Jones said, her gaze warming. "Faith can be grounding, especially for situations like today."

I offered a hopeful smile, thinking I had deflected a deeper conversation, but Mrs. Jones pressed on. "Lena, I'm happy to hear you're finding support, but I want to remind you that you can always come to me if you need to talk. I'm here for you."

"I know that," I replied, though just being back in this room made my stomach twist.

Mrs. Jones always started sessions the same way, examining her subjects like the prey we were before tearing into our psyche.

"How are things at home?" she'd ask, voice flat and scripted, like she was reading from a manual.

I'd sit stiffly, searching for something true to say that wouldn't earn me another empty nod or a printed worksheet. Once, I mentioned I'd lost my appetite, and Mrs. Jones handed me a flyer on self-care, like that could heal the ache of my mother running out on me.

Dad always said talking would help, but with Mrs. Jones, talking felt more like checking boxes. I'd leave her office more hollow than before, having spent the time counting the minutes until it was over.

Now, she paused before continuing, her gaze flicking down to her notes.

"Mr. Hall spoke with Miss Clarke and Miss Lockhart after meeting with you," she said. "We've come to a shared understanding, particularly concerning Miss Lockhart. She'll serve after-school detention and begin sessions with me this week."

My jaw almost hit the floor at the shocking turn of events because, for once, I wasn't to blame. Suddenly, I didn't feel as relieved as I thought I would; instead, I just felt sorry for Lacey. After surviving guidance counseling sessions last year, I knew Lacey had no idea what was waiting for her inside these walls.

Mrs. Jones must have noticed my reaction, because she added gently, "Lena, I know this hasn't been easy, but I'm proud of how you handled yourself today. Still, I want to make sure there aren't any future issues. Retaliation of any kind will result in further disciplinary action. Am I clear?"

"Crystal," I said, relieved that for once, I wasn't in trouble. Mrs Jones rose to her feet finally and motioned to the door.

"Both your father and Miss Lockharts' are here to take you home. If you don't have any questions, you're free to go."

My stomach dropped. *Was Dad already filled in on what happened, or was I going to have to explain it all myself?*

I murmured a quiet *thank you* and headed for the door, only to stop short. Just outside Mrs. Jones' office stood between Lacey and her father, Aaron Lockhart. Lacey remained silent while he spoke to her in a quiet, sharp tone, lecturing her about acting like an adult. Instead, she crossed her arms, and when she saw me, she turned her face away.

Aaron glanced up, and when he noticed me, I watched as he immediately straightened and gave a faint, polite nod. "Lena, I'm sorry to hear what happened."

His eyes flicked between the two of us as Lacey's gaze dropped to the floor.

"Girls," he said, voice tired. "Can we finally put this to rest? Whatever happened between you two... it's time to move on."

"Yes, sir," I answered softly.

Lacey didn't say a word; she just gave a small nod, eyes fixed on the floor like it might open up and swallow her. Her arms remained locked tightly across her chest like she'd built a wall around herself and didn't know how to let it down. The fury and pain in Lacey's eyes last year had been sharper and colder than ever before. I recognized her pain because I'd felt it too. The two of us had once been inseparable, but all of that changed when she started dating Javier.

The girl I once called my best friend disappeared, slowly reshaped into the version of herself she thought he wanted. When I needed her most, she wasn't there. Lacey let Javier consume her, and she hated that I couldn't pretend to like him like everyone else did. She couldn't see the truth, but he had changed her into someone I barely recognized.

Lacey had taken on Javier's dismissive tone and his cruel laugh. Javier Diaz was just a guy who used people for his benefit and left them behind. Lacey was just too blind to see who he was and she kept choosing him again and again. Losing all of her best friends wasn't enough to convince her, but if Lacey didn't open her eyes soon, she was going to lose herself completely. The confident, vibrant girl I used to know was now hidden beneath layers of exhaustion and invisible pressure. Even though I openly said I forgave her, she didn't apologize for what she did.

Deep down, I knew I didn't need to hear Lacey say sorry. I had already chosen to let the past go this summer, realizing that holding on to bitterness was only hurting me. Seeing Lacey now, weighed down by her own inner struggle, only made me feel sorry for her. I knew she wouldn't admit her part in all of this, but somehow, I was okay with that. Her father had asked us to move on, and maybe this was all the closure we were going to get. Lacey had always needed the last word, but this time, her silence said more than words ever could.

We were finished, the war was finally over.

"Good," Aaron said with a nod. "Now go get your things and wait in the car. I need a word with Mrs. Jones before we head home."

Lacey gave a small nod and turned without a word, slipping out of the office. Mrs. Jones stepped forward, gesturing for Aaron to follow her as they disappeared down the hall.

Just then, Dad stepped out of Mr. Hall's office, and the moment his eyes landed on me, his expression shifted.

"Let's go," he said, voice clipped.

I followed, the weight of his disappointment already pressing down on me. I hadn't forgotten the promises I made about this school year, and I knew he hadn't either.

As soon as we were out of earshot, his frustration spilled over like a boiling teapot. "What's going on, Lena? I got a call in the middle of the day saying there was some kind of incident. What is it now?"

My face flushed with heat, but I wasn't about to unpack everything in the middle of the hallway.

"Let's just go outside," I sighed, feeling my heart sink.

Dad sighed but didn't argue as he fell into step behind me. We walked out to the front walkway in silence, and once we were clear of the building, I turned to face him, arms crossed, bracing myself.

"There wasn't a fight," I said defensively. "Something happened at lunch, but it's not what you think."

"Mr. Hall told me what happened," Dad interjected. "He said this wasn't the first incident between you and Lacey this year, but that it would be the last. He told me they have a zero-tolerance policy for bullying and that he's advised Lacey to leave you alone, and for you to do the same."

My jaw tightened as I glowered back at him beneath a furrowed brow. "I've been leaving her alone."

"If either of you had been leaving each other alone, I don't think I'd be standing here right now," Dad retorted, exasperation lacing his words. "This has to stop, Lena. We can't keep doing this. You're a senior. You're supposed to be thinking about life outside of these walls and considering your future. If you're determined to go back down this path—"

"Why do you always think the worst of me?" I shouted, unable to contain myself any longer.

"Because you don't seem to understand that I am fed up with this childish behavior!" Dad shot back, raising his voice. "We have enough going on with your mother—"

The mention of her hit me like a knockout punch to the gut and I lost all self-control. "I'm not her!" I shouted, as my voice broke. "And I'm not trying to ruin my life or yours!"

Dad took a step back, stunned, though his hardened expression softened. "Lena—"

"Don't," I cut him off, taking a step away.

His eyes locked on mine, and I knew that whatever version of the story Mr. Hall had given him clearly hadn't been the whole truth. Dad wasn't listening; he never did. He just jumped to conclusions, and let the past speak for me.

If my own father couldn't see that I'd changed... how would anyone else?

"If you'd just let me talk," I said, struggling to keep my voice steady, "you'd know that Lacey threw tea on me at lunch today. Instead of fighting back, I walked away."

That made him pause, and I watched as Dad's mouth opened slightly, caught off guard by my response.

"A few weeks ago," I added, my voice trembling, "her friends covered my car in pickles and posted it online for everyone to see." My chin quivered, and the dam behind my eyes threatened to give. "You don't know that though, because I can't tell you anything without you flying off the handle. You keep waiting for me to become Mom, but you don't see how hard I'm fighting just to get my life back after she tore it apart!"

My words landed their final blow, and I watched my Dad's expression crumble, though as he took a slow breath, and reached out like he wanted to close the distance between us.

"Lenny... let's just go home and talk," he pleaded.

Pulling away from him, I stepped back again, putting more distance between us than ever. "No," I whispered, shaking my head as a tear slid down my cheek. "I'm not going home. I'm done talking to you right now."

Before Dad could say another word, our argument was interrupted by the sudden creak of the front door. We both turned to see Worthy step outside, instantly picking up on the tension in the air.

"Um... is everything okay?" she asked gently, taking a hesitant step forward. "I heard shouting and saw you out here. I didn't mean to interrupt."

"I'm sorry you had to hear that," Dad said, his tone subdued. "I shouldn't have raised my voice."

Worthy's lips pulled into a polite grin, though her expression remained uncertain. I wiped at my eyes, embarrassed she'd seen me like this, but her presence felt like a lifeline. There was only one place I wanted to be, somewhere I could let it all out without fear of judgment.

"Hey, is your grandmother home?" I asked her suddenly..

Her brows knit together in confusion, but slowly she nodded, though there was a question in her voice. "She should be. Why?"

Without looking back at my dad, I walked up to Worthy. "Can you call her and let her know I'm on my way? I need to talk to her."

"Of course," she said, pulling out her phone. As she dialed, I turned to face my dad briefly, unable to hold his gaze.

"I'll be home later," I said. Without waiting for his response, I headed back into the school to grab my backpack and car keys.

20

Miss Pearl was already waiting on the porch by the time I reached the Clarkes' house. She had wrapped her long cardigan tightly around herself and shuffled down the steps in house shoes as I stepped out of the car. Miss Pearl immediately opened her arms and pulled me into a firm embrace when she reached me as my tears began to fall.

"It's okay, baby," she whispered, her voice soft and steady. "I've got you, you're all right now."

Miss Pearl smelled of honeysuckle and cookie dough, a comforting mix that began to unravel me as she held me.

"I didn't know what else to do," I choked out, pulling away to wipe at my face with trembling hands. "Everything just started falling apart again."

"It's all right, baby," Miss Pearl repeated, her voice like a balm. She tucked an arm around my shoulders and turned me toward the house. "Come on in, Worthy called to let me know you were on your way over and you and me, we'll just go inside and have ourselves a little chat."

She let the door shut behind us as we stepped into her cozy living room. The smell of freshly baked cookies filled the space as Miss Pearl guided me to the couch. She took a seat across from me in a well-worn leather armchair and leaned forward, holding out a box of tissues.

"Talk to me, baby," Miss Pearl said softly, settling her elbows on her knees.

The words spewed out as I told her about how Lacey had ambushed me with her tea and how I walked away, even though she never apologized.

"I was just trying to set the right example and not lash out like I used to," I babbled. "Then I just left, and Lacey got in trouble, but then our parents showed up, and my dad... he was just so mad." With the tissue, I dabbed at my eyes. "I didn't even fight back, Miss Pearl. I didn't want to give Lacey the reaction she wanted. She was trying to start a fight, but when I tried to tell my dad everything, he wouldn't listen."

Miss Pearl studied me for a moment as I struggled to piece my words together.

"Lacey didn't even say sorry when I said I forgave her," I continued. "I don't know what version of the story my dad got, but it's like he didn't know or care that I was trying to do the right thing."

She simply bobbed her head up and down as a small, sad smile pulled at her lips. "Baby, let me tell you something, sometimes we have to forgive people who don't say they're sorry."

I blinked as I choked back a threatening sob. "I'm trying, but how do I know I'm doing the right thing when everything feels so hard no matter what I do?"

Miss Pearl exhaled before climbing to her feet. "First Peter has the perfect advice," she said, moving toward the bookshelf. She pulled down her worn Bible, flipping through the thin pages until she found what she was searching for. I watched while she settled back into her chair and read aloud, her voice rich and steady.

"But even if you should suffer for righteousness' sake, you are blessed. 'And do not be afraid of their threats, nor be troubled.' But sanctify the Lord God in your hearts, and always be ready

to give a defense to everyone who asks you a reason for the hope that is in you, with meekness and fear; having a good conscience, that when they defame you as evildoers, those who revile your good conduct in Christ may be ashamed. For it is better, if it is the will of God, to suffer for doing good than for doing evil."

She closed the Bible and rested her hands on top. "We're going to come into conflict with others, Lena. That's just part of life, but the way we respond, that's what matters. God calls us to give an answer with gentleness and respect."

I swallowed hard, her words settling into the cracks of my heart.

Miss Pearl leaned forward, taking my hands. "You showed people what it looks like to turn the other cheek today. Baby, that's hard, especially when they can't do the same for you." She squeezed my hands, keeping her steady gaze on mine. "But that's what makes grace so powerful. Your actions reflected your heart after God, but don't you ever mistake meekness for weakness, Lena Harris. Meekness is a fruit of the Spirit, and it takes strength to hold your tongue when the world tempts you to lash out."

A lump formed in my throat, and I glanced down, blinking against the fresh wave of tears.

Miss Pearl lifted my chin with a gentle finger. "You going to be okay, honey," she whispered, her voice full of certainty. "I just know it."

Her words hit me hard, clearing a path through the storm in my mind. I sniffled and peered down, twisting the tissue between my fingers.

"What about my dad?" I croaked. "He always thinks the worst of me and never gives me a chance."

Miss Pearl gave my hands another gentle squeeze, cradling them in hers as she locked her gaze with mine. "Honey, you got to look at that daddy of yours with the eyes of Jesus, just like you been doing with everybody else," she said gently. "Y'all been through so much, but he's just a man, flawed and just trying to figure it out, same as you. You don't have to be perfect, baby, but neither does he."

I simpered weakly, drinking in her advice.

"I'll tell you something else," Miss Pearl continued. "Holding on to bitterness will only weigh you down, and you're already carrying more than your share. You need to give it all to God."

Her tender words soothed me, easing the ache in my chest. When tears threatened again, Miss Pearl pulled me back into her arms and cradled me while she whispered a prayer.

"Lord, give this child strength, peace, and guidance," she said, her voice steady and full of faith. "Help her see herself as You see her, and soften the hearts of those around her."

When she finished, Miss Pearl pulled back and gently cupped my chin, wiping tears from my cheeks with her thumb.

"I know this ain't easy," she explained. "It ain't easy for Mr. Tom either, raising you on his own right now. Your daddy's not gonna do everything right, but that don't mean he doesn't love you. Sometimes we hurt the people we love the most, but you can't control him or the things he says. All you can do is show your daddy the same grace you showed those kids at school today. Shine your light."

Her words calmed me down, and I finally felt a little hopeful. Suddenly, the thought of going home didn't feel quite so impossible anymore.

"God's got you, baby," Miss Pearl whispered, her eyes full of certainty. "Believe it."

21

When I arrived home, the gentle light from the living room window illuminated the gravel driveway, and I knew Dad was waiting for me. The comfort I had felt at the Clarkes' home was beginning to fade, replaced by a knot of worry. The hurt in Dad's eyes when I left him at school was still fresh on my mind, and I had no idea what I was walking into. I exhaled slowly and whispered a quick prayer before reaching for my phone. There were no missed calls from Dad, but Carter had been reaching out all afternoon. He'd sent three texts that I hadn't replied to.

> Rosie: Hey Dutch! Call me.
>
> Rosie: Earth to Dutch!
>
> Rosie: Lena? Please confirm you're alive.

I stared at Carter's messages as a wave of regret washed over me, imagining how worried or upset he must be. Carter never called me Lena, and reading his last text left a hollow feeling in my chest. Today had slipped away from me. Between everything at school and my blow-up with Dad, there had been no time to check my phone. Carter didn't know how bad things had gotten, but now, after hours of silence from me, I'd be lucky if he even wanted to pick up my call. I sighed and rubbed my temples, feeling a mixture of guilt and frustration taking over. As much as I wanted to hear Carter's voice, I knew there was someone else I had to face first.

Miss Pearl's prayer swam through my mind the entire drive home.

Look at that daddy of yours with the eyes of Jesus. Show your daddy the same grace you showed those kids at school today. Shine your light.

I held on to her advice as I stepped out of the car and walked to the front door. When I stepped inside, the house was quiet except for the sound of Dad's voice coming from the kitchen. I closed the front door behind me without making a peep and slipped across the living room, pressing my back to the kitchen's adjacent wall.

"Lena isn't doing any of that," Dad groaned. "Since she came home, she's been shutting me out. Lena's either at school, at work, or shut up in her room talking to that boyfriend of hers."

The way he said *boyfriend* made me bristle. My heart thudded as I leaned flat against the wall, just out of sight, wondering who he was talking to.

"I don't know what to do anymore," Dad continued, his voice heavy with weariness. "She was so happy when I saw her at camp. I finally felt like I had my daughter back, but now it's like she's retreating into her shell again. What did you do to break through to her?"

There was a pause before a familiar voice answered over the speakerphone. "Have you tried just listening to her, Tommy?" Lou's tone was calm but firm.

Lou.

I felt a sudden shred of hope, because if anyone could help Dad understand, it was my aunt.

"Of course I've tried," Dad said, sounding exasperated. "I ask her about school and work all the time, but Lena completely stonewalls me.

I felt crushing blow after blow as I listened to Dad talk about me like this, but Lou didn't miss a beat.

"No, Tom. Those are the last places she probably wants to talk about. Have you asked her about Bible study, or about the friends she's been reconnecting with from church?"

Dad sighed, but the way his voice sounded muffled had me picturing him holding his head in his hands. "I haven't."

"Well, start there," Lou urged my father. "Your daughter gave her life to the Lord this summer, Tommy. She's not going to be perfect, but she's trying. Sometimes, instead of tightening the reins, you need to loosen them and give Lena her own space to grow."

"I'm trying," Dad replied, sounding defeated. "I'm just not sure how to be there for her."

My heart fell as I thought of just how much pain I had been causing Dad. Even when I tried my best to keep a low profile and not cause him any trouble, I ended up doing the exact opposite. I pushed myself off the wall to head down the hall to my room when Lou's voice held me in place.

Quietly, she said. "Lena isn't Natalie, Tom."

I froze, as Lou told Dad the exact same thing about my mother that I had earlier at school.

"Both of them both have the same sensitive heart, but they're different." Lou continued, "When Lena's under pressure, she knows how to make the right decision if she's encouraged to use her good judgment. You have to nourish the good qualities she has and meet her where she's at."

There was a long pause before Dad replied, his voice heavy. "You know my daughter better than I do, Lou."

I heard Lou chuckle on the other line. "No Tommy, I just spend a lot of time with teenagers at camp, and at church. Even though I don't have kids, I've been around them long enough to get to know them in ways their parents sometimes don't. I get to be the cool aunt for all of them."

"I know Lena confides in you though," Dad said, the weariness in his voice already sounding lighter. "Thank you for being there for her, *for both of us*."

"You don't have to thank me, Tommy," Lou replied warmly. "I just want to help, however I can."

There was a beat of silence before Lou added. "Lena loves you, if she didn't she wouldn't try so hard to make you happy."

I leaned my head back gently on the wall behind me, feeling overwhelmed with gratitude for the way Lou supported us. Maybe if she had been at school earlier, the conversation would have gone differently.

"Well, hey," Dad said, shifting his tone after clearing his throat. "I don't want to talk your ear off, I know you've got things to do but remind me again about the fall thing."

Lou laughed, cutting him off. "It's the Fall Retreat, Tommy. Oh, and don't forget about the weekend, too."

"I won't," Dad said with a chuckle. "Hopefully, when Lenny gets home, we can clear the air first and then talk about it."

"Just know fall break is short, but this will give her something to look forward to," Lou added. "Plus, the retreat will open the door for the two of you to talk and make plans. Remember, Lena adores you, she just needs to know that you're on her side."

My heart fluttered as I immediately strained to hear more. *Fall Retreat? What was that and why hadn't she mentioned it to me?*

The thought sent my curiosity soaring, and as I heard them say their goodbyes, my heart began to race. I didn't want Dad to think I was eavesdropping, even though clearly I was. Thinking fast, I quickly slipped back across the living room and retraced my steps to the front door. Carefully, I opened the door and shut it loudly enough for Dad to hear, hoping he'd think I'd just arrived. When he turned the corner into the living room, I knew I'd convinced him when I saw the look of surprise on his face.

"Hey, honey," he greeted gently, hesitantly, as if trying to gauge my mood.

"Hey, Dad," I replied a little too briskly. My cheeks flamed as I met Dad's gaze and saw the same concern in his eyes from earlier. Lou's advice blended with Miss Pearl's suddenly, giving me the strength to wave a white flag of surrender first. "I'm sorry about what happened at school, I shouldn't have said what I did...or left the way I did."

Without hesitating, Dad shook his head, putting his hands on his hips. "I'm the one who should be apologizing, Lenny. I've been thinking about what you said all afternoon, and... I know I don't always handle things right but I'm trying, kiddo. Just bear with me, okay?"

A lump rose in my throat, and I worked to swallow it. "I know, Dad, but sometimes it feels like you don't trust me, like you're just waiting for me to mess up."

He rubbed his hand down his face, his eyes filling with defeat. "Honey, that's not true. I do trust you, but I worry, and sometimes my worry comes out all wrong. Earlier, I know I should have heard you out, but you have to understand—"

"Understand what, Dad?" I asked, peering up at him.

He heaved a sigh and stepped closer. "The last couple of years have been rough for us, especially you. I know a lot happened for you this summer, all good things, of course, but I wasn't there. I missed seeing you thrive at camp, and when you came back, you were you again. But, honey, ever since you've come home, I don't know...I've had to slowly watch as you shrink back into yourself."

I opened my mouth to speak but had no words. Dad seemed to sense my struggle as he pulled me into a hug, cradling my head against his chest.

"I'm so sorry, Lenny," he said, his chin resting on the top of my head, "for today, and for all the days I made you feel like you weren't good enough."

"It's okay, dad." I swiped at my eyes, peering up at him.

Tears stung my eyes as I tried to blink them back while Dad smoothed a hand over my hair. "We'll put this behind us and move forward, okay? Just like we always do."

Dad held me tightly against him as though he was trying to carry my pain for me. "We'll talk more and be open with each other, and we'll figure everything out together, Lenny. I promise."

I bobbed my head as Dad pulled me back against his chest.

"I'd like that," I whispered.

Dad pulled back with a warm smile, instantly dissolving our earlier tension.

"Good," he said, stepping back and pulling his phone from his pocket. "Because there's something I want to show you."

I felt my heart pitter-patter as I watched him scroll through his phone. "What is it?"

Once Dad found what he was looking for, he handed me his device, and I stared down at a flyer for New Hope Bible Camp. My breath caught as I read the details.

Calling All Senior Campers!

Join us for the New Hope Bible Camp Fall Retreat

Come refresh your faith and soak in the autumn beauty of the camp grounds.

When: Third weekend in October

Theme: Unshakable - Standing firm in your identity in Christ

Senior Campers (Ages 13-19)

Register By: October 12th

"That's only two weeks away." My eyes darted up to meet his, excitement bubbling in my chest. "Are you saying I can go back to camp?"

Dad grinned, but I didn't miss the relief flashing in his eyes. "Lou said the Harvest Festival is that weekend, too, so if you're interested we'll make it happen."

"I'm in," I said instantly. For the first time all day, I felt a genuine smile spread across my face, and as my heart soared, I threw my arms around Dad. "I'm so in!"

After a day like today, the news felt like an answered prayer. I couldn't believe it, in just two weeks, I would finally be back at New Hope Bible Camp, *my favorite place in the world.*

22

"You're alive!" Carter answered when I called him later that night. "I've been calling for hours. I was about to send out a search party."

I made a face he couldn't see as I wrapped a towel around my damp hair, fresh from a quick shower. "I'm so sorry, I've had the longest, most insane day."

Earlier, Dad and I had spent nearly an hour making breakfast for dinner together and getting everything out in the open. After our argument at school, Dad made me sit down and insisted on knowing exactly what had been going on. I told him everything, but the truth hit Dad harder than I expected because I wound up having to talk him down from marching into Mr. Hall's office in the morning.

"Mrs. Jones said they have a zero-tolerance policy," I reminded him gently. "Everything's under control."

At least, that's what I was telling myself.

Dad still wasn't happy about how my senior year had started, but once I convinced him I was okay, I saw the tension in his shoulders ease. We finally moved on, and I let myself get swept up in the part I was actually excited about—*spending fall break in Meadowbrook.*

Dad told me all the plans that Lou had shared and how she would work it all out for me to come up. Throughout the year, there were different events planned at camp for the youth, but unlike summer camp, the Fall Retreat only lasted for a few days. Once camp ended, Lou wanted me to stay the weekend with her to attend the Meadowbrook Harvest Festival. Putting our heads together, me and Dad constructed the perfect plan. I'd leave for the retreat, stay through the weekend, and be home by Sunday night, just in time for school Monday.

The Harvest Festival always seemed like a scene plucked from a fall postcard. I'd only gone twice as a kid, but I cherished the time I had shared with my grandparents. I could still see Gramps and Grams walking beside me on each side, holding my hands in theirs as we wandered the festival grounds with the smell of caramel apples and hot cider in the air. There was a carousel, a towering Ferris wheel lighting up the sky, fall-themed games, and the hay bale maze. I used to pretend to get lost in the maze just so I could hear Gramps call out my name, laughing whenever he found me. Now, I'd get to relive it all, only this time with my best friends.

The thought of returning to camp quickly turned my day right side up again, despite Dad giving me a checklist to accomplish before my trip; like getting an oil change and my tires rotated and balanced. Even though I didn't leave for two more weeks, Dad was in full prep mode for my five and a half hour solo drive. I didn't mind though, I would have agreed to do whatever it took if that meant going back to camp.

Before I could run through the events of the day again, Carter's voice pulled me back. "So, are you going to tell me why you went full stealth mode on me?" he pried, "or keep dodging my questions about your *crazy* day?"

I grimaced as a knot tightened in my chest. Carter didn't know what had happened today, not at school, and definitely not about the argument with my dad, but I couldn't say anything. Deep down, I was afraid of what he'd think if he knew how bad things were at school because Carter was everything I wasn't.

Confident, grounded, and a varsity athlete who was steady in his faith. He was the guy people respected and admired, and somehow... he had chosen me. I didn't want to think about what would happen if he ever saw the mess behind the girl he thought he knew. *Would he still want to be with me?*

"School was just wild today," I said, shaking away my fears and forcing a laugh that sounded fake even to me. "You know how it is, teachers breathing down your neck if you so much as glance at your phone." I paused, pulling scraps out of thin air. "Then I had a couple of errands afterwards, it was a whole thing."

My voice trailed off as Carter fell silent on the other end, and I felt my stomach sink because this wasn't how I wanted the call to go, especially not when I had the best news to share.

"Look, Dutch... if something happened..." Carter started, trying to find the right words. "Can we talk about whatever's going on? If you're mad at me—"

"No, Carter," I cut in, but my tone was sharper than I meant. "I promise I'm not mad."

Yet, when he spoke again, he still didn't seem convinced. "It's just, I was worried when I didn't hear from you because I thought maybe something had happened. Now, I kind of feel like you're not telling me everything."

The hurt in Carer's voice stung, and I knew how he felt because I felt the same way whenever he was busy with practice or work. Not being around him made me feel like I was missing out.

"I'm sorry," I said as my heart raced, hating the thought that I had hurt him. "Something came up with my dad, and then I went to Worthy's for a while. When I got home, Dad had some news for me though, *good news*," I added quickly. "That's what took so long, me and dad have been going over plans, and I've been dying to tell you."

The shift in his tone was instantaneous. "The suspense is killing me. Spill it, Dutch."

I beamed, unable to hold back my excitement. "So, there's this Fall Retreat at camp—"

Carter let out a loud gasp. "Stop!" he shouted excitedly. "The retreat flyer just came out today, and I wanted to be the first to tell you. Did Lou beat me to it?"

I chuckled, feeling my stomach flip, hearing the happiness in his voice now. "She did, Lou and my dad already worked everything out."

"Wait, so you're going?!" His voice lit up with so much joy, I could hear his smile.

"Yes! I'm coming to camp for fall break!" I nearly squealed. "You'll be there, won't you?"

He scoffed, and I could picture his coy smile on the other line. "Silly Dutch, of course, I'll be there. I tried texting you all day because I wanted to be the one to tell you. The retreat is only a couple of days, but I don't care; I'll take whatever time I can get with you."

"Rosie," I said, trying but failing to hide the excitement in my voice. "I get to see you in two weeks. Can you believe it?"

Carter chuckled, and I was grateful that he finally sounded like himself again. "Two weeks can't come soon enough."

23

Carter was right, the next two weeks dragged on like I was a prisoner awaiting my freedom. As eager as I had been to remain invisible, having my wish granted wasn't as glamorous as I'd been imagining. Worthy and the Show Choir had several competitions that left me alone in the music room for lunch most days. As untouchable as I felt under the school's anti-bullying policy, I had become the leper of Freeport High as everyone kept their distance. As empty as the silence felt, somehow, I felt like God was making a way for me.

Work hadn't been much better for me. Since requesting time off for fall break, Anthony had crammed the weekends with double shifts, like I had to make up my time away even though vacation time was a benefit I'd earned. The long hours spent at the aquarium meant going to church was still impossible for me, but Miss Pearl never complained when our weekly Bible studies ran late. No matter how exhausted I felt after school and work, there was something about sitting at her kitchen table with open Bibles and a cold glass of sweet tea that grounded me. Miss Pearl and Worthy's support felt like coming up for air, and when I mentioned I would miss a week because of camp, they were just excited that I was going to get to go back.

Now, the time had finally arrived, and my heart leaped out of my chest as I shoved the last of my clothes into my suitcase. Dad had helped me arrange everything from an early dismissal from school to a plan to hit the road with just enough time to make it to camp by mid-afternoon. My teachers had been understanding in letting me work ahead, and I only had one lingering geometry assignment left to finish before the weekend was over.

Lately, concentrating on school felt nearly impossible. Carter and I had been counting down the days together. Trading texts about everything from our camp plans to the Harvest Festival and how we would make the best of our time together this weekend. Although Carter checked in often, there was something about the way he fished for details about my day that had me wondering if Lou had said something to him about me. Lou went to church with Carter's family, and even though I knew she was close with his mom, I knew I could trust that Lou wouldn't betray my confidence.

When I truly thought about it, I realized Carter didn't need to be told something was going on with me. He was perceptive and had been since the day I met him. Unlike at Camp, Carter didn't press me to talk, and I wondered if he understood I wasn't ready to open up. So instead we kept our conversations on safer topics, like camp.

Just then, as if on cue, my phone buzzed, and I glanced down, expecting the new message to be from Carter.

> *Jojo: I don't think flannel is too basic for camp, but everyone else is going to wear it too.*

> *Jojo: Wear your green jacket. It's grunge vibes & totally you.*

I laughed, shaking my head as I typed out a response. Earlier, I had texted her asking what people usually wore to camp this time of year. I didn't know if I should dress warmer than normal since Meadowbrook had cooler temperatures than Freeport, but I also worried there might be some sort of dress-up event like the end-of-summer banquet. Jojo had reassured me this weekend was casual, and having styled me before for my date with Carter, she now had strong opinions about my wardrobe.

> Me: Is that supposed to be a compliment?

> Jojo: Duh! You pull off the whole "grunge princess meets comfy chic" vibe.

> Me: Hmm…I'm still not sure that sounds like a good thing.

> Jojo: I'm just saying your style is effortless like you want to be comfy AND cute.

> Me: Okay, Jo but I'm trying to feel flattered here…

> Jojo: You should be! Your style is iconic. OWN IT.

She followed up with a stream of emojis, and I was still laughing when Dad walked in holding my car keys.

"You've got a full tank, kiddo," he said, placing them in my hand.

"Thanks, Dad," I replied, grateful that he'd taken care of getting my oil changed and topping off the gas while I packed.

"Anything for my little girl. Got everything ready to go?"

I zipped up my suitcase and gave its hard shell a solid pat. "All set."

Dad said little as we headed to the car, but I caught the way his eyes lingered on me a little longer than usual. He loaded my suitcase into the backseat with a grunt, and I slid behind the wheel, gripping it with equal parts nerves and excitement.

"You'll call me every hour on the hour," Dad said, trying to sound casual, but I could hear the concern in his voice. "And keep your location on the entire drive."

I grinned and saluted him. "Yes, sir."

He leaned in and gave me a quick peck on the cheek before carefully shutting my door. I buckled up as he adjusted my side mirror, then threw me an approving thumbs up.

I gave him a thumbs up back and blew him a kiss, which Dad pretended to catch in mid-air before pressing it to his heart. He stepped back as I pulled away, and as I glanced in the rearview mirror, Dad was still there, arms folded, watching me just like he always did until I disappeared out of view.

There was always a quiet ache in my chest when we said goodbye, and I knew Dad felt the same way. This time though, leaving felt different from the last. After two weeks of waiting, I was glad to finally be back on the road to New Hope.

PART TWO: NEW HOPE BIBLE CAMP

24

I hung up the last of my hands-free check-ins with Dad, knowing I was on the homestretch. I exhaled a sigh of relief as the familiar highway signs came into view and I knew I wasn't far now. Meadowbrook was just around the corner, nestled between the autumn-covered mountains. I spotted Cobalt Bluff, but the normal blue hues of the mountaintop were now painted in rusty crimsons and golden orange up ahead. I rolled down the window, allowing cool air to rush in to let the chill refresh me. As I neared the *Welcome to Meadowbrook* sign, excitement bubbled inside my chest, a stark contrast to the last time the mountains waved me goodbye.

***

Lou and I had met the Roses for dinner Saturday while I was in town over the summer, and I was shaking with nerves at the thought of meeting my boyfriend's family. Yet, following Lou's lead, I realized I had nothing to be afraid of. From the moment we walked through the door, Carter's family welcomed us as if we belonged. His mom, Amy, pulled me into a fierce hug, while his dad, Jack, greeted me with a warm handshake and a sweet smile; but it was Sadie, Carter's little sister, who stole the show.

"Lena from camp!" she shouted, grabbing my hand and began hauling me toward her room to show off her toy horses.

Carter trailed behind us, amused and looking like a proud big brother. It didn't take long before the three of us were galloping around her bedroom floor on all fours, while Sadie's laughter filled the house.

Dinner that followed was relaxed and full of easy chatter that completely put my nerves at ease. Sadie kept her miniature horses nearby, making them trot between the plates while Jack cracked jokes that had Amy rolling her eyes and blushing while the rest of us bellowed. While laughter filled the air, under the table, Carter reached for my hand when no one was watching, his thumb brushing gently against mine, causing my heart to dance in my chest.

After dessert, Sadie insisted on giving us a tour of the house, and when we reached Carter's room, I paused at the doorway, taking it in. His desk held neatly stacked books and a half-full water bottle. Posters of his favorite soccer team covered one wall, alongside a small shelf of trophies. The nightstand held a lamp, a Bible, and a photo of us before leaving camp. My heart skipped at the sight, realizing my picture was framed by his bed.

I tried my best to hide a smile as I gazed down at my phone screen, where I had the same picture as my wallpaper. Our hair was windswept, his arm over my shoulder, and both of us smiling like we didn't have a care in the world on top of Cobalt Bluff. When I glanced up, I caught Carter grinning at me before Lou called out that it was time to go.

The next day, Sunday, passed by in a blur of goodbyes. After church, the congregation spilled out onto the lawn for a potluck. There were picnic blankets and folding tables stretching across the grass while the scent of warm casseroles, sweet pies, and tangy barbecue floated through the summer air. Lou caught up with old friends while I stayed close to Carter, weaving through clusters of people I hadn't seen in years, pausing every few steps to greet a few familiar faces.

"Well, Carter, have you found yourself a Rivers girl?" an older woman asked, her eyes shining as they landed on me. I didn't recognize her, but she recognized me, especially since my family name *Rivers* meant something around here.

My grandfather had started River Ridge Realty, helped build this church, and served as an elder for years. He raised my Aunt Lou and my mom in these pews, and now here I was, his granddaughter, standing where they once stood.

"Yes, ma'am," Carter said, his voice warm. "This is Lena Harris, Lou Rivers' niece."

The woman's face lit up. "Well, that makes sense. You look just like all the other beauties in your family. I hope we'll be seeing more of you, sweetheart."

"Thank you," I said politely, feeling my cheeks flush as Carter gave my hand a gentle squeeze like always

After we'd eaten, Denny suggested a final round of tag on the playground to stretch out his belly. Jojo rolled her eyes but relented when Theo teased her, and Carter took Sadie's hand to lead her to the swings. From the swings, we watched as Theo darted past Denny, narrowly avoiding a tag while Jojo perched on the merry-go-round, giggling at the two of them.

I sat on a nearby swing, watching Carter push Sadie and sneak glances my way. His smile softened every time our eyes met, and I felt the weight of the coming goodbye settle over me when finally, a text from Lou broke the moment: *Ready to head out?*

"Is it time?" Carter asked, watching me text my aunt back. His eyes fell as I nodded glumly, and he stopped Sadie mid-swing.

"It is," I confirmed with a frown

"Hey Sade," Carter whispered gently, slowing his sister's swing to a stop. "Lena has to leave, so can you say bye and go find Mom and Dad inside?"

Sadie flicked her gaze to me as her bottom lip jutted out. She slid off the swing and ran over, wrapping her tiny arms around me.

"Bye, Lena," her sweet little voice rang out, gutting me. "Can you come back soon?"

Sadie pulled back, her big eyes searching mine, as I offered her a reassuring smile and returned her squeeze. "As soon as I can," I promised.

Carter ushered his sister back to the fellowship hall, watching until she slipped through the door, then he turned and stretched out a hand to take mine, pulling me to the playground gate. The two of us left behind the sounds of Theo, Denny, and Jojo still goofing around but now on the monkey bars.

"Are we just going to leave them monkeying around?" I joked, trying to keep the mood light.

Carter peeked over his shoulder and then simply nodded as we marched on, crossing the parking lot to Lou's SUV. He held my hand until we were both behind the vehicle, out of sight, and pulled me to him.

"I hate this," he whispered against my hair.

"Me too," I confessed, leaning my cheek against his chest.

"I'm not ready to let you go yet," he sighed. Carter pulled away, faced me, then leaned in, pressing his warm lips to mine. The kiss was gentle but deep, filled with what neither of us was ready to say. A clearing throat behind us shattered the moment, and I jumped out of Carter's arms to find Denny standing behind Theo with Jojo, holding up his hands innocently.

"It's just us," he said, "but the adults are coming, so... you might want to leave a little room for Jesus."

I blushed, realizing I hadn't heard them walk up, but Denny simply grinned, causing Carter to roll his eyes, while Theo nudged Denny and murmured, "You're one to talk."

Jojo's cheeks turned bright pink as she poked Theo. "Hey!"

"Real subtle, guys," Carter chuckled, taking my hand.

Just minutes later, Lou approached, and my last few moments with my friends ticked by. We said quick goodbyes, and Lou gave Carter and me one last moment for a final kiss before he tucked me into the passenger seat.

Raising a hand, Carter waved again as Lou pulled out, and I watched my friends from the side mirror, waving from the parking lot until they were out of sight. The further we drove, the faster the tears came as the mountains blurred once Meadowbrook faded in the mirror behind me.

***

Now, as I reached Meadowbrook, its small-town charm wrapped around me like a favorite sweater. Fall had arrived in full force, and I felt dazzled as I drove through witnessing the downtown shops and streets gearing up for the Harvest Festival. The Cupcake Cottage stood out with colorful chalk-drawn pumpkins decorating the windows, and pastel pumpkins surrounding the door. Driving further, I caught sight of Max's Diner, and the old neon sign flickering faintly. A jittery excitement filled me as I smelled the familiar scent of food cooking, drawing me back to the memory of Carter and me sitting in one of those booths on our first date.

A short distance away, the old pawnshop had a storybook quality. Just like the night Carter and I spied inside, the window was a chaotic jumble of trinkets and dusty antiques, each with its own history to share. The mercantile caught my eye next, and as usual was buzzing with people, the store's entrance flanked by whiskey barrels overflowing with a stunning fall flower arrangement. In the front window, a handwritten sign advertised their seasonal specials, welcoming the change of seasons.

Throughout downtown Meadowbrook, there was an air of celebration as volunteers swarmed the town square, setting up vendor tents and decorating for the weekend events. The small-town was so beautiful that my faint childhood memories had never truly done Meadowbrook any justice.

Once I passed through the bustling town, I took the familiar main road to camp. After a short drive, I spotted the iron gate and squealed as I turned onto the gravel driveway. The *New Hope Bible Camp* sign stood proudly, welcoming me back, causing goosebumps to prickle over my skin. The winding road was alive and lined with trees decorated in fall foliage that no picture could do any justice. Camp had completely transformed into a beautiful autumn landscape that made my heart swell as I took it all in. *I was finally here.*

I parked near the gravel lot by the kitchen and checked the time. I was early, exactly as planned. Lou was likely still packing, and the others wouldn't arrive for at least another hour, allowing me to maintain the element of surprise.

Climbing out of the car, I stretched, yawning, as the cool, fresh mountain air filled my lungs. I tucked my hands into the pockets of my warm jacket and let the scenery wash over me again. Camp was so different in the fall; it felt even more magical, somehow, even though nature was preparing for a long winter sleep.

The crunch of gravel and leaves under my boots stirred up a flood of summer memories as I made my way toward the Dining Hall to check in. As I pushed open the door, I paused, letting the smoky scent of the fireplace wrap around me like a welcome-home hug.

"Lena Harris!" Hannah exclaimed behind the sign-in table, clipboard in hand.

Of all the people I thought I'd run into first, I hadn't expected Hannah. She seemed just as put-together as always, but her sleek ponytail and blazer made her seem more professional than when I last saw her at summer camp. Her time working for Lou at River Ridge Realty showed in subtle ways, like how she now held a clipboard instead of a counselor name tag. Hannah looked like she'd stepped straight out of a team meeting and into the woods.

"Hannah!" I squealed back, stepping up to the table.

With a warm smile, she quickly pulled me in for a side hug. "I'm so glad to see you, Lou's beyond excited you're here this weekend!"

I chuckled, holding a finger to my lips. "Don't tell her I'm already here, though; I want to surprise her."

Hannah laughed softly, acting like she was zipping her lips. "Your secret's safe with me, but I can't believe you're back! This weekend is going to be amazing!"

I couldn't stop smiling as I gazed around the familiar space. "I wouldn't miss a chance to get back here."

She grinned, but more dimly than before as she peered down at her clipboard, flipping the pages. "I wish everyone felt the same way, especially with the way attendance is down."

I wasn't sure what Hannah meant, but I tried to offer what little reassurance I could. "Maybe it's just how fall break landed this year?"

Plucking a piece of paper from her clipboard, Hannah grinned, though it didn't quite reach her eyes. "I'm sure you're probably right anyway; it's so good to have you back, Lena. We've all missed you."

Her words made tears prickle behind my eyes, but I pushed them away as Hannah handed me my cabin assignment and a paper name tag to fill in. I gazed down, relieved to find Jojo, and I were back in the same cabin we'd shared over the summer.

"Thank you, Hannah," I beamed, clutching the paper.

She waved it off with a smile. "Be sure to wear the name tag because you'll need it later; oh, and don't forget a swag bag from the table. You can settle in, but I'll be around if you need anything."

Following Hannah's instructions, I collected the welcome bag and stuck the name tag on my front before stepping back outside to find my cabin. As I climbed the creaking wooden stairs and stepped inside, a quiet feeling settled over me, like camp had been waiting for me all along. Inside, familiar details welcomed me back. The same picture frame hung crooked on the wall, its message urging me to unplug and recharge with my Bible. I reached out instinctively to straighten it, then headed into the room Jojo and I had shared last summer. I tossed my bags onto the bottom bunk and, without thinking, grabbed the top mattress and stacked it below, just like Jojo taught me.

I had barely started unpacking when the light shifting outside the window pulled my attention. The lake gleamed in the distance, its surface shimmering with sunbeams. Drawn to the light, I stepped back outside and made my way down the trail, leaves crunching beneath my boots as I followed the gravel path toward the water. When I reached the shore, the sight stopped me in my tracks. The lake stretched out like glass, reflecting the colorful surrounding trees, as Miss Pearl's words about the mountains drifted back to me. I felt awestruck by the vibrant view, taking in what could only be described as God's artwork.

I stepped onto the dock and marched to the end to close my eyes for a moment and whisper a silent prayer of thanks; for the view and the chance to be back here again. As I took in the sights, a memory surfaced of Carter asking me last summer to describe what I saw. I smiled faintly. Standing there, I could picture God speaking all of this into existence, knowing exactly what our hearts would need to find peace in nature's beauty.

Peering down at the water, my reflection stared back at me, and I saw my long sandy hair cascade past my shoulders in loose waves, blending with my warm army jacket and chunky combat boots. I couldn't hide my smile as I caught my reflection inserted into the autumn scene behind me. I had spent most of my life by the beach, with salt in the air, and waves in the distance, but seeing myself now, I couldn't shake the sense that this place is where I belonged.

Climbing to my feet, I wrapped my arms around myself as I gazed back out at the lake until footsteps echoed from a distance on the other side of the dock.

"Hey, Dutch," came a voice behind me.

I turned and immediately felt my heart racing, knowing only one person called me that. Carter stood just a few feet away, a grin pulling at his lips, and in that moment, everything around us faded because *all I saw was him.*

Carter stood there in dark jeans that fit snug over his athletic frame, and the soft gray sweater he wore that made his brown eyes glow in the golden light. That smile, the one that always made me feel seen, pulled at something deep in my chest.

He was really here.

All the weeks apart, the late-night calls, the ache of missing him, all of it crashed into me at once. Without thinking, I ran to him, and Carter caught me mid-stride, his arms wrapping tight around me as he lifted me off the ground. The second I was in his arms, I knew this was real; I wasn't dreaming.

"Man, have I missed you," he murmured against my hair. The feel of his warm breath made my stomach flip-flop like normal when Carter was around.

I opened my mouth to respond, but before I could, his lips met mine in a kiss that was soft and lingering, like we had all the time in the world and wanted to get lost in this moment. When

Carter finally pulled back, he set me down gently, his arms still around my waist.

"I can't believe you found me here," I said, breathless, stealing another quick kiss.

Carter tilted his head, brow furrowed slightly, like I'd said something crazy. "I'll always find you, especially since this is our spot, Dutch."

His words settled over me again, and I wrapped my arms around his neck, pulling him close again.

"I just can't believe it; this is real," I breathed into his neck.

"It feels like it's been forever, doesn't it?" Carter asked, arms tightening around me.

With a small nod, I burrowed into his embrace, clinging to him because forever felt like an understatement. After being apart so long, all I could think was that I never wanted this moment to end.

25

As Carter and I made our way back toward the heart of camp, the familiar clang of the flagpole chain swaying in the breeze caught my attention, followed by a voice that was unmistakable.

"Hey, look who decided to show up!" Denny shouted, standing by the flagpole, broader than I remembered. His dark hair was a little longer, curling at the ends like he hadn't bothered to cut it since summer, but with that charming Denny grin stretched across his face, he uncrossed his arms and held them out like he expected me to run to him.

Before I could say a word, Jojo elbowed him, but Denny smirked and tapped her arm back with one finger, nearly tipping her over. I laughed as Jojo straightened, rolling her eyes dramatically, while beside them, Theo leaned against the flagpole, arms crossed in his usual moody way.

Within seconds, Jojo launched toward me with a squeal that turned the heads of others that had arrived. "You're here!" she cried, throwing her arms around me in a hug that nearly knocked the wind out of me. Her oversized sweater and leggings were as colorful as her personality, and the joy on her face made my heart swell.

When she finally let go, she held me at arm's length, taking me in. "You're really here. And early, too! Wait... did you skip school?"

I grinned, but waved off the idea. "No skipping, I just worked ahead so I could leave early. What about you guys? Did you just get here?"

Jojo shrugged, a sly grin spreading over her face. "We've been here maybe twenty minutes. Theo drove us, and we were about to text, but here you are."

I gawked at her and looked over her shoulder toward the boys. "Theo drove? You carpooled with him?"

Over the summer, I'd learned how much Denny enjoyed being the driver of the group. Carter said Denny was in love with his Jeep, but really, he was a control freak behind the wheel.

Theo rolled his eyes as Denny clutched his chest dramatically. "Don't remind me, my Jeep had a recall, so it's in the shop, but I'll have her back Saturday morning. Until then, we're stuck riding with *Mr. Hands-Off-My-Playlist.*"

Theo shot him a glance. "You signed up for greatness when you got into my car."

"Greatness?" Jojo groaned, rolling her eyes. "That playlist was thirty minutes of pure sadness; I'm never going to get that part of my life back."

I stole a glance at Theo, but didn't miss the flicker of emotion on his face, knowing his break-up with Katie was still on his mind.

"You say sadness," Theo retorted, shrugging, "But you don't know what you're missing. Just wait, I've got a campfire playlist ready for you lovebirds, nothing but screamo love songs."

"You wouldn't dare," Jojo warned, crossing her arms.

The five of us fell into a familiar rhythm, laughing and teasing each other as if no time had passed since summer. Butterflies fluttered in my stomach every time Carter's eyes met mine. He kept sneaking glances, and each time our gazes locked, it felt like we were silently reminding each other this wasn't just a dream; we were both really here.

Denny had just asked about my job at the Aquarium when the rumble of a vehicle coming up the gravel drive drew our attention, and we watched as Lou's sleek SUV pulled into the parking lot.

"Your aunt's here," Theo pointed out flatly.

"Wow, Captain Obvious," Denny murmured.

Ignoring them, I took off running, and Lou had barely made it out of the vehicle when I barreled into her arms.

"There's my favorite niece!" she laughed, hugging me tight. With her hair clipped back, she appeared more polished than ever in a sharp blazer and jeans, having just left the office.

"I've missed you," I murmured into her shoulder, breathing in her warm vanilla perfume.

She squeezed me tighter, voice thick with emotion. "Oh, honey, you can't imagine how happy I am to have you here." When Lou pulled back, she studied me with an expression that was both tender and proud. "Are you doing all right?"

I bobbed my head, grinning. "I'm better now, thanks for making this happen for me... *again*."

"Anytime." Lou ruffled my hair with a playful smile.

"Hey, Lou!" Denny's voice broke through the moment. "You got any snacks in there?"

Lou turned, raising a brow as he put her hands on her hips. "I do, but the snacks are for campers who behave!"

"Guess that means you're out of luck, Dennis," Theo shot back, earning a laugh from the group.

Lou popped the trunk of her SUV, revealing the mother lode of treats, from chips, crackers, and fruit.

"Whoa! Did you bring all of this?" I asked.

Lou winked and pulled out a collapsible cart to transfer the supplies. "They're donations, courtesy of River Ridge."

My heart swelled with pride knowing how much love Lou poured into making camp special. I jumped in to help unload while the others joined us, filling the air with jokes and jabs. Standing there with Lou and my friends, I felt the weight of the world lift.

"Where to, Boss?" Denny asked Lou, peeking around an armful of boxes.

"Follow me," she declared.

***

Entering the kitchen was exciting for the first time ever. During summer camp, I had dreaded the early morning wake-ups to prepare food for all the campers, but now it felt nostalgic. The once-crowded and lively Dining Hall was now eerily empty, its long plastic tables bare instead of having every seat filled. Lou said dinner was late; unlike summer camp, they had a caterer this time, but there was still plenty to do.

I followed Lou through the kitchen, my arms loaded with snack boxes, the cardboard edges digging into my skin beneath the weight. Carter, Theo, Denny, and Jojo had gone back to Lou's SUV to gather the rest of the load, leaving me alone with Lou as we carried the last of the supplies to the back storage room.

"Just set those down by the shelves," Lou instructed as she shifted a crate of bottled water aside to make space.

I stacked my boxes carefully in a pile before wiping the dusty residue from my hands on my jeans. "How's River Ridge?" I asked, glancing at her.

Lou took a deep breath, brushing dust from her own hands. "Good...really good, actually. Hannah's been a huge help; I'm not sure how I've made it this far without her."

I kept my eyes trained on my aunt as I listened, feeling relieved to know that Lou wasn't handling things on her own anymore.

The long hours at the aquarium had quickly taught me just how overwhelming work could get without proper teamwork.

Lou glanced at me as she began opening boxes and stacking items into organized bins. "Business at River Ridge has been steady," she said, grabbing a pack of trail mix to stow away. "But I've been dreaming of expanding, maybe some rebranding, opening a second office, or dabbling in rental properties. The market just isn't playing nice right now. Between interest rates and people holding tight to what they have..."

She trailed off with a sigh, and I paused mid-stack to look at her. "That sounds amazing, Lou," I said quietly. "I know Gramps would be proud of how hard you work, and it helps that you love what you do."

Lou smiled, a little wistfully. "Thanks, kiddo. I love it, both the real estate part and serving others. I never get tired of handing over the keys to welcome someone to their new home."

The word brought a small pang to my chest. *Home.* That's exactly what Meadowbrook had always been to me, like the town had wrapped its arms around me the moment I stepped out of the car. I loved hearing Lou talk about her work and continuing our family's legacy. Even though my future was undecided, I pictured myself doing the same while she spoke.

I imagined standing on a front porch, waving to potential buyers, and then later, placing the keys in their hands and welcoming them into their forever home. Growing up as a military brat, the idea of home looked different for me. Home was wherever the Coast Guard sent us, and even though my parents did their best to make each stop feel special, I knew each place was only temporary. Meadowbrook was different, though. The small town was the one place that had remained constant, no matter which coast we were on.

"I have all these ideas," Lou continued, opening another box. "I think about doing more, but I'm not much of a risk taker like your Gramps was. The man could put a thought on a napkin and make it happen by morning." She gave a soft chuckle. "Your mom is more like him in that way."

When I tensed up, Lou noticed when I saw her eyes flicked to me and she changed the subject. "Anyway, that's just me rambling." She slid a bin across the counter and gave me a gentle nudge. "Enough about me. How are you holding up, sweetie?" She asked, her voice quieter now.

I exhaled, shifting my weight to the opposite foot. "Better," I said honestly. "Not perfect, but... better."

Lou studied me for a long moment before accepting my answer. "I'm so glad to hear that." Then her expression softened as a knowing smile parted her lips. "This weekend, I want you to remember something."

"Okay?" I asked as she stopped to face me.

"You know I always love seeing you." Lou started, "but, I don't want you to just be here, I want you to *enjoy* being here. There will be great lessons you'll hear, so I don't want you to just be focused on Carter and the gang, but really focus on yourself and being back for the *right* reasons."

I swallowed, letting her words sink in as her reminder hit its mark. Even if Lou hadn't meant to, the way she shared her heart helped me see the bigger picture. Camp felt like an escape, a break from Freeport, but this weekend wasn't just an escape from everything waiting for me back home. The retreat was a chance for me to reconnect with the faith I'd found over the summer.

Lou rested a hand on my shoulder, her voice quiet but firm. "This world is going to try and pull you away from who you are in Christ. I know what it's like to leave this place and feel yourself drifting when life gets hard." She gave my shoulder a squeeze. "Let this weekend remind you of the light you have inside and let it spark that fire in your heart."

She wasn't lecturing me, but her words were a firm encouragement to be truly present, and Lou was right. I cast my eyes down, wondering *how on earth I had let the fire in me fade so easily.*

Gazing back up at my aunt, I nodded, accepting all of the above. "Thanks, Lou."

Lou let go of my shoulder and leaned against the shelf, crossing her arms. "So, that reminds me to share a few things. The retreat is different from summer camp. Of course, you know from the flyer that we'll only have only senior campers and some staff, no junior campers. Also, the schedule's packed into just a couple of days, but you'll still have Bible lessons, breakout sessions, free time, and enjoy hanging out with friends... *the usual.* To bring back tradition, though, the directors wanted to bring back the talent show Friday night."

"A talent show?" I frowned.

Lou's smile turned knowing. "Yeah, I told your dad about it. What's wrong?"

I sighed. "He probably forgot to mention it." I picked at the edge of a box. "Not that it matters to me anyway, I can't participate since I don't really have a talent."

Lou raised a brow and tsked. "That's not true, besides, participation isn't optional, hun."

I groaned. *Of course it wasn't.*

Lou scrutinized me. "Lena, you can sing though; you have plenty of talent in that arena."

I let out a dry laugh. "Singing isn't something I do anymore, much less getting on stage in front of people."

The last time I had truly sung a song was in a church pew before my mother left, so whatever talent I'd once had was long gone now.

"What else could you see yourself doing?" Lou asked, collapsing a box over her knee.

I shrugged as a thought came to me. "I could always show others the art of rolling someone's yard. Camp has plenty of toilet paper, right?"

She snorted and picked up another snack box to break down. "Don't you dare, we don't have enough staff or campers this time around to clean camp up."

"Just kidding," I added with a smirk. "I don't even think I'm good at that. Getting caught was the whole reason I was sent here in the first place."

Lou grinned, something soft and knowing in her expression. "Regardless of the circumstances, I'm glad you're here, then and now. Don't sell yourself short, honey. Singing may not be your thing right now, but think about all the times we sang together as a family. You have a beautiful voice, Lena. Don't overlook that, singing is your gift."

I swallowed, my throat tightening slightly at the memory.

As we worked, Lou started humming a tune that was both soft and familiar. I paused to listen as the sound took hold of a memory I had almost forgotten.

Come Thou Fount of Every Blessing.

I swallowed, slowly, peeling at a piece of tape on a box I broke down while I listened to Lou's quiet voice. Grams used to sing that hymn all the time; Gramps, too, in his deep, steady voice. As a family, we used to sing hymns together on the porch at my grandparents house in the evenings, or around the table after dinner.

A bittersweet smile spread over my face as I remembered the way my grandparents used to gaze at each other while they sang, like they were the only two people in the room. "I love that song,"

Lou glanced up, now humming, and scooted a case of bottled water in my direction. "I was listening to it on the way over," she said.

"It makes me miss hearing Grams and Gramps, they harmonized perfectly on that song." I admitted.

Lou's hands stilled for a second while she glanced at me, her expression soft with understanding. "You remember."

I nodded with a smile, and for a moment, we stood there together while the bittersweet memories wrapped around us. Then Lou tilted her head, with a dare in her eyes. "Even if you do something else in the talent show, try singing this weekend, okay?"

My spine stiffened at her request, but I forced a polite grin, then picked up the case of water at my feet, and slid it onto the stack. "I'll think about it."

Lou watched me for a moment, then let it go, accepting my answer for now. "Alright," she said finally. "Just think about it."

We worked in silence for a few more minutes before Lou decided to change gears. "Come on, let's go check on the others and make sure they're not eating all the snacks."

I let out a small laugh and followed Lou as her request pulled at a part of my past I wasn't quite ready to let back in.

26

We spent time unpacking and setting up our bunks before dinner, but the moment I stepped into the Dining Hall, I realized the weekend just got even better. Instead of the regular camp kitchen staff, Max stood behind the counter, handing out bagged dinners like it was just another night at his diner. As much as I wished to run up and say hello, Max was busy with the line, so I decided to wait my turn.

Since the Fall Retreat was much shorter than summer camp had been, I wondered if Max's catering was a better option than the food delivery service we'd had before. As I gazed around the room, I couldn't help but notice just how much smaller the Fall Retreat crowd seemed. Some chairs sat empty, and even the number of adult staff seemed pared down. As I scanned the room, I found the others and took a seat near the center of the room beside Theo and Jojo who were busy unpacking their dinner.

Giving a once over, I took note of the rest of our group. Denny was across the room, helping Preacher Adam fold and stack a few tables, and Carter had made his way up in the line, now nearing the front. My focus drifted back to our table, and that's when I noticed that Theo's name tag was upside down and Jojo's read *Jojo Bean*, clearly written in Denny's handwriting. I grinned, glad to see that some things never changed.

"Theo," Jojo piped up, "did you end up changing the chorus, or are we keeping it the same? I'll need to practice before the talent show tomorrow night."

Theo opened his snack bag and popped a chip in his mouth. "Nah, we're keeping it the same. We'll have the lyrics on hand, though, so no stress."

Jojo gave him a thumbs up, then turned to me. "Speaking of singing, have you thought about joining the show choir yet, Lena?"

I resisted the urge to glare, since Jojo knew I'd only vented to her about joining the show choir in confidence. Worthy had bugged me nearly every day about joining the choir at school, but I hadn't taken the offer seriously and definitely hadn't planned to discuss it here.

"No, not really considering it," I said, trying not to make a big deal out of the question. "Singing isn't really my thing anymore."

Jojo curled her lip like I'd confessed to hating puppies, and joked. "Too busy with other extracurriculars, huh?"

I blinked and tilted my head, feeling lost. "What?"

She scoffed and flashed her bright eyes at me. "Senior pranks?"

Theo perked up, leaning forward at once. "Senior pranks, huh? Do tell, Mermaid."

My heart did a weird reactive flip, but I played it cool, realizing they didn't know the full story. "It's nothing, besides, I had no idea there was even a talent show until I got here, so I'm not sure what I'll do."

Jojo grinned like she'd just had a brilliant idea. "Denny decided at the last minute he needed a partner, so if you want to help, Theo, I could work with Denny."

I made a face and shook my head. "I don't think so, Jo, but thanks. Maybe I'll find the old dusty keyboard in the storage closet and play the Knuckle Song or something."

"That's just crazy talk, Lena," Jojo said like she couldn't believe I wouldn't accept her offer. "I'll always remember that time Lou had a big barbecue at her house and then after, everyone sat around the fire pit and started singing. Your whole family sounded like a chorus of angels, and you used to sing the loudest."

I remembered that night perfectly. Me and my mom had come up for a visit, and Lou threw a barbecue to make it easier for people in Meadowbrook to come by and see us. I could still remember the goosebumps I got, sitting beside my mom and Lou, my voices blending perfectly with theirs, though they had been singing together since they were kids. Those moments stayed locked in a vault, along with my voice, to protect the good memories from the painful ones.

"That's not really something I do anymore." I replied, hoping Jojo would back down.

Theo, who had been emptying his chip bag onto his sandwich paper, tilted his head, clearly not listening. "You sing, Mermaid?"

A short sardonic laugh slipped out as I gazed between the two of them, feeling exasperated. "No! I just said I *don't* anymore. You feeling okay, Lockwood?"

I caught Theo's eyes flicking over to a table across the room, and immediately I followed his gaze to see what had suddenly rattled him. Katie was laughing at something a friend had said, unaware she was being watched, but when I looked back, I caught the faint blush that had crept up Theo's neck and face. He dropped his gaze in an instant and focused a little too intently on his chips, avoiding all eye contact.

"Yes, you do," Jojo insisted, picking back up on the singing thing, unaware of mine and Theo's silent exchange. "Your whole family does. I used to sit behind your grandmother at church, and I'd listen to her to help me learn the songs."

I knew exactly what Jojo was talking about, having experienced the same thing with Grams' myself. I could still hear

Gram's voice as she held the hymnal between us, her finger guiding me along the lyrics, just like my mom learned from her too.

Theo leaned back, brushing off his hands. "Your grandpa led singing at church all the time, too, so, if you sound anything like those two, maybe you can sing."

Jojo grinned, nodding in agreement. "I've heard you, Lena. You sound like an angel, and I think you and Theo would make way better partners."

My cheeks burned as their pestering mixed with bittersweet memories of my grandparents. *Why on earth were they pressing this so hard?*

Theo smirked, tossing one last chip into his mouth. "You're really selling her talent, Jo but don't try getting out of the duet now."

Jojo hesitated, appearing caught, and I felt a sliver of relief to see her mouth drop momentarily. "I just think with Lena, you might have a better chance at winning, that's all."

"Forget about it, I never ever sing." I repeated, trying to make the fact sink in. "Like, ever."

Jojo raised her eyebrows, seeming appalled by my confession. "Well, I hope you sing during song service because God wants us to make a joyful noise, and singing is one of the best ways to praise Him."

I blinked, but tried not to let her get to me. Like Lou, Jojo was dancing on a nerve I wasn't ready to confront. Leaning back in my chair, I sat quietly until Jojo finally got the hint that I was done with this conversation and dug into her sandwich. While the others ate, I stared back at the line wondering where Carter was, but I felt my stomach twist when I saw him standing by the water coolers talking to Riley. Her long blonde ponytail swished as she talked animatedly with her hands, a smile flashing across her face. I hadn't seen her since summer camp... since she had worked so hard to come between Carter and me. Now, here she was, giggling at something he said, standing too close, and acting like nothing ever happened.

I tore my gaze away as my thoughts started to spin. Carter didn't seem to be flirting back, but he wasn't exactly running away from her either. *Why was he even talking to her?*

My gaze flicked back for the briefest second, catching Riley as she crossed the dining hall and slipped into a seat beside Katie and Kelsey. Out of the corner of my eye, I saw Theo stiffen and followed his line of sight again to find his sister, Kelsey, glaring back. The moment our eyes met, she turned away, flipping her hair over her shoulder as if her long locks could block the view of me.

I pressed my tongue to the roof of my mouth and turned my attention back to the table, unsure what had just happened but ready to change the subject.

"So," I started, "what's new with you guys?"

Jojo's eyes lit up as she giggled and eyed me curiously. "Since we talked earlier today? Nothing, but Carter's been telling us how you've become quite the movie buff."

"There's no way he said that." I tsked as butterflies wriggled in my chest at the thought of Carter talking to our friends about me. The sudden irritation I felt seeing him talking to Riley began to evaporate. "Although, I do think Carter can give Denny a run for his money quoting movie lines."

Theo leaned in, eyes filled with doubt. "Rosie's just showing off by making you watch his favorite movies. The guy can quote Forrest Gump like it's Scripture."

I rolled my eyes, unwilling to let Theo tarnish my long-distance date nights. "I like the idea that he can quote something like Scripture."

Jojo grinned, wiping her fingers on her napkin. "Me too, I think it's sweet. I mean, there are worse couple activities, you two could be watching sad movies on repeat."

She whipped her gaze back to Theo, who held up his hand to shush her. "I do not watch sad movies on repeat," Theo protested. "I watch them with purpose, there's a difference."

I raised a brow. "What's the difference, Lockwood?"

Theo leaned in with a straight face. "Sad movies are full of life lessons and character development, but they're also good for songwriting."

Jojo tilted her head and grimaced. "You're allowing sad movies to influence your song writing skills? That explains so much now."

Theo rolled his eyes like Jojo was his exhausting little sister. "You're just mad because I rhyme better than you, little-miss-valedictorian."

I glanced at Jojo, surprised. "Wait...you're valedictorian?"

She gave a modest shrug and wiped her hands on a napkin. "Nothing's set in stone yet, but I'm trying. I kind of need the scholarship because my parents can't really help with college, especially with everything going on with my dad."

My smile softened as I pictured her dad the last time I saw him, happiness dancing in his eyes despite the walker and tremor in his hands. "How is he?"

Jojo's voice was quieter now but I didn't miss the spark of hope in her eyes. "He's okay, some days are harder than others, but that's just part of his life now."

We sat with that for a beat, the air a little heavier until Jojo turned the tables on me. "What about you, Lena? How's the aquarium? I would like to be able to watch all the exotic fish all day"

"I'm thinking about quitting," I admitted, catching Jojo by surprise. "My boss is strict about hours and I haven't been to church in weeks. I feel like I'm being a little taken advantage of because there is so much turnover there."

Before I could say more, Denny dropped into the seat beside Theo, cheeks a little pink from moving things around.

"Hey," he said, reaching into his dinner bag and snagging his cookie first. "Didn't mean to be late, Adam recruited me and a few other guys to help put away extra chairs and tables. There are way fewer campers than usual."

"Really?" Jojo asked as she glanced around. "The crowd is thinner, but I didn't realize that much of a difference."

"There's a *big* difference," Denny said. "Max was asked to cater instead of the directors bringing in the full kitchen crew. With a smaller crowd, that just made the most sense to everyone."

So that explains the catering, I thought to myself.

Just then, Carter returned with two dinner bags and a water bottle in each hand, slipping into the seat beside me. "Sorry, I got caught up at the cooler."

I accepted the dinner and drink he offered me as my eyes flicked to the table where Riley sat with the others, caught up in conversation. Carter followed my gaze before turning back to me, examining my reaction.

He opened his mouth to speak, but I quickly forced a smile, "It's okay, thanks for bringing me dinner. Seeing as how we'd just gotten back to camp, the last thing I wanted was Riley getting between us like last summer. "We were just talking about Theo's questionable movie taste and Denny flipping tables."

"Excuse you," Theo said in mock offense.

Carter's eyes lit up as he pointed at Denny. "Jesus flipped tables too, am I right?"

"Dude, Jesus totally flipped tables," Denny agreed, as he and Carter exchanged a high-five.

I snorted as Carter nudged me gently with his elbow. "Hey, did you see who's here?"

Following his gaze to the kitchen, I saw Max and Lou standing shoulder to shoulder, handing out bagged dinners, moving seamlessly together like a well-oiled machine.

"See?" Carter leaned in, voice low so only I could hear. "Told you, apparently, my mom thinks they're adorable."

A smile slowly pulled at the corners of my mouth, as all traces of Riley-tension disappeared. "They are," I whispered. "Has Lou said anything to your mom?"

"If she has, Mom hasn't said anything to me," Carter said, taking a sip of water. "But I have overheard them chatting before dinner at our place once or twice. Max's name came up, but I didn't catch much."

I nudged his arm, pretending to be disappointed. "Some spy you are."

Carter guffawed. "Yeah, terrible, no stealth skills whatsoever."

"You're lucky you're cute," I teased, bumping his arm again.

He grinned and gave me a playful wink before digging into his dinner.

The five of us sat like that, together, finishing our dinner and picking right back up where we left off as though I had been right beside them all along. I realized just how much I had missed Theo and Denny's banter, Jojo's giggle, and Carter's ability to put me at ease. We sat like a group that belonged together no matter how far we ever were apart.

Later, as other campers started to clean up, Theo stood and stretched. "Alright, who's up for night one Devo?"

"Let's do it," Jojo said, scooping up her trash.

As we gathered our things and filed out, I felt lighter, like this weekend really could be the reset I'd been hoping for.

***

After dinner, the five of us wandered down to the amphitheater, following the crowd as dusk draped itself over camp. I opened the chips I hadn't finished at dinner and trailed behind the others as the boys continued their earlier bantering.

"The soccer team is undefeated this season," Theo announced, beaming with pride. "Back-to-back shutouts, man, nothing gets past us."

Denny waved him off with a scoff. "Quit bragging, dude. You play soccer, not football. Try going up against guys twice your size and see how you fare."

Falling in step beside me, Carter let out a long-suffering sigh, clearly used to these debates. He reached over casually, swiping a chip from my bag. "Here we go," he muttered, chomping down, the sound matching the sounds of leaves beneath our feet.

Theo shot Carter a warning glance before turning back to Denny, raising his brows. "So you want to compare sports now, Dennis?"

I smirked, nudging a pine cone off the trail with my foot and watching it tumble into the brush. "Alright, who do you think will throw something first?"

"Denny," Carter lowered his voice, without missing a beat. "Theo loves to rile everyone up, but Denny lets Theo get under his skin." His voice was dry, but there was fondness in it as he watched them bicker. "Theo's just been...*extra* lately."

I thought about the way Theo kept glancing over at his ex throughout dinner, knowing how painful it must have been for him to sit there without her acknowledging him.

"He's still planning to win Katie back," I said, glancing over, remembering the text Theo sent me about the flower delivery fail.

Carter scoffed, before his expression shifted in a coy smile. "Of course he is."

"You think it's a bad idea?" I wondered.

He slowed his steps before shaking his head. "Not exactly. I believe in fighting for what you want, but you also have to know when to let go. I don't know if he's really trying to win her back... or just trying to prove that he can."

I was quiet for a moment, watching our shadows stretch across the path as the others trailed up ahead of us. "This summer on our hike, Theo told me he wished he had the same extra time we did after camp when I stayed in Meadowbrook. He wondered if things would've turned out differently between them if they had."

"Nope," Carter said without hesitation. "That kind of time doesn't fix what's not there. Our relationship works because we promised to try, it's not one-sided."

I stared back at him then, catching Carter's expression both serious and sure.

"Who would've thought our friends would envy a couple hundreds of miles apart," I joked.

Carter reached for my hand, and I looked over to see the sunset glowing behind him, making my knees feel weak. "Why not? We talk every day, and I'd be willing to bet we know more about each other than Theo ever knew about Katie."

This intrigued me. "You think so? Those two had known each other for years."

Carter shrugged dismissively. "You can know someone for years but not *really* know them."

My ears perked up suddenly as I offered him a teasing grin. "Okay then, tell me what you know about me."

"I know your favorite movie is The Princess Bride because you love the enemies to lovers trope," Carter pointed out.

"That was an easy one." I cut my eyes at him, while my heart pitter-pattered in my chest. "It's kind of our trope, too."

Carter chuckled as I swung our clasped hands back and forth. "I know your favorite color is blue, like a deep-blue, that reminds you of water because that's what calms you."

My smile widened as he continued. "And even though you claim you don't sing, you hum all the time. Especially when you're nervous or focused, because I've heard you on our calls."

I stopped walking just then, overwhelmed by how seen I felt in that moment. "I can't believe you remember all that."

Carter tilted his head, eyeing me peculiarly. "You can't believe your boyfriend remembers stuff about you?"

I shook his hand in mine, feeling antagonized. "I just thought all this time apart meant we were missing out on what everyone else has, but—"

"You were wrong?" Carter asked with a sly smile, as if he were finishing my sentence.

I let go of his hand and gave him a playful nudge, but he caught my elbow before I could pull away. Giggling, he said, "I missed this."

I smiled and slipped my hand back into his. "I missed you, Rosie."

Carter didn't answer right away; instead, he glanced around, making sure no one was close and then he leaned in slowly, his eyes soft and warm as they stared into mine. Yet, just before our lips could meet, a voice rang out.

"Hey, lovebirds! You coming to Devo, or just gonna stand there breaking rules?"

Carter sighed, lingering one heartbeat more before pulling back. We both glanced up the trail to see Theo standing ahead, arms crossed and smirking. I didn't miss the tic in Carter's jaw as he took my hand again, nodding toward the amphitheater. "Come on," he said, voice low.

We made our way down the trail to where Jojo and Denny were the ones bickering now about a cupcake she owed him as we found our spots. I noticed Theo rolling his eyes, clearly feeling like the fifth wheel as he turned to me, flicking his golden blonde hair off his forehead. "So, Mermaid," Theo said, smirking. "When are we going to hear about these senior pranks of yours?"

The spotlight of his question landed squarely on me, and I felt a jolt in my chest. I peered into the nearly empty chip bag as my mind flashed with unwelcome memories of pickles on my car, Javier's cold smile, and tea dripping down my front.

"Um... never because there are no senior pranks," I muttered, munching on one last chip to fill the awkward pause.

Out of the corner of my eye, I caught Carter watching me, giving me the kind of look he wore when he was quietly trying to figure something out. Even after the sweet moment we'd just shared, and all the buildup to being back together, I knew Carter hadn't stopped wondering about what really happened that day he couldn't reach me.

Before Theo or anyone else could ask any follow-up questions, Preacher Adam's familiar voice rang out, warm and commanding. "All right, everyone, have a seat, and welcome to the Fall Retreat!"

His rhyme warranted a chuckle from the crowd as campers settled into their spots. Theo just shook his head and murmured something about Adam and his dad jokes.

"I hope you all enjoyed your bagged dinners." Adam smiled. "Let's take a moment to give a hand to the person behind these delicious meals, Max Adler!"

A ripple of applause broke out, and I turned to see Max and Lou trickling in towards the back of the thin crowd. Max raised his eyebrows and gave a modest wave, appearing both surprised and slightly out-of-place outside the diner. Lou beamed up at him, nudging his arm as if urging him to soak in the recognition, and a smile flicked across my face as I watched them together.

There was an ease between them that had always existed, but the lingering look they exchanged was new.

Adam's voice carried on, pulling my attention back to the front, as he listed the weekend schedule. "Our theme this weekend is being unshakable and focusing on our identity in Christ. Over the next day or so, we're going to explore what it means not only to be Christians, but to truly know who we are, and what it means to stand firm in our faith. We've got lessons, breakout sessions, activities, and plenty of free time. Oh, and of course," Adam added with a grin, "the talent show on Friday night!"

A loud cheer rippled through the crowd, but I felt my stomach sink with the reminder of a performance that I was expected to give but felt completely unprepared for.

"So, with that said," Adam continued. "Let's get started with our song service."

My throat tightened at the mention of singing, and I busied myself rolling up the chip bag as quietly impossible despite the loud crinkling. Singing was the one part of camp I wasn't ready for, *not yet*. Even though I'd hummed show choir tunes under my breath lately, hymns were different. They made me think of family, of how things used to be, and the ache that came with those memories was still too raw.

Carter leaned in, his shoulder brushing gently against mine, and when I glanced at him he gave me a soft smile as if silently checking in. I didn't respond, instead; I laced my fingers through his, and he gave my hand a reassuring squeeze before letting go.

As the sun sank, string lights twisting around the pergola flickered to life as I looked toward the rest of the crowd as some campers huddled on the wide concrete pad of the amphitheater wrapped in blankets, their breath rising in soft wisps though outdoor heaters worked to keep us comfortable.

I took a deep breath, comforted by Carter's warmth beside me, as Mateo, a camper I remembered from summer camp, stepped forward to lead us in song. I glanced at Carter, watching his gaze lock on the projector screen behind Mateo, cast the lyrics to help us follow along. Jojo began to sway gently beside Carter, while Denny and Theo grew uncharacteristically serious, singing on key. The voices around me expanded, rising in harmony to fill the evening air. I'd heard this song countless times, suddenly, lifting the weight I'd been carrying.

How can I keep from singing Your praise
How can I ever sing enough
How amazing is Your love...

I pulled my sleeves over my hands, shrinking into the comfort of my own body. Beside Carter, Jojo drummed her hand softly against her knee as I recalled her words from dinner.

God wants us to make a joyful noise.

I pressed my lips together to bite back the lyrics so I didn't have to worry about letting a song spill out. Every time I heard a familiar hymn, I instantly thought of my mother's face, of the way her eyes used to light up as she sang with all her heart. Before tonight, every hymn I heard made me want to just forget all the memories that were dredged up, but now, as the lyrics pressed around, I focused more on the song's meaning and felt a gentle shift inside.

How can I keep from shouting Your name...

Without realizing it, I tapped my foot lightly against the concrete as a soft hum slipped from my lips, barely more than a ripple. I caught myself, feeling a rush of heat creep up my neck as I froze. When I glanced sideways, I spotted Carter, leaning back, watching me in that quiet way of his, nodding encouragingly for me to continue.

Even though I wasn't ready to raise my voice, I thought about how if God wanted me to make a joyful noise, I still could without singing out. *As long as my heart was in it, isn't that what mattered?* This time, I let the hum slip out on purpose, weaving my voice into the music as the chorus swelled around us.

I know I am loved by a King
And it makes my heart want to sing...

As I listened, the lyrics seemed to crack open a door inside me. Suddenly, I couldn't shake the thought that maybe Jojo was right. Maybe making a joyful noise wasn't about opening a portal to my past, but giving my best back to God. As I listened to the voices all around me, I felt my ears perk up hearing the beautiful soprano sound I knew I could support, even if my voice shook a little. So when the next verse rose, I found their simple harmony and joined in with an offering that only God and Carter could hear.

As the words tumbled from my lips, I turned and saw Carter's mouth curve slightly as though he had been waiting for this moment to arrive. Though a blush crept down my face, I returned my focus to the lyrics in the front and, for the first time in a long, long time, singing didn't feel like losing a piece of myself. Instead, it felt like rediscovering a part of myself I had let slip away.

When the song service ended, a peaceful stillness settled over me until I turned and found Theo's wide-eyed stare fixed on me.

"Okay, um, what was that?" he blurted as his jaw hit the ground. "Lena, you can sing."

"She's back!" Jojo exclaimed.

"What?" I asked, confused by their dramatic reactions.

Carter chuckled beside me. "Everyone and their dog heard you, Dutch."

My cheeks heated again, and I shook my head. "That was nothing; I wasn't even singing, it was just harmonizing."

"Yeah, you're delusional, but your voice makes up for that shortcoming," Theo retorted.

My mouth flew open as Carter shot daggers at Theo, but he didn't bother to acknowledge us. Instead, Theo turned to Jojo beside him, completely straight-faced. "Sorry, Jo, but you're out. Lena, you're my new partner for the talent show. I'm singing a duet, and I need you."

"Way to insult her first, that will win her over," Carter quipped.

"What? No," I protested, dread rising in my chest.

Denny pumped his fist triumphantly. "Sweet! Jojo Bean, you can be my assistant for my magic act."

Relief washed over Jojo's face as she placed a hand over her heart. "Yes, please."

Unwilling to be told what to do, I stood my ground. "No! Look, guys, I'm sorry, but I can't make that any more clear than I already have."

Carter placed a hand on my back and eyeballed Theo. "Maybe let Lena decide."

I peered over at him as his annoyance with Theo began to fade, and Carter began searching my face for answers.

"I can figure something else out," I pressed, feeling exasperated with all of this pressure.

Theo didn't back down, though. "Mermaid, just come with me later to at least hear the song and then decide."

I glowered at him while he pleaded with me. Everyone's eyes were on me, all of them questioning, like they didn't understand why I couldn't help Theo.

"Can you just listen to the song, Lena?" Jojo asked in her sweet voice, showing me a small sheepish smile. "It's actually pretty good."

I sighed, rolled my eyes, and shrugged, pulling my knees to my chest again and wrapping my arms around them.

"I'll think about it," I replied curtly, turning back to face the front.

I felt Carter's hand slip from my back as the group fell quiet around me, suddenly feeling the weight of Theo's performance solely on my shoulders.

27

I sat stiffly with my hands clasped together in my lap, still reeling from the pressure to agree to be Theo's talent show partner. Everyone acted like it was no big deal, but they didn't know why I couldn't sing anymore. They all knew I used to love it, but they didn't know why. I used to sing all the time with my mom, it had become our thing, the one bond we held onto when everything changed after my grandparents passed. Yet, when Mom left, I couldn't do it anymore; singing felt too much like forgiveness, like pretending things hadn't fallen apart.

I forced myself to look ahead just as Preacher Adam stepped to the front, Bible in hand. He peered out and asked, "If someone asked who you are, what would you say? Not your name, but *who* you are."

Adam let the question hang in the air, and I noticed a few kids shifting in their seats as his words landed with a heaviness I didn't know how to shake. Most days, I didn't know how to answer that question, though my thoughts drifted to my family's reputation, the mistakes I couldn't seem to escape at home, and the version of me that lived in other people's rumors. I pulled my knees to my chest, hoping the familiar posture might guard me from the ache rising inside.

"The world already has an answer for you," Adam continued. "It throws labels at you without even asking."

My throat tightened as a rush of thoughts crowded in, words I hadn't chosen, but started to believe about myself. Beside me, Carter sat casually, arms resting on his knees, eyes fixed on Adam. Normally, his quiet strength steadied me, but right now, all I could think about were the things I hadn't told him about Freeport.

Adam raised his Bible, flipping briefly through the pages. "But the Bible tells us a different story. There was a young man named Daniel who was close in age to all of you, maybe younger, when his story begins. Daniel's life was ripped out from under him. His home was taken and his name was replaced; Daniel was forced to learn a new language, and his community was scattered near and far. Babylon did everything they could to erase who he was, but Daniel knew something they didn't. He knew his true identity came from God."

Adam held up a white name tag, the same kind we'd all received at check-in. "Let's talk about these for a second," he said, peeling off the backing and pressing it onto his coat pocket. "These little tags help people learn your name, but what if I asked you to write something else?"

He paused, letting the question settle as his eyes scanned the room.

"What would you write if you had to be honest? Not what you want people to see, I mean the label you've given yourself that you've been carrying around in secret."

I glanced down at mine, still stuck to my jacket, my name scrawled in black Sharpie. In my mind, other labels surfaced. *The alcoholic's daughter. Troublemaker. Loner. Abandoned.* I twisted the drawstring of my jacket between my fingers as Adam read the part where Daniel's name was changed to Belteshazzar, a name meant to honor a god that wasn't his. Next, Adam shared the meaning of Daniel's real name, which meant *God is my judge.*

That fact grabbed my attention as Adam continued.

"Despite the King's demands, Daniel knew God had the ultimate authority, and he didn't forget who he belonged to," Adam said, his voice sure. "He knew his name, but more than that, he knew his God." Adam smiled, the weight of his words lifting a little. "You know what happened as a result? God honored Daniel and his friends. Daniel 1:17 says, *'God gave these four young men knowledge and understanding...' and verse twenty tells us the king found them ten times better than everyone else.* Can you imagine the amazing things our God can do if we only stand firm like Daniel?"

I shifted where I sat, suddenly aware of the cold, hard concrete beneath me. Back in Freeport, I had learned how to hide pieces of myself just to make it through the day. At school, I kept my head down, but at work, I smiled and did whatever was I was told. At home, retreating to my room had become a habit, a way to shut out the noise and lock myself away in my safe little cocoon.

Adam kept going. "Jesus Himself quoted Daniel, that's how powerful his story is. Daniel didn't let the names Babylon gave him blot out the truth of who God said he was. God called Daniel wise, faithful, and most importantly, God called Daniel *His*. Don't we want God to do the same for us?"

My throat tightened with emotion because that was exactly what I wanted but knew I didn't deserve.

"Some of you," Adam said, his voice dipping lower, "came here carrying labels that were never yours, names the world has given you, names pain has given you; but, know this... God wants to give you a new name, but most of all God wants to call you His, just like he called Daniel. You are all who God says you are."

Adam then pointed to the name tag on his chest. "We all wrote our names on these earlier, but if you could do it again, knowing what you know now, what would you write?"

The amphitheater went quiet as the crowd drank in Adam's lesson.

"Would you still just write your name?" Adam asked gently. "Or would it be something else? *Son? Daughter? Forgiven?*"

His gaze swept over the crowd, urging us to reconsider how we thought of ourselves. "Here's what I want you to do. If you're ready, cross out your name and write the one you know God calls you. Let tonight be the night you stop letting the wrong names stick."

No one moved at first, but slowly, others around me started to reach into the baskets Lou passed from the back. Markers clicked open, name tags peeled off, and I watched as other campers scribbled fast, while others sat thinking, like me, about the names they wanted to bear. I sat still, my thumb resting on the edge of the sticker that read: *Lena*.

Even though I only saw my name, beneath it were the invisible words that clung to me like second skin. My heart thudded in my chest; then, like a gentle breeze, I heard Miss Pearl's voice, saying: *Don't forget who you are, Lena Harris. You're not your past anymore, you're a new creation in Jesus.*

I swallowed hard, knowing Miss Pearl was right. I had been shrinking back like my light didn't matter, but God had already given me a new name this summer. Once the truth dawned on me, I crossed out my name and I wrote down in neat, bold letters: *Free*.

After Adam extended the invitation for anyone who had forgotten their name or hadn't yet answered the call to follow Jesus, Mateo stepped forward again to lead the crowd in another song, *He Knows My Name*. I didn't know this song, but one by one, campers joined in, offbeat at first, but then the music became stronger. As I listened, the lyrics pricked me to the core, as the crowd around me lifted up their voices to praise God for knowing each and every name in the universe.

I stared down at the tag on my chest again and read the word I had written down, *Free*. When I became a Christian, I was made free from my past and free from the sins I once bore. Yet, once I left camp, no matter how much I tried, the sense of freedom I had gained slowly slipped away.

As the lyrics continued to swirl, I listened as the song spoke about how God knows our every thought and how He hears us, and never leaves us alone. As much as I tried to cling to the promise of the song back home, I had still struggled. But now, hearing the reminder of how God knows me, *Lena Harris*, in the midst of this great big universe, brought tears to my eyes to know how loved I truly was.

Carter's hand found mine, suddenly, with a soft squeeze that I returned. As the lesson spun around in my mind, the last note of the evening made me feel even lighter.

Adam gave us a moment before stepping forward again. "You've got some free time now, use it," he said. "Talk to someone or find a quiet place to talk to the One who knows your real name. Let God remind you who you are."

I glanced around at the faces nearby, realizing they weren't just acquaintances anymore, they were my family in Christ. When I glimpsed back down at my name tag, hope filled me. I knew I had been drifting, but I hadn't truly realized just how far until now. The guilt I'd been carrying began to loosen its grip, replaced by a quiet, steady reassurance, knowing God had made a way for me to come back to camp this weekend for a reason.

As Adam closed in prayer, I bowed my head and let his words settle over me. Tonight's lesson wasn't just a reminder, but a call to stop living under false names and start walking in truth, and to remember who I was and who I belonged to.

When Adam said *Amen*, Carter leaned in, his voice low, still holding my hand. "That was... awesome."

Pulling myself together, I nodded in agreement because I felt the exact same way. "I know, Adam gives the best lessons. You're lucky he's your preacher all the time."

With a quirk of his mouth, I caught the way his one dimple popped as Carter gave my hand another squeeze once the crowd began to scatter. "I'm also lucky to have some free time with my girlfriend now," he said with a half smile. "Wanna go somewhere?"

I smiled back, feeling lighter than I had felt in weeks. "Lead the way, boyfriend."

28

Branches snapped underfoot as Carter and I walked along the moonlit path in comfortable silence. Even in the dark, I felt safe here at camp, as Adam's lesson still swirled in my head about the name God gave me. I wasn't sure if it was just the thought of the lesson or the bite of cold that gave me goosebumps, but the next thing I knew, I released a full-on shiver and wrapped my arms around myself.

Without a word, Carter reached for my hand and laced his warm fingers through mine.

"Wow! Your hands are freezing!" He exclaimed, wrapping his hand tighter around mine like he was trying to warm me up.

"Cold hands, warm heart." I joked as we marched ahead.

"I like your name," he said, pointing to where I crossed out *Lena* and added *free*.

I smiled and peered down at our joined hands. "Me too, I was just listening to Adam, and the word 'free' just came to me out of nowhere. That man has a gift."

Carter dipped his head slowly as if he completely agreed. "Adam brought the heat tonight, didn't he?"

Another shiver curled through me as I glanced at Carter's name tag to see his name scribbled out, replaced with the word *Son*. My heart melted at the sight.

"Did the lesson get to you, too?" I asked, pointing to his tag.

Carter stared ahead and offered me a casual shrug, seeming unbothered. "Not more than usual, but Adam has a way of reaching into your heart and showing you what's really there."

"And... what did you see?" I pressed.

Beneath a lamppost along the path, I caught a flash of his casual smirk. "Before I was adopted, what I wanted most was a family. When I met my mom and dad, they studied the Bible with me and showed me who I belonged to. Then, when I became a Christian, I knew God had welcomed me into His family and gave me one with the Roses, too."

I swallowed, my throat growing thick as I listened to how important the word *son* was to him in more ways than one. Over the summer, Carter told me how Amy Rose had been his tutor at an alternative school and how she refused to give up on him when he'd given up on himself. He found a family with Amy and her husband Jack. They studied the gospel with him and helped him find a better path. I knew the double meaning behind the word for him after being abandoned by his birth family.

"I think I have your parents to thank, too," I confessed, staring down at my feet to watch where I was going.

"How's that, Dutch?" he asked, eyes on the trail too.

"They taught you about Jesus, and then you taught me." I grinned up at him briefly. "Evangelism 101, right, Forrest?"

Carter chuckled at my reference, his hand finally warming mine as we walked. He gave my hand another gentle squeeze as he steered us toward the Med Cabin.

"Are you bunking here this weekend?" I asked, taking in the sight of how quiet the place seemed compared to summer.

Carter shook his head as his breath came out in tiny wisps of air. "Not this weekend. Since the Fall Retreat is just us senior campers, they only needed Angie on standby in case someone pulls a wild stunt during the talent show. I'm crashing with Denny and Theo at Boys' Camp."

A small smile pulled at my lips for a moment as I pictured Carter keeping the other two in line. "Speaking of the talent show, what's your plan?"

I could barely make out the wink he gave me in the dark. "I'm a solo act, and it's a surprise, but trust me, my performance will blow your mind."

I chuckled, nudging him. "I'm excited to see whatever you do, oh, and thanks for not pushing me to sing with Theo, by the way. He'd probably make me attempt some screamo song or something."

Carter scoffed. "Theo would never embarrass himself like that, the guy's too busy trying to win Katie back. Jojo says his song's pretty sappy."

"That might be a nice change from all the show tunes I've heard lately," I said, thinking of my school lunches with the choir.

Just beneath a second lamppost, I caught sight of the way Carter grinned at me. "You can't hate it, though. The girl I know doesn't stick with things she doesn't like; so, your show choir friends can't be that bad."

I smiled, remembering how I told him about my show choir lunches, and how I'd heard too many renditions from *The Phantom of the Opera* to ever need to see the play. In my opinion, watching the show choir's take on performing the numbers was way better than any musical I had ever seen.

"I'm actually having a ton of fun with them," I admitted, scrunching my nose like it was an embarrassing confession. "They're all so talented, but now my brain is stuck on all these musical numbers from movies I've never even seen."

Carter bit back a laugh as we made our way off the trail, the floodlights from the Med Cabin shining so brightly my eyes began to water. Letting go of my hand, Carter led me over to the porch swing and motioned for me to sit on the wooden seat.

The chains creaked softly as he joined me, giving the swing a slow push as he dragged his right foot on the ground.

His voice softened as he wrapped his arm around my shoulders. "So, besides your secret lunch crew and Bible study, what else is going on in that little beach town of yours?"

"Nothing really," I said, leaning into his side to capture his warmth. "It's so nice to be back here, though."

The light spilling from the Med Cabin illuminated Carter's face, as I watched his expression turn serious. "You know what else would be nice?"

I peered over, catching a mischievous glint in his eyes. "What?"

He nudged my shoulder, smiling. "If you would just tell me if there's anything going on with me."

My stomach twisted as I hesitated, pulling my sleeves over my hands. "I've just missed everyone, leaving Meadowbrook was harder than I thought."

Carter wasn't convinced as he dipped his head, challenging me. "We promised to always be honest, Dutch. You got short with Theo about singing, and I get it, he and Jojo sprung the whole idea on you, but I can't defend you unless I really know what's going on."

His words settled over me, and I glanced away. *How did he always see through me like glass?*

"I know," I said quietly. "When you think about it though, it's not like they're both asking me for a small favor, here. Getting onstage to sing doesn't exactly feel like a walk in the park. Everyone would just be staring at me and if I choke, Theo won't have a chance of winning with me as his partner."

Carter opened his mouth to respond, but laughter down the path caught our attention. I turned toward the sound and recognized the others instantly as Riley, Kelsey, and a few of their friends. Their laughter quickly stopped as the group noticed us, but to my surprise, I watched Riley lift a hand in a casual wave, while I froze, unsure how to react. Beside me, Carter dipped his head in an easy nod, completely unbothered. I swallowed hard, shifting my gaze back to the group just as my eyes landed on Kelsey. Unlike Riley, she didn't look at me, she kept her eyes fixed ahead, and kept walking as if trying to pretend she didn't see us.

So much had happened back home, I hadn't even considered what had been happening here in Meadowbrook. After the way things ended at camp this summer, I assumed Riley was long gone from Carter's world, but clearly I was wrong.

As the group disappeared down the path, I turned to Carter, my brows furrowing. "I think it's my turn to ask what that's all about?"

Carter shifted, seeming uncomfortable for just a second before shrugging. He reached for my hand but didn't hold it, instead he stopped and pulled back. "Riley and I... we're cool now. We talked at youth group and—"

I scoffed, my stomach sinking at the thought of them spending time together, talking, especially after everything that happened over the summer. Before I could think, words tumbled out of my mouth.

"Wait...you guys are *cool now*?" I asked in air quotes.

Carter let out a quiet chuckle, as if trying to lighten the mood. "There's a little more to it than that, Dutch."

I glanced away, trying my best to keep my cool as I tilted my head toward the sky. The last time I saw Riley, she had done everything in her power to get under my skin and ruin the beginning of my relationship with Carter. Now, here he was, talking about her like they had simply moved on, as if she hadn't tried to sabotage us.

Carter sighed and finally turned to face me, keeping his voice steady. "Dutch, I know what happened between all of us hurt, but I have to be civil with Riley. We go to the same church. Sure, she and I have a past, but I'm not going to hold grudges. I refuse to let what happened between us dictate how I treat her."

The way he said that caught me off guard, and when I glanced at him, his eyes were locked onto mine. Carter took both my hands in his, as if trying to tether me to him with the invisible string that constantly pulled me back to him. "Can you understand that?"

By reflex, I squeezed his hands back, forcing myself to push down the unease twisting in my chest. His words stepped all over my toes, but I knew he was trying to do the right thing. *After all, isn't that what I had tried to do with Lacey and Ronni? Put the past behind us? How could I be upset with him for that?*

The last thing I wanted this weekend was drama, so I let out a quiet breath and agreed. "Okay."

Carter didn't hesitate as he hooked his arm back around my shoulder and pulled me into his side. "Good, because there's this really cute girl I haven't seen in weeks, and all I want is to have the perfect night with her."

I smiled as he pressed a kiss to my forehead, drawing me closer under the pretense of needing warmth. We sat there, wrapped in each other's arms, but as much as I fought against them my thoughts still wandered, first to Riley, and then to Kelsey who seemed just as weary about me as I was about her.

When Carter's fingers found mine again, I exhaled slowly and pushed both girls out of my mind. Right now, all that mattered was this moment with the guy I'd missed more than words could describe.

29

I woke to the soft rustle of trees outside my window as the first light of morning filtered in. Last night with Carter still lingered in my thoughts, just the two of us on the porch swing, gazing up as stars scattered across the sky. After months apart, it almost felt too good to be true that I was back at camp. The thought of seeing Carter *again* today had me reeling as I jumped out of bed to get ready, leaving a snoring Jojo still asleep.

By the time I reached the dining hall, the room was already alive with its usual morning chatter and my stomach instantly growled once the smell of eggs, bacon, and buttery biscuits wafted from the kitchen. That's when I spotted Max in the kitchen, cooking like he always did at the diner, surrounded by only a few staff members to help.

"That smells delicious," I greeted Max, walking up to the window.

He peered up briefly and smiled once he caught sight of me. "Hey Lenny! It's good to see you."

"You too," I said, watching as he rolled out a huge slab of biscuit dough. "Sorry I didn't get a chance to say hi yesterday, I didn't want to bother you, you seemed busy."

Max smirked, but kept his focus. "I'm never too busy for you, kiddo. Did you have a good ride up yesterday?"

"I did, I know the way by heart now." I replied.

Max smiled and flicked his gaze at me briefly. "I'm glad, we're all happy you're here, especially your aunt."

"Speaking of my aunt, have you seen Lou yet?" I asked, while Max quickly began cutting out biscuits.

"Not this morning, but I'm sure she's around somewhere."

With no sign of Lou, and Max clearly occupied, I told Max I would see him later and grabbed a bottle of water before searching the room to find an empty seat. I drained my water and kept my eyes on the door for what felt like an eternity before the others arrived.

Denny slid into the seat across from me and leaned in with a knowing grin. "Carter's out running. You know how he is about training."

I nodded, but that didn't stop the nerves from twisting tighter in my stomach. Carter and I had just spent time together last night, but now that I could see him again, the waiting felt endless. Twenty minutes later, I was nearly finished with my breakfast plate when Carter finally appeared, hair still damp from a quick shower.

As if agreeing he was late, Carter held up a steaming cup of coffee in one hand, a banana and protein bar in the other.

"For you," he said, slipping into the seat beside me and sliding the coffee over. "The rest is for me...breakfast of champions."

I laughed, taking the warm paper cup and letting my hands soak up the heat. "You're the one who just ran three miles, I should be bringing you coffee."

"Maybe next time," he said with a wink, unpeeling the banana while already halfway into the protein bar. "Lou let me use some of her pumpkin spice creamer in that. Happy fall, Dutch."

I took a sip and peered up at Carter with wide eyes. The coffee was surprisingly good. Sweet with a hint of spice, the cinnamon blended perfectly into the warmth of the drink. Back when school first started, Carter used to stop by the Ridge Roast before class and send me selfies, teasing me for not knowing what's good for me. I'd tried my dad's coffee blend once but the taste was bitter and belonged in the trash. I vowed I would never look back, but Carter insisted he would convert me eventually. With this cozy, cinnamon-laced concoction, he may have just won me over.

I sat between him and Jojo for the rest of breakfast, slowly stirring my drink as the hum of conversation buzzed around us. Even surrounded by my friends, my thoughts wandered to the one thing still looming over me, tonight's talent show. I felt like everyone assumed I was just going to stand beside Theo and pull off some show-stopping performance, but the truth was, I had no intention of getting on stage tonight. *I couldn't.*

As if she could sense the storming inside me, Jojo leaned in and whispered. "You okay?"

I nodded, forcing a smile. "Yeah, just thinking."

She smirked, sipping her orange juice. "Thinking about what you're going to perform tonight?"

I groaned and set the coffee down. "More like thinking about how to disappear before then."

Jojo giggled, but Theo peered up across the table, catching my response as his gray eyes narrowed slightly. "You don't have to disappear," he said. "You could just do the duet with me before it's too late."

"You're never getting out of this now that he's heard your pipes, Dutch," Carter added, finishing his protein bar.

I opened my mouth to respond, but before I could get a word out, Adam stepped to the front of the dining hall and clapped his hands. "Alright, everyone, listen up!"

The Dining Hall chatter instantly quieted down as all attention was drawn to him. Adam dove into the announcements, rattling off the day's schedule: morning sessions, group worship, small groups, and free time before tonight's big event. Then he gestured to the man standing beside the small platform and I did a doubletake. He looked so much like Theo that it took me a second to realize who the man was..

"As most of you know, Grant Lockwood is our new chairman of the Board, so let's give him a warm New Hope welcome."

Polite applause rippled through the room as Grant stepped forward. He seemed like an older, more polished version of Theo, with the same piercing eyes that were much colder.

"Good morning," Grant dipped his head, taking in the crowd. "I just want to say how grateful I am to be here with you all. Camp has meant a great deal to this community over the years, and I'm honored to serve as your new Chairman."

His gaze drifted toward the back of the room where Lou had finally appeared and now stood by the entrance with Max. "I also want to recognize Max Adler and his team for stepping in to handle meals this weekend, especially while juggling preparations for the Meadowbrook Harvest Festival. I hope everyone will be sure to thank them when you can."

There was another wave of clapping and a few scattered cheers as I glanced back at them. Lou's expression caught me off-guard, while I expected to see her smiling, she just seemed reserved beside Max who only offered a polite nod in response.

Grant continued, his tone shifting to tend to business. "For those of you familiar with summer camp procedures, I want to mention there is no cleaning service this weekend. I expect everyone to do their part. If you see trash, pick it up and if you make a mess, clean it up. Let's work together to keep New Hope in tip-top shape."

With that, Grant stepped back and allowed Adam to return to center stage.

"Alright," Adam grinned, his tone and demeanor already brightening up the room again. "Finish up breakfast, everyone, and then get ready for your first sessions. Today is going to be a great day!"

The Dining Hall instantly filled with noise again as others began to clear their tables. Across from me, Theo sat stiffly, eyes fixed on the napkin he kept folding. He hadn't looked up since his dad spoke but when I leaned forward to ask if he was okay, I stopped because I knew the answer.

Instead, I offered a gentle nudge. "Earth to Lockwood."

It took a second of me waving my hand in his face before Theo finally glanced back up. When he saw me waving, he let out a breath like he'd been holding it in.

"What's up, Mermaid?" he asked, at first he gazed at me with narrowed eyes but then restrained his face to seem bored.

"Just checking to see if you were okay, but nevermind." I said dismissively.

Theo leaned on one arm, stroking his chin as if an idea just hit him. "You know what would really make me okay?"

I instantly cut my eyes at him. "Don't say it, Lockwood."

"Come on, Lena. Have you thought any more about singing with me? Come on, Jojo wants to perform with her boyfriend, do the short fry a favor."

When I gazed over at Jojo, I expected to see her protest, but instead she just shrugged and poked out her bottom lip.

Turning back to face Theo, I found him now giving me puppy dog eyes. I couldn't even look over at Carter, so instead I dropped my gaze, shaking my head as I sighed. "It's not that simple for me, Theo. I don't think you realize what you're asking me."

When I felt brave enough, I turned back, surprised to see Theo give me a small nod, as I spotted the tiniest flicker of concern in his eyes. "Just... think about it, okay? The talent show is tonight, and I would love an answer by lunch."

I offered a weak smile, agreeing as he turned to Denny, who leaned in with a whispered comment, and the two of them quickly slipped into conversation. Beside me, Carter's hand found mine. Eyeing him, I saw something searching in his gaze, like he was trying to silently figure out what I wasn't telling him.

Picking up my coffee cup, I stared down at the ring it left on the table and sighed. This weekend was supposed to be a chance for me to get away from all the pressure, and drama, but somehow, the talent show had become its own kind of burden. None of my friends could understand why the idea of singing again felt impossible for me, because no one knew that the day my mom walked out was the day my voice disappeared.

30

Just as we were about to head down to the amphitheater for this morning's breakout session, Adam flagged us down. "Hey guys, I need a few strong arms to help me prep the pool area and move some chairs," he explained, acting quickly. "Mateo brought a friend he's been studying the Bible with and the young man has decided to get baptized."

Despite the talent show tension, I felt my heart warm back up hearing the news. Whatever Adam had said in his lesson last night must have struck a chord with Mateo's friend. As the guys started heading to the pool, Adam asked Jojo and me to tell others so we could all go support the young man's decision.

Jojo shot me a salute before sprinting off to gather the crew on the front lawn. I turned the other way, planning to do a sweep through the dining hall and the kitchen in case anyone was still lingering. The dining area had mostly cleared, and the kitchen was quiet except for the hum of the fridge and the lingering scent of breakfast. Clean chafing dishes were stacked beside the sink, and the floor still glistened from a fresh mop. I was about to turn back around when a voice caught my attention.

"I still think about that marshmallow plumbing disaster," Lou said, giggling as she and Max headed to carry supplies to the storage closet.

I paused just beyond the pantry wall, hidden from view as Max followed my aunt with an arm load. "You mean when I spent almost all night in my cabin with a wrench and a prayer? I still can't eat marshmallows to this day."

Around the corner, I heard Lou gasp. "Oh, and we can't forget the canoe fiasco of 2005. I honestly believed your whole cabin was getting banned from camp after that."

"They should've made them sign a safety waiver," Max said, dryly. "Those boys were menaces."

I leaned against the doorframe, with a small smile as their laughter carried across the kitchen. For a moment, they weren't the adults running this place, but two former counselors, trading their own nostalgic stories.

When Lou's voice softened, I sensed the shift in her tone. "We've come a long way, haven't we? Back then it was chaos, but it was our chaos. Is it really so bad that I just want to hold onto what my Dad built? I don't want to see everything slip through my fingers." There was a pause before she finished. "I don't want this place to change, not more than it already has."

Max didn't answer right away, and I felt something tighten in my chest at the weight of her words. I pressed closer as her words made my head spin. *What did she mean camp was changing? What did Gramps' have to do with New Hope?*

"Then we won't let it, Louie," Max said at last. I peered around the corner and caught Max leaning in, gently tucking a strand of Lou's hair behind her ear.

Their gaze was locked on each other for a quiet moment, but then Lou cleared her throat, and as her gaze shifted, it landed on me in the doorway. Her eyes widened in surprise as a blush crept onto her cheeks. Whatever moment I had just stepped into, I had definitely interrupted.

Watching Lou take two huge steps back from Max, I offered a smile that was more like a wince and an awkward wave. "Um... Adam sent me, he wants everyone to head to the pool. There's going to be a baptism in a few minutes."

Lou's expression instantly brightened. "That's great!"

Max turned toward me, arching a brow as he tapped his digital watch. "At the pool? The water's going to be freezing, it's fifty-three degrees out."

"Says the fisherman," Lou teased with a nudge to his ribs. "Since when did you worry about cold water?"

Max held up his hands in surrender. "Point taken."

Lou tilted her head knowingly. "Exactly, and you know the temperature doesn't matter when someone's ready to give their life to Jesus."

Dipping his head briefly, Max replied. "You're right, as usual...."

"Good man," Lou said with a reactive brush of his arm before turning to me. "Lena, honey, let's go grab some towels from the storage closet down by the pool. The boys will need them."

"Should I bring coffee?" Max asked, already moving toward the counter.

Lou paused, thinking for a moment before she agreed. "Yes, but only what's still left in the pot. Bring enough to warm the boys up a bit. Oh, and don't forget about the cocoa packets in the closet if you need more."

Max offered a two-finger salute as Lou slipped her arm around my shoulders and guided me toward the back door.

"Is the pool really freezing?" I asked, suddenly worried about Mateo's friend catching hypothermia than the moment I just interrupted.

Lou shook her head and chuckled as we strolled onto the porch and down the stairs, the chilly morning air already packing a punch. "I wouldn't exactly say *freezing*, but it wouldn't be too far off to say this young man was about to do a polar plunge."

"We don't have another way for him to be immersed?" I asked.

Lou shook her head as we walked, our feet crunching over the gravel. "Do you remember when you studied the book of Acts, and all those people became Christians? What did they all have in common?"

I thought about all the accounts I'd studied, especially the three thousand and the Ethiopian eunuch. The three thousand heard Peter's sermon and were baptized immediately, the same as the eunuch.

"They obeyed the gospel?" I asked, unsure. "I'm thinking of the eunuch and the three thousand, but is that what you mean?"

Lou let her head bob around a little, like she kind of agreed with me. "You're right, but there was also no hesitation. Once they heard the gospel, they acted immediately. When we think about the sin that stands between us and Heaven, we should act quickly to ensure nothing stops us from being with the Lord."

Just then, I considered my own decision to obey. As soon as I was ready, Lou, Jojo, and the others were there, making sure nothing stood in the way of me getting to Heaven one day. I didn't realize it then, but I knew now that act of urgency mirrored the examples in Scripture. When I saw it from her perspective, I understood Lou's point. Nothing, not even bad weather or cold water, should get in the way of someone's decision to follow Jesus. As unpleasant as it might feel, immersion only lasted minutes, while eternal life with Jesus was forever.

"There is a towel warmer in the storage closet we can plug in so we can wrap the guys in warm towels," Lou said. "Thank God for modern technology and the blessings that come with it."

We reached the pool just as Carter and the other guys were clearing chairs and making space. Carter glanced up and smiled over at me just as I offered him a quick wave, before Lou and I slipped into the pool's storage room. The scent of chlorine and must lingered as Lou retrieved the towel warmer from a haphazard pile of towels on the back shelf and plugged it in. With a nail-biting screech, the machine finally whirled to life.

"Give *Old Faithful* a few minutes," Lou said, brushing dust from the warmer off her hands. "Feels like just yesterday we were here for your baptism."

"Just a few months ago," I said, the memory still fresh. I could still feel the weightlessness of the water and the joy of dying to my old self and rising into a new life in Jesus. "I almost can't believe it... I feel like I still have so far to go."

"We all do," Lou said. "It's a journey, not a sprint, Lena. That's the beauty of it."

"When were you baptized?" I asked thoughtfully. "I don't think you've ever told me your story."

She chuckled as she opened the towel warmer, shaking her head in disbelief. "Forever ago, it feels like."

Lou placed a towel inside and pressed a button, as a gentle hum filled the storage room. I watched her as the memory seemed to take shape behind her eyes.

"I was eleven," she began, her voice laced with nostalgia. "Sitting on the porch with Mom and Dad. That afternoon they had been teaching me *How Great Thou Art*, and something about the lyrics just... hit me on full blast." Lou paused, eyes distant. "I had been asking really deep questions for awhile because I never missed a church service, youth group event, or Bible bowl, and spent all my time at camp. The routines were burned into my brain, but I found myself wrestling with the why and how of it all.."

That surprised me. I had always envisioned Lou as being someone firmly planted in her faith, unmovable even; but, hearing how she had questioned things made me feel less alone in the guilt I carried for sometimes doubting.

Lou smiled gently, still reliving the memory. "We had this beautiful backyard. Do you remember how we could see the bluff in the distance from your grandparents house?"

I nodded, smiling as I pictured my grandparents' view while Lou continued. "There was the old pond where Dad taught us to fish and the tire swing your mom and I used to play on." Her voice caught. "That day, we were singing together on the porch, and I stared out at the view and it hit me, God made every single tiny detail all the way down to the atom but somehow, God wanted little old me."

I felt my chest almost cave in beneath the weight of her beautiful story, because I knew exactly how it felt to realize just how much God gave just so I could choose Him.

Swiping at her eyes, Lou sniffled before she added. "I felt this sudden overwhelming gratitude and told my Dad I wanted to be a Christian and spend eternity in Heaven."

As Lou spoke, I pictured everything so vividly, the same backyard where I'd run barefoot and pick wildflowers. The back porch where I'd spent countless summers eating sliced watermelon while the bees zoomed around. I had always thought Grams' and Gramps' house was magical, but now their old home place felt like holy ground..

"I talked with them that night, and we went down to the pond where I made my confession, and my dad baptized me right then and there," Lou said.

There was a quiet peace that settled between us as I imagined my grandpa pulling Lou from the pond and embracing her. That old house had been layered with memories of my mom, and for so long, her presence made we want to bury all the moments far enough into my brain that I would never have to remember the pain they carried. But hearing Lou's story reminded me of the goodness that had existed long before the pain was there. I wanted to replace all the hurt with the strong roots my grandparents planted from all the time I spent in their home, in my heart.

I glanced at Lou and for a moment, her profile reminded me so much of my mother that it made my breath catch. They had the same cheekbones, the same soft eyes holding both joy and sorrow. To me, the biggest difference was the light in their eyes. Lou's were still bright, having never gone out, even with all the hurt she faced, too. Suddenly, I admired her strength and craved her secret.

"How did you feel about singing after Grams and Gramps passed?" I asked quietly. "We sang as a family so much, was it hard to keep going without them?"

Lou exchanged towels in the warmer and looked back at me. "At first? Yeah, it hurt," she said honestly, and I felt a strange sense of relief in her vulnerability. "I felt like I had lost part of myself, including my voice." She paused, then smiled faintly. "But over time, I began to hear them in the music again. Not physically, but in the way the tenors raised their voices like Dad or when I would see someone tap their foot, like Mom always had. Singing became much more than a way for me to remember them, but a way to honor their legacy, too. Over time, I truly believe music also helped me heal."

I swallowed against the lump in my throat, picturing how she could see the beauty even though she had lost her parents. Suddenly, I felt struck knowing that I let my pain pull me under, just as it seemed to do to my mom.

"Music does that, though," Lou said, opening up further. "If tied to a certain moment or person, a song can take us right back to that time, but music is also a gift that can point us to the One who gave it to us."

I nodded slowly, her words soaking in like warmth to the towels in her hand. *Could I ever feel that way about singing again?* As my thoughts spun, excited chatter filtered in from outside, pulling my attention toward the door.

I glanced at Lou. "Is it time?"

With a soft smile, she dipped her head. "I think so. We can come back for the towels, let's go join everyone."

I pulled the door open just as the first few notes of a song rose into the morning air. Sunlight danced along the pool's surface and softened the bite of the autumn chill. The crowd had already formed, taking me back to this past summer where I first witnessed the group gather. The outpouring of love and celebration was exactly what I could picture happening in Heaven when someone decided to choose Jesus and leave their old life behind. Now, as voices blended in reverent harmony, I stood in awe as the music wrapped around the crowd.

Then, the door to the boys' locker room creaked open and Mateo, Adam, and a boy I didn't recognize stepped out. Adam wore fishing waders while Mateo's friend walked barefoot in a T-shirt and shorts, trying his best not to shiver. He didn't know it yet, but soon he would be warm again, wrapped in fresh towels and the arms of everyone here today.

Adam and the boy made their way to the ladder as the singing softened, giving space for Adam's voice to carry.

"This morning, we have Reggie," he began, smiling at the boy beside him, "a young man who's been studying with Mateo and has come to understand what it means to follow Jesus."

Reggie stood tall despite the cold, shifting slightly. He looked both nervous and certain, like he knew he was about to make the most important decision of his life.

"Reggie and I have talked, and he's ready to walk with Christ," Adam continued. "We're going down into this freezing pool and bringing up a brother into new life. Are you ready, my friend?"

We all watched as Reggie bobbed his head without hesitation, and together, they stepped into the shallow end. Water lapped around Adam's waders as Reggie braved the cold, his face tight with determination as Adam guided him gently.

"Reggie, I just have one question for you," Adam said once they were in position. "Do you believe that Jesus is the Son of God?"

"Yes, sir," Reggie answered immediately.

"With that confession," Adam said, beaming, "I now baptize you in the name of the Father, the Son, and the Holy Spirit for the remission of your sins."

Reggie braced himself as he inhaled and clasped his nose, before allowing Adam to lower him into the water.

A moment passed, still and reverent, before Reggie rose again, gasping as he broke through the cold surface. His eyes were bright with joy as he reached for Adam, who wrapped him in a hug as cheers erupted around the pool. Tears pricked my eyes as I remembered that feeling, the moment I came out of the water and Carter pulled me into his arms. There was an overwhelming freedom, once I realized I wasn't the old Lena anymore. I had been washed clean, and now Reggie had that same new beginning.

A familiar melody floated above the noise, voices joining again in song that caused stole my breath once I recognized the words:

I've been bought with blood,
I am mine no more.

Lou took my wrist in hers and led me back into the storage room to retrieve warm towels. Together we quickly marched back to the pool's edge as Lou reached Reggie first, wrapping both towel and arms around him while I handed Adam his towel, offering a quiet smile. Then I stepped aside, watching as camper after camper formed a line to hug Reggie, to welcome him into his new family. He shivered but there was no hiding his radiant smile as camper after camper embraced their new brother in Christ.

As the song continued, I had to fight harder to stifle my tears as the lyrics pricked my heart. Home had been hard, school, work, but also the fear that met me once I returned to Freeport. I had let the weight of everything pull me away from the joy I'd felt after my own baptism. Now, standing here watching Reggie, I realized I might not have lost my faith, but I had let it fade.

I had forgotten just how much Jesus had done for me, to give me the grace that covered every shortcoming and His blood that was shed to wash me clean. I had been so caught up in staying busy and out of the way that I'd forgotten I wasn't mine anymore, my life belonged to Jesus.

My eyes scanned the crowd of campers and landed on Theo then. His arms wrapped around Reggie in a warm, brotherly hug, and suddenly it hit me. I didn't know what Theo was going through with his dad, but I could see what he tried to hide in his eyes. He carried quiet weariness, but still showed up anyway. When I looked honestly at the pain I carried, I saw flashes of moments I'd buried. Sitting beside my mom in a church pew, her voice guiding me through a hymn. Singing together at my grandparents' house as the sun dipped low. Holding Mom's hand in the hospital, whispering words of a song, praying she could hear me through the haze of her addiction.

For so long, I had associated my voice with her, with what we shared and what she left behind. I thought walking away from singing was protection, but maybe, deep down, I was blaming her for something I hadn't let myself grieve.

Lou's words reached all the way down into my heart, then. *Singing became a way to remember them... and overtime, a way to heal.* Next, I heard Jojo again, *God wants us to make a joyful noise and singing is one of the best ways to praise Him.*

As the final notes of the song faded into the cool morning air, a peace settled over me. I had spent so long letting pain hold me back from worship, from joy, and from living in the light, but God had never stopped deserving my praise. When I thought about how much I was losing by clinging to the negative memories, I knew I was holding myself back and maybe others too.

I glanced back at Theo, talking with another camper, and noticed how his smile didn't quite reach his eyes. Then it dawned on me, maybe singing with him wasn't about the talent show. Maybe it was about facing what needed to change in me and helping someone else know they weren't alone. For a long time, I had let pain and old memories silence me. I tied my voice to people I couldn't forgive and moments I didn't want to face. Staying quiet felt like protection, but really, my silence had kept me stuck. Now, seeing Reggie's decision in action made me wonder. *If God had already let go of my past, why was I still clinging to it? Why was I letting my pain stand between me and obedience?*

The truth finally hit me at full force as I realized I had only been holding myself back. If I was honest with myself, there were things in my life I still needed to change. Not singing kept me from fully praising God, my job was pulling me away from church, and those decisions fell on me. The guilt I felt was a sign I couldn't keep ignoring everything, it was time to make a change. I couldn't keep asking for deeper faith while giving my best to everything but God.

Maybe Lou was right, maybe music wasn't meant to remind me of what I'd lost but to help me find healing. Maybe now was the time to stop hiding, and the moment I chose to sing again and give God what I'd always said I would, *my whole heart.*

As I looked out at the crowd still celebrating Reggie's new life, his decision reminded me of my own, that my life was meant to reflect the light of Christ. As the song said, *I wasn't mine anymore*, my life belonged to Jesus.

I tipped my face up toward the sky as the sun's warmth touched my face, and in that moment, four simple words stirred in my heart: *How great Thou art.*

Suddenly, I felt so grateful for all the Lord had done and for all He was still doing for me. In that moment, I knew I could use my voice as the gift I had been given.

31

The first notes of the song service floated up into the clear fall sky. Two more campers had made the decision to follow Jesus after Reggie, each stepping into the cold water and rising again, drenched but smiling, into their new life. The breakout session for this morning had to be cut due to time constraints, but when the group had gathered for the morning song service, the amphitheater was filled with hearts on fire.

I sat between Carter and Jojo, our knees barely touching, the warmth of their bodies anchoring me in the cool air. Denny sat a few feet down, tapping a rhythm on his knee. The first few songs were lighthearted camp favorites that made Jojo sway side to side, her voice bright and complementing mine. At first, my voice came out dry until I warmed up and muscle memory kicked in. Singing had never truly left me, but had been resting dormant, waiting for me.

Yet, once the next song began, a lump formed in my throat. I had never heard this song before, which felt impossible given how many hymns we once sang as a family. As soon as the lyrics drifted onto the projector's screen though, I felt my heart clench reading the song title, *Light the Fire*.

I froze as the opening verse hit so deep, I didn't feel like I was singing anymore. The lyrics felt like a prayer I should have said a long time ago, but it was the chorus that truly gave me goosebumps. These weren't just any lyrics, in that moment, the lyrics felt more like confessions, asking God to renew my spirit and light the fire in my heart once again.

When I left Meadowbrook over the summer, my soul had felt weary, but back home, I had let my flame go out, no matter how hard I fought to keep it lit. More than anything, I wanted that spark back, I knew the Lord knew exactly what was on my heart, and as I sang the next verse about the power of God's healing, I felt like I was pouring out my soul. As the music swelled, I closed my eyes and imagined God holding me. Though I couldn't see or hear Him, I knew He was there with us. I wanted a faith that stood firm, not one that disappeared the moment life got hard. I wanted people to see beyond the broken parts of my story and know that I belonged to the One who never let me go.

The next line sent another chill down my spine. I sang about how God breathed a new spirit of life into me, even when I didn't deserve it, even when I pulled away, even when the weight of my mom's absence felt too heavy, and even when I stopped singing. God never left me, He simply made a way for me to find my way back to Him each and every time.

As the last note dissolved into the trees, a hush settled over the crowd again. I opened my eyes to find the sky a few shades brighter, as the sun shone through the pines. My throat was dry, my hands cold and my nose was likely bright red, but most importantly, my heart felt full.

Jojo glanced over, arms wrapped around her knees, and grinned like she was genuinely happy to hear my singing voice again. I smiled back, and it was the kind that stretched through my whole chest. From my left, Carter's hand found the small of my back and started rubbing slow circles; but when I looked back at him, his eyebrows were raised, like he was waiting for a confession.

"So what are you thinking, Dutch?" He asked.

Holding up my hands in surrender, I gave in. "Okay, okay, I'm going to do it. I'll sing with Theo."

His eyebrows as shock covered his face. "What made you change your mind?"

I exhaled a sardonic laugh and tilted my head, scrunching my nose as I said, "Singing again. Can you believe it?"

Carter pulled back, slowly nodding his head as he processed this. When he looked back at me, he just offered me a tiny shrug. "That is ironic. What's going on in that head of yours, Dutch?"

I stared ahead at the trees swaying just beyond the amphitheater. The mix of this morning combined with singing had somehow been just what I needed, to refocus on what truly mattered.

"I've just been…holding back," I said slowly, "from letting myself really feel happy singing again, but when I saw Reggie in the pool, it all finally clicked."

Carter bobbed his head like he understood, but didn't speak. He just waited while I continued.

"I used to love singing," I admitted. "It felt like a part of me, but somewhere along the way I stopped loving it. I couldn't separate singing from the way a song made me feel, but also, there were certain memories I had that I didn't want music to be tied to, so I just stopped. I actually promised myself I would never sing again."

Carter's chocolate eyes met mine as he listened. "I get that more than you probably think."

I glanced at him as he offered a half-shrug.

"Soccer wasn't something I loved at first, it was just a way to get out of my biological father's house and away from all the fighting."

I blinked, caught off guard by the honesty in his voice. Carter didn't talk about his past often, but when he did, his story always put things into perspective for me. Compared to everything he had been through, my struggles with my mom sometimes felt small. After his mom got trapped in an abusive relationship with her dealer, Carter had been sent to live with his biological dad, Dan. Carter had no idea that Dan already had a new family and no place for Carter. One day, Carter came home and Dan had simply packed up the house and left him behind, but Carter's teacher, Amy, stepped in. Her decision changed everything for Carter.

"But the more I played," he continued, "the more I realized I wasn't bad, and when I let myself be all in, soccer became something I loved instead of just being my escape."

"That's exactly how I feel," I said, before I could second-guess it.

Carter wagged his head slowly from side-to-side, offering a new idea. "Maybe taking this first step will help you fall in love with singing again."

Hearing the words tumble from his lips, made my heart skip at the phrase *fall in love*. I knew he meant the music, and he was right, but something about hearing those words in his voice made my chest flutter.

He smiled, and then bumped my shoulder lightly with his. "Besides, I can't wait to see you on stage, Dutch."

I rolled my eyes, but I couldn't hide the smile he caused if I tried. Just the thought of Carter in the crowd, cheering me on, made my heart flip in ways I could never explain.

***

My heart was still full from the morning's song service as Carter and I made our way toward the canteen. Up ahead, Carter spotted Theo leaning against the porch railing by the Craft Cabin, deep in conversation with his friend Asher. I hadn't seen Asher since summer camp, where he and Theo had been the unstoppable duo on our sports team. Since then, Asher had shot up taller, and the way his flannel hung on him made him look older than your average teenager.

I took a steady breath, unsure why I suddenly felt so nervous, but as I walked up to him, Theo's gaze met mine, and he raised a brow.

"Hey," I said, stopping in front of him. "So... I'm going to do the song with you."

Theo dipped his head, somehow amused. "Oh yeah?" He glanced at Asher like he needed someone else to confirm this was actually happening. "And... what exactly changed your mind, Mermaid?"

I shoved my hands into my coat pockets, rocking slightly on my heels. "Honestly? You kept bothering me about it."

Carter tried to hide his smirk as Asher chuckled, shaking his head. "Yeah, that sounds about right."

Theo grinned, pushing off the railing. "Fine by me. Meet me at the old shelter past the archery range during free time, and we'll run through it a few times."

Before I could respond, Carter, who'd been quiet beside me, spoke up, shooting a wink my way. "Maybe I'll stop by and be your first audience."

"No." Theo pointed at him immediately, narrowing his sharp gray eyes. "You'll distract her, and we have no time to nail the song down."

Carter held up his hands, and barked out a laugh. "I wouldn't—"

"You absolutely would," Theo cut in flatly. "No boyfriends."

Asher simply shook his head at the three of us, and I rolled my eyes, nudging Carter with my elbow. "I'll find you after, I promise."

"Don't be late," Theo called after me, already turning back to his conversation with Asher.

As Carter and I walked away, he reached for my hand, his fingers warm against mine. Before I could react, he gave me a gentle squeeze and pressed a quick kiss to the back, without a care that anyone might see. "I'm proud of you," he murmured.

When I met his gaze, warmth curled in my chest, taking in the soft, gooey look in his eyes. "Thank you, for always being there for me."

Carter smiled, giving my fingers one last squeeze before letting go. "I pinky promised, didn't I?"

That made me chuckle, but before I could say anything else, he leaned in slightly and lowered his voice, a playful glint danced in his eyes. "If I remember correctly... we sealed that promise with a kiss."

"The unbreakable vow," I said in the worst possible British accent. Suddenly, I realized we had been planning, but never got around to the Harry Potter marathon we had talked about.

Carter simply nodded. "One hundred percent, a pinky promise is just the muggle version of the unbreakable vow."

"It's been a while since our last pinky promise," I teased, nudging him gently. "I might need a reminder on how we're supposed to seal those."

He raised an eyebrow, as his grin spread slowly across his face. Carter tipped his head, but I didn't miss the faint red blush that touched his cheeks. "Challenge accepted, Dutch."

32

As the final morning breakout session ended, I slipped away from the crowd, weaving through the campers still hovering close by. I followed the narrow path that curved past the amphitheater, worn and slightly overgrown, until the old shelter Theo told me about came into view. The wooden beams creaked in the breeze, and I caught the way the structure was beginning to sag. My stomach rumbled at the idea of lunch, but the granola bar in my pocket would have to do for now. I peeled it open, and took a bite, when I finally spotted Theo perched at the far end of a weathered bench, his acoustic guitar resting on one knee. His head was down while he worked to twist his tuning pegs. Once I stepped on a dead patch of leaves, the crunch instantly made him whip his head in my direction.

"Hey," I greeted, stepping into the shelter.

"You're late, Mermaid," Theo said, shoving a sheet of paper with handwritten lyrics at me before fiddling with the guitar again.

I rolled my eyes and dropped my shoulder bag onto the worn bench across from him. "Yeah, sorry about that," I replied, not even trying to sound apologetic. "It was just a little nerve-wracking making my way down here and all. I wasn't sure if we were here to practice or if you were luring me to my untimely death."

Theo bit down on his guitar pick and met my gaze, waggling his brows. "No murder yet, I still need you to win this thing."

I reached over and swiped at his guitar strings until Theo recoiled, furrowing his brows. "Whoa now! Only I can touch Jolene."

I scoffed. "Jolene?"

"My guitar," he clarified, as if it were obvious. Gently, he patted the body of the instrument as if trying to soothe it.

I snorted. "I never would have guessed you were into country music."

Theo responded by strumming a few chords before he slapped the strings still. "Never said I was, *Jolene's* just the first song my grandpa taught me to play," he said. "Now, as for what we're singing, here goes nothing."

Without another word, he started strumming a melody, and as he sang, the lyrics struck me. They were sad but beautiful, like Theo had poured his heart into the music, singing about a love built over the years, and begging for more time together.

When Theo stopped just shy of the bridge, he looked up and shrugged. "The song's a little rough, but it's from the heart."

I stared at him, still feeling a little stunned. "Theo, it's really beautiful. Did you write that for Katie?"

His gaze flickered briefly before he replied, "Nope. Wrote it for Denny."

I narrowed my eyes at his sarcasm, but I knew that was just Theo's way of protecting himself.

"It's how I felt, or...I guess I should say, still feel," he admitted, breathing out a deep sigh as he leaned over his guitar. "I don't know, Katie said she just wanted to be friends, but she never gave us a real shot. We were so great this summer, and then as soon as we left, it was like she got cold feet or something. I know everyone thinks I'm wasting my time, but I'm not ready to give up on her without one last try."

I hesitated, not wanting to discourage him, but also, not wanting to see his heart ripped to shreds...*again*. "Are you sure you want to do this?"

Theo's usual confidence slipped for a moment before he offered an almost hopeless shrug. "I have to try, at least while she's right in front of me. Then, if she says no again, I won't have to wonder if there was something else I could've done."

His honesty surprised me because, for once, Theo was allowing himself to be vulnerable, instead of hiding behind his sarcasm. Seeing the real him reassured me that I'd made the right choice to join him in performing tonight. He definitely needed a friend for this.

"If she says no, you're really going to walk?" I asked gently, knowing how tough it felt to have to face things head on that weren't easy.

Theo's mouth twitched but he raised his brows admitting this was his final act to get her back.

I asked and leaned forward, putting my hands under my thighs. "How are you doing with all of this? Being here at camp with Katie, I mean, that's got to be tough, right?"

Theo let out a dry chuckle and leaned over his guitar, as if searching for the right words. "Being near her while she avoids me feels a lot like getting my heart run over, and then backed over... and then run over again and again."

I grimaced, trying not to picture what Theo described. "That was incredibly graphic."

Theo raised an eyebrow as if he doubted I could understand.

"When I got home, I felt stuck in this weird, torturous state of limbo." I shared. "It feels kind of hard to explain, but I felt trapped between the girl I was before summer camp and who I am now."

Theo stopped plucking at his strings and looked at me. "Well, don't we just make a winning team?" he joked. "The guy trying to win back his ex and the girl who is, *once again,* trying to rediscover who she is."

I scoffed but couldn't help grinning at his dry humor. "When you say it like that, we sound like the making of a pretty sad country song."

Theo grinned and gestured around us. "Look around, we're in the perfect place to write one. If we found a harmonica or maybe a violin I'm sure we'd have a great song on our hands."

I scoffed, then squinted at him. "You sure you're not into country music?"

"Neo-mellow and alternative rock," he corrected me, as if I should know. "But, I'll let that slide since you're clearly rusty on your music knowledge."

I shook my head as he strummed a few notes. As much as I enjoyed teasing him, my thoughts drifted back to what he'd said about Katie and how it felt to lose someone. I knew where he was coming from, especially when I thought about my mom and how my breakdown had led me to camp last summer. When I'd first arrived, I thought New Hope was the worst place on earth, but spending the summer here proved me wrong.

"You know," I said, treading carefully, "it's kind of crazy that camp was the place I wanted to run from, and now it's the one place I want to run back to."

For once, Theo didn't joke. "I know a little something about that myself."

"Oh, really?" I teased. "Theo Lockwood can relate to me being all sappy?"

Theo sighed and leaned over Jolene, wincing as he opened up. "Since we're spilling our guts and all, I'm not exactly thrilled my dad is now Chairman of the Camp Board."

I tilted my head as his news came out of left field. "Why?"

"He's probably going to make a lot of changes around here," Theo said. "My dad doesn't get what New Hope is about, and when he gets the chance, he will run this place into the ground."

I sat up straighter, feeling suddenly alarmed. "You really think your dad would ruin camp?"

Theo narrowed his eyes, offering a slow nod. "Of course I do, I've seen it back in Meadowbrook with the way he runs things as mayor. My dad hates change, and if it were up to him, Meadowbrook would stay this picture-perfect little town that never moves forward. The city council's been pushing back lately though, but it's not the first time he's faced some kind of backlash."

His words shook me as a flood of memories I hadn't pieced together until now, hit me all at once. I remembered the way Theo reacted to his dad's announcement earlier, like he didn't want to hear what he had to say. Then, over the summer, Grant had a tense but short-lived exchange with my Dad, but what struck me most is when Grant called me Natalie, *my mom's name*. I didn't know how he knew who my mom was, but I remembered the steely way he said her name.

Then there was Lou, when she mentioned the changes coming to camp while talking with Max in the kitchen. I hadn't pieced it all together before, but now I couldn't shake the feeling that whatever was happening with Grant becoming the new Chairman may not be the best thing for New Hope.

"Camp's the one place I've always been able to be myself and get away from my dad for a little while," Theo said. "Seeing him take over feels like just another way he's trying to butt into my life."

While Theo spoke, I suddenly remembered what he'd said over the summer about tension between our families. Back then, I'd been too wrapped up in everything with Lou and my mom to give it much thought, but now, Theo had my wheels turning, especially the part about something weird between his dad and my Gramps.

"I don't think he and my dad always saw eye-to-eye." Theo had said.

My grandfather had always been the kind of man I looked up to, the type of guy who helped out without expecting anything in return. I could still picture him holding an umbrella over Grams when it rained, not caring if he got soaked as long as she didn't. Once, I had seen him stop what he was doing just so he could help an elderly woman outside the Meadowbrook Mercantile load her groceries. My Gramps was kind and had more heart than anyone I had ever known. If there was bad blood between our families, I knew it hadn't started with him.

My thoughts shifted to Kelsey next. For some reason, from the moment I arrived, she'd acted like she couldn't stand me.

"Do you feel like there's still beef between our families?" I wondered out loud. "I mean, hearing the way you talk about your dad possibly ruining camp, just made me think about Kelsey who for some reason seems to think I'm public enemy number one..."

Theo gave me a quizzical look as he slowly shook his head. "I have no idea, I try to stay as far out of my own family drama as possible, so it's hard to know if there's beef with anyone else."

I felt myself deflate a little with Theo's lack of help. He must have picked up on this, as he sighed and nervously scratched the back of his neck.

"Listen, I love my sister," Theo explained, "but she's a troll and can be the worst sometimes. Is that what you're getting at?"

"I thought it was just a Lockwood thing," I joked, as he shot me a look. "No, really, I mean, Kelsey acts like I've hurt her somehow."

Theo shrugged, frustration flickering across his face. "I don't know what's been going on with her. She's been weird with me since Katie and I broke up, but I think there's more to it." He glanced over my shoulder, then back at me. "There's always been this pressure in our family, but things have only gotten worse since Kelsey started college. I think she's trying to prove herself this weekend because college kids can still come to camp, but as staff, not campers like us."

I nodded, thinking about how Hannah was here as staff this weekend, too, and I wondered if Kelsey's new role explained her sudden intensity this go around.

"She's not here as a camper this weekend," Theo added. "Kelsey helped plan the retreat. She's been buried up to her eyeballs trying to make everything perfect with Dad watching, and that kind of pressure messes with her."

"What kind of pressure?" I asked.

He scrunched his face. "The men in my family are supposed to live up to the Lockwood legacy. Grandpa was mayor, and now my dad, so of course I have to fall in line. Kelsey always wanted to make my dad proud and would kill to be in my shoes. She hates that I'm the next in line for the Meadowbrook throne."

"So, she's upset with you because she's not being pressured into a life you don't even want?" I balked.

"Yep," Theo quipped. "Crazy, right? I've always said Kelsey can be mayor, if she could even get elected. She declared political science as her major this year and has been crushing it, but, whenever she tries to tell my dad about her plans, he just pats her on the back. Then dad tells me to start applying to colleges and think about my future in Meadowbrook like there are no other options."

"Is that what you want?" I asked, wondering about the kind of pressure both Theo and Kelsey were under.

"No," he replied flatly.

His gaze drifted out toward the trees as he sighed but Theo didn't say anything more, he just went back to strumming. I knew how to take a hint, and to be honest, I was still working to process everything he had just shared with me. My thoughts spun with uncertainty about how camp could change. I didn't know if Theo was right, but I couldn't shake the dread pooling in my stomach. New Hope was my safe haven, a little slice of Heaven away from the rest of the world, and the idea of losing this place made me shudder.

As Theo strummed the opening chords of his song, I looked down at the sheet of paper he handed me earlier, reading the lyrics along with the melody. As the words jumped off the page, I felt the longing behind the words and somehow related to Theo more than ever before. I knew he had written the song for Katie, but as I read the lyrics, I knew how it felt to want something that seemed out of reach. To cling to a distant place, and to the memories built from hardship and love because that's how camp felt to me.

Even though I didn't have any answers for Theo about his future or his family, right now, that didn't seem to matter. What mattered was showing up, now that I understood the hurt he was carrying, because I had carried something similar. The more that I thought about how Theo was just bottling everything up, the more I realized I had been doing the same. I was suddenly grateful for the friends that surrounded me even when I still had my guard up and that helped me see Theo's situation differently.

Maybe getting onstage wouldn't help him win Katie back, but I hoped singing with him could help him feel less alone. Because, deep down, if the tables were turned, I hoped someone would stand by me, and beneath all the snark, I had a feeling I could count on Theo for that.

At that moment, I cleared my throat and sat up tall, ready to shake off my *what-ifs* and dive in. "So, Lockwood, are we actually going to practice or are you just going to keep up this broody musician thing you've got going?"

Theo's head snapped up as he immediately cast a sardonic smile my way. "Broody? Mermaid, I don't brood, it's called charm, and I exude it."

"Whatever you say," I replied with an eye roll. "Now let's practice, because if I'm going to sing with you, I'd rather not butcher this song in front of the entire camp."

Theo held up his hands in mock surrender. "Fine, okay, but when we win the talent show, *and we will win*, I'm taking all the credit."

I could only shake my head and glower as he took the pick from his mouth, and placed it over the guitar strings. "Just play the song, Lockwood."

Theo began strumming the chords again, and for once it was nice to be shouldering someone else's burden for a change.

33

After nearly an hour of practicing Theo's song, my throat was dry and my water bottle was empty. I was definitely out of practice, but learning a new tune also meant trying to control my breathwork. Grams' had taught me the importance of breathing with my diaphragm to hold just the right amount of air when singing. Now that I had the hang of the song, I had to focus on hitting the notes with the proper breathing. When Theo finally started tucking his guitar away, I was relieved to see him packing up, beyond ready for lunch.

"Not bad, Mermaid," Theo commended me as he gathered his things.

"That last run-through was better, right?" I wondered. The lyrics were as sweet and simple as the melody, which made learning Theo's song a breeze. The two of us wouldn't be ready for a reality show audition, but for the camp talent show, I felt well prepared.

Theo nodded. "Yeah, you're picking it up fast. You know... you kind of sound like your grandpa."

With a look of horror, I asked. "Is that supposed to be a compliment?"

Theo barked out a laugh, setting his guitar case upright beside him. "I just meant you've got the same tone as old Walt, like he taught you a thing or two."

Deciding to let that little quip slide, I folded the lyric sheet and tucked it into my pocket as I remembered Gramps behind the pulpit, guiding the congregation like a conductor. When he led the audience, he commanded the room with his ability to fill the room using only his booming voice without needing a microphone. Gramps hadn't been a professional, but he didn't need to be, he truly loved to praise God through singing, so that's what he did.

I knew Theo was just joking, but he didn't realize how much his words meant to me. Sounding like Walt Rivers wasn't just a compliment, it was a gift I got to carry with me every day. Suddenly, our earlier conversation came back to me as a question resurfaced.

"Theo, do you remember over the summer when you mentioned the weirdness between our families?"

Theo paused, hand resting on the latch of the guitar case. "Yeah?"

"It's just..." I hesitated. "Our grandfathers were church elders, right? You'd think they would have worked together, or maybe even been close."

A breeze abruptly stirred the trees, rustling Theo's golden hair as he stared at me straight on. "You're wondering what really happened, huh?"

I nodded, because I couldn't make sense of anyone not getting along with Gramps.

Theo gave a small shrug, looking unsure. "I wish I knew, but it's just been one of those old family feuds no one talks about; like our own little Meadowbrook version of the Hatfields and McCoys."

"The Rivers and the Lockwoods," I said quietly, wondering if the truth was really that bad.

"Exactly," Theo said. "I've asked my dad before, but he always brushes it off and says something vague like they had differences in opinions or whatever. I've never gotten a real answer from him."

"I'm sorry," I said softly, though I wasn't sure why. I didn't know what had caused the rift between our families, and maybe it didn't matter. Somehow, sitting across from Theo, I felt like my Gramps would be proud, and it hit me that we didn't have to let the past define the future. I didn't push any more, even though I had more questions than answers. Before either of us could say more, a familiar voice rang through the trees.

"Hey, rockstars! It's lunchtime!"

I turned to see Carter strolling down the path, with his soccer ball tucked under one arm. He kicked at a rock on the trail as I watched that easy smile of his light up his face, giving me butterflies once Carer reached my side.

"You sound amazing," he said, his voice low and warm.

My cheeks instantly flushed, as Theo gagged and picked us his guitar case. "Okay, that's my cue to get to lunch before I lose my appetite."

Carter chuckled, reaching out a hand to pull me to my feet just as Theo stopped short in front of me. I bumped into Theo's back, but before I could ask what his deal was, I heard the crunch of leaves as a sharp voice cut through the air.

"There you are." Kelsey called out. "I've been looking everywhere for you."

When I found my footing, I caught Kelsey's jaw drop as she laid eyes on me, then Carter, before zeroing in on Theo.

"You can't be serious, little brother," she said, crossing her arms. "Haven't you done enough already?"

Confused, my gaze flicked from Theo to Carter who seemed just as lost as I was.

Theo tensed. "Kels—"

She shook her head furiously, blonde curls bouncing in the sunlight. "You really think singing one song is going to fix everything between the two of you? Katie didn't dump you over one fight, she broke up with you because of her."

My stomach twisted, then sank like a stone. "What?"

Kelsey turned her glare on me, suddenly out of nowhere. "Look, this is none of my business, but I'm getting really tired of my friends getting hurt. Is this just what you do, Lena?" she asked, voice dripping with disdain. "Theo and Katie were great until you showed up. Remember all that the texting you two did after summer camp? Guess what? Katie knew and you came between those two just like you did with Carter and Riley. Why can't you just leave them alone?"

Her words felt like being splashed with cold tea all over again. I had no idea there had even been anything going on between Katie and Theo until the soccer game when Carter told me they broke up. Now I was to blame? Just for talking to a friend? Did Katie think me and Theo were sneaking around behind everyone's back? I suddenly felt sick to my stomach and even worse when I felt Carter's hand slacken in mine, then fall away. The loss of his touch stung more than any words Kelsey could hurl at me and when I gazed over, he wasn't looking at me.

"The drama just needs to end right here, right now," Kelsey demanded.

I opened my mouth, but no words came. I was speechless. This whole time I had just been trying to be a good friend to Theo and help him get Katie back. *How had things become so tangled?*

"Kelsey, stop," Carter demanded. "You know that's not true. Riley and I were done way before Lena ever came into the picture, and we're not doing this again."

I looked at Carter then, searching his face. His jaw flexed, but he looked fed up, like this was something he'd faced before.

Kelsey blinked, caught off guard by his tone, but before she could fire back, Carter reached for my hand and pulled me forward. "Come on, Lena. We're leaving."

Hearing him say my actual name made my heart pinch, he never said it, Carter always called me Dutch. Yet, even as he held onto my hand, I hesitated, glancing back at Theo who wouldn't look at me. But I couldn't read Theo's expression, he just chewed on his bottom lip, staring back at Kelsey who stood like an immovable stone statue. Whatever this was didn't feel like a fight anymore; it felt like a sibling boxing match that I hadn't asked to be tapped in for.

"Good," Kelsey snapped. "Go to lunch, that's where we're all supposed to be anyway, not hiding out here in the woods."

Her demands didn't make me flinch, though, they just irritated me because I had no idea what this girl's problem was. I didn't ask for Katie and Theo to break up, and I certainly hadn't tried to come between Riley and Carter. The way the two of them were standing off, I didn't want to leave Theo. I wanted Kelsey to hear us both out and understand what really happened.

As I worked to find my voice, Theo finally looked at me with coldness flickering in his gray eyes. "Seriously," he muttered, "just go."

Carter's hand brushed my elbow, and then without a word I let him lead me back up the path to leave the siblings behind.

Just as we crossed into the trees, I pulled back from Carter's grasp and stalled. "Wait," I whispered, feeling my dry throat crack. "That was so insane. I had no idea Kelsey or Katie thought any of those lies about me."

Carter slowed and turned, as his eyes locked on mine. He looked contemplative for a second, and I wondered what he was truly thinking about what Kelsey accused me of. "Don't worry about her. Kelsey had no right saying any of that to you."

I almost sank to my knees with relief, but I couldn't shake the feeling that he was upset over what Kelsey had said. In my mind, I went over the way I had seen him wave and smile at Riley and couldn't stop the little green monster of envy from invading my thoughts. Still, Carter had to know nothing ever happened between me and Theo. "You're not mad at me, are you?"

His head tilted slightly, like the question caught him off guard. "At you?" He let out a soft scoff and shook his head. "No, Dutch. Not even close."

Still, something about the way he raked a hand through his hair made me feel uneasy. "Kelsey completely crossed a line."

I shoved my hands into my coat pockets and slid my boot through the gravel, unintentionally stirring up rock dust. This weekend was supposed to be drama free, and here I was again, somehow hurting others without trying to.

"I can't believe Kelsey blames me for their breakup," I whispered. "That's the last thing I would want to happen."

"Hey," Carter said gently. He set his soccer ball on the ground and stepped forward, pulling me into his arms. Without hesitation, I sank into him, resting my cheek against his chest.

"I don't even know what just happened," I started unraveling. "Where did that even come from? I've never really even had a conversation with Kelsey, and she just has this idea of me that's not even true."

Carter sighed as he rested his chin lightly on my head. "Knowing Kelsey, I'd bet that has nothing to do with you and everything to do with Theo."

I pulled back just enough to look up at him. "But, she said I came between Theo and Katie and ruined everything for you and Riley too. Kelsey blamed me when I had nothing to do with any of it."

"Because it's easier to blame someone else than deal with what she's actually feeling," Carter said, putting his hands on top of my shoulders to steady me. "You're not the problem, Dutch. She's angry, but not at you. This is what Kelsey does, she stands up for her friends fiercely but sometimes does it without having all the information first."

I gulped as I met Carter's gaze. "How do you know that? She clearly said—"

"I just know," Carter interrupted. "Trust me. It's best to keep your distance and let Theo sort it out."

I nodded slowly, trying to let his advice soothe me, but I couldn't shake the fact that there was something else going on, especially when Carter looked at me the same way he did last night outside the Med Cabin. *Did he know something that I didn't?*

"You mentioned last night that there was more to it. What did you mean?" I asked, fishing for details.

Carter's gaze drifted as he glanced away for just a moment before turning back to me. "I was talking about Riley stuff, but I told you she and I are cool now. Can we just go to lunch and forget about all this Kelsey stuff right now?"

The way he said the words with a flash of annoyance made my heart sink. *Were we having our first fight?* Last summer when Carter and I first met was the first time I heard him seem frustrated by me when he had to escort me around because of my ankle, but this was different. I couldn't tell if he was upset by Kelsey or me, *unless...*

"Are you mad? About me and Theo talking?" I gaped at him. The last thing I wanted was there to be tension between us when we didn't have a lot of time left together this weekend. "Carter, he asked for advice about Katie, that was it."

Carter looked at me and for a moment, I couldn't tell what he was thinking. Then slowly, he placed his hands on his pockets and shook his head. "No, I'm not upset. I trust you, Dutch.

Theo's your friend, and I'm not the kind of guy who's going to tell you who you can and can't talk to. That's not how this works."

Still, something between us felt... unsettled. "So it doesn't bother you that me and Theo text sometimes?"

Carter chuckled as he dipped his head and raised a brow slightly. "Should it?"

Without pause, I shook my head, keeping my gaze on Carter's perfect chocolate eyes. "Never, we're just friends. That's it."

Accepting this, Carter offered up a small shrug. "Then I'm not mad. I said I trust you, and if Theo's your friend, that's okay. I've been in relationships before where an ex tried to control who I could talk to or be friends with. I'll never do that to you."

I didn't think it was possible for him to get any more perfect but there he went. "Okay, good, because I never want to do anything to mess up what we have."

Carter reached out and brushed his thumb across my cheek. "You and I are okay, Dutch, but don't let Kelsey get in your head, okay?"

Just then, I caught the way the sun flickered through the trees, turning the messy ends of his hair a shade of gold. I reached up and held my hand over his, so thankful for the way God brought him to me.

"Thank you," I whispered, smiling up at him, "for pulling me out of whatever that was."

Carter cupped my cheek and pulled me close. "I don't want anything ruining this weekend for us."

I nodded in agreement as he pressed his forehead to mine, but I had no idea what to do about Kelsey or Theo. Just when I had finally given in to the talent show, Kelsey came barreling in, making me doubt myself again.

As Carter and I walked toward the Dining Hall, each step felt like sinking into the quicksand of uncertainty. The steady ground New Hope felt like to me was beginning to shift and I had no idea where to stand anymore.

34

The warmth of the Dining Hall embraced me like it was fighting away the afternoon chill outside. Chatter and laughter rebounded off the walls and straight to my head. When the smoky, sweet aroma of barbecue drifted from the kitchen, it went straight to my rumbling belly reminding me that I was starving, despite the run-in with Kelsey that made me feel sick to my stomach.

Through the kitchen's serving window, I spotted Lou with sleeves rolled up and hair tied back helping Max in the kitchen. The sight of my aunt instantly put me at ease, she had been there for me with the social media disaster back home, and if anyone could help me make sense of the Kelsey drama, I knew Lou could.

"Carter," I called to him before we could find a seat.

He turned, raising his eyebrows expectantly.

"I'm going to go catch up with Lou," I motioned to the kitchen with my thumb. "I'll come find you though, okay?"

His gaze trailed off to the kitchen before settling back on me. The way he searched my face told me he was looking for more than I was letting on, but instead of asking, Carter just dipped his head once. "I'll find Denny and Jo," he said, a second later. "I'll save you a seat."

Carter said it so casually, but I could hear the question lingering in the air between us.

"Thanks," I said quietly, offering a small smile, hoping I could convince him everything was okay. "I'll be over soon."

Carter gave a small nod then turned to find his seat. As much as I wanted to follow him and have lunch without a care in the world, I couldn't just let the Kelsey thing go like Carter wanted me to. She was accusing me of lies that weren't true, but on top of that, there was a history between our families that I wanted answers to. Somehow, I felt like Lou was the key to figuring out what happened.

The moment I stepped into the kitchen, Lou looked up from the prep counter where she was filling a dish with fries and beamed.

"Well, there's my favorite niece," Lou said as she wiped her hands on her apron. "How are you, Lenny?"

"I'm alright," I said, already moving toward her. There were several unopened bags of sandwich buns on the counter, and a tray of cooked barbecue that still needed to be put together. "Can I help?"

Lou nodded, scooting over as her gaze flicked up briefly to check on me. "You're *just* alright?"

I grabbed a pair of nylon gloves from the table and slipped them on, settling in next to her. Max darted past to grab the pile of fries and cheered when he spotted me. "Perfect! An extra set of hands in this jungle. What's up, Lena?"

"Hey Max! Lunch smells amazing," I said, forcing a smile.

He smirked, like I'd said something obvious. "Of course it does, I'm cooking."

Lou rolled her eyes but kept working, assembling sandwiches like a pro. "Everything okay?"

I pursed my lips but shook my head, getting busy with the task in front of me. Grabbing a fresh bun, I filled it with a scoop of barbecue and added it to the fresh tray to serve. "Kelsey Lockwood just chewed my head off."

Lou froze to stare back at me with wide-eyes. "She did what?"

I looked around, making sure no one could overhear me before filling her in. "Me and Theo were down at the old shelter practicing for the the talent show—"

"Oh honey, that's great!" Lou exclaimed. "Are you singing the duet with him?"

"I am," I shared before continuing. "When we were done, we were heading to lunch, and then Kelsey just appeared out of nowhere. She started blaming me for his breakup with Katie and accused me of ruining her friend's relationships."

She slowly shook her head, letting out a groan loud enough to get Max's attention. "What now?" he asked.

Lou waved him off and lowered her voice. "She just started accusing you?"

I shrugged, helplessly. "Kelsey thinks Katie dumped Theo because of me."

"But you have a boyfriend," Lou said, frowning. "A boyfriend who is also Theo's friend and teammate, Kelsey knows that."

Scooping another pile of barbecue on a bun, I tucked another completed sandwich into the tray, feeling much better at how ridiculous all of this sounded to Lou, too. Still, as wild as Kelsey's outburst seemed, there were other questions I had.

"I think there's more to it, Lou," I admitted, eyeing her carefully.

She paused, her scoop hovering midair as she flicked her gaze at me. "Like what?"

I finished another sandwich and lowered my voice. "Theo said something about our families having a falling out."

Lou's hands stilled, and I watched her mouth pull into a tight line as she glanced toward Max.

"What is it?" I glanced between the two of them, slowly placing another sandwich on the pile.

Max set his tray down and walked over, facing my aunt head on. "Tell her, Louie. If the Lockwood kids are dragging her into this, Lena deserves to know what she's walking into."

Then, with a sad shrug, Max picked the tray back up and slipped through the swinging doors, leaving me and Lou to talk. Around us, a few of Max's staff bustled around, filling trays and stacking dirty dishes in the sink, but the space between me and Lou felt still, as if she were frozen.

She had a bleak look on her face, as if my question had filled her with dread. I felt my heart speed up as I stripped the gloves off my hands to grab a nearby stool to sit on. "Lou, what's going on? What don't I know about the Lockwoods?"

Lou sighed as she stripped off her own gloves and ran the back of her hand down her face. She took the other stool nearby to sit and face me. "Lenny, don't think for a second that you're to blame for other people's relationships. This is much bigger than that."

I sat up straight and leaned in, trying to still the nerves building in my chest. "I've figured that much," I said, looking at her. "Theo told me our families didn't get along, but Kelsey's acting like I showed up here just to wreck everything, like I'm the only one to blame."

Lou nodded slowly as her eyes grew weary. "That's because Kelsey's repeating what she's heard her whole life. The family stuff goes back decades, sweetheart, all the way back to your grandpa Walt and Theo's grandfather."

My eyes widened. "Wait...all the way back to Gramps? That's how long something's been going on?"

Her eyes filled with regret as Lou slowly nodded. She folded her arms and leaned back against the counter like she was making herself comfortable. "Your grandpa Walt was a good man. He loved Meadowbrook deeply, but he didn't grow up here. When he and my mom passed through Meadowbrook on their honeymoon, their car broke down just outside the city limits." Lou paused, smiling faintly, as if she were picturing it. "That's how they met Harold Lockwood."

"Harold..." I tilted my head, trying to place the name. "Is that Theo's grandfather?"

"Great-grandfather," Lou corrected. "He owned the old Soda Shoppe back then, it was the local diner favorite before Max's was even a thought. My parents stopped into the Soda Shoppe to wait for a tow truck, but they met Harold and their lives completely changed."

"Because of Harold?" I asked, trying to follow.

"Exactly," Lou said, crossing one leg over the other. "Harold and his wife invited my parents to their house when their car repairs took longer than expected. Harold offered them a place to stay and that night, he ended up talking to my folks about Jesus."

"You're kidding." I said, feeling bewildered. It seemed ironic that my Gramps' faith was inspired by the Lockwood's, considering the encounter I had with Kelsey before lunch.

"Scout's honor," Lou continued. "The next morning, Harold helped my parents get back on the road, but they never forgot his kindness or Meadowbrook. So, a few months later, my parents changed course. The two of them left South Carolina behind to move to Meadowbrook for good."

I blinked, trying to picture my Gramps as a young newlywed, starting a life in a place he had never planned on settling down in. If he seemed so happy in Meadowbrook, I wondered where everything went wrong.

"So... did something happen between him and Harold?" I pressed.

Lou shook her head, though her eyes filled with a wistful look. "Not between them. Harold and my dad were so close, no one would have known they weren't father and son. Harold was the type of man who would give a stranger the shirt off his back without ever asking for a favor in return. He had money because he invested, but Harold also believed in investing in people. He helped others see their potential, and your grandpa was one of those who Harold truly believed in."

She paused for a moment as if recalling a painful memory. I felt a knee-jerk reaction to reach out to her, but Lou looked back up at me, seeming more steady.

"I don't know if your mom ever told you, but when my dad came home from the war, he wasn't the same. My dad carried his experiences with him everyday, but he never talked about what happened. Harold gave him more than just a job, he gave him direction and taught him a sense of community, but mostly, Harold gave my dad something to believe in again. Eventually, they started River Ridge Realty together."

"I didn't know that," I murmured, feeling shocked as I processed just how deeply intertwined our family was with the Lockwoods.

Lou shifted in her seat, nodding slowly. "But when Harold passed away, his death hit your grandpa hard. Though, I think what hit even harder was when Harold's son, Teddy, came back to town. That's when everything really changed."

"Teddy?" I asked, trying to keep up. "That's Theo's grandfather, right?"

Lou nodded again, but this time the light in her eyes dimmed, and I didn't miss the way she folded her arms tightly across her chest.

"Teddy had been gone for years, off in the city building a career. He didn't come home until after Harold died, and when he did, it was like he expected to step right into his father's shoes." She said.

"Are you saying Teddy didn't?" I asked, wondering what happened next.

Lou's lips tightened as she shook her head. "Oh he most certainly tried, but he and your grandpa clashed from the outset. Your grandpa believed in Harold's vision of growth for Meadowbrook. Harold saw our town as a place that could expand without losing its heart. Your grandpa believed in progress that meant reaching more people, just like what Harold has always done."

I leaned forward again, feeling the tension grow. "So what happened with Teddy?"

Lou let out a slow, heavy sigh, like she didn't want to say. "Teddy thought changing things meant compromising. He didn't want Meadowbrook to change because he viewed outsiders coming in as a threat. For Teddy, preserving Harold's legacy meant keeping things exactly the way they were and leaving it alone. But your grandpa wanted to invest in outsiders who wanted to make Meadowbrook their new home, just as Harold had done for him and my mom."

My thoughts were spinning as I processed our family history. I had never heard any of this before, and the way both mom and Lou had always talked about their love for Meadowbrook, I would have never guessed there was any family feud between ours and the Lockwoods.

"So that's what started the rift?" I asked, searching Lou's face for more answers.

I watched as my aunt nodded, leaning her head on her hand. "Teddy and my dad had two completely different visions for Meadowbrook's future, and neither one was willing to bend back then to make any sacrifices."

When I pictured Gramps coming to blows with Teddy, it was impossible for me to see him being confrontational. I had never witnessed any other version of him than the one who sang with me, who taught me how to fish in his pond, and who led me proudly through the streets of downtown Meadowbrook like I was the apple of his eye.

"Did things get worse between them?" I wanted to know. Something had to explain the weird tension besides a difference in opinion.

Lou scrunched her face as if she didn't want to say but carried on anyway. "Things between them really soured after Harold's will was read. They found out he'd left a portion of his estate to your grandpa because Harold's will stated my dad was like a second son to him."

I sucked in a breath, knowing it really did get worse. "Teddy didn't take that well, did he?"

"Not even a little," Lou said, pursing her lips. She glanced toward the floor before continuing. "Especially not when your grandpa started talking about Harold's dream for the Soda Shoppe. My dad wanted to turn the Shoppe into a pay-what-you-can café, a place where people could work for their meals, with no questions asked. He saw it as a way to honor Harold while still keeping the Soda Shoppe operational."

My brows lifted suddenly when I thought about seeing the old Soda Shoppe every time I was in Meadowbrook, in the heart of downtown. "Isn't it a historical landmark now?"

"It is," Lou said, but her tone was flat. "But that wasn't what Harold wanted. Teddy turned the place into a monument so the building would always stand tall and no one could ever change it."

To me, the Soda Shoppe had always been a beautiful pit-stop when touring Meadowbrook. Everyone loved to stop in and tour the old restaurant because of its history. The Shoppe was a deep-seated Meadowbrook treasure. "The building is amazing, was it really so bad to preserve the Shoppe?"

Lou's lips twitched, but not with amusement. "Sure, it is amazing, but imagine giving someone your final wishes and watching them do the opposite of what you asked."

The hypothetical question was crushing. "I'd be heartbroken."

She wrinkled her nose sadly before explaining further. "That's exactly how your grandpa felt. He took Harold's final wishes seriously, but it only got worse when Teddy began selling off Harold's other properties. Places your grandpa and Harold had talked about turning into affordable homes or rentals for local families. These were dreams they had shared, hoping to one day make them a reality."

"All because Gramps was in the will?" I asked in disbelief.

Lou's eyes met mine, sure and steady. "Because Teddy had a hard, bitter heart. Harold always prayed Teddy would come home and fall in love with Meadowbrook. He wanted Teddy to carry his vision forward, but Teddy never saw Meadowbrook the way Harold or your grandpa did. He just saw a small town that couldn't give him what he truly wanted."

"Was that it?" I grimaced. "All the business stuff and the inheritance is what started the feud?"

Lou scrunched her face again and closed her eyes as she shook her head from side-to-side.

Sitting across from her wide-eyed, my jaw dropped. "You mean there's more?"

"Their paths crossed almost everywhere," Lou shared. "Both Teddy and my dad served as elders in the church later, and the hurt just got deeper and deeper, spreading through business, church, and further down the road to camp, too." She paused, and I noticed her voice grow soft. "When your grandpa finally used part of his inheritance to start New Hope, he actually invited Teddy to be a part of it. He wanted to heal things between the two of them, and finally build something lasting in Harold's name."

My eyebrows rose once the shock set-in. "Gramps started camp?"

A small, proud smile spread over Lou's face. "He did. Your grandpa thought that if he and Teddy could finally work together, then they could really build something lasting, like Harold had wanted all along."

"The name New Hope...." I trailed off, still working to put two-and-two together. "Is camp named for the hope of a new beginning between our families?"

Lou chuckled but shook her head. "Some people speculate that's why, but those who really knew your grandpa know the real truth. He named camp, *New Hope,* for the place it was meant to be. These grounds were meant to be a refuge from all the craziness we all face in our everyday lives. Camp was meant to be a place for us to find a new hope that is only found in Jesus, not in the world.

Pride bloomed in my chest as I thought about Gramps and all the effort he poured into making this camp my favorite place in the world. When I pictured myself walking the grounds he had found and worked so hard to build from the ground up, my heart soared. Yet, as I thought about the way Theo said his dad could run camp into the ground, I felt a wave of panic and wondered if Gramps' plan worked out as he'd hoped.

"If Gramps and Teddy built this place... why didn't Gramps' plan work to bring them together?"

Lou leaned forward, her expression darkening slightly. "Once people in town and in church found out about their differences, everyone started taking sides." She exhaled slowly, before saying. "Your grandpa stepped down as an elder before the conflict could drag our family through the mud."

My stomach sank. "But why? None of this sounds like it was Gramps' fault. He was doing the right thing. Teddy just sounds so...*impossible*."

Lou leaned in, and I caught a flicker of determination in her eyes. "Sometimes, faithful people have to make the worst choice, especially when a personal battle threatens to become a spiritual one." Pursing her lips, she added. "Your grandpa knew what God's Word says about church leaders. In his position, your grandpa was to be above reproach, temperate, gentle, not quarrelsome, and a peacemaker. So when his and Teddy's disagreements started to cause division in the church, he felt like he was no longer eligible to continue in a church leadership role."

My head was spinning as I imagined my grandpa silently stepping down to keep the church in one piece. I had loved him while he was alive, but knowing Gramps was gone now, I wished I could have told him just how much he meant to me, and still did.

Her eyes dropped to the countertop as Lou continued. "Your grandpa didn't believe he could serve effectively without living peaceably with others, so he stepped down to protect the people he loved and be obedient to God."

I swallowed hard, fighting tears prickling behind my eyes. "I never knew any of this, Lou."

Just then, Lou reached out to me, cupping my chin gently in her hand. "That's the kind of man your grandpa was," she added. "Humble, faithful, and willing to lay down his position if it means making sure no one stumbles in their Christian walk."

My chin quivered as I thought about Gramps and how much I admired him more and more. "What happened with Teddy?"

Lou winced and could only offer me a tiny shrug. "He carried on as an elder but his bitterness ran deeper than I think any of us ever realized. Now, it seems Grant, Teddy's son, shares his father's opinions of our family."

I swallowed, my pulse pounding. "And Kelsey?"

"I believe she's only ever heard the version of the story she was told," Lou said softly. "To her, the Rivers are the reason her family has been disrespected, we are the threat to the Lockwood legacy. I'm sure Kelsey's just trying to protect what she believes is right."

I leaned forward, resting my elbows on the counter, still trying to process just how far down the rabbit hole our two families' ties went. Camp was supposed to be my safe place, or at least that's what I thought. Now I realized, camp was my family legacy, a place my Gramps had built from the ground up. *How had everything been turned upside down?*

"Lou... does this mean I have to choose?" I whispered, my heart feeling heavy. "Between being friends with Theo and being loyal to our family?"

Quickly, she shook her head and reached across the counter to hold my hand in hers. "No, honey, don't ever feel like you have to choose between anyone because of history that's not yours to hold onto."

Leaning forward, I ran my fingers through my hair before placing my head in my hands. "I don't know what to do, Lou. Kelsey has the wrong idea about everything, and I think she's trying to turn Theo against me. Should I just take a lesson from Gramps' playbook and walk away?"

Lou gave me a sad smile and reached out to push the hair out of my eyes. "Lena, no. Think about it like this... what if you're exactly where God wants you to be? What if He wants you to be a bridge, or a light even, to show others there is a better way to move forward?"

I let out a shaky breath and stared at the floor, trying to make sense of everything. Camp was supposed to be my place of peace, my escape, but now, because of Kelsey, it was beginning to feel like a game of tug-of-war where I was caught in the middle. My thoughts were spinning a million miles per hour, but when I looked at Lou again, I remembered what she said about her fears that camp would change, and I had to know what she meant.

"Theo said Grant's had a lot of push-back in town over business decisions. Are his decisions affecting River Ridge?"

Lou's mouth pressed into a tight line, though reluctant at first, she answered. "I run a business, sweetie. When the mayor makes decisions, sometimes they affect lives and the livelihoods of local businesses. They won't always make popular choices to say the least."

Theo's concern made more sense now. "So... what does that mean for camp?" I asked quietly. "If Grant's in charge now, what will happen to New Hope?"

Lou squeezed my hand again. "Camp isn't going anywhere. I only told you all of this so you could hear the truth from me, not Kelsey, or anyone else. This is for your ears only, okay?"

I squeezed her hand back, promising not to breathe a word of this. "I just... wish I'd known sooner."

Lou turned toward me, brows lifting. "Why would you have treated Kelsey or Theo any differently?"

My gaze wandered around the kitchen as I shrugged, feeling uncertain. "I wouldn't have but I also wouldn't have agreed to do the duet with Theo. The last thing I need is more drama, especially not at camp."

My aunt studied me for a moment and reached out to turn my head, forcing me to look back at her. "Lena, you can't change the past or control what Kelsey thinks, but what you can control is how much power you let her have over you."

I blinked, voice barely above a whisper. "But what if Kelsey's right? I mean, what if without trying I really have ruined everything?"

Lou's face softened. "Lena, honey, stop. I know how much you've been through this year, but don't let your pain or anyone else's convince you that you're a problem. Kelsey's just telling her version of the truth, but that's not the full story."

I nodded slowly, though the knot in my chest didn't untangle. "What should I do now?"

Lou gave a small laugh. "I can't tell you how to move forward, honey."

Before I could protest, Lou held up her pointer finger, silently asking me to let her finish. "But what I will say is think about Theo. Think about the kind of friend he's been and ask yourself if he's ever treated you any differently because of the family name you bear."

I hesitated and considered Lou's advice. Even when Theo mentioned weirdness between our families, he never treated me differently.

"No," I said honestly. "He's only ever treated me like everyone else. Well, except for Denny. He treats everyone better than Denny."

Lou chuckled. "Then pay attention to the truth you see, not what you've been told. That's how you make your choice."

I nodded as I heaved a deep sigh, soaking in every word.

"Remember what Adam said last night," she added. "You know why you're here. Don't let Kelsey or anyone else convince you that you're anything other than who God says you are."

"I needed that," I replied, feeling my voice crack.

Lou's smile reached all the way up to her eyes. "My dad used to tell me when I was younger, we don't get to choose what others say or how they treat us, but we do get to choose how we treat them." She paused to turn her head and sniffle before looking back at me, her eyes brimming with tears. "When you told me about buying that girl a new tea in the cafeteria that day at school, all I could think about was my dad, because that's exactly what your Gramps would've done."

I felt my eyes swell up then. "Really?"

Lou nodded as she swiped at her eyes. "He wasn't a perfect man, he had many flaws, like we all do, but my dad lived with integrity. If someone ever accused him of doing wrong, no one believed it. You're walking in his footsteps, Lena. If he were here, he would tell you to keep your eyes on Jesus and let Him guide your path."

"Thanks, Lou." My voice wavered, her encouragement radiating through every part of me. Now that I knew the truth, I knew I had a choice to make, but one thing was crystal clear. I wouldn't let the past decide my future.

35

My head was still swimming after lunch as I made my way down to the amphitheater with Carter. After all I heard from Lou, my appetite had been squashed though I managed to choke down a sandwich before Carter came to find me and we helped Max and Lou clean up. Thoughts whirled around my brain like the fall breeze gently rustling the colorful trees around us. I still had no idea what to do about the talent show and the thought of running into Kelsey or Theo made my stomach sink. My first instinct was to run and hide, but after yesterday's lesson and hearing all my family history, that was the last thing I wanted to keep doing. Shying away from my problems had never truly solved them in the first place.

Interrupting my racing thoughts, I felt Carter reach for my hand, his cold fingertips pulling me out of my head.

"You're quiet." He pointed out, eyeing me with curious interest.

"Sorry, I'm just thinking." I said, making a spinning gesture to describe my head.

Carter chuckled, "I can see that, Dutch. We can talk about it, you know? Whatever's on your mind."

I gave him a sheepish smile as the chatter beyond the treeline came within earshot. Carter had told me earlier that he wanted to forget what Kelsey had said, but there was so much more to the story now that I just couldn't, not when it affected how I would move forward with the talent show and even my friendship with Theo.

As we reached the end of the trail, Carter gave my hand a squeeze before letting go once we were no longer alone.

"Maybe later." I told him, while we both searched the crowd.

I couldn't see any of our friends until Jojo popped up and started frantically waving both arms as if stranded on an island and signaling a rescue team. Carter chuckled as the two of us found our way over. Denny was seated on the ground next to Jojo, but next to him sat a quiet Theo. I felt my heart pick up speed, all of a sudden, feeling anxious at the sight of him. He sat hunched over with his elbows resting on his knees, slowly turning a yellow leaf between his fingers. Theo didn't look up once as Carter and I sat on the complete other side of Jojo, he merely kept his gaze locked, spinning the leaf in his hand.

My brain felt like the leaf in Theo's hand as my head spun around and around. I had never lost friends before because of family history, so trying to navigate this new territory felt foreign to me. I couldn't help but wonder what they had talked about when Carter and I left Theo and Kelsey at the shelter. *Had they fought? Was he going to avoid me now? Were we even friends anymore?* The more I wondered, the more I found myself stealing glances at Theo, trying to somehow get a read on him. Yet, Theo never looked up, he just kept turning that leaf as if in a trance.

Before I could get lost any deeper in my thoughts, Preacher Adam stepped to the front of the amphitheater. His presence alone was enough to silence the crowd's chatter as he opened his Bible and began this afternoon's lesson.

"We're continuing in the Book of Daniel, chapter three," he shared, scanning the crowd. "This chapter highlights one of the most valiant moments we read about when three young men choose to stand firm in their identity in God, even when it meant defying an entire kingdom."

There was a rustling of pages as campers began to flip in their Bibles while Adam carried on.

"Shadrach, Meshach, and Abednego were faced with an impossible choice, they could either bow to a golden idol or stand boldly for God. These young men had to look beyond their survival instincts and decide whether they would keep their allegiance to God or fall before the king.

The word *allegiance* grabbed my attention as Adam spoke. In a way, I felt like I had a similar decision to make, to choose between friendship or walking away. Yet, as the lesson continued, Adam's message became even more clear. Daniel and his friends weren't just choosing sides, they were determined to stand firm in their faith to God no matter what it cost them.

Adam read on, "Daniel 3:17–18 says '*If we are thrown into the blazing furnace, the God we serve is able to deliver us from it... But even if He does not, we want you to know, O king, that we will not serve your gods or worship the image of gold.*'"

Even if He does not.

I felt goosebumps hearing those words the more Adam drove his point home. Shadrach, Meshach, and Abednego's faith stood boldly because they understood the power of God. The three of them knew God didn't promise He would rescue them, but they knew Who was with them even when life felt impossible. They never quit, even if God didn't show up in the ways they hoped. The lesson pierced me to my core, bringing my earlier chaotic thoughts to a halting stop.

Adam raised his voice, as she went on. "Daniel and his friends chose to stand and not bow because they knew they served a God far greater than any earthly kingdom, even if their decision cost them their lives."

I glanced sideways and caught Carter's eyes on me. He lifted his brows slightly, and he dipped his head as if asking if I was okay. I gave him a small nod, then turned back to Adam, though my eyes briefly caught sight of Theo, who still hadn't moved.

When I faced the front, I tried focusing on Adam, but Lou's earlier words came back to me. *We don't get to choose what others say or how they treat us, but we do get to choose how we treat them.* Theo hadn't once treated me like I was enemy number one, even when Kelsey clearly believed I was. In his own sarcastic way, Theo had only ever made me feel like I belonged, even when I wasn't sure I did.

As the lesson sank in, I felt a familiar guilt settle in my chest as I thought about how much I was letting Kelsey's lies shake me.

"Because the three young men didn't bow, the king ordered the fiery furnace to be heated seven times hotter than usual," Adam continued, pulling me back to the present. "The fire was so hot that the flames killed the guards who threw them in. But then, in verse twenty-five, scripture tells us that King Nebuchadnezzar jumped to his feet and said, *'Look! I see four men walking around in the fire, unbound and unharmed, and the fourth looks like the Son of God.'*"

A stillness settled over the amphitheater, and I gulped, feeling like I was standing in my own fiery furnace.

"These young men weren't alone in the fire," Adam said, his voice filled with awe. "God didn't just intercede and pull them out of the flames, He met them inside the fire. Scripture tells us when the king called them out of the fire, they walked out unscathed. Not a hair on their heads had been singed or even their clothes. They didn't even smell like smoke."

He paused, letting that truth settle into our hearts. A moment later, Adam's voice softened as he said. "After that, the king who once mocked their faith now praised their God. He promoted Shadrach, Meshach, and Abednego, and declared that no one could ever speak against a God that saves His people from the flames."

I felt a lump in my throat as I sat in awe thinking of the God who meets us in the middle of our most difficult challenges and never lets us walk through the fires of life alone. The God who never lets us be consumed by the troubles of life, but saves us, and gives us a way out.

Adam closed his Bible gently and lifted his gaze to meet the crowds. "So, what does that mean for us?"

No one said a word as Adam gazed into the crowd.

"It means that standing up for God may cost you something..." he said, pausing to let those words sink in. "But your choice will never cost you God, no matter what fires we face in this life, we know that God will be with us and will provide us with a way out."

His words struck me and I couldn't help but wonder, *is that what was happening to me?* Everything that had happened this year at school, and now Kelsey and Theo, and our family's past, was it all a fire I had been walking through? Even though I'd been trying to escape, was I supposed to stand in the flames and wait for God to make a way for me?

Adam threw out another thought-provoking question. "So, what about you? What fire are you standing in right now? Who or what is asking you to bow?"

I felt my stomach twist as I thought about how camp was supposed to feel like an escape from the fire I left behind in Freeport. Instead, I'd stepped straight into another blazing inferno here at New Hope, one I never saw coming.

"What are you choosing to stand firm in instead of your faith?" Adam asked. "Is it comfort? Are you trying to control the situation on your own? Or, are you seeking the approval of others?"

Each question chipped away at me. *How many times had I let fear decide my path for me? How many times had I kept quiet just trying to keep the peace?* Little by little, I'd bowed at school, at work, and even here at camp instead of standing up for what I knew was right.

As Adam's lesson hit home, I knew I didn't have all the answers, but I was done letting my fears control me. I didn't want to bow to Kelsey's lies or stay trapped by the past I couldn't change. I wanted to stand boldly in my faith and do what was right, no matter what it cost me.

As a gentle breeze brushed a few fallen leaves across the pavement, I looked up as the trees in the distance billowed, watching more golden leaves float to the ground. The thing about leaves was they didn't resist change, their nature was simply to let go.

When I pictured all the battles I'd been trying to fight silently, I realized I was trying to be in control instead of surrendering each situation to God. As I watched leaves fall in the distance, it hit me that letting go didn't mean giving up. Letting go meant standing quietly in surrender to make room for God to bring about something new.

What Adam said next made my heart soar. "Isaiah 43:2 says, *'When you walk through the fire, you will not be burned; the flames will not set you ablaze.'* You don't have to fear the fire when the One who walks beside you commands it."

The verse felt like confirmation as I thought about the fears I was holding onto, they couldn't hold a match to the God who went before me. At that moment I knew I didn't need Kelsey's approval to stand, and I didn't need to explain my friendship with Theo or apologize for a family feud I had nothing to do with.

I let my gaze drift back over to Theo once more, but I noticed the leaf he had been spinning had slipped from his fingers. The golden stem now rested on the ground before him, like he had finally let go of whatever had been bothering him too.

In that moment, I knew it was time for me to start choosing faith over fear, and as the final prayer was spoken, I bowed my head and prayed. I prayed for Kelsey and for all the pain that made her believe I was her enemy. Then, I prayed for Theo, for the quiet battles he was fighting that I might never know; and finally, I prayed for myself. I asked God to help me stand boldly just like Daniel, even if the outcome wasn't what I hoped for.

With each worry and fear I prayed for, I felt lighter and lighter, surrendering my fears like leaves scattering in the wind. I knew God had brought me this far, and I trusted Him to walk with me into whatever came next. As I clung to His truth, I knew I had no control over Kelsey's heart, but I did have control over mine.

36

While Carter, Denny and Jojo stood cackling beside me, as I watched Theo disappear into the crowd, quietly slipping away after the lesson. I didn't know what had pushed him to leave like that, but I wanted to make sure we were okay. Before my nerves could get the best of me, I pulled out my phone to message him.

> Me: Still on for the talent show?

My thumb hovered cautiously for a moment before I took a deep breath and hit send. To my surprise, the screen immediately lit up with three dots, then a reply.

> Theo Lockwood: I'm still game if you are.

I breathed a sigh of relief but still wanted him to know that his sudden, elusive behavior was confusing.

> Me: I wasn't sure if you changed your mind.

I pressed send again, hoping for some reassurance that Kelsey hadn't turned him against me, especially if I was going to feel comfortable singing with him onstage tonight.

> Theo Lockwood: I don't care what Kelsey thinks, I have something to say.

I paused, and felt my stomach sink as I read his text. Theo's reply didn't exactly bring me comfort, but before I could worry anymore over the cryptic text, Jojo squealed in excitement, almost making me drop my phone.

"We've got free time!" She announced. "Which means we're going to the craft cabin!"

Denny groaned. "Jo... why?"

Jojo stepped in front of Denny and planted her hands on her hips. "Because it's fun and I want to paint pumpkins."

Carter smirked and nudged Denny. "Or, we could hit the ropes course."

"Yes! Finally, a good idea," Denny said, throwing his hands up. "Way better than painting pumpkins."

Jojo squinted at her boyfriend. "Okay, compromise. Crafts first, then the ropes course."

Carter and Denny exchanged a look, then sighed.

"Fine," Carter said, winking at me.

"But only if there are no rules against smashing the pumpkins after," Denny added.

Jojo rolled her eyes but grinned. "You can smash your own pumpkins, not mine."

As we started down the path, Carter placed a hand on my shoulder and leaned in quietly. "Are you still thinking about Kelsey?"

I shook my head, because the truth was, I was worried about Theo. "I was just making sure Theo and I are still doing the duet tonight."

Carter made an *Oh* shape with his mouth, as if he hadn't realized what happened in the woods with Kelsey and Theo may have altered my talent show plans. "You guys aren't letting Kelsey ruin your plans are you?"

With a flash of a grin, I shook my head again, finally feeling brave enough to stand on my own. "Not even a little bit."

That made him smile. "Good."

Suddenly, Denny stiffened and stopped in his tracks, forcing me and Jojo to side-step so we wouldn't run into him. His eyes locked on a camper taking a slow bite of what looked like a small pastry.

"Is that—" Denny whispered.

The three of us followed his gaze, as Carter clapped a hand on Denny's shoulder. "That's an apple turnover, my friend."

Denny cupped his hands around his mouth and called out, "Hey dude, where'd you get that?"

The camper looked up and around until he spotted Denny, "The canteen." Then he took another bite and made his way down the hill.

That was all Carter and Denny needed, because without another word, they spun on their heels and bolted toward the canteen at breakneck speed.

Jojo sighed, shaking her head. "They're unbelievable."

I chuckled and shrugged, feeling lighter than I had in hours. "Maybe they'll bring us one back."

"I'm not waiting to find out," she replied, yanking on my elbow.

Jojo and I reached the craft cabin just as others were filing in. Inside, a long table was set up with mini pumpkins in orange, yellow, and white, alongside jars of acrylic paint and paintbrushes in all shapes and sizes.

I picked up a mini-pumpkin, rolling the stem between my fingers. "These are so cute."

Jojo grabbed a brush, inspecting the bristles. "They're way better than last year's pinecone turkeys."

I giggled and once we picked our colors, we found a seat at a nearby table. Jojo glanced at me, lifting a brow. "So, how did practice with Theo go?"

Dipping my tiny paintbrush into a bright red, I swirled it along my pumpkin and replied. "The song he wrote was easy to pick up, but now Kelsey's making it a whole thing."

Jojo's brow arched as her lips pressed into a fine line. "Carter mentioned something about that at lunch, how typical of her."

I glanced up, not expecting her to say that. "Typical how?"

She gave a small shrug as she picked up her pumpkin and began brushing paint across the top. "When I was a freshman, Kelsey and I were actually best friends. She's a year older than me, so it was fun to be friends with the cool girl who didn't mind hanging out with someone her brother's age. We used to be so close I even told her I liked Denny, and when we all started hanging out, we all had a ton of fun until out of nowhere Denny asked her out and she said yes."

My jaw hit the floor. "Wait, really?"

"Yep," she said, emphasizing the P as she dipped her brush in paint to sweep another swirl across her pumpkin. "The date wasn't even the worst of it."

I frowned, focusing solely on Jojo instead of my pumpkin. "Why? What happened?"

Jojo gave me a half-smile, but it didn't quite reach her eyes. "I had to hear all about their first kiss the next night at youth group"

The hits just kept coming. "I can't believe it. Did you ever confront her?"

She shrugged again, surprisingly seeming unphased. "I didn't, because there was nothing I could do about it, so I just decided to love Kelsey from afar. I couldn't trust her anymore, but it didn't matter because she dumped Denny a few weeks later."

I shook my head in disbelief, then grimaced at the thought. "The idea of the two of them together is bizarre."

Jojo chuckled. "Right? Thankfully, we can laugh about it now."

As I carefully painted a golden sun on my pumpkin, I found myself hoping everything with Kelsey could be something to laugh about in the future just like Jojo could. Still, knowing her history with Kelsey, I couldn't help but wonder what her opinion of the Lockwood family was.

"Earlier, when Theo and I were practicing, he opened up about his family." I glanced at her. "What do you think about them?"

Jojo set her brush down and leaned back to stretch and flashed her eyes at me. "I feel kind of sorry for Theo, and even Kelsey, in a way."

I tilted my head, curiously. "Why?"

"Because they're just... a product of their family," Jojo said, her voice softer. "My parents always told me that when people act like Kelsey, there's usually something deeper going on. Like one minute she's your best friend and then the next she'll stop at nothing to get what she wants. Their family seems so perfect from the outside, but they work way too hard to keep up that image."

I let that sink in and finally understood what Theo meant when he said he wanted to escape his dad sometimes.

"But Theo isn't like that, right?" I asked, dragging my brush to paint another sunray on my pumpkin.

Jojo immediately shook her head. "Theo can go into dark mode sometimes, but I think it's just because of how much his family bugs him. When he gets like that, we just give him space and try our best."

I let out a small laugh, shaking my head. "Easier said than done." I hesitated before adding, "The Lockwoods really are a piece of work, huh?"

Jojo let out an exaggerated sigh, dipping her brush into soft green paint. "That family is far from perfect, no matter how much they want people to believe otherwise."

As she painted, I felt the weight of her words because I knew how it felt for people to have opinions about family problems, but I also knew how tough it was when those opinions were true.

The sound of hurried footsteps on the stairs made us glance up. Carter and Denny stood in the entryway, both wearing victorious grins. Carter's eyes found mine, and he lifted a brown paper bag, bouncing it up and down before they raced over to us.

Denny reached in and pulled out two apple turnovers, wrapped in napkins. "We figured you two might need a snack before we conquer the ropes course."

"Still warm," Carter added, waving one in front of my face with his dazzling smile

Jojo accepted the other from Denny and gave him a playful look. "Took you long enough."

Carter turned to me just as I took a bite, and let the flaky appley goodness melt on my tongue.

Jojo let out a satisfied groan as she beamed. "I love fall!"

"This is delicious," I said, brushing a crumb from my lip, glancing back at Carter "Thanks for thinking of me."

I watched as a dimpled smile spread over his handsome face. "I always think of you, Dutch," he said sincerely. "But in all honesty, I just wanted to see you smile."

His words warmed my heart as I watched him take a bite of his pastry, as a crumb tumbled onto his shirt. Carter looked down to brush it off, and that's when I noticed a shiny glint of the ocean wave necklace wrapped around his neck. The sight of the pendant made my stomach flip flop and suddenly I reached up and felt my own beneath the neck of my t-shirt. I smiled at the reminder of the promise we made to each other feeling happier than I had all day.

37

The rest of the afternoon was picture-perfect. After painting pumpkins, Jojo and I left ours to dry while Carter and Denny bought a couple to shoot at the archery range. Not only was Carter a soccer star, but he was a great shot; Denny, on the other hand, turned out to be a pro. Afterwards, the four of us hit the ropes course, which turned out to be more fun than I expected, even though my hands ached from gripping the paracord like my life depended on it. When I lost my balance near the final platform, Carter reached out and caught me in his steady grip.

"You're okay, Dutch. I've got you." He said, pulling me safely to the platform.

As I looked into his cocoa eyes for a moment, my heart raced, whether from my near slip or Carter's closeness I couldn't tell, but for a second, I thought he might kiss me in front of everyone. His save stayed with me all day, making my heart race each time I replayed the catch in my head.

Later, while Jojo and I took a break, we sat together on a bench while the boys raced on the course, sipping hot cider we had purchased from the canteen, and going over Theo's song one more time. Singing with her felt easy, and as our voices blended seamlessly, for a few minutes, it was just the two of us harmonizing together beneath the autumn sky.

When free time wrapped up, the four of us walked to dinner together, and across the field, I spotted Theo finishing up a pickleball match with Asher and a few others. He seemed like he was having fun and I was glad to see it, but I also wondered if he was purposely avoiding me. The thought lingered as we stepped into the Dining Hall, but by nightfall, the noise in my head finally quieted down as the final session of the Fall Retreat began.

The crisp night air carried the scent of the crackling bonfire at the center of our circle. Beyond the dancing flames, the lake shimmered in darkness washed in moonlight. Carter and Denny sat to my left, nudging each other as they both tried, unsuccessfully, to stoke the fire with twigs without drawing Adam's attention. Jojo was on my right, wrapped in a colorful quilt she brought from home, and quietly, Theo had rejoined us on Jojo's other side. I pulled my sleeves over my hands, holding them out to the fire, then when Adam rose, I noticed the glow from the fire cast flickering shadows across his face.

"This weekend, we've discussed who we are in Christ," Adam spoke, his voice echoing into the treeline. "Tonight, we're going to talk about what happens when that identity is tested, and when following Jesus can bring us real risk and true fear."

As he spoke those words, the fire snapped, emphasizing his words.

"Daniel knew what it meant to follow Jesus in the face of danger. In chapter six, we read that he was so faithful, the people around him even used his faith against him. When King Darius signed a decree making it illegal to pray to anyone or any God but him, Daniel had a choice to make."

Adam opened his Bible then and read slowly from the pages. "*'Now when Daniel knew that the writing was signed, he went home, and in his upper room, with his windows open toward Jerusalem, he knelt down on his knees three times that day, and prayed and gave thanks before his God, as was his custom since early days."*

Looking up, Adam let his gaze fall over the circle, continuing. "Daniel didn't run in fear, he didn't hide, and he never stopped praying for safety or to avoid conflict. Daniel never changed a thing, because his trust in God was greater than his fear of man."

The fire hissed, sending sparks into the sky as if highlighting the danger Daniel faced. No one moved and the circle stayed as still as the lake stretching out before us.

"Daniel was arrested," Adam continued, "and thrown into the lions' den, for once again, standing firm in his faith. Even though the king didn't want to punish Daniel, the law was the law. So Daniel went into the den, knowing fully he was standing in the midst of a den of lions ready to devour him, but he never lost faith and fully trusted in God's plan." My breath caught in my throat as Adam leaned closer to the fire. "The next morning, King Darius immediately ran over to the den and called out, *'Daniel, servant of the living God, has your God, whom you serve continually been able to deliver you?'* And Daniel answered: *'My God sent His angel and shut the lions' mouths. They have not hurt me, because I was found innocent before Him.'*"

I felt a wave of relief, knowing that God had once again spared Daniel's life, waiting to hear what happened next.

"We can see again how God went with Daniel into the lions' den," Adam said softly. "He was with him every step of the way, meeting the danger head on, protecting Daniel through it. God used that moment to not only increase Daniel's faith but to change the hearts of those who saw God deliver His servant."

For a third time, Adam's lesson cut me to the core, reminding me that nothing could overcome the power of God.

Adam spoke again, but quieter this time. "We've talked this weekend about what it means to stand firm, but even when we know the truth, sometimes we still allow fear to creep in. Maybe that fear comes in the form of a test we're dreading, a championship game that could cost a team's title, or maybe it feels like pressure from people we care about. In those moments, it can be easy to make decisions to avoid our fears." He slowly looked around the circle, eyes hovering over each of us. "But when we stop letting our fears control us and put our hope in God, we can stand in any fiery furnace, or lions' den, and know God is with us, meeting each challenge head on."

From a small bag beside him, Adam reached in and pulled out a handful of slips of paper to hold up. "Tonight, I want everyone to walk in Daniel's shoes. Imagine you are walking into a dangerous den like he did, but I want you to write down what lions you face. Think about what is testing your faith? What are you afraid of? What's standing in the way of you fully trusting in God?"

Once the paper slips made their way around the circle to me, I took one. The slip was feather-light in the palm of my hand, but the weight I carried on my shoulders made it feel like a stone. All around me, I watched others scribble their metaphorical lions down as I thought carefully about the lesson.

Before camp, I saw Freeport as my fiery furnace. I'd carried the weight of my past, the ache of loneliness, and the heartbreak of my mom leaving me behind, but my encounter with Kelsey revealed family secrets I had never heard of. The thought didn't make me feel like I was standing in the middle of a fire anymore, I felt like I had slowly walked into my own lion's den completely unaware. Yet, as I looked around the circle to those seated right next to me, I didn't feel abandoned or afraid. I saw proof that God was with me, and then it dawned on me. Back home, Worthy stood by my side; but here at camp, Carter was always right next to me, then Jojo and Denny, and finally, in his own quiet way, Theo.

I had wondered why God allowed me to face so many heartbreaks, but sitting there, surrounded by my friends beside the campfire, I saw God in every detail. *This whole time, I was never alone, I'd been surrounded.*

When Jojo reached over after finishing, she handed me a pen. I took it, clicked the ballpoint in place, then slowly, I named each lion head on. *Fear. Anger. Judgment. The unknown.*

Each word was a lion I had faced, clawing at my peace, and making me question my faith. As I finished writing each word, I folded the paper in half and stood just as others had done. The once weightless slip now carried the name of each fear I wanted to lay down and surrender to God. Over the summer, I vowed to live like Jesus, but I couldn't keep that promise when I still clung to my fears. Letting go meant choosing trust, knowing God was standing next to me no matter what I faced next. Then, as I exhaled a deep, steady breath, I stepped up to the fire and released the paper into the flames.

38

After the final prayer, Adam doused the fire in sand while campers gathered their things and started back up the trail to the heart of camp. Carter hadn't moved, still sitting beside me, resting his elbows on his knees, he looked over at me with a quizzical stare.

"Judgment, huh?" He asked, studying me.

I blinked, caught completely by surprise. "Wait... you saw what I wrote?"

Carter sat up tall and offered a small shrug, as his eyes filled with concern. "Not all of it. Just that word... and fear." He looked at me, his gaze steady. "Was that about Kelsey? Or... something else?"

My heart began racing in my chest as my mouth dropped open, but I wasn't sure how to answer him. I bore my soul on that slip of paper, but I hadn't realized Carter had been watching. As I stared back at him, I could have kicked myself because Carter was way more observant than I gave him credit for.

Still hesitating, I watched as Carter shifted slightly beside me, lowering his voice. "I've been trying not to push, and I know I've already asked you a few times," he said. "But whatever's been going on...I'm here, Dutch. You can talk to me."

I turned to face him. "I know," I said quietly. "Of course I know."

The flicker in his eye made my stomach sink. Of course I knew I could talk to Carter, last summer he proved that he was more than trustworthy but we had come so far. It was one thing for him to know the truth about my mom and my past, but for Carter to know about the present was something I couldn't stomach. I didn't want all our efforts to go to waste once he found out how my senior year had really been going. The truth was, I didn't think I could face him if he ever found out just how low I fell on the social chain at Freeport High.

"You sure?" Carter asked, still holding my gaze. "Because I just feel like, I don't know, like there's something you're not telling me."

I turned away because hearing the hurt creeping into his voice made me feel sick with guilt. "I told you I missed everyone," I said, keeping my voice steady as I gazed out at the lake. "Being back at camp this weekend, it's been good for me, though; it feels like the reset I didn't even realize I needed."

Carter didn't answer at first, but when the silence between us stretched far too long, I glanced back to see a slow smile spread over his face.

"I know what you mean." For a moment, he was perfectly still, his eyes flickering out to the water's surface but then something shifted. I watched as he traced a circle in the sand at his feet before turning back to me.

"You should know," Carter said, raking a hand through his hair, "when I was writing my own stuff down, there was something I wanted to—"

"Lena!" Theo's should cut through the moment as he jogged up, guitar case bouncing heavily over his shoulder. "There's still time for one last run-through for the talent show tonight. You in?"

Carter leaned back, but I didn't miss the way his face fell. I felt physically stunned to see Theo talking to me like nothing had happened earlier; but I couldn't just ignore whatever was on Carter's mind, not when it felt like he had something to tell me.

"Can you give us just a minute?." I held up my index finger to put Theo in pause before turning back to Carter whose expression was now unreadable. "What were you going to say?"

Carter's eyes flicked to Theo then back to me, and I caught the slightest flair of his nostrils at Theo's interruption. "It's, uh—"

Theo groaned dramatically, and snapped his fingers like we were wasting his precious time. "Come on, guys. You'll have the rest of the weekend to give each other the googley-eyes but right now, I need Mermaid to keep her eye on the prize. Please just spare me until the talent show's over. Please!"

With a sigh, I looked back at Carter who gave me a helpless shrug. "Just go, Dutch. We're fine, you and I can catch up later," he said.

He gently brushed a hand over my shoulder and I stood hesitantly before murmuring, "Okay."

Even though I wanted to stay exactly where I was, I knew I had this one thing to do for Theo and then Carter and I could have the rest of the weekend together, just as Theo had said.

***

Theo led me toward the gazebo centered at the heart of camp, but far enough away from anything else to be overheard. Working quickly, he pulled Jolene from his guitar case and began strumming like the clock was working against us. I listened while Theo launched into the melody, but something was off. It sounded like the chords were off from the last time he played, and I noticed his hands shaking. When Theo began to sing, his voice was softer and more flat as he sang the lyrics about traveling a tough road thinking about moments that never happened.

On the last note, I heard his voice crack and then I knew something was wrong. Reaching out, I laid my hand over his holding the guitar pick until he stopped. His fingers froze, but when he peered up at me, Theo looked more vulnerable than I had ever seen him before.

"Are you okay, Lockwood?" I whispered. The string lights overhead flickered softly, casting shadows over his darkened face. Theo didn't answer right away, but he didn't have to, the answer was obvious. His usual sarcasm was gone, replaced by worry.

"She hasn't spoken to me all weekend," Theo admitted slowly. "I've been here one night and an entire day, but Katie won't even look at me, much less talk to me."

My heart sank, and I wondered if he was ready to give up. "Did you try talking to her?"

Theo let out a dry laugh that held anything but amusement. With a deep sigh, he looked out into the night before glancing back at me. "I've texted her twice. Once was just to joke around. I said her shoe was untied hoping to get her attention with some witty one-liner but she never responded. Earlier when we had free time, I texted again to see if we could talk while there was time, but again, she said nothing."

Looking back down, he plucked gently at his guitar strings, playing a few melancholy notes that reflected the current state of his heart. I knew his pain, I knew how much it hurt to feel invisible by someone you once counted on. I felt it again when Ronni left me behind at Lacey's to save her own skin, and I felt it when Lacey kept tormenting me this year, even when I wasn't fighting back. Then I felt it still when my Dad buried himself in his boat restoration instead of making time for me like he used to. But even though I knew how much it hurt to be let down,

I knew what it was like when others showed up for me when I needed them most. Now, sitting beside Theo, I knew he needed me to show up for him.

Leveling with him, I asked. "What do you want to do, Lockwood?"

Theo paused his strumming to look up, his brow arched in confusion. "What?"

Repeating myself, I asked again. "What do you want to do?" Then I reached down and plucked a string on the neck of his instrument.

"We've been over this," he muttered, narrowing his eyes at me.

I rolled mine back. "Relax, okay? I'm not trying to play your precious guitar. I just needed your attention. Now tell me, do you want to get on that stage tonight and sing for Katie or not?"

Theo looked stricken by how direct I was but answered, still seeming unsure. "It's not like I can back out, now. The talent show isn't optional."

"That's not what I meant." I said firmly, hoping Theo could see I wanted to help him face this lion head-on. "I'm asking what kind of heart you're bringing up there."

Wincing, he flicked his gaze away for a moment searching for the right answer.

But I couldn't take this anymore. "All weekend, we've talked about who we are in Christ and who we'll be when we leave camp. Earlier, you told me you had something to say, and to me it sounded like you were ready to stand on that stage tonight and speak your truth. But right now, you sound like you've already been defeated."

Theo turned back to me, and although I couldn't read him, I knew I'd found a crack in his armor. I knew how it felt to be the one in hiding, now, watching Theo trying to shrink himself away to avoid the pain and hurt, I knew I couldn't let him keep going like this. Just like I knew I couldn't keep trying to make myself small just to try to make others happy.

"I don't recognize this version of you," I said gently. "You look like you've already lost. So tell me, when we go up in front of the entire camp tonight. Am I going to be singing with the Theo who's ready to put his heart on the line, or with the one who's already quit before even trying?" Theo held my gaze silently for a beat while a chilly breeze swirled by and I raised my brows, waiting for an answer. "Well, are we in this to win it or not, Lockwood?"

The final question was all it took for Theo to look at me like he was in awe. "Wow, I didn't know you had that little speech in you." He said, sitting taller but when I saw the spark in his eyes return, I knew Theo was back. "Let's win this thing."

I smiled and cleared my throat. "Good."

We ran the song twice more, and by the end, Theo seemed like himself again, voice steady and each chord hit perfectly. Sitting next to him, I felt confident thinking whatever doubts Katie still had over getting back together, wouldn't stand a chance after our performance.

After our final run-through, a sudden applause near the stairs made us both jump. Jojo appeared, beaming. "You guys sound amazing!"

Theo groaned, slipping his guitar pick between his teeth. "You weren't supposed to hear that yet, Jo."

She cut her eyes at him. "You know I know this song by heart, right Theodore?"

Theo gave her a look and mimicked her words in a high-pitched voice.

Jojo stuck out her tongue. "That's not what I sound like and you know it." She turned to me, holding out her hand. "Come on, we've got less than an hour to get ready."

"It's already that late?" I blinked, pulling out my phone to check the time. Jojo was right, there was less than an hour until showtime.

Theo snapped Jolene's case shut before he flicked his two fingers from his eyes to mine. "Just remember, look the part of a tortured artist, that's our vibe tonight."

Wincing playfully, I added. "Don't you think I look tortured enough?"

Jojo giggled and grabbed my hand, pulling me behind her. "Don't worry, Theodore. I'll make sure she looks like a rockstar."

As Jojo drug me across the lawn, I glanced back toward the Dining Hall. Under a lamppost, Denny was juggling a soccer ball on his pointer finger, while Carter stood supervising. When Jojo blew Denny a kiss, he grinned and waved then dropped the ball as his gaze followed Jojo crossing the lawn. When Carter noticed Denny's looming gaze, he caught sight of me grinned, like he was trying not to look like the cheeseball Denny was. The lightness in Carter's dark eyes made me feel relieved, even though our earlier conversation had been interrupted. The way his eyes locked on mine conveyed a silent message that we were really okay.

After running through Theo's song again and again, the lyrics replaying in my head suddenly struck me. In the final verse, Theo wrote about a darkening sky holding a flicker of light, and no matter what kind of storm hit, the light was always there, always breaking through.

From the very first time Carter and I sat by the lake together, I realized he was the silver lining in every dark cloud threatening to rain down on me. Although Theo was going on stage tonight hoping to win Katie back, I knew that when I stood before the camp, I wouldn't just be performing a song; I'd be singing the lyrics to Carter, who had kept my heart safe through every storm.

39

The air outside the Dining Hall was buzzing as campers started filling in for the talent show. Outside, I waited on the porch with trembling hands, quite literally, shaking in my boots. *Why had I agreed to this again?* Each time I peered into the front window, it looked like the crowd grew larger and larger despite the small number of campers. My eyes were likely paying tricks on me, but when I caught my reflection in the mirror, I relaxed but only slightly. Even if I got up and made a fool of myself in front of everyone, at least I would look okay doing it.

Jojo had worked her magic on me again, in record time. She gave me a nice smokey-eye, bright red lips, and lent me an outfit that was both comfortable and rockstar worthy. I was dressed in a black-and-white striped bodysuit tucked into a rust-colored corduroy mini skirt paired perfectly with black tights and ankle boots. Jojo called me an indie rock goddess, and for a moment, I felt like it until my nerves started getting the best of me while waiting for Theo.

When he appeared, crossing the front lawn, I had to do a double take. He looked every bit like a brooding musician with a flannel shirt layered over a faded tee and messy blonde hair. I could tell he'd spent extra time getting ready for Katie, but when his eyes landed on me, he looked just as taken aback to see my new look as I was his. He adjusted his guitar case over his shoulder as he gazed at me, brows raised and eyes only getting wider as he took in the sight of me.

I raised an eyebrow, hoping he would stop staring. "Are you going to be alright there, Lockwood?"

Theo blinked, trying his best to snap out of it. "Sorry, it's just...um, you look, uh...you clean up well, Mermaid."

I scoffed, punching his arm playfully despite the heat of embarrassment spreading up my neck. "You said rockstar so Jojo delivered."

Trying not to look at me, Theo cleared his throat and only *mmhm'ed* before motioning toward the entrance. "After you?"

Together, we stepped inside, where the Dining Hall had been completely transformed. Streamers hung from the rafters in a tangle of glowing string lights. A small black stage, barely a foot off the ground, stood near the front of the room ready for the night's performances. Across the room, Jojo and Denny were impossible to miss. Denny had layered a shiny black cape draped over his usual jeans and T-shirt. To top off his look, he paired the cape with a top hat and a fake plastic wand. Jojo sparkled in a sequin dress, long white gloves, and the brightest smile I had seen her wear.

While we were getting ready she'd told me about packing the dress just in case Denny needed help with his act. Even though she planned on singing Theo's song for her performance, I could tell she really wanted to be onstage with her boyfriend instead. Now, seeing them together, I was glad I agreed to help Theo so her and Denny could shine together. The pair of them instantly made me miss Carter and as I turned to search, I finally spotted him.

He stood near the med table, chatting with Angie, who was on the scene for tonight just in case someone's act went horribly wrong. Dressed in his Viking soccer warm-up uniform, backwards hat, and stylish high-top shoes. One glance from him was all it took to send my stomach flipping like hitting a dip on a roller coaster ride.

"You didn't want to dress up?" I asked as he approached.

Carter grinned, gesturing to his outfit. "You'll understand soon enough." I watched as his gaze swept over me, followed by a faint blush. "You look incredible, Dutch."

My nerves seized, causing my heart to pitter-patter in my chest, but before I could say more, Jojo and Denny strolled up, and Theo nudged Denny's shoulder with a grin. "You two look *magical*."

"That's the idea, dude!" Denny joked.

Jojo beamed, though she seemed fidgety. "Let's just hope I make it through this in one piece." She winked at me just as Hannah, one of the senior staff members, stepped onto the stage, microphone in hand, just as the lights dimmed.

The five of us slipped into seats near the back as the talent show began. A pair of campers kicked things off with a skit poking fun at their counselors, followed by a solo ukulele performance that earned standing applause from the crowd. By the time Denny and Jojo's names were called, the Dining Hall was in full hype mode, cheering on each performer.

"Ladies and gentlemen!" Denny announced, striding onstage and flinging his arms wide. "Prepare to be amazed and feast your eyes on the show!"

Carter coughed to stifle his laughter beside me, which only made me giggle.

"He's so into this magic thing." Carter chuckled, his tone laced with admiration for our friend.

"I never knew but it's the best!" I replied, smiling as I watched my friends onstage.

Denny's first trick was the classic scarf-from-the-sleeve act. He started strong, slowly pulling the fabric through, smiling at the crowd like it was the nearest trick in the book, but when the fabric got stuck, Jojo pitched in to help, just as the sleeve of scarves landed in a heap onstage. Everyone watched as Jojo threw her hands up and reached down to begin pulling apart the sleeve, tossing the scarves into the audience like confetti as if the mishap were planned.

"Voila!" Denny declared, sending the audience into a roar of laughter and applause.

His next act was a disappearing coin trick that quickly unraveled when Denny fumbled and accidentally dropped the coin. We all watched as the coin rolled off the stage, until Jojo twirled over to him, reached behind his ear, and retrieved another coin to present to the crowd as she floated back across the stage.

"Presto change-o!" Denny cheered, as Jojo winked at the audience before pointing back to her partner. As they finished the act, everyone climbed to their feet in a standing ovation. Carter and I looked at each other, exchanging smiles, and I couldn't help but think Denny and Jojo really were the perfect pair.

Next, it was Carter's turn. I watched as he rose from his seat and grabbed his soccer ball, casually dribbling it once before climbing onstage. I had no idea what he planned on doing, but when I remembered seeing him and Denny spinning the ball on their fingers earlier, I wondered if that was his act.

Carter found his place center stage, holding his ball beneath his arm, then nodded to Hannah by the bluetooth system to cue the music. A beat dropped over the speakers, and suddenly the Dining Hall was pulsing with vibrant energy. Hitting the beat just right, Carter tossed the soccer ball into the air, caught it on his knee, and flicked it behind him with total control. A few others around me gasped, and so did I, cupping my face with my hands in shock as Carter launched into a freestyle soccer routine. He juggled the ball with quick footwork, balancing it on his head, before flicking the ball from his knee to catch it on top of his finger for a spin, all perfectly timed with the music.

With the next beat drop, Carter stepped up his moves, spinning the ball on one finger, rolling it across his shoulders in a deep bend, before catching the ball behind his back like he had done the move a million times before. A giddy laugh escaped me while I watched, mesmerized by Carter's routine. I knew he was amazing on the soccer field, but his moves were beyond amazing.

When he reached his final act, we all sat and watched as Carter planted his hands on the stage floor, kicked up into a handstand, and somehow, balanced the ball on the sole of his shoes. Then, with one controlled flick, the ball flew out into the audience as a camper by the front caught it. Carter landed back on his feet and straightened with a grin as the song ended. The Dining Hall erupted as campers leapt to their feet, hooting for my boyfriend as he made his way off the stage.

He slid back into the chair beside me, his face red, with sweat prickling at his hairline. Flicking me a shy smile, he asked. "Well, what did you think?"

I could only shake my head, grinning like an idiot. "I'm speechless," Staring at him like he was a mystical creature. "You were amazing! Where on earth did you learn to do all that?"

He just grinned and pulled me into a hug. "I've got moves, Dutch, but, you're up next, so break a leg."

I scoffed and tapped his arm, playfully. "Don't wish another injury on me, Rosie."

Carter chuckled but flicked a finger as me and Theo headed for the stage. "Hey, that injury brought us together."

Theo gave me a slight push towards the stage before I could reply, and suddenly my heart was pounding. Once we made our way to the front, the string lights suddenly seemed to grow brighter, making me squint before the crowd of campers. To my right, Hannah joined us for just a minute, moving quickly as she slid two microphone stands into place. Beside me, Theo adjusted the strap of his guitar, getting into position then, standing at the ready, he looked up to make sure we were on the same page. My stomach clenched as I avoided looking out into the sea of campers, but when I turned to Theo, his face fell and then he froze. Following his gaze, I looked out into the crowd wondering what he had seen, and that's when I knew.

Katie.

She stood near the back, with her arms crossed, whispering to Riley, who stood next to her. Somehow, just seeing the two of them whispering was enough to bring me back down to earth, even from center stage. Watching Theo shrink back when he was about to bear his heart on the line, gave me a new perspective. Watching Theo tense up and freeze, I wondered if I was feeling how Worthy had all year at school. From the dumb senior prank in the parking lot to the tea throwing in the cafeteria, Worthy had been by my side every time. Now, it was my turn to do the same for Theo.

When he took a step back from the mic stand, I reached out and placed a gentle hand on his shoulder so he wouldn't budge.

"Just look at me," I whispered, covering my hand over the microphone in front of me.

Theo looked at me then, sadness and uncertainty filling his eyes, but as I held his gaze, I gave him a small, encouraging nod. Still hesitant, he reached out to his guitar strap like he was going to take it off but I shook my head, trying my best to be discreet.

"Lockwood, just keep your eyes on me, okay?" I pleaded quietly. "Say what you came here to say."

As soon as my words hit him, Theo let go of his guitar strap and found the strings again. The opening chords came out perfectly as he stepped up to the mic stand and launched into the first verse. I stared out at the crowd, catching the way a few campers near the front were swaying in their seats. When I looked back just before I needed to jump into the chorus, I found Theo's eyes on me, his foot tapping, and by the time we reached the bridge, I could see he was back, performing even better than we had practiced. Once we reached the chorus, I unleashed my voice, joining in.

Theo smiled as we heard the cheering, then we both turned and gazed out into the swaying crowd, feeling their vibrant energy. As the lyrics rose in my chest, I searched the crowd until my gaze landed on the only person on my mind while I sang. Carter didn't grin when I found him, he simply sat back in his chair watching me, his eyes filled with pride. Singing about the unending light, I hoped he knew he was the only one on my mind. Then, when we reached the last verse, Carter grinned, and I felt my heart flutter, knowing he realized I meant every word I sang, *for him*.

When I turned back to Theo, we ended the song together, our voices blending seamlessly until fading out. Facing the crowd, there was a brief moment of silence before the entire Dining Hall erupted as campers jumped to their feet, cheering and applauding. Denny and Carter were the first to rise, clapping and hollering like we'd just headlined a major tour. When Theo faced me once more, I chuckled at the look of disbelief on his face before giving him another quick pat on the back. Theo and I had pulled off a performance in less than twenty-four hours that had been better than either of us expected.

"We did it, Mermaid!" He shouted over the crowd, shaking his head as the cheering continued.

"Lockwood, we might actually win this thing!" I replied, feeling astonished at the audience's reaction.

Theo merely shrugged as Hannah bounded back onto the stage, clapping as she took the mic. "Great job, you two!" she congratulated, gesturing for us to return to our seats. Just as we were told, Theo and I stepped off the stage and made our way back to our table. We slipped into our seats as Hannah explained that the judges would be deliberating. Around the room, campers grew restless as the minutes ticked by, watching the group of adult staff huddled near the sound system voting on each performance. Time stretched thin with anticipation until finally, Hannah returned to the stage, as a hush fell over the crowd.

"All right, everyone! The judges have made their decision," she said, holding up a folded slip of paper like it was the final rose on a reality show. "Can I get a drumroll, please?"

On cue, the room burst into a roaring drumbeat that nearly shook the building down.

"In third place," she began, "our ukulele player—Hayden!"

The crowd erupted as Hayden, the younger boy who had nervously strummed a folk tune earlier, stood to meet Hannah onstage. His friends cheered wildly, pounding the table, while he retrieved his ribbon.

Hannah raised her voice above the applause. "In second place, with his insane soccer skills—Carter Rose!"

The crowd went wild again, and I joined in, cupping my mouth to *whoop* as Carter climbed to his feet, getting his back thumped by Denny as he made his way to the stage.

After Carter received his ribbon, he sat back down beside me, and I leaned in, wrapping my arm through his. "Not bad, Rosie."

He grinned, and for half a second his smile caught my breath. "Guess I do have some talent after all."

Then Hannah lifted the last slip of paper, dragging out the moment with one last dramatic pause. "And finally," she said, voice rising, "our first-place winners—Lena Harris and Theo Lockwood!"

My stomach flipped and for a moment, I felt frozen to my seat. *Did she really just call my name?* When Jojo screamed beside me, I knew Hannah had named me and Theo as the first place winners.

"You did it, girl!" Jojo squealed, throwing her arms around me with so much force, I almost fell out of my seat. Theo didn't move at first either, like he needed a second to process the news. Then, slowly, he climbed to his feet and motioned for me to follow him.

We stepped forward together, and Hannah greeted us with wide eyes and whispered, "You two crushed it," as she handed over our ribbons.

The buzz in the Dining Hall resumed as campers dispersed, still riding the high of the talent show. Theo and I lingered near the stage, dumbstruck as we soaked in the unexpected win. Just when I thought camp could get any more magical, I felt the air shift around and turned just in time to see Kelsey Lockwood push her way through the crowd. Slowly, she waded forward, her normal blonde curls were pulled back in two braided pigtails following her jump rope bit, her eyes icy cold.

"Congratulations, little brother," Kelsey said coolly, before cutting her eyes to me. "Looks like you won more than just the talent show tonight."

Theo sighed as he brushed a hand over his face.. "Kelsey, can you not—"

She cut him off with a glance toward the door, and when we both followed her gaze, we watched while Katie slipped outside with Riley holding an arm around her shoulders.

"She's done," Kelsey spat at her towering little brother. "Guess that's what happens when you finally make a choice."

To my surprise, Theo didn't argue or stare her down like he had in the woods earlier. Theo simply shrugged. "You have no idea what you're talking about," he said quietly. "And I'm done explaining myself to you."

I didn't know if it was the excitement of winning or months of trying to walk away, but before I could second-guess myself, I stepped in. "Kelsey, why are you doing this?"

With a tilt of her head, her eyes widened like she hadn't expected me to speak up. "Doing what?"

"This." I waved my hand in a circle, motioning between the three of us. "Why are you acting like Theo just set fire to your whole world? Katie and Theo's relationship isn't yours to protect or ruin. He's your brother."

But instead of helping, my words only poured out like oil on a fire.

"Don't talk to me about family," she snapped.

The way her icy glare landed on me sent chills down my spine. Kelsey stared at me like I had no right to tell her not to treat her brother like dirt, when all I wanted was for her to realize she couldn't keep treating people like she was the morality police. Before I could respond, Carter came up behind me and stepped in. "Kelsey, just give it a rest already."

She scoffed, but grinned maniacally, like he was the last person on Earth she would take advice from. "Oh, yes, and here's Carter Rose, coming to his girlfriend's rescue. What a white knight he must be!"

"Enough," Carter said firmly. "None of us came here for this."

Kelsey rolled her eyes and turned as if she were leaving, but then spun on her heel to face me once again. "Actually, before I go," she said slowly, her gaze sharpening, "if any of you hurt my brother, I won't just stop at a photo next time."

At first I didn't catch it wondering how she could accuse either me or Carter of hurting Theo. But, then the mention of a photo caught my attention, and I stared back at her. "Wait... what photo?"

She smiled, but it didn't reach her eyes. "Maybe you should ask your boyfriend...or better yet, your aunt. I'm sure either of them would love to explain what I'm talking about."

Kelsey's gaze shifted to Carter, then to me, like she knew exactly what she was doing, and then she turned and stalked off.

Theo was shaking his head as I looked back at a horror-stricken Carter. The look on his face told me something was wrong. While her words spun around my head, I tried to piece together what she meant.

Photo. Aunt Lou. Carter.

Then it hit me, like getting struck with a lightening bolt, and the pieces began clicking together like a puzzle I had never wanted to solve. I thought back to the photo Lou had shown us at the end of the summer. The one of me and Carter sitting on the dock. The photo that lived in the orb hanging from the necklace Carter had made for me.

Lou has said the photo was sent anonymously, but we had all assumed it was Riley. At least, that's what made the most sense, but now, as the truth dawned on me, I knew Riley wasn't to blame.

It was Kelsey.

My eyes locked on Carter as the realization settled in. "Wait... did you know?"

His expression shifted instantly, first to guilt, then regret. "Lena, I tried to tell you—"

But I could barely hear him as my heart started pounding in my ears. This wasn't just about Theo and Katie, or Carter or Riley, or any other moment. There was something truly broken between my family and the Lockwoods, buried beneath years of silence. Kelsey wasn't just acting out of petty drama, this was personal, I just hadn't realized it until now. This was a grudge she was hanging onto, caused by a family feud that started long before I ever stepped foot in Meadowbrook, and somehow, I'd walked straight into the middle of it.

My cheeks burned hot as my stomach twisted, and when Carter reached out, I pulled my hand away before he could reach me. When I looked up at him, I saw the hurt flicker in his eyes as I brushed him off. He hadn't said a word to me, and when Kelsey confronted me earlier, he asked me to just forget it. Tonight, I had sung to him about being the light, but now, he seemed like a catalyst in Kelsey's raging storm. Carter had promised to be honest, but tonight he had done the exact opposite, and I couldn't even look at him without feeling another wave of humiliation. Without a word, I spun on my heel and walked away, feeling my heart splinter with every step.

40

Breaking free from the Dining Hall, I felt the night's chill hit me with its brisk blow. The cold air felt like a relief as the heat of embarrassment rose up my neck and flamed my cheeks. Leaning near the porch railing, Aunt Lou stood talking with Max until she caught sight of me.

"Lena, you were wonder—" She was mid-compliment as I watched her smile vanish, immediately replaced by concern. "Sweetie, are you alright?" she asked gently, already stepping toward me.

I was still reeling after going toe-to-toe with Kelsey again, but this time, the revelation about Carter was too much for me. As I gazed at Lou, her worried eyes searching mine, I couldn't help but wonder if she had known all along too.

"I know it was Kelsey," I said, my voice raw, whether from tonight's performance, or the emotion thickening in my throat, I didn't know. "She's the one who sent you the photo of me and Carter on the last day of summer camp."

Lou's lips pressed into a tight line. "Honey—"

"Did you know?" I stared at her down, but Lou didn't answer, she didn't have to. I knew what she would say without her evening having to tell me.

"It's fine," I said too quickly, trying not to feel betrayed by everyone in one night. Lou's position was a little different than Carter's though, and to an extent, I understood why she kept quiet. "I get it. You couldn't tell me, with your role here. I'm not mad, I just..." I swallowed hard, trying to steady myself. "Kelsey did it to get back at me and Carter, didn't she? In there, she didn't even try to hide it, she just blurted it out in front of all of us."

Lou's shoulders sank as she watched me motion to the Dining Hall. "Lena, tt wasn't my place to tell you—"

I let out a sardonic laugh and shook my head. "Right, because keeping things from me has worked so well for us in the past."

"No," she said, her voice flat. "What I was going to say is... yes, you and Carter broke the rules. That's true, but you two weren't the only ones who broke them that night, and if Kelsey's still stirring things up with you, I need to have a chat with her."

"Please don't," I begged. "The last thing I need is for Kelsey to cause more drama this weekend than she already has."

Lou nodded slowly, placing a hand on my shoulder as she leveled her gaze on me. "Remember what I told you about her," she said softly. "Don't let her have any power over you."

I bit the inside of my cheek and looked down at the porch as Lou's words wrapped me in a verbal embrace. Tonight, I tried to stand up for a friend, but it completely backfired. Instead, I had just uncovered more secrets and cracks in my relationship with Carter. Although I knew Lou meant well, no part of me felt powerful or victorious, I just felt defeated.

"I think I'm gonna head to the cabin," I said after a long pause. "Start packing up."

Lou tilted her head, pursing her lips. "I can come with you if you want some company."

I shook my head, wrapping my arms to brace against the fall chill. "Thanks, but I just...I need a breather."

Worry lingered in Lou's eyes as I turned and hurried down the stairs. As the hum of the Dining Hall faded behind me, the quiet rhythm of the night amplified my spinning thoughts. I walked in silence, my boots chomping softly against the gravel path as I made my way toward Girls' Camp. The cool air pressed against my skin, making me shiver as I picked up my pace.

Then, through a break in the trees, a shimmer caught my eye. Moonlight danced across the lake's surface as if waving an invitation. Without thinking, I veered off the trail, drawn to the water and the peace I always found nearby. An owl hooted overhead, and the sound reverberated through the trees, until I found the shoreline. Stepping onto the dock, I heard the familiar creak of the wooden boards beneath as I walked to the very end, and felt the cold breeze roll off the lake and brush against my skin.

The water below was still and glassy, a perfect reflection of the night sky above. I usually felt closest to peace when I was by the water, but tonight, my thoughts wouldn't settle. My mind kept churning with thoughts I couldn't push away—*Carter's secret, Kelsey's accusations, the Lockwood feud*—the weight of it all pressed down, refusing to let go.

The thoughts made me shiver again, and when I reached up to pull my hair around my neck, I felt something cool against my skin. Tracing my neck with my fingertips, I touched the necklace I was still wearing, *always wearing,* that Carter had given me. For a second, I let myself trace the small pendant, feeling the curves of the mountain range met by the smoothness of the tiny orb in the center.

Holding onto the pendant, I looked out picturing the way the lake held some of my favorite memories from summer camp. Early morning sunrises, evening sunsets, and shared moments with Carter in between, where his voice anchored me when everything felt like it was falling apart. The lake was where we first really saw each other, where I finally felt like myself again, and felt the peace that had once seemed so out of reach. But tonight, everything was unraveling all over again, and I wasn't sure how to hold all of it together anymore.

I tucked the necklace back into my shirt and lowered myself onto the dock, wrapping my arms around my knees as I looked out at the water's dark surface. A single leaf drifted across the water, spinning slowly before landing flat and still. I watched the leaf sit idly in the water and saw myself. When I arrived for the Fall Retreat, I felt carefree, as if floating on air without a worry in the world. Yet, once the leaf hit the surface, it froze, trapped in the current. Once the thought hit me, I leaned forward and reached out, and pulled the dripping leaf out of the water. As it sat resting on the dock next to me, I felt another gentle breeze stir as a new thought drifted by.

I wasn't meant to carry any of this alone. If I wanted to let the pain go, I had to surrender my hurt to God.

I held my breath for a moment, trying to hold back my tears until I looked up at the crescent moon. As I gazed up, I felt so small and wondered how a God who could create something as great as the moon could create me, too. *What value did I have? Why did He want me too?* Yet, as soon as the thoughts appeared, they were brushed away as I remembered Miss Pearl telling me about Worthy the first night I had dinner and Bible study at their house.

You're already shining as an example for all the Lord is doing in your life. If you don't believe me, just look at that girl inside, she had said, pointing to Worthy in the kitchen window. I didn't see it then, and I still didn't completely understand now, but I wondered if all this pain was for a purpose so that others could see the Lord in me. Even when I didn't understand why, I knew I could go to God and ask Him for the strength I didn't have. Then, bowing my head, I surrendered.

"I don't feel strong, God," I whispered out into the cool night air. "I feel like I could fall apart at any second, but I know You've brought me this far, so please... help me keep standing. Help me give grace when I'd rather disappear. Help me keep going when the odds are stacked against me and please, please, give me direction, because I don't know what to do next."

Another breeze stirred across the lake as I lifted my head, tilting my face upward to the pale glow of the moon. Everything up there looked so steady, so calm and orderly, unlike the chaos happening down here. I sat like that for a moment longer, arms still wrapped around myself until I heard footsteps on the dock behind me.

I turned, flinching at the unexpected sight of Carter standing a few feet away. The moonlight cast soft shadows across his face, and I could barely see the way his head was bowed as if uncertain if he should come any closer. When I saw him, Carter didn't speak right away but instead, he slowly inched forward and lowered himself onto the dock beside me. I watched as his eyes drifted toward the lake, fixed on the way the moonlight shimmered over the water's surface as if searching for the right thing to say.

The silence between us settled thick and heavy, like fog, full of secrets we should have never kept. Then, Carter let out a slow, jagged breath, and dragged a hand along the back of his neck. Even in the moonlight, I could see the tension in his shoulders, like he was bracing himself just to talk to me. It hurt to see him like this, but it hurt even more knowing he had kept things from me.

"I'm sorry," Carter said at last, not meeting my gaze. "I know it probably feels like I lied or kept the whole Kelsey thing from you, but I promise, that wasn't my intention."

I didn't look at him, instead, I kept my eyes locked on the water beyond, not sure if I was ready for his apology yet, not when I still had so many questions. "Then why didn't you tell me?"

Carter hesitated, then out of the corner of my eye, I watched him scoot closer beside me. The dock creaked under his weight, followed by his loud sigh. "Because I didn't know how. Riley told me about the photo a few weeks ago during Devo night at church. She didn't even know about it until after Kelsey had already sent the picture to Lou. Riley said she didn't want to make things worse than they already were so she didn't say anything until she apologized to me."

I hugged my knees closer, trying to shield myself from the truth because his honesty still hurt. Not only did I have to hear about him spending time with his ex, but he had known about the photo for weeks and never said anything to me. When I finally glanced at Carter, the moonlight shone dimly but just enough for me to make out the flicker of guilt in his pleading eyes and the tense set of his jaw.

"Kelsey thought she was protecting Riley and punishing me," he said, his voice a little more even. "You got caught in the middle, and I'm so sorry for that, but when I found out... I wanted to tell you, I really did, but I didn't know if the truth would just make things worse. You always seemed so distant during our calls, and I kept wondering if I did something wrong, or if..." He broke off, shaking his head as he turned away for a moment as if the confession wounded him. When he faced me again, he admitted, "I didn't want this to be how you found out about the photo."

I stared down at the dock, blinking hard as the sting built behind my eyes. The hurt in Carter's voice was palpable, making my heart throb, and the closer he slid to me, the more I realized he was aching to reach out but didn't. My heart sank deeper as I noticed how close we were even though he still felt so far away.

Carter slid closer once again, and I felt his knee brush against mine. "Dutch," his voice cracked. "Please...say something."

But, I couldn't, the words felt caught in my throat, and as I looked up, meeting his gaze, the expression on his face sent a pang through my chest.

"This isn't fair," he said gently, his voice thick with hurt. "I've been honest with you about everything, but it's like you're always holding something back. Ever since you left Meadowbrook after summer camp, something's been different. I can feel it, but you won't tell me."

I couldn't look at him then, so I turned, facing the water, trying to force my nerves to calm down, but he sighed again, this time the sound was mixed with a frustrated groan. "Lena, what will it take for you to let me in?"

The way he said my name, *Lena, not Dutch*, made my stomach sink. He never called me by my first name, and I knew I couldn't stay silent any longer.

"I'm not trying to keep things from you," I whispered, with a trembling voice. "It's just... being home isn't like camp. It's harder, so much harder, and I don't know that you could ever understand, I don't think anyone can."

"Okay, so help me understand. Why is home so much harder?" Carter's voice was gentler now, and I could hear the relief my reply brought him as he pressed. "Just talk to me."

I looked away, biting down on the inside of my cheek, fighting a new wave of threatening tears. "Because I'm not you, Carter. I'm not some golden boy or star athlete destined for greatness. If we went to the same school, you wouldn't even notice me."

Carter looked stricken as his face twisted with confusion. "Why would you think that?"

I offered a hopeless shrug and looked him in the eye. "That day you couldn't reach me... something happened."

He leaned in, his lips pressed, into a tight line as he listened. "What happened?"

"Lacey's boyfriend and his friends covered my car in pickles," I said, voice cracking. "I know it sounds stupid, but they call me *Pickle* at school to torment me about my mom's drinking."

Carter's mouth opened slightly before his lips pressed into a tight line. I watched as he turned his head to look out at the lake and caught his jaw flex once more. As if he needed a minute to compose himself, he faced me once more. "Lena, I'm so sorry."

When I looked up again, I felt shame flaming my skin. "Is that what you wanted me to tell you? That I'm a joke? You're dating Freeport High's biggest joke."

Carter's jaw tightened again as he shook his head, not accepting my truth. "Don't say that," he said, quietly but unwavering. "Not to me."

"Why not?" I asked, choking out a bitter laugh. "It's true, I wanted to believe it wasn't, but after everything with Kelsey this weekend, I don't just feel like a joke, I feel like a complete and total fool."

"Lena... you're not—"

"Why didn't you just tell me?" I interrupted.

Carter exhaled hard, running both hands down the sides of his face. "We live almost six hours apart. That's not exactly a FaceTime kind of conversation."

"That's all we have!" My voice broke. "You said we would be fine as long as we both tried and were honest, that was our promise. But you—"

"Stop." He cut me off before I could finish. "You think I was okay with what Kelsey did? You think it didn't mess with me, too?" He turned toward the water, running his hands through his hair once again. "When I found out, I was relieved she was off at college, but then I kept thinking about what you'd say and how you'd see me. I didn't want Kelsey dragging you into her mess while you were trying to grow in your faith. I thought, maybe if I waited to tell you in person, I could protect you from getting hurt."

I scoffed, but didn't say anything, because in that moment, all I felt was hurt.

When Carter looked back at me, his eyes had darkened. "You know, now that we finally have the chance to be honest with each other, face-to-face, you should know that I've been scared to tell you."

"Scared of what?" I flicked my gaze at him, feeling bewildered.

"Scaring you off," he said quietly, like he was fighting to stay calm. "You wouldn't open up about what was happening back home, but I knew there was something going on. The less you told me the more I felt like I was already losing you."

"Carter—" I tried.

"Why did you call me that?" he interjected. "A golden boy. Why would you say that to me?"

I blinked, watching his eyes narrow further. "I don't know...because you have this perfect life. You have a family that actually cares about you, great friends, and an amazingly bright future."

Carter shook his head, somehow exasperated by my compliments. "Have you forgotten where I came from? Who I was before all of this?"

"No," I said quickly. "But—"

"But what?" His voice broke. "I never hid my past from you. I trusted you enough to lay everything out there, and I thought you trusted me the same way."

"I do," I said, feeling completely misunderstood. "But I didn't want you to see me differently."

Carter's expression shifted as he shook his head. "I wouldn't have, Dutch. Don't you get it? From the very beginning, you were different. When everyone else saw me as this new guy with a past, you saw me for me."

I stared at him, unsure how to respond, but the way he called me Dutch again calmed something deep in my heart.

"The more I got to know you," Carter said, "the more I admired you."

"You admired *me*?" I asked, stunned by his confession.

He nodded, and I didn't miss the way the corner of his mouth tilted into a smile. "Yeah, Dutch, you kept showing up, even when life kept trying to knock you down."

His words sent a reassuring warmth through my chest as I felt my defenses begin to fall.

"And I still admire you," Carter declared. "You're so unlike anyone I've ever known, and when we got to know each other this summer, you never judged me. You saw me for who I was trying to become, not the broken kid I used to be."

Each word felt like Carter was taking a chisel to the brick wall I had thrown up earlier around my heart.

"When we met," Carter went on, his voice softer now, "it didn't feel like a coincidence. I felt like God was moving mountains for us. Remember when you joked that we trauma-bonded?"

A small laugh escaped me as I nervously reached up to tuck a loose piece of hair behind my ear. "Of course I remember."

"Well, maybe we did," Carter threw his hands up. "But who cares? I've never felt the connection we have with anyone else."

Just then, he reached for my hand again, and as if on instinct, I slowly opened my palm, letting our fingers intertwine.

"I don't know if you remember," he said, his thumb tracing a slow circle across my knuckle, "but there was one night we were watching a movie, and you told me you didn't feel seen."

My breath caught as I flashed back to that moment when he quietly looked at me over our FaceTime call. The way he said the words made my heart race. "I remember."

Carter lifted his gaze to meet mine, and even in the sliver of moonlight, I saw the same knowing look from that night. "I see you, Dutch. You're not a joke to me. You're amazing, but I just wish you could see yourself the way I see you."

My eyes dropped to our hands, and I suddenly clung to the warmth he offered me. I didn't think I could ever feel more known than I did at this moment. For so long I felt invisible, unseen, and unheard, like I was expendable to everyone. But just like he had this summer, Carter had a way of reaching down through the rubble of pain that buried me, and yanking me free.

"Forrest Gump," I said suddenly, keeping my eyes strained on our locked hands.

"What?" He asked, quietly.

"The movie we were watching that night," I clarified, looking up at him now with a faint smile. "It was Forrest Gump."

Carter released a soft chuckle as his thumb brushed over mine again. "That's right, I almost forgot."

"I'm sorry, too," I said quietly. "With everything at school, and this weekend with Kelsey, it all just built up, and when I thought you'd lied to me... I freaked out. Honestly, I just didn't know what to do."

Carter nodded, like he understood. "I get it. Trust me, I do, but I need you to know I'd never intentionally hurt you. *Not ever, Dutch.*"

"I know," I murmured, shifting closer to him until we were side-by-side, thighs and shoulders touching. "I wouldn't either."

Just then, he dipped his head slightly, leveling me with his gaze. "But this only works if we're honest with each other, Dutch, about everything, the good, the bad, and the ugly."

A lump rose in my throat as I looked down, feeling a wave of anxiety rush over me. "I just didn't want to disappoint you," I said finally, my voice barely above a whisper. "Or make you think less of me for still struggling."

Carter opened his mouth like he was about to speak but then paused. He leaned back and took my chin in his hand, offering me a slow, reassuring smile. "Our relationship can't survive without trust, Dutch."

He didn't mean it to hurt me, he was being honest, and I knew he was right. We would never make this work if we couldn't be honest with each other. I had lived enough life to see the aftermath of buried secrets and the hurt they caused.

"Following Jesus doesn't mean we don't mess up," Carter reminded me gently. "It just means we don't give up when we do. I've made mistakes, especially tonight, and I'm sure I'll make more, but I hope you know that even when I mess up, it's never because I don't care. I'm just not some perfect *golden* boy."

He leaned in, nudging me playfully with his shoulder as the tension from earlier finally melted away.

"I needed that reminder," I said quietly, smiling up at him.

Carter's gaze softened as he brought my hand to his lips, pressing a gentle kiss to my knuckles. "I want to be there for you," he said. "Like really there, Dutch for everything, even if I can't always show up physically, know that I'm always here for you."

I gulped hard as my voice caught in my throat. As hard as it would be for me to fully trust someone enough to them completely, I knew Carter was someone I could count on to not let me down. "I promise I'll do better."

Carter reached up then, and brushed a strand of hair from my face, inching closer. "Speaking of promises," he said, "do you remember what I told you on the last night of summer camp?"

I flashed a small smile at him. "That you were willing to try and that you were willing to make this thing work between us if I was willing, too?"

He nodded, smiling softly as he lowered his voice. "So here we are again," he said. "On the last night of camp, let's make the same promise, but this time let's keep it. Okay?"

Slowly, I looked into his eyes and agreed. "Okay," I said. "Deal."

Carter inched closer until I leaned back abruptly, catching him off-guard.

"Wait," I added, arching a playful brow, "there's only one way to seal a promise."

Carter chuckled and immediately held out his pinky. I looped mine through his, and for a heartbeat, we just sat there together beneath the moonlight, pinky fingers locked, hearts open wide. Then, feeling that same invisible string tying us together, we both leaned in, and pressed a kiss to our joined hands.

Promise sealed once again.

41

That night, I tossed and turned and barely slept a wink. Even though Carter and I made up, the night had flown by faster than I had hoped, and I knew when I woke up, morning meant goodbye. All night I laid awake, wondering how I could make time slow down, but it never did. By the time the sun rose, I had barely drifted off. Groaning, I got up but moved slowly as if somehow I could make time stop. Across the room, Jojo was sitting on top of her suitcase, using all her might to zip the hardshell closed.

"Jo, stop or you're gonna break it," I scoffed, watching her ridiculous antics. When she finally succeeded, I watched her throw her hands up in the air with success. "Ha! Take that zipper!"

I shook my head and chuckled as I found the shoes I set aside and pulled my socks on. Looking around, I took a moment to drink in our room one last time. Bunks empty again, and clothes once strewn across the floor were zipped away. While the room looked empty, our hearts weren't, and just like at the end of the summer, I felt transformed by camp once again.

As I pulled on my shoes, Jojo turned to me and pulled a long strand of my hair through her hand. "You okay?"

Sitting up straight, I offered her a bittersweet smile. "This weekend just went by way too fast."

Jojo nodded, taking a second to look around herself. "It always does, doesn't it?"

Climbing to my feet, I bent down to grab the handle of my suitcase to set the shell on its wheels before offering her a small shrug. "Camp is a part of me now, I hate leaving this place behind."

Those words were truer now, than they had ever been before. When I left over the summer, I didn't know about all the work Gramps had put into making camp so special. He had built this place from the ground up, New Hope wasn't just a special place anymore, camp was a part of me.

Pulling her suitcase behind her, Jojo wrapped one arm around my shoulder, pulling me into a one-armed hug. "You're not leaving camp behind though, Lena," she said softly. "Camp will always be here, like always, just waiting for you to come back."

Summoning all my courage, I followed Jojo as she dragged her suitcase from our room. With one last look, I turned, taking in the sight of our empty bunks one more time, and then closed the door.

At the front door, Jojo turned, beaming brightly, she said. "Remember that we're not saying goodbye yet, we still have the whole day together."

She was right. Today was the Harvest Festival, which meant I had one last day to spend with my friends and enjoy all Meadowbrook had to offer in the fall. As Jojo and I stepped out onto the porch, the crisp mountain air hit first, followed by warm, morning sunlight. I paused for one more moment, and spun to take in the weathered cabins covered with colorful fall leaves. Just beyond the treeline, the lake shimmered beneath the glow of the sunrise, as if waving me goodbye.

I didn't notice them at first, but just a few feet away, Carter and Denny stood beside a golf cart near the edge of the path. Without even trying, Carter looked handsome as ever in just a jacket and jeans. I followed Jojo as she handed her case to Denny, who loaded it into the back of the cart. Beside him, Carter stood holding a cup of coffee in each hand before offering one to me.

"I don't know if you slept as bad as I did, but I wanted to bring you coffee while I still had the chance," Carter said.

"You're a lifesaver," I murmured, taking a sip immediately. The caramel sweetness hit my tongue as I glanced back up at him with a small smile.

"What do you think?" He asked, itching for praise.

"You might just make me a coffee drinker out of me yet." I said, taking another long sip.

Turning to her towering boyfriend, Jojo crossed her arms and tapped her foot. "Where's my present?"

Denny grinned, as he leaned down to boop her nose. "Right here." Before she could brace herself, Denny slung Jojo backwards, landing a kiss on her cheek with a loud smack of his lips.

Jojo gasped once he released her and swatted his arm. "Denny Mayhew!"

Unfazed, he grinned wider. "What? I'm the gift that keeps on giving, Jojo Bean." With a wink, he hopped in the golf cart's driver's seat and turned the key. "Besides, I got the Jeep back this morning, so all is right in the world."

Jojo rolled her eyes but climbed into the front seat beside him as Carter slid into the back row. Unlike Denny, not everything felt right in the world to me. Though there were four of us here together, there were normally five. Carter patted the empty space beside him as the golf cart rumbled to life. Once I slid in, I leaned in close to him and whispered.

"Have you seen him?"

Carter grimaced, knowing exactly who I meant as he lowered his voice to whisper back. "Theo left early this morning, he said he had to help set up for the festival with his dad."

I nodded slowly, though my stomach sank with regret at the thought of leaving Meadowbrook without checking to see if Theo was okay. All I could do was hope to catch him before the day was over.

As Denny drove us along, we passed the Dining Hall then the pool where so many lives had been changed. I tried to memorize every bit of camp, from the grounds, to the smiling campers, clinging to every moment.

By the time we reached the parking lot, Lou was already there, loading the last few bins she had brought from the kitchen into her SUV. She waved as Denny came to a stop behind her vehicle.

"Good morning, everyone! You guys all set?" she asked.

I climbed out and gave her a big hug. "We just have to load up the cars and head into town. Do you need a hand?"

"I've almost got it," Lou said, moving back to her trunk to lift one last bin inside. "I'm heading straight to the Harvest Festival to help Hannah set up the River Ridge tent."

"I'll stop by," I promised.

Lou smiled, but there was something else in her eye that I couldn't quite catch. "I'd love that. Just… remember to have fun today."

I nodded, though the idea of fun still felt faraway. As the others loaded their luggage into separate vehicles, the weight of goodbye made each step feel heavier, as I followed their lead, dragging my suitcase to my car.

Before I could lift it, Carter stepped beside me, and slid the case into my back seat and shut the door. Turning to face me, he tucked his hands into his pockets and asked. "Are you ready for the best day ever?"

I offered a small smile, trying my best to put on a brave face even though I felt anything but. "As I'll ever be."

With an outstretched hand, Carter leaned in to push a strand of loose hair from my face before reaching to open the door for me. "Just follow me, okay?"

I climbed into the driver's seat, as he handed the coffee cup I had left on the golf cart back to me. Dropping to level his gaze at me, Carter smiled and asked. "You know what's been the best part of camp for me, twice now?"

"What?" I asked, squinting beneath the morning light to see him.

Carter leaned in and gave me a quick peck on the cheek before adding, "Knowing I don't have to say goodbye to you yet."

He smiled and closed my door, and I watched Carter walk back to his car, and it hit me that he was right. This time when I watched his red tail lights, I wasn't saying goodbye, I was following him to Meadowbrook where we still had the entire day ahead of us.

As Carter pulled away, I pulled my car around, then shifted into drive as followed close behind him. Sunlight streamed through the colorful trees, casting shadows across the drive as I kicked up dust behind me. In the rearview mirror, I watched while camp slipped away, but this time, saying goodbye felt different than the last.

Even when this weekend unearthed family secrets, I still didn't want to leave. While I couldn't pretend that things were still the same, I realized change wasn't something I needed to fear. As I traveled down the gravel path, change felt like something new, and even though camp might never feel the way it once did, this place was still the refuge Gramps had created it to be. When I reached the end of the long gravel road, I slowly watched as New Hope disappeared out of sight. Silently, I whispered farewell for now to the place where the leaves fall, and where I was leaving a part of my heart behind.

42

By late morning, it seemed like the whole town of Meadowbrook had arrived for the Harvest Festival. After saying goodbye to camp, I felt my heart warm again as I walked the festival streets with my favorite people. Main Street seemed like something out of a fall postcard. Cornstalks and hay bales sat at the base of every lamppost, while pumpkins lined every street corner. The mountain air carried the scent of fried apple fritters, kettle corn, and the smoky scent of slow-cooked barbecue. A bluegrass band was playing beneath the gazebo, but not loud enough to drown out kids squealing with joy at the nearby bouncy houses.

"Let's get this party started!" Denny roared, and the three of us bounded downtown, throwing ourselves into everything the Harvest Festival had to offer.

Denny signed up for the pumpkin pie-eating contest, making that our first stop. Carter, Jojo and I cheered him on from the crowd as he raced to eat slice after slice. When the final bell rang, he stood victoriously, beating his hands against his chest, while pie crust and pumpkin filling slid off his face.

Jojo shook her head as he barreled offstage and handed him her water bottle. "You are a mess!"

Denny leaned in and waggled his face in front of hers. "All I hear is you want a hug!"

Jojo's eyes went wide as she leaned away from him. "Don't you dare—"

But she was too late as Denny lunged, and began chasing her through the crowd with his pie smeared face.

Carter and I followed suit as the rest of the day blurred by in a whirlwind of laughter and fall activities. Together, the four of us tried but failed at apple fishing, but made almost every ring at the pumpkin toss. When we reached the pumpkin patch cutout, Carter posed as a goofy farmer while I slid into the frame below as an overgrown pumpkin trying to run free. Later, while the boys tackled the corn maze, Jojo and I had our faces painted like scarecrows that were quickly smeared from giggling so hard. As the sun began to set, string lights flickered to life above us and the four of us climbed onto a hayride through Meadowbrook as the day wound down. We rode down the decorated streets of downtown Meadowbrook, catching a glimpse of all the fall spirit the small-town had to offer.

After the hayride, Jojo and Denny stood deliberating on which dinner booth to visit next when Carter gently pulled me aside. "Come on," he said with a quiet smile. "I never leave the festival without buying my favorite treat."

With my hand in his, Carter pulled me along through the crowd until we reached a tiny booth where cinnamon sugar filled the air. Fresh from the fryer, Carter ordered us a funnel cake to share that we devoured in mere minutes, both of us covered in powdered sugar.

Carter leaned in but stopped as he glanced down at his dusted hands. Chuckling, he motioned to my cheek. "Dutch, you've got some, um...sugar."

I frowned and rubbed at my face with the back of my hand. "Did I get it?"

"Here." He said, retrieving a napkin from the booth to hand to me, but before I could grab it, Carter reached out and brushed the sugar away himself. His eyes lingered on mine as he gently wiped my cheek.

"Oh wait," I murmured, feeling lost in the moment. "You have some sugar there, too."

Carter raised an eyebrow, clearly amused. "Do I?"

As I stepped in closer, I whispered, "Allow me." Then I leaned in and kissed him, short and sweet.

When I pulled back, his eyes flashed with a bright smile. "Did you get it, Dutch?"

I tilted my head, pretending to study him as I leaned in again. "You know... I think I missed a spot."

This time, he didn't wait. Carter cupped my face in his hands and kissed me again, this time slower as the sugary taste lingered between us. My heart was still pitter-pattering when he finally pulled away, to grab our empty plate and toss it in a nearby bin.

"Come on," he said, reaching for my hand. "Let's find the others and head to the Ferris wheel."

We found Jojo and Denny as evening settled over the festival. Together, we made our way over to the Ferris wheel, noticing the way the flashing lights made the day feel even more magical. As Carter pulled me into one of the cars, the wheel lifted us higher into the night sky. As we gazed out, Meadowbrook glowed beneath us in a tangle of string lights that felt like home.

"Did you enjoy today, Dutch?" Carter asked quietly, tracing circles on the back of my hand with his thumb.

I peered up at him, and to my surprise, I felt completely at peace before I rested my head on his shoulder. "Today was everything I needed."

Carter kissed the top of my head and held me close as we circled the night sky. Once the festival crowd began to die down, we ended the night in the funhouse, catching our reflections in warped mirrors. We were all doubled over laughing as we reached the exit before tumbling into the cold night air.

As I caught my breath, I gazed out into the crowd and felt my stomach sink. Just across from us, I spotted Theo standing beneath the city council tent, all by himself.

I reached out and touched Carter's arm, gently pulling his attention from whatever joke he and Denny were cackling over and motioned to the booth.

"I'll be right back." I said softly,

Carter followed my gaze, and offered me an encouraging nod as I turned and began weaving through the crowd.

I offered him a reassuring smile before slipping away, weaving through the thinning crowd. The way Theo stood by himself, tore at my heart strings. I knew how it felt to standalone in a crowd, but I couldn't leave Meadowbrook without making sure my friend was going to be okay.

43

A couple holding a tiny dog stepped up to Theo's table before I could, picking up a few brochures. Slowly, moving through the crowd, I saw Theo offer the couple a polite smile, and it surprised me to see his full row of teeth. I'm not sure any of us ever caught him smiling like that. Yet, as I caught sight of the city booth he was holding down, it was obvious that Theo was just keeping up appearances for his family. As the couple waved goodbye, I watched Theo roll his eyes as if returning to his normal sarcastic self. He straightened the pamphlets once again until he glanced up and caught me standing right in front of him.

"Hey, Mermaid." He greeted me, flicking his brows like he wasn't expecting me to be standing there.

"Hey Lockwood," I flicked my head in acknowledgment as I offered Theo a stiff wave. Staring down at the table, I noticed all the election propaganda with his dad's face scattered on the table before him. "So this is where you've been hiding all day."

Theo slowly tipped his head from side-to-side and held out his hands like he was carefully weighing two objects. "You say hiding, I say tortured into talking to random strangers all day with no other option."

I grimaced, scrunching my face, though the explanation did make me feel better. Earlier when Carter shared that Theo wasn't joining us today, I wondered if it was because of me, but now I knew, it was most likely because of his dad. "That does sound like torture."

Theo pointed at me like I hit the nail on the head before shoving his hands into his coat pockets. I didn't notice it before, but his long blonde hair wasn't falling in his face like usual. He had the sides combed back a little like he tried his best to seem professional, but it made me wonder if the decision was his or if he was told to. For a moment, we stood there awkwardly until I offered him a sympathetic smile. "Are we, um, you know...are we *good?*"

Dipping his head, Theo narrowed his gaze at me playfully. "That all depends on whether you really came all this way just to check on me or if you were just looking for one of these?"

Reaching down, Theo swiped a pin from the tabletop that read *Re-Elect Mayor Lockwood.*

Batting the pin away, I snickered and crossed my arms against the chilly breeze. "I just wanted to make sure you and I were okay after...um... all the Kelsey stuff."

Theo set down the campaign pin and nodded, and somehow his eyes seemed brighter than before. "We're good, Mermaid. No sister drama's going to mess that up."

"Good," I grinned, feeling my shoulders relax a little. "I didn't want to leave without making sure."

Scrunching his face, he reached over the table and nudged my shoulder as if I were being ridiculous. "No need to get sappy on me now."

I chuckled softly. "Too late."

Theo's smirk widened before all traces of sarcasm faded. Reaching up, he tucked a loose strand of hair behind his ear, eyeing me thoughtfully. "We're good, Lena. Don't worry."

After the weekend we just endured together, his words made my heart feel full. I didn't want to go home tomorrow knowing there were still things left unsaid, without trying to make the effort. Friendship, even Theo's, had become precious to me, and I was going to hold onto every last one for dear life.

"I'm glad," I replied, finally. Thinking back to the talent show, I opened up. "I didn't know what happened after the whole Katie debacle, but I was worried about you last night. Are you okay?"

Theo leaned back against the table, his arms folding loosely across his chest as he looked past my shoulder, pondering last night's events. After everything he had been through over the last few months, trying to cope with their long-distance relationship and win her back, I was surprised to see him appear so...*calm*.

"Honestly? I'm alright." He shrugged like he was already moving past it. "Katie and I... we weren't right for each other. If she couldn't handle who my friends were, or constantly saw any other girl as competition, then things were never going to work between us."

Hearing him say that brought a wave of guilt as I pictured Katie being upset over being friends with me. The last thing I had wanted was to come between them or even be a threat to Katie, as I thought about all the advice I tried offering Theo, it hit me that Katie may never know I had only ever been rooting for the two of them.

"I didn't mean to mess things up for you." I said, shifting my weight as I stared down at my boots.

"You didn't," Theo said, shaking his head as I glanced back up. "Forget about what Kelsey said to you, she had no clue what she was talking about. Last night, when I watched Katie walk out the door after hearing my song, it didn't hurt like I thought it would." He paused, then added with a hint of peace in his tone, "Strangely enough, I think any other girl in the world would have stayed, but she didn't, and I'm okay with that."

I searched Theo's face, surprised to see just how at peace he truly did seem.

"You sure?"

Theo dipped his head in acknowledgment. "Speaking of last night, I should be asking you. Are you okay?"

I felt my stomach churn slightly as I realized he was talking about me and Carter. When Kelsey spat her venom at me, I had almost forgotten Theo was there to witness the whole thing.

"We're fine," I said with a sheepish smile. "We talked everything out last night."

Crossing his arms, Theo smirked while eyeing me thoughtfully. "It's funny how communication can solve a lot of problems in a healthy relationship, huh?"

I bit my lip, trying not to wince as I offered him a helpless shrug. The first time we practiced Theo's song, he opened up about how Katie ignored him and wouldn't give him the time of day, no matter how many times he tried. Carter and I weren't perfect, and there were still things we had to work on, but we always tried to put our best foot forward, and that was the best we could both do.

"Oh well," Theo said. "So when do you head back to the beach?"

"In the morning." I said, feeling a shiver run down my spine at the thought. "I've got to get back before school."

"Well, as the boomers say..." Theo joked, "don't be a stranger, or whatever." Then, before I could respond, Theo stepped around the table and pulled me into an unexpected hug. At first I wasn't sure what to do because of how stand-offish Theo had been all weekend, but then it dawned on me. This weekend Theo and I had walked through fire together and came out on the other side unscathed. Warmth settled deep in my chest as I realized that no matter what relationship drama or family feud threatened us, Theo was my friend regardless.

But I barely had time to return his embrace before a familiar voice cut in.

"Sorry, bud, but Dutch can't vote if she's not technically eighteen or a Meadowbrook resident." Carter smirked, pointing down at all the election advertisements, but behind his poker face, I caught his watchful gaze as I stepped to his side.

"Lucky her," Theo replied dryly, as he stepped away from me and found his way back behind the table again.

Carter turned to me then, and on instinct, intertwined his fingers with mine. "Should we go find, Lou?"

I nodded, staring into his sweet chocolate eyes. "Yeah, let's go find her." Turning back to Theo, I waved. "See you around, Lockwood."

"See you, Mermaid," he said briefly before another visitor made their way over to him.

As Carter and I walked back through the crowd, my heart felt lighter knowing that finally, all was right in the world, and I could leave in the morning without any regrets.

44

The River Ridge tent was packed with visitors once we reached the other side of the festival where Lou had set up. Like most other booths, Lou and Hannah had decorated with pumpkins and hay bales, but the banner with River Ridge's tagline was my favorite touch, reading: *Welcome home.*

In the center of the crowd, I found my aunt laughing so hard she threw her head back, greeting her visitors from all over town. She was dressed in a beautiful peacoat, with chunky gold earrings that looked elegant with the way she had thrown her hair up. When she peered over and spotted me, her face somehow lit up even more.

"Lena!" she called, waving both Carter and me over. "I want you to come meet some of my dearest friends."

Brushing past a few people, I moved toward her and came face-to-face with an white-haired older woman to Lou's right. She stared back at me with wide-eyes at first before her face then fell into a bright smile. "Well, I'll be…" she muttered, stepping closer to me. "This must be Walt and Barb's granddaughter."

"Yes, ma'am," I said, smiling though I felt the prick of her words on my heart at the mention of my Gramps and Grams.

The woman reached for my hand and held it like she had known me all her life. "You look just like your grandmother," she said. "Just as beautiful too. Barb was one of my best friends, and boy do I miss her so."

A sad lump formed in my throat as I pictured my grandparents, especially now, being here at the festival for the first time without them. "I miss them too."

The woman released me to turn back to Lou. "You keep fighting the good fight, honey."

"Oh, you know I will, Betty," Lou said with a grin.

The woman I now knew as Betty pulled Lou in for a hug, but before she released her, I heard her whisper. "Your parents would be so proud of the way you carry on their legacy. Thank you for keeping the Rivers name alive."

Lou reached out and took Betty's hand, giving her a tender squeeze before she turned and walked away. Lou turned as others stepped up to the booth, hugging each person, greeting those who were strangers to me, but close friends to her. Standing beneath the tent, watching while everyone gathered around my aunt, laughing together and sharing stories from years before, I couldn't help but notice the stark contrast between the empty Lockwood table and Lou's. I loved seeing how everyone gathered here together, but what I loved most was the fact that they were all here for her.

Suddenly, behind me, I heard my name. "Lena!"

Then I turned just in time to brace myself for Carter's little sister Sadie to fling herself into my arms.

I giggled as I twirled her in my arms, giving her the biggest squeeze. It had been months since I had seen her, and somehow she had grown much taller. "Oh, Sadie! I've missed you!"

She giggled and beamed up at me as I set her back down. Her sweet curls had started turning dark blonde and as I gazed back at her brother who took her small hand in his, I couldn't help but notice the way Sadie resembled Carter even though they weren't biologically related.

Behind her, Carter's parents approached, both of them waving at everyone before their gaze settled on me.

"It's so good to see you again, sweetheart." Amy said, pulling me into a quick hug as I felt Jack give me a gentle pat on the back.

"You too," I replied, feeling an unexpected blush creep over me. I wasn't sure I would ever get over just how kind Carter's parents were to me.

Before I could say anything else, Max appeared next, joining in on the celebration, grinning and balancing a tray of piping hot drinks.

"For the lady." Max dipped his head, handing a cup to Lou.

"You're a lifesaver," She replied with a wink, before taking a quick sip.

The two of them shared another silent exchange as he watched Lou swig the hot liquid. When she dramatically buckled at the knees, I knew she had satisfied his curiosity that whatever he had delivered, confirming it was delicious.

As everyone was busy chatting, I took a step back for just a second to soak in the moment, watching all of the people I cared so much about in the small town I loved. Each smile was met with the sound of laughter, hugs were exchanged, and I felt the silent pull of belonging as I took it all in; as though I was slowly being stitched into the beautiful tapestry that was Meadowbrook.

Quietly, Carter appeared back at my side, wrapping his strong arm around me, pulling me into his side. I felt his lips brush my ear as he leaned in and whispered, "Is everything okay, Dutch?"

Looking up into his beautiful face, I nodded, wanting to remember this moment, and never let it go. With a quiet smile, I leaned my head on Carter's shoulder, and wrapped my arm around his waist, snuggling as close to him as I could get. As we stood there holding each other, I reached up and slowly traced the small mountain pendant still hanging faithfully around my neck.

"Yeah, everything is perfect."

45

Two weeks had passed since leaving Meadowbrook, but I had left a part of myself behind. Some mornings, I'd wake up expecting to smell the fresh mountain air rolling off Cobalt Bluff, only to be met with the salty breeze from the Freeport shore. Now, as I sat on the fully restored *Gone With the Wind*, I rocked gently with the rhythmic ocean waves. Today had been the first warm day since I'd gotten back, and Dad had surprised me with a ritual I thought he had forgotten. We sat together on the boat enjoying sandwiches on paper plates, just like we used to on our Daddy-Daughter dates.

Dad leaned back on the bench seat, brushing crumbs from his fingers as he finished the last of his bread crust.

"So," he said, squinting beneath the sun. "Was your first day better than expected?"

I smiled, brushing crumbs from my lap too, and nodded, feeling hopeful. "I think I'm going to be really happy there."

As I tucked a strand of hair the breeze caught behind my ear, I caught the aroma of coffee grounds still lingering on my hands from my first shift as a barista earlier. Leaving camp again, I was more determined than ever to truly start fresh and not let anything stand in the way of the promise I made to live boldly in my faith. The first step forward was to find a job that allowed flexibility for church, and with Worthy's help, I had made it happen.

Dad sat up then, but I didn't miss how at ease he seemed by my news. "I'm proud of you for finding a better fit, Lenny. I know leaving the Aquarium wasn't easy."

"The aquarium was great," I shrugged nonchalantly, "but the coffee house gives me Sundays off. Church is going to be my priority this time around."

Flashing a grin my way, Dad warned. "Just remember not to drink more than a cup of joe a day or you'll never sleep again."

His quip suddenly made me think about the horrible bland coffee he bought compared to the deliciously fancy options I had already explored and fallen in love with in just one shift at the coffee house.

"Carter has given me so many combinations to try now that I have all the coffee resources at my fingertips." I replied, but when Dad cut his eyes at me, I held up my hands innocently. "You're right though, I'll pace myself."

Dad nudged my knee. "If you join the show choir, you might need the extra boost. Have you decided if you're going to take Worthy up on her offer yet?"

Since returning from camp, Worthy had been pestering me non-stop after hearing me finally sing again at church. Once again, she reminded me that the show choir was open and with the Winter Showcase coming up, they needed all the help they could get.

I took my place and slid it down at my feet before pulling my knees to my chest. "I'm just not sure it's for me."

With that, Dad sat up straight and eyed me curiously. "Honey, you used to sing all the time. Do you remember that time when you were little, we went out for Italian and you used a breadstick as a microphone?"

I rolled my eyes and palmed my forehead. "Of course, you never let me forget."

"Stop that," Dad said, pulling my hand from my face. Resting his elbows on his thighs, he leaned closer, eyes steady on mine.

"You used to be so fearless, Lenny. I see flickers of my little girl every time you come back from camp, but remember to let that side of you live here too. This is your last year of high school, and I don't want to see you squander it just because you're afraid of what others might think of you."

Dad's words pulled at my heartstrings, and I knew he meant well, but Freeport would never be my happy place. I could survive here, but Dad didn't understand that I felt most alive sitting beside my friends while we worshipped together beneath the stars. My happiest moments were found with Carter, side-by-side on the edge of the dock, opening our hearts to each other. New Hope was the place where I could be myself and truly feel like I belonged. Camp reminded me of whose I was, but also who I wanted to become. Every time I left, my faith was reignited, reminding me of the life I wanted to lead every day, that I hoped one day my Dad could too.

Turning to face him, I said, "At camp, we studied Daniel."

Lifting a brow, Dad tilted his head and asked. "The lion's den guy?"

I laughed and peered out at the water for a moment before shifting my gaze back to his. "Even when Daniel was forced into a life he never asked for, he never gave in. He chose to stand firm in his faith but also for God. The best part was that God honored him."

"That's great, honey." Dad said, but it wasn't enough.

I knew I couldn't force my faith on anyone and would never want to, but I just wanted him to hear me and to have the same hope I had.

"Would you ever want to talk more about God?" I asked, not knowing how this would go. "With me, I mean."

Dad chuckled. "Aren't we doing that right now?"

I sighed then and cut my gaze at him. "We are, but I mean, maybe we could do this daddy-daughter date more and talk then."

Sitting up straight, Dad stared out beyond the horizon. Taking a deep breath, he gazed back at me. "Lenny, I've wrestled with faith for a long time. I'm glad to see you stepping into yours, but I've got a long way to go."

Another breeze cut across the boat, and I stuck my hands in my pockets to warm my hands. Nodding, I was trying my best to understand, but I couldn't meet Dad's gaze. Then, as if he could see me struggling, Dad reached out and lifted my chin with his finger.

"Anytime you want to talk about anything," He said, keeping his voice low. "Faith, school, work, whatever, Lenny, you've got my undivided attention."

His statement felt like a verbal hug, but it was still hard to see where he was coming from. I knew how it felt to experience spiritual hurt, I had run from my faith before I realized God wasn't to blame for the pain caused by others. I had no idea what Dad had experienced in his life that made him so hesitant to talk about things, but I also knew I couldn't push.

Taking the olive branch Dad offered, I nodded with a small grin. "We've got a deal."

Letting go of my chin, Dad patted my knee before climbing to his feet. "Should we head back?"

Saluting the captain, I began picking up our loose trash as Dad found his spot behind the wheel and started the engine. Turning to face the sea, I caught the way the sunset dipped into the ocean as we headed for the shore. As the cool breeze whipped around me, I realized for the first time in a long time, I felt truly anchored in who I was.

On the drive back home, I rolled down the window of Dad's old pickup and leaned my head out breathing in the scent of seaweed and salt marsh. Making our way through Freeport, we passed the same familiar sights, but unlike last time, Freeport no longer felt like a cage I wanted to escape. When I had come home after summer camp, this place once felt so different, but now it dawned on me, it wasn't Freeport that had changed, *it was me.*

When we pulled into the driveway outside our house, Dad pulled all the way through to the backyard and then cut the engine. Motioning to the back, he asked. "Can you grab some of this stuff while I unhook the boat?"

"Sure," I said, opening my door.

Flicking his head to the right, he pointed toward the road with his thumb. "Oh, and honey, can you check the mail, too? I forgot about it earlier."

"On it." I replied, already gathering the cooler and beach blanket.

The evening was still and quiet aside from the clinking from the chains as Dad unhooked the boat in the backyard. As I walked toward the house and out onto the loose gravel, a few stray leaves breezed by brushing the top of my foot. When I reached the mailbox, I pulled the metal flap down and grabbed at the stack inside. Adjusting the bag on my shoulder and the blanket on one arm, I shuffled through the mail piece by piece, before a single envelope caught my eye. My breath hitched as the sight of the familiar handwriting stopped my heart.

The name on the return address read: Natalie Harris.

My mother.

I stared at the name on the envelope as the rest of the world seemed to fade in the background behind me. The only noise I could hear was my pulse pounding in my ears as I swallowed hard, tightening my grip as though the envelope in my hand weighed way more than paper should. Then, as if on autopilot,

I turned toward the house with trembling hands, staring down at the unopened slip of mail, unsure what to do next.

ACKNOWLEDGEMENTS

When I wrote The Summer Away, I could have never imagined the number of people who would walk alongside me on this journey. I told myself, if just one person reads my book and is inspired, then I have accomplished my goal. The outpouring of love and encouragement I have received, often in moments, when I need it most, helped me keep going, even when I considered letting The Summer Away be a standalone novel. That love and encouragement helped me keep Lena's story going. Where the Leaves Fall brought new challenges, I hadn't anticipated. As I was writing, I realized I needed to incorporate new story elements to drive the plot, and to be honest, as a self-proclaimed amateur, I hope I did the story justice. Writing a series proved to be far more complex than I ever expected, but also exciting in ways I never imagined.

This year's diagnosis of Anterolisthesis challenged me in ways I never saw coming. The sequel took much longer to write than I planned when being at the keyboard meant pain. Yet, the outpouring of love and encouragement I received truly helped me press forward, and looking back, I realize how blessed I am. As a result, I have so many of you to thank!

To my husband Homer, thank you for being my unofficial ARC reader, my biggest cheerleader, and my personal tax man. While this may be the only book you read this year, I know that's a huge deal for you, and I love you for always supporting me.

To Sara, thank you for being so willing to continue this journey with me and for being my second set of eyes. Forgive me for any grammar or punctuation gremlins I may have overlooked or missed in proofreading, they are no reflection on you. I hope I've done your editing justice this time around, but more importantly, I'm so grateful to you for ensuring God's word is conveyed truthfully. You help me keep my goal to inspire others with the gospel at the forefront of my mind, and I truly appreciate you so much. Lastly, I can't forget your keen eye for math because I certainly don't have one. Thanks to you, my readers will understand the distance between Freeport and Meadowbrook without having to imagine Lena driving a spaceship. (Iykyk)

To the great Jackie Dras, thank you so much for giving my books their beautiful covers to help me tell the story and for always being up for the challenge. Without you, I wouldn't have a book or an amazing website, and I just can't thank you enough for your dazzling creativity and beautiful imagination.

To Casey, Kyla, my sister, Amber, Amber C., Lauren, Elizabeth, Kate, and Brooke. Thank you all for your cover votes. The choice was way too hard for me to do on my own and I am so grateful to each of you for your help.

To my Forrest Park family, thank you for all of your support, even when I'm far away. You all were my very first virtual book club, and I will never forget that. Your love and support has made a huge impact on my journey as an author, and I'm so thankful to have each of you.

To Lilly, my best hype girl! Thank you for your incredible reading blog for The Summer Away and for every like, comment, share and piece of social media advice you always help me with. Far or away you've got my back, and I am so thankful for all you do. I miss you oodles, my friend!

To Naomi, thank you for however many copies you bought of The Summer Away you bought and for sharing, and helping spread the word for me. I am so grateful for your support, and I can't wait to see your Instagram flourish!

To my AMAZING Bookstagram community, there are so many of you to thank that I'm scared to name you all in case I miss someone. Please know that I sincerely appreciate every like, share, comment, post, repost, story, recommendation, and review! Because of each of you, my books reach others, which is the greatest support you can offer an indie author like me. I love each and every one of you, and there just aren't enough words to articulate how thankful I am to each and every one of you.

To my reviewers, your thoughts not only help my book stand out and be discovered, but they make me better. Thank you all for taking the time to support little old me.

To my sweet furbabies, Delta Bean, Ozzie, and Bravo. You three are the best writing companions a girl can have, whether it's a 4:00 a.m. writing session or a light night one. You're always by my side and you deserve credit too.

To my family, Mom and Dad, thank you for dreaming big with me and for always encouraging me to reach for the stars. Your support of my imagination keeps the wheels turning and means the world to me. I love you both! Next to Aunt Rose, MAA, Nana Hayes, Miss Lois, and all my extended family, thank you all for buying extra copies of The Summer Away, donating, sharing, and believing in me. It takes a village and I am so glad you are mine!

Lastly, I want to thank YOU, the reader. Thank you for picking up this book, especially when you could have picked up thousands of others. You are the reason I write. When I was younger there were stories I longed for but could never find, and if this book is that for you, know that you were on my heart and I hope this story goes beyond the page. I hope the story fills you with hope and encourages you to seek the Lord with all your heart. As I continue writing stories, you are in my prayers, and I hope the New Hope Series always points you to Jesus, the One who loves you most.

From the bottom of my heart, thank you all SO much.

Hymns/Songs

"They'll Know We are Christians (by our love) by Fr. Peter Scholtes

"How Can I Keep From Singing? ("My life flows on in endless song") by Robert Wadsworth Lowry

"He Knows My Name" by Tommy Walker

"I Am Mine No More" American Folk Hymn of unknown author and composer

"God Will Take Care of You" by Civilla D. Martin

"Come, Thou Fount of Every Blessing" by Robert Robinson

"Light the Fire" by Bill Maxwell

"Somewhere Over the Rainbow" by Harold Arlen

Scripture References

"Fear not, for I am with you; Be not dismayed, for I am your God. I will strengthen you, Yes, I will help you, I will uphold you with My righteous right hand."
Isaiah 41:10 NKJV

"Blessed be the God and Father of our Lord Jesus Christ, who according to His abundant mercy has begotten us again to a living hope through the resurrection of Jesus Christ from the dead, to an inheritance incorruptible and undefiled and that does not fade away, reserved in heaven for you, who are kept by the power of God through faith for salvation ready to be revealed in the last time. In this you greatly rejoice, though now for a little while, if need be, you have been [b]grieved by various trials, that the genuineness of your faith, being much more precious than gold that perishes, though it is tested by fire, may be found to praise, honor, and glory at the revelation of Jesus Christ, whom having not seen you love. Though now you do not see Him, yet believing, you rejoice with joy inexpressible and full of glory, receiving the end of your faith—the salvation of your souls."
1 Peter 1:3–9 NKJV

"Then Jesus said, 'Father, forgive them, for they do not know what they do...'"
Luke 23:34 NKJV

"You are the light of the world. A city that is set on a hill cannot be hidden. Nor do they light a lamp and put it under a basket, but on a lampstand, and it gives light to all who are in the house.

Let your light so shine before men, that they may see your good works and glorify your Father in heaven."

Matthew 5:14-16

"Repay no one evil for evil. Have regard for good things in the sight of all men."

Romans 12:17

"But even if you should suffer for righteousness' sake, you are blessed. And do not be afraid of their threats, nor be troubled. But sanctify the Lord God in your hearts, and always be ready to give a defense to everyone who asks you a reason for the hope that is in you, with meekness and fear; having a good conscience, that when they defame you as evildoers, those who revile your good conduct in Christ may be ashamed. For it is better, if it is the will of God, to suffer for doing good than for doing evil."

1 Peter 3:14-17

"As for these four young men, God gave them knowledge and skill in all literature and wisdom; and Daniel had understanding in all visions and dreams. Now at the end of the days, when the king had said that they should be brought in, the chief of the eunuchs brought them in before Nebuchadnezzar. Then the king interviewed them, and among them all none was found like Daniel, Hananiah, Mishael, and Azariah; therefore they served before the king. And in all matters of wisdom and understanding about which the king examined them, he found them ten times better than all the magicians and astrologers who were in all his realm."

Daniel 1:17-20

"If that is the case, our God whom we serve is able to deliver us from the burning fiery furnace, and He will deliver us from your hand, O king. But if not, let it be known to you, O king, that we do not serve your gods, nor will we worship the gold image which you have set up."

Daniel 3:17-18

"Look!" he answered, "I see four men loose, walking in the midst of the fire; and they are not hurt, and the form of the fourth is like the Son of God."

Daniel 3:25

"When you pass through the waters, I will be with you; And through the rivers, they shall not overflow you. When you walk through the fire, you shall not be burned, Nor shall the flame scorch you."

Isaiah 43:2

"Now when Daniel knew that the writing was signed, he went home. And in his upper room, with his windows open toward Jerusalem, he knelt down on his knees three times that day, and prayed and gave thanks before his God, as was his custom since early days."

Daniel 6:10

"And when he came to the den, he cried out with a lamenting voice to Daniel. The king spoke, saying to Daniel, "Daniel, servant of the living God, has your God, whom you serve continually, been able to deliver you from the lions?"

"Then Daniel said to the king, 'O king, live forever! My God sent His angel and shut the lions' mouths, so that they have not hurt me, because I was found innocent before Him; and also, O king, I have done no wrong before you.'"

Daniel 6:20-22

DISCUSSION QUESTIONS

1. Lena dreads heading back to Freeport and facing her past. She feels like she no longer fits in. Have you ever struggled to fit in? If so, how did you overcome these challenges?

2. Lena struggles with the past mistakes she made and how others treat her as a result. Can you relate? How do the opinions of others impact how you see yourself?

3. Reflect on Psalm 139:14 and 1 Peter 2:9. How do these scriptures encourage you?

4. Lena reconnects with her old friend, Worthy, who she feels turned her back on her when Lena needed her support. Do you face challenges with forgiveness regarding your own friendships? If so, how do you move forward to forgive those who have hurt you?

5. At camp, Lena studies Daniel's journey in the Bible and is pricked to the heart over his bold faith. Do you ever experience challenges standing boldly in your own faith? How does Daniel 3:18 and Romans 1:16 encourage you to stand boldly?

6. After learning about Daniel being sent into the Lion's Den, Lena thinks about the lions she's faced too. What lions do you face that get in the way of you standing

boldly in your faith?

7. In order to stand boldly, what is something you need to let go of to fully step into your Christian identity?

8. Lena faces different challenges at this point in her journey but learns to truly lean on God. What can you do to keep your heart and mind focused on the Lord?

9. How may the Lord be preparing you for a difficult season in life?

10. What can you do to encourage others in your life to live faithfully?

About the Author

Aiessa Holland is an Enneagram two, fur-mom, and avid reader. She was born in Bangor, Maine, and raised in the small town of East Bend, North Carolina. Aiessa graduated Summa Cum Laude from American Military University with a Bachelor's of Business Management. She is married to her high school sweetheart and is an active duty military spouse. Wherever the Air Force sends her family is where she calls home.

As a lifelong reader with a fervent desire to serve God, Aiessa decided to write her debut novel, The Summer Away in 2024. Her hope is that the story helps readers to find an inspirational book that also serves as a compass, pointing them to the Lord. When Aiessa isn't reading or writing, you can find her serving the military through non-profit work, volunteering in her local community, spending time with her husband and furbabies, and enjoying the great outdoors.

ALSO BY AIESSA

Book 1 in the New Hope Bible Camp Series
Link to Amazon: https://a.co/d/hXYDSi1

To connect with Aiessa, please visit:
Website: https://aiessaholland.wixsite.com/aiessaholland
Instagram: iesuh000author
Join Aiessa's Facebook group - iesuh's inside circle:
https://www.facebook.com/groups/1702121220531467

Made in the USA
Coppell, TX
13 February 2026

72026664R00203